Mermaids of Eriana Kwai
Book Two

ICE CRYPT

Rogue Cannon Publishing
Canada

First published in Canada in 2016
Rogue Cannon Publishing, Abbotsford, BC

tianawarner.com

Discover

ICE MASSACRE

Book One in the Mermaids of Eriana Kwai series

tianawarner.com/books/ice-massacre

★ "… thought provoking and intelligent … fresh and thoroughly entertaining … Warner does a fantastic job creating a tight plot and masterfully creates a sense of atmosphere through subtle yet potent descriptions … Ice Massacre is a truly exceptional book."

— *Foreword* Clarion Reviews, 5-star review

★ "Fascinating, unique, scary and written with a beautiful economy of words…"

— 23rd Annual Writer's Digest Self-Published Book Awards

Winner: 2016 Best Indie Book Award, Young Adult
First Place Winner: Dante Rossetti Awards 2014
Foreword 10 Best Indie YA novels of 2014
Foreword Reviews' 2014 INDIEFAB Book of the Year Finalist

CHAPTER ONE
The Massacre Committee

Hanging from the crooked branch of a maple tree wasn't that glamorous—not what my people would expect from an honoured Massacre survivor. Legs swinging to try and get a foothold, strands of hair clinging to my face, I heaved myself onto the next branch.

This would have been easier if I'd had the use of both hands.

Out of breath and halfway up, I paused, deciding how best to continue. The tree had forked and my legs were splayed, one foot against each trunk. In my fist, the owlet gave a feeble hoot.

I glared at him. He could hardly be called cute, with his sparse white fluff and oversized feet.

"Your family reunion better be worth all of this," I said.

I pushed off one trunk and wrapped my limbs around the other, then shimmied higher until I was level with the nest.

Two owlets peered back at me, identical to the one in my fist.

"Gaawhist," I said. *Home, sweet home.*

I placed my rescue next to his siblings, where he toppled sideways and blinked a few times. I poked him to make sure I hadn't squeezed him too tightly. He ruffled himself and settled in.

Maybe I couldn't help everyone survive, but I could, at least, save this one life.

I just hoped the mother would return soon.

I leaned against the trunk and caught my breath, my thoughts turning back to what I'd come here for. I inhaled slowly, letting the sweet scent of maple buds calm me.

From this height, the wooden, mossy cabin below seemed less imposing. I could see how these grounds might have once been used for camping—back when seaside camping was not a life-threatening activity. Now, this cabin was one of many classrooms at the Safe Training Base. Once a place to connect with wilderness, now a place to learn the best way to slaughter a sea demon.

The Massacre trainees had all gone home for dinner. The woods settled peacefully when not filled with the buzz of girls discussing battle tactics. Leaves whispered in the summer breeze, insects chirred in my ears, and a thrush somewhere near enjoyed an endless conversation with one several trees away.

Then voices cut through the forest, and the thrush fell silent.

A small group approached the cabin. I stayed still, hidden partly by leaves and partly because they wouldn't bother looking up here.

My father led the group, conversing in a low voice with Anyo, the training master. A tough, solemn man, Anyo bore a scar where a mermaid had once torn half his scalp off. His eyes stayed downcast, hiding any indication of whether or not he was in a good mood. He was my key target. He was the one who made the ultimate decisions concerning the Massacres.

Hassun followed—a tall, muscled man in his late twenties who had also survived the Massacre, back when we were naive enough to send men. In fact, Hassun was the last ever man to survive it. It was shortly afterwards that the Massacre Committee decided to switch to female warriors.

After him came Mujihi, the thick, severe-looking father of my least favourite human being on the island.

A thirty-something woman trailed behind. I was fairly sure she was the lead seamstress for the Massacre uniforms and the widow of a former warrior.

The group entered the cabin and shut the door.

I turned back to my owlets. They blinked at me.

"Stay in your nest as long as you can," I said. "Trust me."

I shimmied down the trunk.

For the millionth time, I reviewed what I would say. Annith and I had rehearsed so I wouldn't come across as an eighteen-year-old girl trying to act like an adult, but rather an enlightened warrior. It was an ongoing struggle.

I was part way down the tree when footsteps crunched nearby and Annith strode into view. She stopped outside the cabin door, glancing around.

I landed lightly in front of her on the spongy forest floor. She didn't flinch. After a lifetime of friendship, it was as though she'd expected me to arrive via tree.

We stared at each other, my anxiety reflected on her shiny, freckled face.

"You won't have to say anything," I said.

"I'll jump in if you need help."

Leaving the soft glow of the forest, we entered the dimly lit room and the collective stare of half the Massacre Committee. Where were the rest of them?

We sat at the far side of the long table. The hard wooden seat and musty cabin smell brought back memories of my years in the training program.

I wiped my sweaty palms on my jeans and squared my shoulders.

To my left sat Hassun, rocking his chair back on two creaky legs and gazing out the window like he had better things to do. Beside him was the training master, and then the widow. An empty chair remained across from me. Mujihi stood behind everyone else, squinting down at us. Then there was my father, drumming his knuckles on the table, avoiding my eye.

No one spoke.

I swallowed, a nervous gulp that was far too loud.

"Thank you, everyone, for agreeing to meet with us."

… *finally,* I thought bitterly.

I kept my eyes on my father and Anyo. Neither of them looked at me.

"We were approached by the mermaids' king," I said, my words strong. "He offered a bargain."

There. Now, they were looking at me.

"Which brings me here with my fellow Massacre warrior, Annith, to propose a new strategy for freedom from the sea demons. After decades of war, it's clear the Massacres are not working."

This was met with raised eyebrows, crossed arms, and unconvinced frowns. My father's face was unreadable. He had already shown infuriating hesitation at home. But he, of all people, should have been eager to listen to a plan that might end the Massacres. He'd experienced the horrors first-hand at my age. He'd lost his son—my older brother—to one. He'd nearly lost me two weeks prior.

"We're still starving," I said, "we can't go near the water, and we risk the lives of twenty warriors per mission each spring. Annith and I have a plan but we need help. According to the king, there is a lost legend about Eriana Kwai. If we can uncover it, we can use its power to bring peace—"

Hassun raised a hand. "You're telling me the demons' king just swam up to you and told you about this legend?"

I glanced to Annith. "Not exactly."

What was I supposed to say? My secret, treacherous friendship with a mermaid led to this? My people would sooner throw me out to sea with a rock tied to my ankles than accept that I'd befriended a sea demon.

"He swam up to you and you didn't shoot him?" said the widow.

"I didn't have my crossbow."

"You were unarmed?" said Hassun.

"No. The mermaids pulled me into the water to speak to him."

"What—?"

"Let me finish," I said.

Why were they being so difficult? Anyo, especially, might have been interested in a new strategy that didn't involve all his students dying. His own daughter had started training. I tried to catch his eye without success.

Hassun gave a lazy flick of his hand.

Before I could continue, the door creaked open. Everyone turned.

A tall, thin girl with a high ponytail entered. She stepped into the dim light and shut the door, lips quirked as though amused by something. She would have been better groomed than I'd seen her since the Massacre, except her hands, arms, and shirt were splattered in bright, wet blood.

"Sorry I'm late," she said, not sounding sorry at all.

The front legs of Hassun's chair hit the floor.

"Dani," said Mujihi, clapping his daughter on the shoulder. "Please, come in."

The widow squeaked. "What happened?"

"Oh, this?" said Dani, lifting a red hand as though inspecting a manicure.

"Dani's been out hunting," said Mujihi. "Caught a healthy doe this morning. Real beauty. Took a bit of time to clean her up, eh kiddo?"

"Mm," said Dani.

I clenched my teeth. My father had mentioned Dani's recent involvement in the Massacre Committee. Here I'd been waiting for a trial, for any sort of punishment for her crimes—but two weeks had gone by, and still she walked around freely like a war hero.

Dani swaggered to the table, brushing a hand across Anyo's shoulders and leaving a smear of blood. She waved to Hassun, who perched forwards in his chair, suddenly more interested in the meeting. Barf.

She pulled out the empty chair across from me and plunked down. Her smile went out like a snuffed flame as she fixed me with her gaze.

"Hope I didn't miss anything exciting."

She purred every word, low and sinister. It brought to mind a mountain lion I'd once seen purring as it devoured a large and bloody carcass.

"Nothing you'd be able to add value to," I said.

Annith cleared her throat. "We were getting to the bargain offered to Meela by the sea demons' king."

"Oh," said Dani, speaking to the room, "so they've already mentioned their little plot to stop the Massacres?"

This was answered by grunts. Hassun rocked his chair back again with a creak that filled the small cabin.

So this was it. That was why nobody had been surprised when I announced that the plan involved stopping the Massacres: Dani had already told them. But what, exactly, had she told them? The frowns around me left no doubt that it had been a twisted version of events.

"It's not a plot," I said shortly. "It's a plan to stop our warriors from being killed."

Dani fixed her pale eyes on me. "Noble intent as always, Metlaa Gaela."

I turned to the others, ignoring Dani. "King Adaro is looking for the Host of Eriana, a lost legend and an important part of our people's history. Has anyone heard of it?"

I scanned their faces for signs of recognition. My insides seemed to deflate as I met more frowns. I'd been hoping for some hint, even a tiny shred of information to work from.

Nothing.

I pushed on.

"Adaro has been trying to drive us away from the island so he can find it. His bargain is that he'll call off the attacks if we hand it over. It must be a powerful weapon. We think it's something he can use to control the seas, and if we can use it—"

Hassun barked out a laugh. "That's not how sea demons work, girls. They're attacking because they feed on human flesh, not because they're commanded to."

"See, that's where we've been wrong," I said, leaning forwards. "They have battle plans, formations, human-like thoughts and behaviours."

"Meela," said the widow. "It's all right to be scared. The Massacre is a high-stress battle that would leave anyone paranoid."

"I'm not paranoid. This is fact. Mermaids are intelligent. Why do you think they're targeting us? Adaro wants something from our island. He's not attacking the rest of the world like he is us."

"The demons are an invasive species," said Hassun. "We need to drive them out of the Pacific if we want our freedom back."

"No, we don't. The king is the problem. We can make peace."

Why didn't any of them understand this?

Surely Dani understood, having made elaborate plans against the mermaids on our Massacre. She'd talked like they were intelligent. Yet here she remained silent, picking at her blood-encrusted nails.

Annith must have sensed my discomposure, because she continued. "Of course, Adaro's promise to stop attacking our beaches can hardly be called a peace treaty. So instead of making an alliance with a sea demon, Meela and I plan to find this weapon—the Host—and use it against him."

"If we kill Adaro, we stop the attacks," I said.

Their faces read solemn and unimpressed. The widow's mouth gaped open. My father looked away. Anyo stared at the wall behind Annith, which incensed me because the training master's opinion mattered most.

Dani sighed and leaned back. "That is a well rehearsed story if I ever heard one."

Hassun smirked.

Dani glanced around pointedly before turning back to me.

"Why on the Gaela's earth would a sea rat know an ancient legend about Eriana Kwai? One that its own people aren't familiar with?"

"We think the legend has been lost over time," said Annith, "but we're willing to put in the work to find it. In the meantime, we're hoping to stop the Massacres so we avoid—"

"And you're telling me," said Dani, as though Annith hadn't spoken, "that Meela just happened to be singled out by the king to hear this bargain?"

Annith raised her eyebrows at me in a "maybe you should tell them the whole story" sort of way. I returned an almost imperceptible shake of my head. I couldn't say anything more without revealing that Adaro had sought me out specifically— that he'd pulled me into the water because he knew about my relationship with one of his warriors. The other half was that he'd return Lysi to me if I found the Host.

"This mermaid king, Ada-what's-his-name," said Hassun. "You say he came to your ship while you were slaughtering demons, and he told you about this Host of Eriana?"

"Yes."

"How did you communicate?"

"He speaks Eriana," I said.

"He speaks Eriana."

"Yes. And English and Spanish, I think."

They exchanged glances, and I realised I shouldn't have said that last part.

The widow spoke up. "If this Adderall merman—"

"Adaro."

"Yes. If he came to your ship as you claim, what makes you think he was telling the truth? You're prepared to trust the word of a sea demon who can speak Eriana?"

"Well, we know Meela's always been quick to trust a nice mermaid who can speak her language, hasn't she?" said Dani.

My father's head snapped up. Annith sucked in a breath.

I held Dani's gaze as her lips pulled into a sneer.

"So you have mentioned," said Mujihi.

No, I thought desperately.

The room seemed to cool as everyone stared. They knew.

"This plan does conveniently stop the demons from getting slaughtered, too," said Hassun.

Sweat prickled beneath my skin. Dani must have found out from one of the girls who'd seen Lysi. Was it Texas? But how much did Texas know? Did she realise how much history Lysi and I had?

No, she wouldn't. As far as the girls on the Massacre knew, Lysi and I had spoken once, and then she'd saved my life. My crew didn't understand why, or for how long we'd known each other.

I had to keep it that way. My people couldn't know about Lysi. Not ever. They would hate me for it—worse, those I cared about would be disappointed in me. No one would love a girl who loved a mermaid. Eriana Kwai was my family, my history, and I could never alienate myself like that.

But Dani and Texas had obviously mentioned Lysi. And now my people would never trust me enough to support my plan.

Dani flashed her most charming smile around the room.

I narrowed my eyes. If she wanted to get nasty, fine. I wasn't the only one with a black smudge of betrayal in my past.

Mirroring her venomous tone, I said, "Tell me, Dani, why weren't you around when Adaro came to the ship?"

Annith's head snapped from Dani to me.

"You were a little isolated at the time, were you not?" I said.

Dani's face went hard as stone.

Mujihi stepped forwards. "Enough. Dani has a point. This young lady"—he pointed a thick, calloused finger at me—"is keen to stop the Massacres. It sounds like she has enlisted her friend here to help pitch this tale."

"It's not a tale," I said, temper flaring. "Most of us in this room know what it's like out there. Why send more girls on the Massacre when there's a way we can avoid it?"

"Metlaa Gaela," said Anyo, finally opening his mouth. "It is a noble goal to protect the future girls of Eriana Kwai. But—"

"But the Massacres are looking up," said Mujihi.

"How many times have we said that in the past?" I said. "Sending women instead of men might be a more successful strategy, but it doesn't change the fact that a lot of them are going to die before we get anywhere—*if* we get anywhere!"

No matter what, I couldn't let another Massacre happen. Adaro's rising desperation, along with my failure to find the Host in time, meant the next Massacre would end worse than ever—for the warriors aboard the ship, for my people, and for Lysi.

My heart ached to think about it. Lysi was his hostage right now. I had no idea where she was, or what he was doing with her.

"We have a newer strategy yet," said Mujihi. "A new training master."

I opened my mouth, but his words hit me like a rock to the head. I spluttered.

"New—what—new training—?"

Anyo flicked his gaze to me before lowering it to the table. I caught a glint of apology in his dark, tired eyes.

Mujihi clasped a huge, calloused hand on Anyo's shoulder.

"Since your departure in May, I have taken over the training program. We have been working on new strategies and experimenting with a deadlier range of weapons."

"No," I said before I could stop myself.

Mujihi's expression darkened, giving him the appearance of a hawk on the hunt.

"It's just—Anyo has always been the training master. You can't change that."

I felt Annith's eyes on me. This, we had not planned for.

"With Anyo's daughter in training," said Mujihi, "the committee felt there was a conflict of interest. Besides, many have been pushing for a change in the program for years."

I narrowed my eyes. "And I suppose you had a vote on the new training master."

"It was an obvious choice," said Hassun. "No one else had a plan for new weapons, better training—even the idea to send women in the first place."

Mujihi puffed out his chest. I caught a glimpse of Dani in his expression.

I turned back to my father, waiting for him to offer any shred of support. He was watching Mujihi, jaw tight.

"Girls," said the widow, "I think I speak for all of us when I say we appreciate your ideas for helping our people. But we have no evidence of the Host of Eriana. This legend isn't substantiated by anything, which gives us no reason to pursue it."

"If we had some help, and gave our best shot at finding it ..." said Annith, but not a single face showed interest.

My father drummed his knuckles on the table. "Have you exhausted all potential sources of evidence?"

"The library is ... limited," I said, shifting in the rigid chair.

Since returning from the Massacre, Annith and I had read every book on our people's history, including essays, newspaper archives, a reference book on local fungi, even a picture book called *Ern the Eagle Learns to Fly*.

"Certainly, there are pieces of history we don't know about," said my father. "Many legends have been passed verbally and lost over time. I suggest you find proof, and then—"

"It doesn't matter," said Hassun. "We need to keep fighting. If we stop the Massacres, we're surrendering."

"We want to stop the Massacres, not give up," I said. "We'll still use the trainees. They'll help us find the Host. Just don't send them to sea. Adaro's army is getting stronger and the mermaids will probably sink the ship within the first few days."

At this proclamation, the silence in the room thickened. Either the idea scared them, or they were wondering why I knew so much about Adaro's army.

"You have nearly a year before the next Massacre," said the widow. "I suggest you do your best, and if you haven't found this Host before then, we'll keep doing what we know works."

"But the Massacres don't work!" I said, slapping the table. "They're a death sentence! These girls will be doomed the second their ship hits open water."

"Can we wrap this up?" said Hassun, watching Dani fix her ponytail.

I stood. "No. This committee was formed to protect our people and save us from sea demons, and you're ignoring a real solution."

"Meela, sit down," said my father.

"I think we should end this meeting before tempers get out of hand," said Mujihi with exaggerated calmness.

I dropped into my chair. "I'm fine."

"No, we're done here," said Hassun. "I have to go close up the foundry."

I clenched my fists. I couldn't believe what I was witnessing.

"So you're willing to send a girl out to fight for our people," I said, "but you're not willing to listen to what she has to say?"

"It's not like that," said my father, but I didn't want to hear it from him. I wanted to hear it from the others.

"You're using us," I said. "You're training us to fight this war because it's the only way to battle the sea demons, but you won't take us seriously. We trained for five years and spent a month on the fringe of being eaten alive. We deserve to be treated like adults."

"Then as an adult," said the widow, rising, "you understand we cannot base a decision to stop training for the Massacres on a myth for which you have no evidence."

I sat back, scanning their indifferent faces. My insides quivered with anger, disappointment, and regret for letting myself think they might listen.

"I have to get back to planning my lessons," said Mujihi.

He, Anyo, and the widow made for the door. Hassun leapt up to walk beside Dani. I could have gagged.

My father remained at the table with Annith and me.

Amid the scuffling feet and creaking chairs, he leaned in. "Metlaa Gaela, I understand your empathy for the Massacre trainees. But it's in your best interest to give the new program a chance."

I stood, refusing to look at him, and stormed out the door. Annith trailed behind me as I headed in the opposite direction of everyone, deeper into the woods. The cold evening air stung my burning cheeks.

The people I'd fought for didn't believe me. They thought I was paranoid. My own father wouldn't stand up for me. Anyo, who'd become as close as an uncle throughout my time in the training program, hadn't said more than a few words.

I stomped on a fat mushroom, which exploded into brown powder.

When we'd retreated a safe distance from the cabin, I rounded on Annith.

"How could they possibly—how could they even think—how can they ignore—"

I twisted my fingers in my hair, at a loss.

"I can't believe no one told us about Anyo. Six weeks, Dani's father's been the training master."

"Unbelievable," said Annith, crossing her arms. "Anyo must have been sacked, like, the day we left."

I rubbed a hand across my face.

"They *like* Dani," I said weakly.

Of everything that happened during the meeting, I'd found this to be the most disturbing. How could they let Dani attend their meetings, charm them with her fake smile, speak as though worthy of being listened to? Didn't they understand what she'd done on the Massacre? Every girl who survived could attest to it: Dani was a murderer. She had killed Shaena and hadn't faced so much as a scolding since we had come home.

"It's because Mujihi's her father," whispered Annith. "I mean, new training master? This is totally why she hasn't had to answer for what she did."

I stared at the ground, speechless. Somewhere overhead, a saw-whet owl whistled. The other birds had fallen silent, tucking in for the night.

"That's why Dani's so opposed to stopping the Massacres," I said. "No doubt she'll be offering opinions on how the girls should be trained."

"But what's up with the rest of the committee?"

"They don't trust me," I said.

"That's not true."

"It is. They know I trusted a mermaid."

Even if they did believe me, they dismissed the idea that sea demons could be intelligent. My people had never been willing to believe mermaids had minds like ours. But they did. Mermaids fought like humans, laughed like humans, and loved like humans.

Over and over, I'd pictured the expressions on my parents' faces if I told them my feelings about Lysi—my mother crying, my father yelling himself hoarse about how I'd shamed the family and the memory of my older brother.

It didn't matter. Standing there in the woods, my heart ached at the thought of Lysi, like Adaro's giant, webbed fist was clenched around it, pulsing every so often to remind me how easily he could end it all.

Annith squeezed my shoulder and I looked up. She was watching me closely.

"We'll get your friend back," she said.

I stared back into her hazel eyes.

My friend. Even though Annith knew about Lysi, I'd kept the details of my feelings to myself. Annith didn't know Lysi was more than a friend. Even I didn't know whether Lysi was more than a friend, or if she felt the same. The realisation of it embarrassed me.

Trying to talk about such a complicated feeling with Annith would achieve a level of awkwardness I never wanted to face. Even talking about crushes on boys made me uncomfortable, never mind this.

"Now what?" said Annith. "None of them believed us. Did you see their faces? They think we're totally nuts."

I frowned. "Maybe they don't believe us, but that doesn't change anything. We need to go after Adaro."

The owl whistled again, and I lifted my gaze to the maple tree.

Even though Annith stood by my side, loyal as ever, I felt alone.

"We're going to have to find the Host without their help," I said, my words crisp in the silence.

I waited for Annith to argue, anticipating that she would turn homewards and leave me. But she straightened, facing me with a gleam in her eyes.

"Where do we start?"

With a grim smile, I turned in the direction of the ocean. The woods had stilled enough that the swishing waves carried faintly to where we stood.

I had been thinking about it for a while, though I hadn't brought it up. It would be dangerous. But we could do it without the help of the Massacre trainees.

"Skaaw Beach."

CHAPTER TWO
Adaro's Prisoner

My escape might not have gone so well, if I wasn't trained in the art of punching someone's face in.

I left Katus hunched with his hands over his nose. Blood clouded between his fingers. Ladon would be working out how he got stuck inside my prison cell.

Arms held tight to my sides, I shot towards the kelp forest. My body waved smoothly, tail beating quick strokes in the open water.

The current pushed against me. A short drop below, plankton drifted forwards. I dove, finding the favourable current and letting it propel me faster.

Of course, the guards were also trained in combat, and their thicker frames would be to their advantage if they caught me. That wouldn't happen. Mermen had brawn, but nothing could match the speed and agility of a mermaid.

The kelp forest towered ahead. Its lush, weedy scent wafted towards me. Trees faded into the blue on either side, anchoring to the rocks and rising into a canopy above. The dense tangle would mask me from my guards. The swaying plants and darting fish would stop them from sensing me.

Shouts rang in my ears. Their presence closed in on me like an oil slick. They were too close, and swimming fast.

Still, I was faster.

I exploded through a school of herring, sending tremors and bubbles in all directions.

I reached the forest and didn't slow down. I adjusted my rhythm, my tail making quick, small movements, getting me through the trees at breakneck speed. Blacksmith fish scattered, little blue blurs that moved hardly fast enough. If I were hunting, they wouldn't have had a chance.

Buoys on the kelp pummelled me as I darted by. The greenery thickened, the world darkened, the water warmed.

The sound of my pursuers faded. They must have been slowing down. No way could they navigate the kelp this quickly.

I dove abruptly, letting my wake hit the trees and dissipate.

The darkness intensified. The forest isolated the outside noise, like a cavern closing around me. I stopped before I hit the rocky bottom.

Water gulped against my ears. Any life had scattered, leaving me isolated in every direction.

Heart pounding, I waited. I pushed down my anxiety in case they felt it, swaying with the trees, forcing my pulse to slow. I focused on the vibrations brushing my skin.

There was nothing more here than flapping fins and twirling comb jellies.

Somewhere, I smelled the blood from Katus' nose. They weren't far.

As soon as I lost them, I planned to zigzag back up the currents to the Gulf of Alaska. I refused to float around, a pathetic hostage, while Meela carried out her end of Adaro's bargain. I had to help her.

I ached to think of home—of Meela on Eriana Kwai, of my family in Utopia. I'd never travelled this far from them in my life.

Ripples hit my senses. A face appeared beside me.

I recoiled, blowing bubbles in surprise.

A sea lion. His playfulness tickled my senses, an aura I felt beneath my skin. He stared at me with huge black eyes, then blew a bubble from his nose, returning my gesture.

No, I thought. *Get lost.*

He zoomed back and forth in front of me. The surrounding plants swayed.

I drove a current at him with my tail. Katus and Ladon couldn't find me because of this.

The animal poked me with his nose and looked away as though to pretend it wasn't him.

On an ordinary day, I might have welcomed the game. But he was going to betray my position.

I snarled, letting my eyes fill with blood and my teeth lengthen.

The sea lion froze. His eyes widened. With a flip of his fins, he shot backwards into the forest.

I waited until I lost the feel of him, and then sank into the rocks. My state remained predatory, ready to fight if the guys had felt the movement.

My muscles were tired, weak. My lungs ached. I hadn't breached in a quarter-tide. But I couldn't surface now. Not yet.

"Over here!"

Ladon's voice bounced off the trees. I tensed, trying to gauge which direction to flee.

"That's not her, fish face. That's a sea lion."

I opened my mouth in silent protest that he could mistake this body for that fat, hairy animal.

"Oh. You sure she didn't flounder?"

"She never got breath. Give it time. She'll have to surface."

"We don't have time. What'll happen if the king finds Lysithea's cell empty?"

Silence. Then, with an air of panic, Katus said, "Maybe she'll stay low and black out on us."

He might have been right. Each thud of my heart brought me closer to running out of oxygen. My chest burned. I floated limp, trying to save the tiny puff left in my lungs.

A crab passed my nose on its way up a rope of kelp. It paused, seemed to decide it would rather stay near the bottom, and changed direction. I watched it, envying a life so simple.

My skin prickled in the heat, like I'd landed in a pit of toxic algae. Wherever I was, it was much too hot. I guessed they'd taken me to the Fractures—the coast of what Meela called California.

Not for the first time, I cursed Adaro. I'd taken an oath, trained for years, and fought his war against humans, and this was how he thanked me?

I reminded myself how quickly I'd broken my oath when I found Meela on the ship I was sent to destroy.

As though triggered by the thought of Meela, my lungs spasmed with pain.

Maybe I was lucky. At least Adaro had kept me alive. Still, I didn't trust him or his promise of peace. He knew Meela would do anything to save her people.

If I could get to Eriana Kwai, I could help her. This thing Adaro called the Host must have had the potential to control the seas. Why else would he want it? With that power, we could instate a new queen or king.

Desperate for breath, I glanced towards the surface. Beams of sunlight peeked through the canopy, illuminating patches of greenery and leaving others in shadow.

I had no choice. If I swam further, they would feel my movement. Plus, the exertion would use up my last breath in a single heartbeat.

My lungs gave a desperate squeeze. I couldn't bear it any longer.

Rockfish cleared out of my path as I shot upwards. An otter paused to watch me dart by.

Halfway to the top, a pulse hit me from above.

"No," I whispered.

A body eclipsed the sun.

Without pausing to think, I bent at the waist and dove— and stopped short. Another presence closed in from below.

Ladon streaked towards me, wooden spear in hand.

"You made it far this time," said Katus from overhead.

I darted blindly sideways and collided with a tangle of weeds.

Ladon reached for me. I slammed him with my tail, knocking the wind from his lungs in a stream of bubbles.

Lights popped in my vision.

Air.

I tore through the weeds, scrambling to reach the surface. My senses clouded over.

Up.

For several desperate heartbeats, I knew only the shimmering light above.

Finally, my head broke through the canopy. I took a long, gasping breath.

The harsh sunlight blinded me. I coughed out seawater, panting hard, too dizzy to do anything but inhale.

Ripples hit me on either side.

My next breath came as a sob. I didn't have time to inhale deeply. I had to dive—but I was too late. A webbed hand grabbed my hair.

I shrieked, squirming to get away.

"I've had it with these seal hunts," said Katus, dragging me like a dead tuna. "I'm gonna ask if we can cut off her fin."

His nose had stopped bleeding. I tried to punch it in the same place. Ladon's fist closed around my arm. I twisted, trying to sink my teeth into either of them.

"Babe, you gotta understand," he said. "Our lives will be on your hands if you escape."

I thrashed, hitting them with my tail and fists. But Adaro had obviously chosen these guards for their size. They were easily twice as thick as me, and pulled me away from the canopy with ease.

Both of them oozed smugness. I bristled at the closeness, not bothering to hide my disgust.

While a mermaid's upper body resembled a human in its everyday state, mermen never left the state that earned us the nickname *sea demons*. Sharp teeth, long ears, webbed fingers, solid red eyes, and skin like rotting seaweed. Even then, a merman was more reptilian than a transformed mermaid—thicker and stronger, skin faintly scaly, a lipless mouth, nose blending into cheekbones like the face of a common fish.

Nineteen and at the peak of fitness, Katus and Ladon embodied the hulking crocodile appearance better than anyone. Some mermaids went for that. I sooner would've kissed an anglerfish.

As they dragged me back, the vibrant ripples of the kelp forest gave way to a dirty, lifeless city. Stone pillars towered beside us, barely visible through the murk.

With Utopia nearly finished, Adaro had begun colonising further south. Most of this city was under construction, the surrounding coral beaten and dead. Even the water tasted sour, the result of constant stirring of dirt and grime.

Ladon held my prison entrance open with his spear.

I tried to bite Katus but he leaned away, shoving me into the cave with extra force.

"I'm warning you, fish face," he said. "We'll knock you out next time. Drag you back by your pretty golden hair."

I blew bubbles in his face before the curtain of tentacles fell closed.

Jellyfish didn't usually bother me. Their sting was painful, sure, but after feeling the molten burn of iron in the early years of my life, it was hard to get worked up over those soft, slippery creatures.

These jellyfish were an exception. I recoiled as they swayed towards me. Their tentacles fell two fathoms deep. Above, their guts were visible inside the pulsing bells. I wouldn't have been able to wrap my arms around one if I tried.

I backed against the rocky wall, feeling the jellies' sting without touching them. My prison was barely a cave—an indentation, really—and I had to be careful where I drifted. A tiny pocket of air at the back served as my oxygen supply, and I had to bend my neck painfully to get it.

The first day, I'd braced myself and tried to blast through the tentacle curtain before anyone knew what had happened. I'd blacked out before I made it to the other side.

Since then, I'd discovered easier ways to escape—like hauling my guard through the curtain instead.

"Babe, it's in your best interest to give up," said Ladon.

I snarled. "Feel free to take a break if you're tired."

"He's serious," said Katus. "Keep going and you'll get sent to the labour camp."

"Better than being here."

They laughed.

"Never heard about the labour camp, babe? No food. Rationed air. Depths that make your eyes feel like they're about to pop. The only creatures that survive down there are the scavengers feeding on the corpses."

"Don't forget the viperfish," said Katus. "They'll tear you piece by piece for breakfast."

"Still sounds like better company than what I've got here," I said, not buying the intimidation.

Ladon shrugged. "If you think digging into rock until your fingers bleed is better than here, I'll be sure to tell—"

The guys' sneers vanished. They whirled around. I caught a whiff of fear.

"Now, if a captive repeatedly escapes, ought I to punish the captive, or her guards?"

I froze. The jellies' sting blinded my feel of the current, so I never sensed his approach.

"We have her under control, Your Majesty," said Katus.

A third merman drifted between them like a dark ghost. Larger, thicker, more impressive in every way, he brought everything to silence. Anyone would recognise that black hair, long and matted, anchoring the black crown on his head.

I dropped my gaze as he fixed me with his crimson eyes.

"Open it," said Adaro.

Ladon pushed the tentacles aside.

"Your Majesty," I said, heart pounding.

"Lysithea. You have convinced me."

Two thick bodyguards floated behind him. They gripped stone clubs rough with barnacles. The left one held a coil of slime-encrusted rope.

I'd heard Adaro had started taking bodyguards everywhere. I'd also heard the guards once ripped the arms off a group of mermaids who had refused to sink a sailboat. I hoped the limb-ripping part was a rumour.

"Convinced you of what, sir?"

"Of letting you go."

He was too calm. I waited.

"You have a certain quality," he said.

"If being a slippery eel can be considered a quality," mumbled Katus.

"Whatever it is, it seems to get her past my guards," said Adaro, a dangerous flare in his eyes.

Katus shut up. He and Ladon exchanged looks.

"It would be a waste not to utilise those skills," said Adaro. "Your academy training was, after all, expensive."

I didn't miss the threat. "The battlefront?"

Adaro flashed his yellowed fangs. "Not Eriana Kwai. You clearly cannot be trusted near humans."

I opened my mouth. A silent "oh" escaped in a bubble. He was going to make me fight below the surface.

He knew I would have no chance against mermen. Mermaids were trained to fight above water, and mermen to fight below, and there was reason for both.

"Must be a relief, babe," said Ladon. "In our battles, you don't need to worry about iron."

Right, I thought, *I only need to worry about a merman cracking my skull.*

"A shame," said Katus. "No chance to add more texture to that cute little waist."

He reached for the scar on my side—the iron-made burn earned from a friendship with a human. It had become my tattooed reminder of why I needed to fight Adaro's rule.

I grabbed Katus' wrist before he could reach me, letting my eyes fill with blood.

"Don't touch me."

I barely got the words out before Ladon swiped me across the face with the end of his spear. I let go, but refused to back away.

"Take her to the south military base," said Adaro. "She will depart for battle with the next detachment."

The strand of hope that had remained—that maybe I would be sent to the same military base as my big brother—snapped.

"South?" I said. "Why south? I thought you were battling for India."

His aura darkened, and I added, "Sir."

"If I ask you to fight in the south, you will fight in the south," he said. "If I ask you to fight for a wisp of volcano at the bottom of the Mariana Trench, I expect you to fight until you have either won it, or died trying."

I said nothing. After a moment he added, with a threatening note, "Am I clear?"

"Yes, sir."

"So, men," said Adaro, backing away. "Get moving, if you want to arrive before sundown."

The bodyguard handed Katus the slimy rope. My back collided with the rocky wall of my cell.

"You're supposed to keep me alive," I said. "That was your deal with Meela."

Whatever Adaro sensed in my mood made his lip curl.

"It is not in my hands whether you live or die in battle."

"Please," I said. "I don't want—"

I stopped myself.

Adaro's eyes widened. "You don't want?"

Behind him, the two bodyguards drifted closer.

"That's not what I meant."

Of course not. Fighting Adaro's war was the only *want* anyone should have. Even as a prisoner, I felt nothing but the deepest loyalty to my king.

I thought of this as I stared him in the eye.

A mermaid I'd gone to school with came to mind. Her family had claimed she couldn't enter the army because of an illness. The day after admitting she couldn't fight, she disappeared. Her parents said the illness finally took her—but something was never right with them after that.

"I do not need to remind you that you are sworn under oath," said Adaro.

"My life is dedicated to your reign."

He studied me, as though trying to dig beneath my mask of sincerity. Afraid of what he'd find, I recited the oath I'd taken at thirteen years old.

"I swear that I shall be unconditionally obedient to King Adaro, ruler of the Pacific Ocean and all merpeople within. I shall be ready to give my life for the quest to unite the seas under one kingdom, one rule, with King Adaro the deserving wearer of the absolute crown."

He revealed nothing.

When I spoke again, my lips felt numb.

"Your Majesty, I would be honoured to serve in the south army."

After a long moment, the king turned away. He nodded to his bodyguards. They followed him into the depths.

I watched them go, feeling their presence long after they disappeared from view.

My attention snapped back as Katus and Ladon reached into my cell. They hauled me into the open and forced my hands behind my back. Could I break loose as they tried to move me? With full lungs, I could make it further into the kelp this time.

Ladon wrapped a fist in my hair to force me to stay still.

"Watch out for lice," said Katus. "I think one bit me coming back from the weeds."

I rolled my eyes. "Can't that shrimp-sized brain of yours come up with a new insult?"

He bound my wrists, wrapping the rope all the way up my forearms so I wouldn't be able to snap it. He yanked it tight. It dug into my flesh.

"He has a point, babe," said Ladon. "Heard of a comb? Have some respect for the men in the world."

He disappeared to get supplies, leaving me at the end of Katus' rope like an otter on a leash.

I ignored his comments. I'd spent my whole life teased by other mermaids. These guys had nothing new to say.

While the average mermaid spent half the day obsessing over her appearance, any ribbons of seaweed in my hair likely got there by accident while I was chasing a dolphin. My parents had tried for years to get me to care. They gave me the latest makeup and hair products, with kelp paste and ground pearls and farmed caviar. One day, after spending most of my life without friends, I decided I'd try it. I woke up before sunrise, spent a quarter-tide on my hair and makeup, and went to school. I somehow got teased even worse than when I'd gone to school with knots in my hair. My day ended early when a group of girls told me I missed a spot and shot squid ink in my face. I went home and threw out all the makeup—except the caviar, which I ate. Then I got sick because it apparently had been farmed for beauty, not eating.

Ladon returned with a sack of food and two stone clubs. Katus pulled the rope, forcing me along behind them. I pried my wrists, subtly trying to pull my arms apart with all my strength. The rope groaned, but didn't snap. If I could stretch it loose, maybe I could pull free, grab one of those clubs and—

"Don't," said Katus. "I'll tie you to a rock and leave you there. The king won't know the difference."

I glared at him, but said nothing, knowing he could very well do that if he wanted to.

So I followed, trailing at the end of the rope. We left the city behind and crossed the empty wilderness.

Several times, I promised to swim without fuss if they let me go. To my frustration, they were smart enough to distrust me.

After our first breach, I discreetly tried to work my arms through the rope again. But it was bound too tightly and, before long, my arms were chafed in the effort.

Then we reached open water, and I had to stop struggling to keep up. We swam at high speed the whole way, breaching every few strokes.

I hated the open water. In every direction was nothing, nothing, and nothing. Ripples and sound carried for leagues, so a ghostly symphony played against my senses the whole way: the long, low moan of a grey whale, the clicks of a pod, a groaning tanker, and a blend of vibrations I couldn't identify. They might have been schools of tuna, giant squids, or humans, for all I knew.

At one point, we passed close to a pair of orcas. We gave them a wide berth because they were the transient kind—dead silent and mean, with a taste for big bait like seals.

Few things could kill merpeople. The only way a human had done it was by using iron. Merpeople had also managed to kill each other for millennia. Being chopped to pieces in the jaws of a whale or shark also did the trick.

That was the only time I was thankful to be with Katus and Ladon. The whales noticed us, slowed down, seemed to think about giving chase. But there were three of us, and those mermen might have had scum for brains, but they were too brawny to be whale food.

The encounter wouldn't have gone so well if I'd been alone. Though I could outswim a whale, the pods had clever hunting tactics, and they surrounded and killed mermaids more often than anyone cared to admit.

Finally, the floor grew shallower, and sand became rock. The water tasted sweeter in the presence of coral, anemones, and fish. Pulses grazed my skin from a nearby octopus. The city would be close, now.

I tried to relax the knot between my shoulder blades. Our trip through the open left me as twitchy as a guppy.

The guys stopped and I bumped into Katus. Ladon smacked me away with his spear.

I peered between them. A guard floated upright, a stone mace wrapped in his webbed fingers. More treaded on either side, stationed out of sight but close enough to feel. We'd arrived at some kind of border.

I glanced around, feeling my surroundings. Guards to either side. Shallow, rocky bottom. Empty ocean behind and in front.

How was I supposed to get back home if I had to cross a military line?

Ladon pulled out a roll of rawhide.

"Royal guardians on a transport order," he said, puffing himself up.

Could I risk the empty ocean alone? Maybe not, but if I didn't flee now, I might not be able to once we crossed this border. I tensed, preparing to jerk away from Katus' grip. If I could catch them by surprise, disappear into the distance, maybe I'd find something sharp to slice—

A sharp blow on the back of my head made a rainbow of lights pop in my eyes.

"I swear," said Katus, "I'll knock you out and drag you."

I snarled at him, the back of my skull throbbing.

The guard grunted. He slapped the roll of rawhide back into Ladon's chest without bothering to read it. I wondered if he could even read.

His eyes raked over me like I was a sub-par dinner delivery.

"This is a girl."

I wanted to comment on his superior observational skills, but I held my tongue.

"She's to serve below surface now," said Ladon.

The guard scowled at me.

I would have been wary, too, seeing a mermaid stationed so far from humans. What could I have possibly done?

I flashed the guard a wicked grin, letting my eyes bleed red.

He broke his gaze and motioned for us to continue.

Katus tugged the rope. I followed, a wave of fear passing over me. Had that been my last chance? Between the emptiness behind us and the military zone ahead, an escape attempt now would get me killed.

I wondered, with a hollow feeling in my stomach, if I would ever see home again.

CHAPTER THREE
Training Base

Black pants, black kohl around the eyes, dark hair braided under the hood of a black sweater. I'd given myself the best chance at not being seen.

I peered out my bedroom window. The night was cloudy, of course. I could always rely on the skies of Eriana Kwai to block any hint of moonlight.

Annith had promised to meet me at the end of my driveway at dark—eleven thirty, at this time of year. I checked the clock. I was a minute late already.

"Going to Annith's," I said as I strode from my room.

The sound of my mother brushing her teeth carried down the hall.

"Ish mishle o' nigh'!"

I pulled on my boots. "What?"

A pause while she spat. "It's the middle of the night!"

"Yeah. She had a fight with Rik."

An easy lie. Boyfriend issues had been a regular occurrence for Annith since we were about twelve.

Silence. I thought I heard a deep sigh. "Don't be too late, honey."

"Love you."

Face buried in the neck of my hoodie, I stepped outside and shut the door. I turned around—and walked straight into someone.

I let out a small scream, and before I knew what'd happened, Tanuu was stumbling backwards with his hand on his cheek.

"Ow, Meela! What the hell?"

I gasped and dropped my fists, pain throbbing across my knuckles. "Tanuu, I'm sorry! I didn't … I didn't see you."

"'s okay." He let go of his face, eyeing me.

"I was just going …" I motioned vaguely across the yard. "Are you okay?"

"Yeah."

We stared at each other until the silence became awkward. Above us, a noisy assortment of insects and moths that were easily the size of my palm bounced off the porch light.

"I've wanted to see you," said Tanuu. "I've tried to come by but you're never home."

"I've been busy."

"Doing what?"

I stuffed my hands in the pocket of my hoodie and buried my chin, mumbling something about "settling back in" and "homecoming dinners". It was partly true.

"I've only seen you once since you got back," he said with a note of accusation.

"Twice," I said, as if that made it better.

"The day you got home doesn't count, Meela. The whole island was there."

I didn't reply. Moths continued to flutter in the porch light. Not knowing what else to do, I started to walk past Tanuu.

"Meela, please. I just wanna know if you're all right. If *we're* all right."

I turned.

"I just need some recovery time."

He nodded once, but his eyebrows stayed pinched. "I get that. The Massacre's a lot for anyone to handle. You don't have to grieve alone, though."

I held his gaze. The dim light made his pupils huge, so I felt like I was staring into the face of a baby seal.

Footsteps crunched behind me. Annith was barely visible, all in black with a hood casting her face into shadow.

"You coming or what?" she said.

She stopped at the edge of the porch light, scrutinising Tanuu with black-lined eyes. "Is he coming, too?"

"No," I said, at the same time as Tanuu gave a hearty, "Yes."

Annith and I exchanged a glance.

"Annith and I have plans," I said. "We can talk tomorrow."

Not that I wanted to have a conversation about my feelings with him the next day, but I thought that might make him more inclined to leave us.

"Where ya going?" He followed us down the driveway, away from the soft glow of my house and onto the dead-end dirt road.

"We're having a girls night," I said. "We'll be talking about periods and stuff. You won't like it."

"Like hell you are. Since when does *girls night* involve dressing all in black and leaving the house under the cover of darkness?"

"You can't come with us," I said.

"Why not?"

"This isn't your fight!"

"Ha! This has to do with the Massacres, doesn't it? Heard you girls want to stop them. Are you trashing the training area?"

Annith snorted. I shot Tanuu a glare he wouldn't see.

"We don't want to *vandalise* anything," I said. "We're working on a better method. A way to make peace."

"And?"

I said nothing, kicking a rock so it bounced off a tree trunk. The sound cracked through the air.

"Whatever you're doing, I wanna help," said Tanuu.

I glanced sideways at Annith.

"He could keep watch for us," she said. "I mean, it won't look good if we're caught."

True, we had been under higher visibility since we'd gotten back. No Massacre survivor could go out in public without attracting attention.

The potential for disgracing my family dawned on me. My father had survived the Massacre, Nilus had died for it, and my mother had supported all three of us through training and departure. With that level of involvement, our family had achieved a level of recognition on Eriana Kwai.

We arrived at the path leading into the woods and stopped. Without the crunch of our footsteps, every chirp, every hoot, every whistle rang clearly.

I removed my boots. In pitch darkness, the forest would be easier to navigate in bare feet.

"Meela, I want our freedom, too," said Tanuu. "I sat at home while you girls fought the sea demons. Yeah, I would've been lunch in seconds, but still. Every minute you were out there was torture. Now I have the chance to be useful, if you let me."

I crossed my arms. An owl swooped low over our heads, the night so silent that I heard the swoosh of its wings.

I scrutinised Tanuu's outfit. His windbreaker had reflective strips on the chest.

"Take off your coat. You'll stand out like a lighthouse."

He did, with enthusiasm. His shirt underneath was grey.

"All right," I said. "You can keep watch."

He thrust a fist into the air, and then balled up his jacket and tossed it next to my boots.

"What am I watching?"

"We're going to borrow a couple of things from the training base," I said. "Crossbows. Ammo. Anything else that might be helpful."

"You didn't get to keep your Massacre weapons?"

I huffed.

"They took them back for the next round of trainees," said Annith.

A stiff silence followed. Unfortunately, the girl who actually should have been stripped of all weapons still had access to them.

"Why don't you borrow my father's hunting bow?" said Tanuu. "I could—"

"Oh my gosh, Tanuu," said Annith, "we need *iron* weapons. A hunting arrow will just bounce off a mermaid's skin."

"Oh. Right."

We entered the forest. After the empty dirt road, the dense rainforest wrapped me in warmth and comfort. We followed the narrow path, me in the lead, guided by the carpet of moss on either side. I extended a hand to brush the passing saplings, feeling them shake off cool droplets under my touch.

"Doesn't your father have a crossbow?" said Tanuu.

"We can use the ammo, but the bow's a piece of junk," I said. "Tried it last night. The bolts don't even leave it in a straight line."

"We should bring it, anyway," said Annith. "It's still iron."

"I think the poker from my fireplace might work better."

My eyes adjusted quickly to the blackness. I sprung onto a fallen tree and ran up the sloping log a few steps before landing on the ground again, nimble on the balls of my feet.

"So you're gonna steal some weapons and fight the mermaids on your own?" said Tanuu.

His tone suggested that was about as good an idea as a man deciding to go for a dip in the ocean.

"Don't be ridiculous," I said. "We need something to keep us safe while we search the shoreline. We're going to look for a cave."

I pretended to concentrate on stepping over roots and logs. If he was going to help us, he needed to know the story. But after our meeting with the Massacre Committee, I didn't feel up to sharing the plan anymore.

Annith picked up my hesitation.

"I think Tanuu will have a better reaction than they did," she said.

"I can hardly imagine a worse reaction."

Tanuu waited.

"All right, I'll tell it," said Annith.

I said nothing. She took this as permission, and gave Tanuu a tame summary of how I'd met Adaro. For Tanuu's sake, she avoided mentioning the part where I'd gotten hypothermia and nearly drowned.

The woods thickened, the moss warm beneath my feet. It pressed in from all sides like a giant pillow, muffling our voices and footsteps. A shape leaned across our path, blacker than the backdrop. I touched it as we ducked beneath, the log soft and springy beneath my palm.

When Annith got to the part where we planned to double-cross Adaro and kill him, Tanuu stopped walking.

"You're both nuts," he said faintly, as though in deep awe.

Annith laughed.

"Not going to argue," I said.

His shoes padded softly as he jogged to catch up. "What exactly is the Host?"

"Adaro said it's like a pet," I said. "Something playing host to Eriana's soul. She was bound with it when she died. That's all we know."

"Have you tried the library?"

Annith sighed. "What do you think we've been doing in the last two weeks?"

"And?"

"There's plenty of material on the last two hundred years of international relations," I said.

"Boring," said Annith.

"There was one book that mentioned the goddess Eriana," I said. "That's the one we all read in grade two."

"A bit less boring."

"But there was no mention of her pet anywhere."

"No idea where it is?" said Tanuu.

"None whatsoever."

"So," said Annith, "we decided we need to hunt for the Host ourselves."

Skunk cabbage met my nose, and I veered right to avoid traipsing through a marshy patch.

"Adaro thinks the Host is somewhere beneath the island?" said Tanuu.

"Right," I said. "We're thinking it's in some kind of cave."

"And the crossbows are for?"

"Skaaw Beach."

Tanuu made a noise between a gasp and an "oh!"

"Yeah," I said.

None of us had been to Skaaw Beach. As with every beach on the island, access was forbidden. We knew about it through word of mouth, as a landmark on Eriana Kwai. *Skaaw* was the old-language word for lava. A million years before, molten lava had oozed from cracks in the earth and cooled quickly, forming hundreds of peaks, valleys, and jagged columns along the stretch of beach.

"On the way there," said Annith, "we'll be able to check out other places, too. Like the cliff below Meela's house."

I didn't tell her I already knew what the cliff below my house looked like, because I spent half my childhood there.

Ahead, water trickled. I led us to the narrower part of the stream. We hopped over it, moving quickly through mud that was sure to house a swarm of mosquitoes.

"What happens once you get this mermaid king out of the way?" said Tanuu.

"He's, like, the whole reason we're being attacked," said Annith. "He's been trying to get rid of us so he can find the Host. Once he's gone ..."

"We'll be able to go fishing," I said.

"So you're sure freeing this thing's a good idea?"

"Adaro won't stop trying to get it," I said. "This is what he's after, and he'll keep attacking us until he gets it—or until we kill him with it."

Tanuu said nothing for a long time.

"Okay," he finally said. "I might believe you."

"That's a start," said Annith.

"The committee didn't, then?"

When neither of us answered, he added, "You'd think they'd wanna avoid losing more warriors."

I glanced back, trying to see Tanuu's face through the darkness. Annith was right: he had reacted better than the committee had. At least he was entertaining the idea.

"The committee thinks the change in training masters will fix the problem," I said. "But even if they do turn out better warriors, Adaro's army is also getting stronger."

A long silence passed, filled by the distant hoots of a saw-whet owl and the scuffing of Annith and Tanuu's boots. My bare feet were soundless over the moss.

"You still have time to change your mind if you think we're nuts," I said, offering Tanuu an escape.

"No," he said. "You're right for trying to find this Host. I don't wanna see anyone else die because of the Massacres either."

"I totally knew you'd feel that way!" said Annith. "You're a step ahead of Rik, you know."

I turned my head sharply. "You told Rik?"

"Obviously. We tell each other everything."

After a few seconds of meaningful silence from me, she added, "Almost everything."

I hoped she was being truthful.

We stopped talking, drawing near the training base. When we reached the clearing where the Enticer sat, we stopped. The rotting fossil of a ship was the island's most famous landmark—if only because no one could figure out how a ship had ended up in the middle of a forest. It now made up the centre of the Safe Training Base. The weapons stayed here, locked away when not used for target practice.

"You know Mujihi isn't gonna take it lightly when he realises someone broke into his weapons shed," whispered Tanuu.

"That's why we're only taking a couple," I whispered. "And if he does notice, he won't be able to prove it's us."

The crumbling outline of the Enticer loomed like a black hole in the glade. Around it, the cabins remained dark and empty.

Something big slunk through the bushes across the way, but I couldn't see what it was before it retreated into the forest. I caught myself hoping it was just a mountain lion, and then realised how ridiculous that was. This side of the shoreline, a mountain lion was the worst animal to encounter. Running, hiding, and fighting were all useless, especially at night. Still, somehow I would have rather fought a mountain lion than faced the shame of being caught breaking into the training base.

"Wait here," I whispered to Tanuu. "If you see anything suspicious, make an owl call."

"How will you know it's not a real owl?" he said.

He stood hunched, arms crossed. I heard his teeth chattering.

"Make another sound, then," I whispered impatiently.

"What about this?" He tilted his head back and made a ridiculous, guttural cry. "*Rrree-ah! cah! cah!*"

Annith and I stared at him.

I whispered, "How will I know it's not a real velociraptor?"

Annith stifled a laugh in her sleeve.

We left Tanuu shivering at the edge of the clearing. The air felt thinner, cooler as we left the insulation of the bush. Stepping cautiously over the forest floor, we crept past the

Enticer and towards the wooden shed containing the training crossbows.

Annith stumbled over something and grunted.

"Some idiot's been having a bonfire."

I glanced back. An ashy fire pit lay in the middle of the clearing. Annith had tripped over an iron rod dropped beside the charred logs.

"Maybe the trainees," I said. "Or else some kids trying to have a party."

The dark outline of the shed came into view at the top of the shooting range. A bit taller than me, curved on top with double doors in front, it might have passed as the garden shed of a sweet old lady.

I removed a pin from under my ponytail and slid it confidently inside the enormous lock. It reminded me unpleasantly of the time I had to do the same thing while locked inside the brig on the Massacre. *Traitor*, my crew had called me.

The task was easier here, surrounded by still woods instead of a mermaid-infested ship crashing through angry seas.

As I wiggled the pin around, pushing the buttons inside, I kept my ears strained for weird noises.

At last, the lock clicked open. I removed it hastily.

Crossbows lined the walls, hanging on pegs. A pile of extras littered the bottom, along with quivers and bolts.

"Grab them from the floor," whispered Annith, "so they don't notice any missing."

I reached down just as a noise split the air that made my blood run cold.

Tanuu.

I whirled around to see the whites of Annith's eyes. What had he seen? I'd honestly not expected Tanuu to be useful.

Who could be creeping around the training base at this time of night?

We gaped at each other.

Should we abandon the crossbows and run? Put the lock back on? Hide inside the shed and wait it out?

Annith seized my wrist and pulled. "Come on!"

I grabbed the first thing I touched and sprinted after her.

We made it not two steps before I heard a click, an electric buzz, and Annith's black camouflage became useless as she was bathed in the orange glow of a floodlight.

We stopped dead in our tracks.

A girl stepped into the clearing, arms crossed, lips curled in an expression of savage triumph.

A crossbow was slung across her chest. I considered running—but then a man stepped out from the darkness behind her, face purple with anger. He put a hand on his daughter's bony shoulder.

"My goodness, ladies," said Dani in her usual purr. "This doesn't look good at all."

CHAPTER FOUR
The South Pacific Army

By the time Katus and Ladon slowed down, we must have been halfway to the equator. Every piece of me ached from being stuck without my arms for so long.

A mountain range sprawled ahead, crackling with plants, fish, and shrimp. The movement tickled my skin, and beyond it, something larger.

While I couldn't see through the blue, every angle and divot materialised as a tiny swirl in the current. At first, I thought this might be another city under construction, Adaro's kingdom expanding towards the South Pacific. But the water didn't have that same dirty scent. Coral breathed on every surface, mature and healthy. Stone buildings grew into the mountain range like they'd been there for centuries. They towered high above the reef. The architecture was curved, ancient, unlike the blocky structures of Utopia.

"The Moonless City," I whispered.

In school, we learned that Adaro had made a peace pact with Queen Evagore when he crossed the Ice Channel into the Pacific. Adaro stayed north and built Utopia there, while Evagore remained in the Moonless City.

"Is the military base here?"

Katus and Ladon ignored me.

"Hello?" I said. "Are we there?"

"Yes," said Katus, not looking at me.

They both oozed exhaustion. I felt a smug satisfaction at the thought that the trip had been as gruelling for them as it had been for me.

As we drifted closer, I doubted the queen would suddenly be all right with Adaro's army storming through her city. It didn't sound like part of a peace pact.

Anemones swayed below. Small fish darted inside, brightly coloured in ways I'd never seen. In other circumstances, I might have plunged to the bottom for a closer look.

To my right, a turtle flapped along, the only creature indifferent to the three predators passing through. I slowed, feeling her presence.

She projected tranquility. I'd never felt it at such a deep level. I wanted to swim closer, but the rope tugged sharply.

A ridge materialised ahead. It rose from floor to surface, a natural wall of coral and rock. The current told me the other side was a grotto, like a circle carved by a meteor a million years ago. Activity buzzed inside of it—the deep voices and laughter of mermen. I couldn't tell how many.

My nerves tightened. Situated just outside of the city, this had to be the military base.

We rounded the ridge. I stopped short.

Hundreds of soldiers bustled inside the grotto, darting into caves and emerging with freshly sharpened blades, scarfing down handfuls of eggs, wrapping seaweed around their foreheads to tame floating locks of hair. I sensed weapons of wood, slate, argillite, chert, bone, coral, shells, and barnacles.

This crater must have been an apartment at one time. Plateaus at the surface offered plenty of space to rest. The walls blocked the currents while camouflaging its inhabitants. It would have also been a haven for food, except all fish and other animals seemed to have scattered.

Two mermen guarded either side of a gap in the ridge. They looked me up and down with the same scepticism as the guard at the border. Ladon handed the roll of rawhide to one of them before they could say anything. The guard unfurled it, scanned it, and waved us through.

I swam as discreetly as I could, flanking Katus as though I could blend with him.

As Katus unbound me, a few stares turned our way. Everyone fell silent. I kept my eyes down, but the change in the surrounding activity was palpable.

By the time the rope was undone, the attention of the entire vicinity was on the three of us.

Not us, I thought. *Me.*

"A *girl*," someone said. "What's a girl doing here?"

"You complaining?" said another.

"Sugar, what'd you do to end up down here?"

I dropped an arm to my waist, a habit I'd formed over the years to hide my iron scar. Being a girl was enough reason to stick out, never mind having—

"Gross! Check that thing out."

"Bet she's too ugly to lure humans so she had to come below surface."

"Whatever. I'd still get with that."

"You'd do a lingcod if it had blonde hair."

A ripple of laughter.

"Shut it, all of you."

A slim merman with dark hair approached, fist wrapped around an axe with a large chert blade. His bright red eyes flicked between Katus, Ladon, and me.

"What's this?"

"The king told us to bring her," said Ladon.

"Why?"

"Whatever you need her for," said Katus, shoving me towards him.

"She should be fighting above surface," said Slim.

"She blew her chance at that."

Slim narrowed his eyes.

I held my tongue, trying to read him. Though his face was a little beaten, hardened from battle, he had an aura of kindness.

"You need to keep her here," said Ladon. "King's orders."

"She'll be killed in the first battle."

I opened my mouth to defend my fighting skills, but decided against it.

Ladon shrugged. "Not our problem."

Slim flicked his gaze between us as though searching for another argument.

"We done here?" said Katus.

"Yeah," said Slim.

Ladon sneered. "Enjoy the battle, babe. Been fun dragging you back to your cell every day."

I twisted and smacked him across the face with my tail. He raised his spear to strike back, but Katus grabbed his arm, and Slim grabbed me.

"Save it," said Slim.

Whistles and laughter rose from the surrounding soldiers.

Katus and Ladon turned away. I watched them until they disappeared into the blue. Then I looked at Slim properly. He'd drifted away a little, sizing me up.

He softened. It was more compassion than I'd felt in a long time. I hoped I wasn't imagining his kindness out of desperation.

"Why the rope?" he said. "Were they afraid you'd try and escape?"

When I said nothing, he turned and drifted towards the reef. Still feeling dozens of eyes on me, I followed closely.

"I recommend you don't try that here," he said.

I grunted. I'd already accepted that my escape would need to be carefully planned. I'd have leagues of open water and that patrolled boundary to deal with—not to mention capital punishment for deserting the army if I was caught.

Around us, soldiers returned to their business and the grotto filled with chatter.

At first I thought the loud conversation and grinding stone weapons muted the soothing crackle of the reef outside. But as we swam further in, the coral paled and the tiny creatures inside disappeared. The army was suffocating the reef.

"The commander will need to assign you a position," said Slim. "We're heading south tonight."

I groaned. I'd hoped for a bit of rest.

"What's your name?" he said.

"Lysi."

"You know how to fight, Lysi?"

"Yes. I was in the Battle for Eriana Kwai."

He looked at me sharply. "You got hauled away?"

I said nothing. He raised an eyebrow.

After a beat, he said, "Even with those qualifications, the commander likely won't give you a weapon. You'll be destroyed in hand-to-hand combat."

"I know how to—"

"You're half the size of everyone else."

I frowned. The thought made me uncomfortable—not because I'd be pummelled in combat, but because I was the only girl in the entire unit.

"We've got the injured repairing and sorting weapons in a cave." He scanned me up and down. "But I don't think he'll waste your abilities on that."

"Good," I said.

His mouth twisted in a small smile.

Behind us, someone said, "Coming through, Coho."

Slim pulled me aside in time to let a group pass. An enormous great white shark swam passively in the centre, guided by four ropes over her snout and tail. Between her gaping jaws, serrated teeth sliced the water in a way that made my skin tingle. She projected nothing but the desire to swim towards dinner. Like all sharks, her presence was basic, instinctive.

I watched them go with my jaw unhinged. Then I turned to Slim. "What are they—how did they—what … Your name is Coho? Like the salmon?"

"Yes. Have you had experience working with animals, Lysi?"

"Uh …"

I watched the mermen gently steer the great white into a corral, which was bounded by a familiar kind of enormous jellyfish.

At least fifteen animals floated in adjacent cells. I saw a stingray, a mako shark, and two spinner dolphins. Below them were several billfish, including black marlin, sailfish, and the most enormous swordfish I'd ever seen. The billfish were no doubt here for their speed, which contended with that of a mermaid.

"Can I have a dolphin?" I said, blurting it out before I could stop myself.

I bit my lip, reminded of when I was four and asking my parents for a firefly squid for my birthday.

"If you haven't worked with dolphins before, then no," said Coho. "They need experienced handlers."

The spinners turned circles in their corrals, chattering to each other. I'd always loved dolphins. They were the only animals whose auras showed as wide a range of emotions as a mermaid's. The pair in front of me gave off an air of amusement, like they didn't mind trading their service for food.

"What are they for?" I said.

"They're trained in offense."

I considered making a case for how many wild dolphins I taught tricks to on a regular basis, but decided against it. I'd never taught them to be an assault weapon.

Harnesses lay on the rocks below them, fitted with short spears on all sides. The dolphins must have looked like a pair of ballistic pufferfish with those on.

"I'd swim the other way," I said.

"Most do. King Adaro's tactics are more advanced than any other kingdom's."

"How nice for him."

My tone made Coho glance sideways at me. I pursed my lips.

Coho motioned to a cave as we passed it. "Weapons are made by civilians in the Moonless City. This is where we sort the delivery and repair anything broken."

I peered inside the dark cavern. Stone scraped against stone as nine soldiers laboured over a pile of broken weapons.

My focus locked onto one merman in particular, hunched over a work surface. He was lanky, much leaner than the average warrior, with hair like he'd licked an electric eel.

"… stole this one right off a dock," he was saying. "I had to fight the fisherman bare-handed. He had one of those bazooka guns, you know? Iron core. I gave him a left hook and backflipped away. Got his legs out from under him and pinned him down."

"Spio!" I said, voice high with surprise.

He looked up. When he saw me, he blinked a few times, and turned to the guy beside him.

"I told you not to let me eat any more of those pink anemones, dude."

"Spio," I said. "I'm actually here."

His jaw slackened. I grinned.

After another moment, his face broke into an expression of total glee. He dropped the club he was holding and shot towards me. We hugged.

"You look awful," he said, slapping me on the back.

I ran my fingers through my hair, got them stuck in a knot of seaweed, and gave up.

"I know."

I didn't want to get into details with so many ears around.

"You know each other?" said Coho with unmasked surprise.

I smiled. "Classmates."

"Good. Stay here. I'll go find the commander."

He left. Around us, the others continued their work, though I felt their attention on us. Waves gurgled against the cave walls. Deep inside a crevice, some creature I didn't recognise clicked loudly.

The wide, pointy-toothed grin never left Spio's face.

"Beating up humans wasn't enough, huh? Gotta come down here for denser meat? I'm surprised, Lysi. I knew you were feisty but I never thought you'd get bloodthirsty."

"I don't … I … yeah," I said, not sure how to respond.

I peered around him into the dim cave. The other mermen had a miserable, beaten air. I smelled blood.

I scanned Spio's lanky frame. "Are you hurt?"

"No. I'm not supposed to be here. But I didn't want to deprive these folks of my genius ideas."

He tapped a finger to his blond head.

"Of course," I said.

The guy nearest Spio grimaced and turned away.

"You hungry? Need anything?" Spio waved me deeper inside.

I glanced around, both starving and exhausted, but I didn't quite feel like eating or sleeping.

Spio must have sensed my energy level because he said, "Best napping place is on the other side of the camp. Crawl up the ridge and you'll see what I mean. The waves on this end will squash you like a jelly in a propeller. But on the other side … bliss. You'll probably get a suntan. Hey, check this out."

He held up a stone club with a hook the size of my face tied to the end.

"I call it the Iron Hook of Doom."

I gaped at it. The hook was solid iron. Its impurity prickled my skin.

"Don't worry," he said. "I have certified experience in irontechnics."

"Iron what?"

Instead of responding, he picked up a pair of wooden hooks. He used them to tighten the rope, carefully keeping his flesh away from the iron. His work surface was littered with rocks, bone blades, coral, and, perplexingly, a sea cucumber.

Anyone who grew up with Spio knew he would end up destroying things professionally one day. He already had an iron-made gash on his shoulder from trying to slingshot himself aboard an American military vessel. He'd said he just wanted to chat up the female captain. When we were twelve, he singed his hair off trying to figure out a way to bring fire underwater. In school, he once stashed several days' worth of lunches then used them to lure a salmon shark the size of a small whale into class. It was chaos. He got suspended, and it would have been worse if he hadn't been so convincing in telling the teachers it was an accident.

So I wasn't surprised when he handed me the hook weapon and said, "I've got another."

I was about to thank him when a stiff presence closed in behind me, and a hand ripped the club from my grip.

"Fascinating craftsmanship, as always."

I whirled around to see a square-faced merman holding my weapon. He wore a placid smile that mismatched his aura.

"I see you continue to use materials outside the authorized list."

"Come on, dude," said Spio. "Iron can't be illegal if we use it on the enemy."

"I am sure His Majesty would be interested to know how you acquired the iron."

Spio said nothing. The others in the cavern froze, watching. I stayed quiet, trying to gauge this merman's personality.

He continued to smile faintly.

"Now, did you trespass a human wreckage during a mission, or did you smuggle this in?"

"Actually—" Spio said, and then seemed to decide silence was the better option.

"I will ensure this is disposed of properly. If you have any more illegal—"

"Look, I already committed this one to Lysi," said Spio. "So you should probably hand it back to her before the theft detection device goes off and it kills all of us."

The guy nearest Spio shrank back in alarm. The square-faced merman wasn't fooled. His expression hardened.

"Perhaps, instead, you ought to fix this with your bare hands. It might remind you that His Majesty forbids such human filth."

Spio waved away the threat. "The king can fix it with his own bare hands if he cares that much."

For a heartbeat, the cavern stilled.

I realised Spio's mistake the same moment the merman reacted. With a pulse of fury, he spun the weapon and slammed the stone end into Spio's chest, knocking him into the wall. A large bubble left Spio's mouth. Before he could recover, the merman closed the distance between them and pinned Spio to the reef, forcing the air from his lungs. Spio seized the guy's wrist, trying to pry himself free.

I shot towards them. "Hey! Stop!"

The merman raised the weapon to Spio's face, almost touching him with the iron hook. "Never insult the king in my presence."

Spio seemed unable to speak. Air escaped his mouth in large bubbles.

I snarled. This jerk might have been twice the size of me, but I couldn't let him treat my friend like this.

"I said, stop!"

Without slackening his grip, the merman turned to me. He scanned me up and down like he was looking at a whale carcass.

"Decide what company you wish to keep, girl. Here, your life might depend on it."

The bubbles leaving Spio's mouth were diminishing. Real fear seeped from his pores.

My eyes filled with blood. "Let him go."

The merman swelled, as though he thought he could intimidate me.

I reached to pull the weapon away from Spio's face.

In an instant, the merman's energy changed. I propelled backwards before he could act. He released Spio and swung the iron hook at me.

The other mermen scattered, fear clouding the water like blood. But fighting against iron was nothing new to me.

I snatched a bone blade off Spio's work surface as the merman swung again. I shot beneath his arm. Before he could follow, I locked my arms around his neck and pressed the blade to his throat.

The iron hook sliced through empty water.

"Drop it," I said.

He chuckled. "Your skill speaks of the academy. How long ago were you in the Battle for Eriana Kwai?"

His muscles tensed for another swing. I pushed the blade to his throat harder.

"Darling, that would not even break skin," he said. "What is it, a human leg?"

I rubbed a finger along the bone, letting the density, oils, and minerals penetrate my skin. "Feels like whale to me. Care to find out?"

He struck. I dropped the blade before the iron touched me and grabbed the stone handle with both hands. The force swung me around with it. I swiped him with my tail, using his own force to hit harder. He grunted at the impact. I took the chance to pry the club from his grip.

I retreated, holding the weapon between us. He lunged for it, but I swung hard. The iron nearly grazed his cheek.

He didn't try again.

For a moment, everyone stayed suspended. No one made a sound.

"Ah, mermaids!" said a voice. "About time we had a few ladies around here."

I whirled around to find an older merman floating up, flanked by Coho. He had a long, dark beard flecked with rubies—the stone of a commander.

"Thank you, Officer Strymon," he said. "This is just what we need. Did I not say our assaults could use more speed, less force?"

The blood drained from my head, dizzying me. I glanced to Spio for confirmation.

"Officer?" I mouthed.

Spio grimaced. I noticed, then, the emeralds braided into the merman's blonde hair—the stone of an officer.

"Sir," said Officer Strymon, composing himself. "I was reprimanding these soldiers for possessing an illegal weapon."

My heart pounded. How did I louse up this badly in the first few moments of being here?

The commander drifted further into the cave.

Would I be sent back home? Punished? Imprisoned again?

But as he glanced around, I caught an air of hopefulness.

"What, just the one lady?" he said.

"Yes, sir," said Coho. "She needs a position."

"Commander," said the officer more loudly. "She shows an unmanageable temper and a blatant disrespect for—"

"Yes, well, she knows how to fight, doesn't she?" The commander turned back to me. "Is that your weapon?"

I looked down at the dropped iron hook.

"Uh …"

"If I may, Commander," said Spio, with the sudden maturity of Coho in his voice. "Lysithea was in the Battle for

Eriana Kwai and faced opposition deadlier than this. She has been battle-trained for longer than most of us and demonstrated proficiency in beating me up at the age of fifteen. If you observe the scarring along Lysithea's waist"—he motioned with a flat hand, like I was a science exhibit—"you can see for yourself that we are dealing with one badass shrimp."

The commander leaned back, scanned me up and down, and nodded. "Very good."

Spio grinned.

I let out some breath, and my skin reverted to my preferred, human-like shade. The webs between my fingers disappeared. The teeth pressing against my lips retracted.

The commander picked up the iron hook, examined it, and passed it to me. "Hold onto this, Lysithea. It'll fare better than the standard weapons."

"Commander, that weapon is iron," said the officer, the flat smile back on his face.

"So it is."

"The king has strictly forbidden—"

"The way I see it, Officer Strymon, any weapon that improves our chances against the enemy is welcome in my unit."

"I think it should be confiscated, sir."

"And I think you should remember that His Majesty has granted me the authority to make these decisions," said the commander, a dangerous finality in his voice.

I avoided Spio's eyes.

A deep moan met my ears, coming from where I'd been dropped off. Every head turned towards it, conversations stopping abruptly.

"Time to go," said the commander. "Gather the troops, Strymon."

The officer passed me with an air of such bitter revulsion that my stomach churned. I forced myself not to back away.

"I'll get my gear," said Spio.

I tightened my grip around the stone club, the iron hook weighing heavy at the end.

"Commander," I said, finding my voice. "Does this mean—?"

"It means you're a soldier now. Welcome to the South Pacific Army."

CHAPTER FIVE
Red-handed

The floodlight shone down on Annith and me, casting everything outside its yellow glare into shadow. I straightened and faced Dani with clenched fists.

I wanted to demand what she was doing there in the middle of the night, but stopped myself. It wasn't me who had the right to make demands. She and her father could have been doing any number of things, now that they owned the training base.

Annith panted as though from a sprint. Where was Tanuu? Had he run?

Refusing to let panic take over, I kept my own breaths slow and deep.

"Follow me," said Mujihi, in a voice so strangled it sounded like someone had seized him around the neck.

I considered making a run for it. But whether we faced our consequences now or later, it didn't matter. At least if we followed quietly, we might be able to lessen the blow before word got out.

So Annith and I followed Mujihi and Dani across the clearing, avoiding eye contact. I finally glanced down and saw that I'd managed to swipe nothing more than a splintered wooden crossbow from the shed. I tossed it aside, hoping Dani and her father had been too focused on our guilty faces to notice it.

Mujihi led us into a classroom and flicked a switch. The yellow lights quivered on after a pause. Once a ten-person cabin, the dingy wooden building now held desks, chairs, a bookcase, and a morbid pile of decaying First Aid dummies.

Dani held out an arm to let us enter first, cheeks tight with barely restrained smugness.

Annith and I sat at adjacent desks. Mujihi trembled with anger, purple-faced and breathing hard. I wondered if I was about to need self-defence.

He placed the tips of his fingers on my desk and leaned over, face level with mine. I fought the urge to recoil from his putrid breath.

"You think you can sabotage my training program?" he shouted, making me jump.

My heart thudded, but as Dani prowled the room behind her father, I gritted my teeth, determined to look composed.

"We weren't trying to destroy anything," I said.

Mujihi didn't seem to hear me. He jabbed a thick finger into his chest. "I am the training master now! Anyo's time here is done."

"Papa—" said Dani, but Mujihi continued yelling.

"My warriors are better than Anyo's ever were. I am not letting a couple of stupid teenagers ruin this Massacre."

I bit my tongue. Whether he or Anyo held the position of training master was not my business, admittedly. But he had no right calling us stupid teenagers.

"If you truly wanted to help your people," he said, "you would be asking to help train our warriors."

"No amount of training will save those girls," I said.

"Papa," said Dani, peering around her father in a way that reminded me of a cowering dog. "They were trying to steal the weapons for a reason."

He waved a large hand in her direction.

"Quiet."

"But they wanted them for something. It's probably to do with—"

"Quiet, Dani!"

"But Papa—"

Abruptly, he turned and brought his hand hard across Dani's face. It cut the air like a thunderclap, and Dani stumbled backwards. She made no sound.

Mujihi's cold eyes found mine once more. I looked past him to Dani, who fixed the back of the man's head with a glare of utter hatred. Her face reddened where she'd been struck. She turned and swept from the room, slamming the door behind her with enough force to rattle the small building.

Mujihi bored into us, breathing hard. I clenched my fists automatically. This guy had something coming if he dared touch Annith or me.

"I'll be reporting your actions to your parents, the Massacre Committee, and the police," he said.

"The police?" said Annith in a high voice.

"Because we want to borrow a few things?" I said, much louder than intended. "Yet Dani didn't get reported—"

Annith kicked me under the desks. I ignored her. I found myself on my feet.

A vein throbbed in the man's temple. "Dani risked her life as a warrior of Eriana Kwai. I would hope you, of all people, would be aware of how much pressure falls onto Massacre warriors."

"So much pressure that any witnesses to a crime are deemed unreliable, right?"

Annith kicked out again. "Meela!"

I shot her a glare. Her eyes brimmed with tears.

A yelp came from outside. All three of us snapped our heads around to look at the door.

No further sounds came. I turned back to Mujihi.

"Fine. Report us," I said. "I'll be sure to explain the *tremendous pressure* we're under as former Massacre warriors. That seems to work around here."

His lip curled in a way that reminded me he was related to Dani. He fixed me with his cold eyes for a moment before sweeping past us to open the door.

"If I see you anywhere near here again, you will regret it."

Annith and I left the cabin quickly.

The police. The Massacre Committee. My parents.

No doubt Mujihi would tell them we'd been trying to break into his training base in some kind of childish act of rebellion. I became furious at myself for not planning this out more carefully. Finding the Host was hard enough without Dani and her father getting in my way.

We passed the Enticer, where Dani's shadow lurked by the wooden shed we'd broken into. Her crossbow was in her hands, as though she'd just used it. Something lay at her feet.

I stopped.

"Dani, what did you do?"

"Got what we came for," she said.

At her feet, caramel fur ruffled in the breeze. A spreading pool of blood glinted in the floodlight. Realisation sucked away any words I might have said.

A hunting arrow jutted from the dog's ribcage.

"The trainees have been leaving food for it," said Dani. "You should know better than anyone, Meela, that soft Massacre warriors are toxic."

I couldn't look at her. I didn't care that she was provoking me.

Moments earlier, in the classroom with her father, I'd almost—almost—pitied her.

Annith wrapped a hand around my arm. I let her pull me away, my words still lost.

All of the trainees, who were already living with the knowledge that they'd soon be fighting for their lives, would arrive in the morning to learn that this animal had been killed because they'd been caring for it. Was Mujihi so determined to punish any act of compassion? The dog had been hungry, just like us, and those girls had been guilty only of empathy. What kind of training master were we dealing with? Anyo had been strict, but without his kindness and encouragement, the training program would have broken me at thirteen.

My toe caught on a root, pitching me forwards. I blinked, trying to focus on the path. The darkness pressed closer.

"Where do you think Tanuu is?" I said weakly.

Annith took a second to answer. "Hopefully he ran back to your place."

We walked in silence for a long time. Mujihi's words looped in my mind. The police. My parents. My people would all know. They would look on with pity, sorry my parents had to deal with the shame I kept bringing the family.

A foul word burst from Annith's mouth so abruptly that I leapt in surprise.

"I've never met such a sick pair of human beings," she said, voice shaking. "No wonder where Dani gets it from. He's so … He's completely …"

The dead dog still lingered in my vision. I blinked it away. Dani and her father wanted to turn out ruthless warriors, ones who associated compassion with death. Like Dani, they would learn to dismiss the feeling as a weakness.

I believed it would happen. The new training program would be different, after all.

The forest thinned as we neared the road. I hadn't remembered passing the creek or the skunk cabbage or any other landmarks as we ducked beneath the fallen log.

"He might've already called our parents," I said. "Prepare for that when you get home."

Annith groaned. "I can't believe we pissed off the new training master. My parents are going to totally hate me."

I pulled my hood up, hunching against a deep chill. "Think the whole island will know by tomorrow?"

"Maybe not. He might find it an embarrassment, or bad publicity."

We broke through the trees and stopped on the side of the road.

"Or," I said, "he'll boast about catching us to everyone who'll listen."

I pulled my boots on.

"Meela, how are we going to hunt for the Host without any weapons?"

I suspected her note of unease had more to do with the idea of opposing Dani's father than anything else.

The earth crunched behind us and we whirled around. Tanuu emerged from the trees.

"We have one weapon."

He held out a crossbow. Iron, relatively new, intact.

My mouth fell open. "How did …"

"Snatched it and ran. Sorry, I shoulda grabbed more. I panicked."

"No. You did great, Tanuu."

His white teeth flashed at me through the darkness. "We're going anyway, then?"

I ran my hand along the crossbow, feeling the grip, the trigger, the sinew. Suddenly, Dani and her father hardly seemed like a setback. We could search the shoreline as long as we had one functional crossbow.

I grinned. "Let's go find this Host."

Annith's shoulders relaxed, as though the decision came as a relief. Tanuu nodded, looking energised.

"You sure you want to come, Tanuu?" I said. "If a mermaid—"

"I'm coming."

I stared into his dark eyes. He earned the right to come by getting the crossbow. I couldn't tell him no after he'd done that much for us.

I nodded once. "We go at low tide. Meet here at noon."

Once home, I hid the stolen weapon in a cavern of tree roots I'd once used as a fort. Then I snuck around to my father's shed, retrieved his old crossbow and ammo, and stowed that, too. It would be easier the next day when I'd need to grab it all in broad daylight without drawing my parents' attention.

I opened the front door to find my parents waiting for me in the kitchen, my mother at the table and my father leaning against the counter. Both were wrapped in faded bathrobes, looking weary under ruffled hair. They surprised me, at first, but then I realised I'd been stupid not to register the lamplight glowing through the window. I glanced at the old clock on the wall. Three in the morning.

I faltered in the doorway, as though ready to turn around and flee.

"Come inside, Metlaa Gaela," said my father.

I narrowed my eyes, not trusting the calm tone of his voice.

"Now," he said.

I edged sideways into the kitchen, keeping my distance.

"Mujihi called."

My mouth dried up. I'd had the whole way home to come up with an excuse, and I'd spent it thinking about finally getting Lysi back.

"Well?" said my mother. "What do you think you were doing?"

"He isn't a good person," I said, the words flooding out. "He should never have been made training master."

My parents exchanged a meaningful glance.

After a moment, my father said, "That's not for you to decide."

I huffed. I hoped my vague statement would serve as an answer, like maybe we'd been trying to investigate his training program.

My father stepped closer. "He's going to inform the constable and the rest of the Massacre Committee first thing in the morning."

I swiped my hood back, hot with anger.

"It's not fair! Dani's—I mean—she actually—" I closed my eyes for a second, trying to bring my voice down. "Dani *murdered* someone, Papa. She killed Shaena on the Massacre and your committee won't even acknowledge it."

"It happened on international waters, Meela."

"International—what kind of excuse—I don't understand why everyone on that stupid committee even *likes* her!"

"If you put aside her crime, she comes across as a sweet girl, very helpful around the training—"

"Dani is not sweet!" I bellowed.

My mother put a hand over her heart. "Honestly, Meela."

I stared at my father, aghast. My whole life, adults had always thought Dani was a polite, kind girl. I never understood how no one saw her for what she was.

"Look, Meela," said my father. "She made a mistake on the Massacre. Heat of battle, fingers too tight over the trigger, and the girl happened to be in the wrong place at the wrong time."

"The girl's name was Shaena," I said. "And I saw her get murdered."

My father rubbed his balding head. "I never said I'm fond of Dani. I tolerate her for the sake of keeping harmony."

"She's—"

"Meela," my mother snapped. "Quiet. Let your father finish."

I crossed my arms, glaring at them.

"Right," said my father. "Let's agree that Dani made a mistake."

"But—"

"The *same way* you made a mistake by putting your trust in a sea demon."

I scoffed, hiding my embarrassment with anger. "So why am I the one getting all the suspicion? Why is a murder completely overlooked, but my ..."

I waved a hand, heat rising to my face.

"This brings me to the issue at hand. After Mujihi called, your mother spoke to Annith's, and we all agree on something. Yes, Dani was granted a pardon. Yes, her actions on the Massacre were ignored because she's a former warrior and Mujihi's daughter."

My mother looked away, failing to hide an ugly expression.

"You and Annith are also Massacre warriors," said my father. "It would be unfair to punish you for this incident while allowing Dani's actions to go unanswered."

I stared at him, my brain working to process what he said.

"Are … are you serious?"

My father nodded once. "But if this has to do with your Host story—"

"It doesn't," I said, deciding it would be best to lie.

He crossed his arms, glancing to my mother. "Well, I was going to say, an old campsite seems an odd place to start looking. If I were searching for a legend, I would try the island's sacred landmarks. The things that make Eriana Kwai what it is."

"Oh."

Sacred landmarks. Yes, that was exactly why we were headed to Skaaw Beach. His words sparked a tiny flame of hope in my chest.

"Enough, now," said my mother, scowling. "You won't be excused if you cause any more trouble."

I took this as my dismissal. As I turned away, I wondered if Annith was having the same conversation with her parents. Was I lucky to be getting off this easily?

"I'm sorry," I said, keeping my back to them.

"Take that stuff off your eyes," said my mother. "You look like a drunk raccoon."

I washed the kohl, dirt, and sweat from my face, then pulled off my clothes and slid into bed.

Away from their disappointment, I could think more clearly. I was sorry for being caught, and for causing them stress. But I wasn't sorry for going there in the first place. More than the crossbow, I'd come away with a better understanding of our new training master.

If I could help it, he would not hold the title for long.

Rather than scare me away, Mujihi had given me another reason to keep going. Finding the Host meant ending the need for Massacres, and ending the need for his training program.

I fell asleep with one thought in my mind: Adaro was going down, and our new training master was going down with him.

CHAPTER SIX
The King's Plan

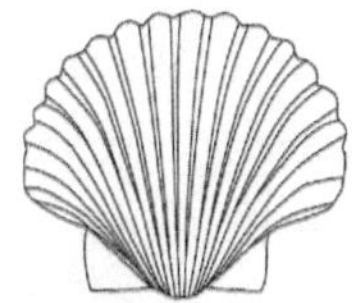

The army assembled near the grotto entrance, moving with stiff discipline. The commander and Officer Strymon left to join them.

Spio crashed around at the back of the cavern, throwing stuff into a rawhide bag. Most soldiers had some kind of bag with them. I had nothing but the Iron Hook of Doom.

Coho moved to join the rest.

I remained where I was.

"Can I travel with Spio?"

Not that I didn't like Coho—I was grateful he'd come to my rescue—but I wanted to stick close to the only guy in the unit who I knew wouldn't throw me to a shark.

Coho hesitated, but seemed to find nothing wrong with that.

"See you out there, soldier."

He disappeared into the crowd.

Soldier. Once again, I found myself in Adaro's army. I might die at the hands of a merman instead of a human in these battles, but my overall mission was no different. I was still fighting for a cause I didn't believe in: the expansion of Adaro's empire.

I waited for Spio while everyone gathered at the grotto entrance. The cavern gurgled, muffling the hum of the crowd. I rubbed my burning eyes. My body wilted from exhaustion, and my growling stomach sent shooting pains into my ribcage.

"Snack?"

Spio appeared beside me, his bag jammed full, the contents of which I could only guess. He offered me a dead cod. It was a testament to how hungry I was that I accepted it. Spio's food generally tasted like it was found on a beach, mangled by pollution and regurgitated by a seagull, and then skinned and stored in his armpit for several days.

"Thanks," I said. "I haven't eaten in ... What are you wearing?"

Spio lifted a hand to the leather cap on his head. It had flaps on the side, which stuck out awkwardly over his bulbous ears. He pulled down a front piece, two plastic holes that made his eyes protrude like a goldfish. Algae had turned the plastic an opaque green.

"It's style," he said, pulling the piece back up to his forehead. "I found it on a dead guy."

We stuffed our Iron Hooks of Doom inside his bag. I would have carried my weapon in hand, but I was afraid of mindlessly hitting myself with the iron end while we swam.

Besides, carrying iron so close to my scar made it sting— like opening a fresh burn all over again.

Spio pulled the bag across his back and we joined the crowd. The rumour that a girl had arrived was spreading.

Heads turned—and then, blissfully, their gazes fell to Spio with his ridiculous hat and overstuffed bag.

We left the grotto. Spio and I became two insignificant bodies in a line of soldiers stretching further than I could see.

To our right, a rocky cliff dropped into nothingness. We followed this, sticking near the surface for easy breaching.

The city sprawled out to our left, its limits spanning much further south than I'd expected. The population must have been tens of thousands.

I travelled close to Spio, constantly feeling for threats in all directions.

Being this far south didn't change the reality that I needed to get back to Eriana Kwai. I wondered if Spio would help me. That was a big favour to ask. Too big. I'd be asking him to risk imprisonment, if not death, for helping me commit such a crime as desertion.

But would he want to leave, too? I hadn't been able to gauge his feelings about the army. He seemed too excited to be given permission to destroy things.

Vibrations brushed my skin from the city beside us. I wondered if the merpeople inside felt us passing, as we felt them. They must have. Were they hiding, or ignoring us? Did they even support Adaro's army?

I wondered what it was like inside the Moonless City. Given that my life had been limited to the young kingdom in the North Pacific, it must have been more beautiful than I could imagine.

"Makes home feel like the Great Pacific garbage patch, doesn't it?" said Spio.

He must have noticed my attention on the city.

"Have you been inside?" I said.

"Nah. The officers are jerks if you try and leave the military base."

He pulled back an earflap to show me a partly healed gash on his neck.

I grimaced. Yes, my escape would need to be planned carefully.

"Is the city all right with the army setting up camp here?" I said.

Spio didn't answer right away. He studied the empty depths below.

With a slight change in tone, he said, "The Moonless City is part of Adaro's kingdom now."

I frowned. "What about his pact with Queen Evagore?"

"From what I've heard, the queen left the throne years ago. Hey, a devil ray!"

It was. We watched it flap below us for a moment.

Spio didn't elaborate. I tried to read his mood, but he revealed nothing. Was that a practiced skill?

The city ended to our left. Coral, greenery, and chattering fish thinned as the floor deepened. We dove, following the cliff.

I wondered why the queen left the throne. Was she too old to keep ruling? Had she and Adaro come to some kind of agreement?

Overhead, daylight faded. The setting sun cast an orange glow across the surface. Activity picked up beneath us as the deep-sea fish, jellies, and squid rose for the night.

"Where are we going?"

Spio rolled onto his side to face me. "They not teach you anything about the army up there?"

"My mission was above-surface. Did they teach you about that?"

He paused for a long moment. "I assumed your mission was *lure, kill, and eat.*"

At a basic level, he wasn't wrong. I wrinkled my nose and fixed my gaze ahead. "We had strategies."

Spio flipped back over. "I heard a rumour."

I raised my eyebrows.

"I heard you fought women."

I relaxed. Someone this far south wouldn't know that I had saved Meela's life in front of everyone. Still, word spread like algae.

"It's true," I said. "Eriana Kwai is training girls."

"That must have sucked."

"It was easier when we just lured the warriors." *And when one of them wasn't Meela.*

"How'd you get 'em in the water?"

"Careening their ship. But the girls had their own strategies. We had to take them down in combat."

"Awesome."

"Not awesome! If you'd seen the way it was up there—"

"All right, all right," he said. "I was picturing a bunch of girls wrestling around together, but if you want to take that away from me ..."

I shoved him.

The army broke the current to catch a stronger one pushing southeast. It helped pick up our pace, but we moved slower than when we'd started. The surrounding chatter had grown quieter.

"Why are we moving south?" I said, steering the conversation back to my question.

"Part of the king's plan," said Spio. "He has three army divisions below the surface. One's stationed at the Ice Channel, where they probably spend most of their time beating away polar bears. The biggest army's moving west. Those poor cods have to poke their way around all those human-infested islands and the Mariana Trench. Then there's us, heading down to the sea of crazy fish and tropical babes."

I envisioned Adaro's plan on a map. The first army trickled through the cracked ice across the top of North America. The second swelled across the Pacific into Asia, where my brother was stationed. The third pushed towards South America.

"They're all closing on the Atlantic," I said.

Spio grinned. "Sharp, Lysi."

Adaro had been planning to take the Atlantic from Queen Medusa for a while, but I never knew how close he was to actually taking it. The troops stationed up north were probably instructed to wait on the defensive until the rest of us had pushed as close as possible to Medusa's cities. I imagined once we rounded the tip of South America, Adaro would tell the northern troops to attack, and the assault on the Atlantic would begin.

"We've got a long ways to go," I said.

My energy dropped thinking about the journey. The strong currents at the equator would be no easy feat to swim through. After that, we still had an entire continent to pass.

"One bite at a time," said Spio. "We've got an army to slay, first. There's one coming from the south." He made a wide swing with an invisible weapon.

"How's their skill?" I said.

"It's numbers you should worry about. They've got three times the soldiers."

"So? In the Battle for Eriana Kwai we outnumbered them by a tidal wave. It didn't matter. Their skill and weapons ..." I grimaced, remembering how many comrades had been killed.

Someone shouted up ahead. Voices rose. The water churned. I reached for my weapon in Spio's bag, but something shiny flew past.

Spio pumped a fist. "Mackerel!"

Sure enough, the army ahead closed around the glistening swarm of fish. The smell of blood wafted over.

"Let's get in there before it turns into a frenzy," I said.

Already, the fish spun like a whirlpool, trapped between the army and the surface. Gulls dove in and snatched their meals from the top. The school tightened into a huge baitball that could have sunk a ship.

Mermen jostled for a place, elbowing each other out of the way even though there was plenty to go around. Spio and I ducked beneath the baitball to snag our share from the bottom.

A tuna shot past as I ate. Turbulence hit me as several more joined in. I was hungry enough to eat a tuna, but these ones were as big as me. Maybe I could have caught one on an ordinary day, when I wasn't such a sleep-deprived mess.

I looked on with jealousy as a couple of huge mermen managed to catch tunas the size of my upper body.

A mako shark rose beneath me, jaws open. With nowhere to go and no time to think, I propelled forwards, straight into the baitball.

Mackerel pummelled my face, shoulders, and arms. The world became nothing but swirling silver bodies writhing to get away from me. But as they pushed out, the feeding predators directed them inwards. I caught glimpses of expressive eyes as they shot past my face, and pointed mouths opening and closing. The whirlpool muffled the outside world. I heard only slopping water and bodies bumping into each other. The current all but disappeared. I couldn't help laughing at the sensation.

I burst out the other side. The mackerel swirled and the predators continued feeding as though nothing had happened.

Behind me, Spio let out a whoop. I turned to see him fly by, arms wrapped around a thrashing tuna that probably weighed more than he did. The tuna turned sharply, plunged downwards, and rose again. I wondered if Spio was steering. It wouldn't have surprised me, considering he once stole a speedboat and actually drove it for a while before crashing into a rock.

The tuna spun a tight circle, Spio hanging around its middle. Then, with a gnash of Spio's teeth, it stopped struggling. A cloud of blood spilled from behind its skull.

"Want some?" said Spio, relaxing his hold.

"No, thanks. It's your catch."

I didn't need his pity. I could take care of myself.

Spio pulled a bone blade from his bag. An octopus tentacle fell out and floated away.

"I can help you wrangle your own," he said.

"I don't need help."

Unfortunately, that was the moment I made a swipe for another mackerel and missed completely.

I blew a bubble in exasperation.

Spio cast me a fleeting glance. He used the blade to cut the tuna into pieces.

"If you need help, ask for it," he said.

"I don't."

The jostling worsened. The current roared. Between the swirling bubbles, my senses picked up a marlin. I decided to get out before someone shoved me into that needle-sharp beak.

With new determination, I snatched a fish in each hand.

"Lysi," said Spio.

"What?"

I was prepared to defend my hunting skills—but something changed in the current.

Spio looked up.

I sensed a blank, single-minded focus.

The frenzy had masked all signs of their approach. They travelled in complete silence. Ripples of movement faded before reaching us.

The world darkened.

A hundred hammerhead sharks eclipsed the remaining daylight.

CHAPTER SEVEN
Skaaw Beach

I spent the morning scrubbing slime from the side of the house, fighting spider webs and overgrown Ravendust bushes. Despite what my parents had said, my mother was obviously punishing me. Ravendust, unique to Eriana Kwai, had tar-black leaves that stained skin, and roots so thick I was sure even a mermaid would have a hard time pulling them up.

The afternoon's plans loomed ahead. I had to be crazy to risk facing mermaids again. But I had to explore the shoreline. Searching the safe, comfortable library had gotten us nowhere.

With each thrust of the wire brush, I thought of all of the people I owed this to. Warriors who didn't need to die. Others who could still be saved. Eyrin. Linoya. Holly. Shaena. Adette. Anyo. Nilus. Lysi.

Lysi.

Lysi.

I scrubbed harder, sweat beading on my face. I kept going until my dead crewmates, the girls in training and their families, Lysi and her family—even those I didn't know by name—were all a part of the rhythm, filling me with purpose.

By the time I made it around the perimeter, my arms were ready to give out. I hauled myself to my feet with a groan like a bear trying to knock a tree over.

Overhead, a sliver of sun peeked through the clouds. Noon. Annith and Tanuu would be waiting for me any moment.

I'd just washed my hands—a several-minute ordeal—when someone knocked on the door.

I opened it to see Blacktail, ears sticking out from a high ponytail, a typically solemn expression on her face.

"Heard you got caught stealing."

I blinked. "Hi, Blacktail."

She crossed her arms. "Why did you want weapons?"

I glanced over my shoulder. My parents were still cleaning the shed. Waving her inside, I shut the door softly behind us. "How did you know?"

"My father's the constable."

"Right."

"So what's going on?"

I hesitated. "Are Annith and I going to be punished?"

"Don't be stupid. Dani never got punished."

I let out a breath. "That's what my parents said, too."

Blacktail waited, arms crossed.

"This isn't really … I can't explain it," I said.

"I want to help."

I studied her earnest face.

"You can't, Blacktail. I'm sorry. This is dangerous."

"I gathered, or you wouldn't need iron weapons. Come on. I'll be useful."

I considered. Blacktail was smart, good with a crossbow, and the only other Massacre survivor I trusted. I might have trusted Fern, but she was friends with Blondie, and Blondie had been in allegiance with Dani on the Massacre.

"I kept my iron dagger," said Blacktail, motioning to the hidden waistband of her jeans. "Told them I'd lost it."

"Why do you want to help so badly?"

"I don't think the Massacres should continue, either. Whatever plan you have, it has to be better than sending girls out to deal with … that."

I chewed my lip. Her skill and the iron dagger would be useful on the beach. Besides, she had stuck with me on the Massacre during times when I didn't even have Annith.

"All right," I said. "Yes. We could use your help."

I invited her into the kitchen, cautioning her to keep our conversation low so my parents wouldn't hear.

"I'm meeting Annith and Tanuu in …" I glanced at the old clock on the wall. "… ten minutes."

She raised her eyebrows. "Your boyfriend is coming?"

I busied myself making a sandwich. "He helped us break into the training base."

"It's not a good idea," she whispered. "If a mermaid comes at us, he's most at risk."

I shook my head. "He's not going to sit back while three girls go out and put themselves in danger."

"We're capable!"

"It's not about that. It's chivalry. That's Tanuu. Want a sandwich?"

She shook her head.

"Tomato and basil on bannock," I said, waving it under her nose. "If you close your eyes it almost tastes like pizza."

Her eyes widened. "Where'd you get basil?"

"Our garden. The tomato is still a little green, but it's good."

"Sold. Thanks."

I sliced a biscuit lengthwise. "Someday I want to learn to cook properly. For now, it's fake pizza."

"Better than my lunches. I'll puke if I see another dandelion leaf salad."

Sandwiches in hand, we left the house. I shouted goodbye to my parents from across the yard and disappeared before they could say anything.

We retrieved the two crossbows and ammo from my tree fort, and set off down the hill. We stuck to the bush in case a neighbour came up the road and saw us with a bunch of weapons.

As I explained our plan to find the Host, Blacktail asked the same unanswerable questions as Tanuu.

"To sum up, we know nothing about it," I said.

"Wish I had something helpful for you," said Blacktail.

"You think the shoreline is a good place to start looking?"

She thought for a moment. "We might find something on Skaaw Beach or in a cliff face. Is it low tide?"

"Yes."

We arrived to find Annith and Tanuu already waiting at the side of the road.

"Blacktail!" said Annith.

"What's she doing here?" said Tanuu.

I raised my eyebrows, wondering where the rudeness came from.

Blacktail grinned at Annith, ignoring Tanuu. "If it isn't the other lawbreaker."

Annith groaned. "Does the whole island know?"

"Not sure about the rest of the island, but I have my sources."

Tanuu scoffed.

The three of us turned to him.

"Oh, please," said Blacktail with uncharacteristic iciness. "You're still on about that?"

"My father could've lost his hunting license."

"But he didn't."

"What if he had? My family aren't the only ones that woulda starved—"

"He should have thought of that before he trespassed."

I stepped between them. "Guys! Cool it."

They recoiled in alarm, and I realised I was brandishing a crossbow. I dropped it.

"Blacktail's going to help us," I said. "Let's forget about whatever issues we have, and … and focus on what matters."

Blacktail and Tanuu eyed daggers at each other across my outstretched hands, but they nodded stiffly.

I glanced to Annith, who mirrored my bewilderment. I didn't know Blacktail and Tanuu had ever spoken, never mind had a beef with each other.

After a silence, Annith said, "What've we got for weapons?"

The others dropped their weapons next to mine, forming a pile. We had two crossbows, ammo, Blacktail's dagger, and the poker from Tanuu's fireplace.

"Who gets the good crossbow?" I said.

I looked up to find the three of them staring at me.

"You, obviously," said Annith, picking up the defective crossbow.

Blacktail slid the dagger back through her belt, nodding. "You're the best shot."

"Plus," said Tanuu, brandishing the fire iron like a sword, "I have a better chance of fending off a demon with an old-fashioned beating stick. My aim with a crossbow sucks."

"That inspires confidence," said Blacktail.

Tanuu glared at her. "I have a good swing. I play baseball."

"Baseball won't help when a mermaid tries to lure you."

"If you're trying to get me to volunteer to stay back—"

"You don't have the proper training. Besides, men are vulnerable to the allure. You shouldn't be coming."

"He's not going to listen, Blacktail," I said. "Persistence is his most endearing quality."

She huffed. "If he gets hauled into the water, it's on you."

"Fair enough," said Tanuu. He thrust the fire iron into the air. "To the beach!"

Annith and I slung the crossbows over our chests and stuffed ammo in our pockets. My pants sagged under the weight.

I led us downhill towards the beach, peeling away from the main trail.

Behind me, Blacktail moved in silence, her small body gliding through the deer path. "Any hunches about what the Host actually is?"

"I bet it's a giant seahorse," said Tanuu. "And Adaro wants to ride it into battle."

"That," said Blacktail, "is the stupidest thing I have ever heard."

"Well, what do you think it is?"

She considered for a minute and then said, "A kraken."

"Ew, it better not be," said Annith. "Can you imagine octopus suckers the size of your face?"

I had, plenty of times. I hoped the Host was nothing like that.

"It could be a spirit. Like the spirit of Eriana," said Blacktail.

I shook my head. "Adaro called it a pet. It must be a living creature."

But it was an interesting theory, a break from the various animals I'd been imagining. How much did Adaro know? Could the Host actually be something inanimate?

We came to a ravine, where a fallen hemlock acted as a bridge. Ferns crowded the foot of the log. I pushed them away with the crossbow, clearing a path for us to cross on our hands and feet like monkeys.

"Maybe it's a giant anglerfish," said Tanuu.

"Gross," said Annith. "Stop being so pessimistic. It could be something beautiful, like a water fairy."

The sound of the ocean met my ears. Light poured in ahead, indicating the edge of the forest. I stomped through some saplings towards it, grateful I'd worn shoes this time.

We emerged to find a thick layer of driftwood.

I stopped. A salty breeze blew wisps of hair around my face. I'd been too distracted by the conversation to note why the path to the beach felt so automatic.

There was the tide pool where Lysi and I used to tackle each other—and beyond it, the place where Lysi had been shot by the crossbow now slung across Annith's chest.

My throat tightened. How many times had Lysi and I met on this beach? Would we ever meet here again?

Tanuu was staring at the grounded fishing boat. "Yikes."

Out of habit, I had averted my eyes from the ghostly sight. Mermaids had killed the sailors on board and the boat washed onto our shores, never to be touched again.

Annith must have seen something in my expression, because her gaze never left the side of my face.

"We'll go this way," I said, stepping through the driftwood. "We can check the cliff face on the way to Skaaw."

Blacktail craned her neck. "We're below your house?"

"Yes. That's east. Haida Gwaii is over there."

I pointed across the empty water with an iron bolt, where the Canadian land mass would have been visible if we were up higher and the sky wasn't so cloudy.

The others scanned the cliff face, eyes following every crack in the stone. I removed the crossbow from my chest, cranked the lever, and dropped a bolt against the shaft.

"Keep your eyes open for anything out of place. Anything that looks like it could be manmade, or—"

"A giant neon arrow that says *This Way to the Host*," said Tanuu.

We started along the pebbled beach, staying as far from the shoreline as we could. We searched as we walked, heads swivelling between the cliff face and the water.

Outside the dense forest, the waves were the only sound. I listened to the way they roared towards us then trickled back. Every pebble had an influence on the water, giving each wave a unique song.

Blacktail frowned at the rocky face towering over us. "It's grim down here."

"Something about the water," said Annith. "It's so …"

"Empty," said Tanuu.

I said nothing. With the entire underwater world stretching before us, existing so far beyond what our eyes could see, I felt anything but empty.

"I've been having nightmares since we got back," said Annith. "This sound is always the background."

I'd also been having nightmares. But the ocean was never the villain.

We trekked across the beach until my hips protested from the slanted surface and my ears rang from the wind. After an hour, we arrived at a stretch piled with too much driftwood to climb over. Behind it, a steep slope led up to the tall, bald trees that had been pushed backwards from constant wind.

Getting around the driftwood meant either climbing the bank, or edging dangerously close to the water. We opted for the bank.

Finding no secret cave entrances, we rounded the next bend in the shoreline, where the cliff rose again. The beach narrowed. Our path became a slab of solid rock no wider than an arm span.

"Now we're getting somewhere," said Annith.

Both light and dark lines decorated the cliff face—millions of years of layers reminding me how ancient the island was. It gave me hope that at least one secret had yet to be discovered.

At least thirty eagles flew in slow circles above the cliff top. I scanned the water with a tightened grip on my crossbow.

"Keep your weapon between you and the water," said Blacktail.

Tanuu was the only one carrying his weapon in the wrong hand. He switched his grip on the fire iron. "If the cliff attacks me, I'm blaming you."

We hopped over a stream between two boulders, continuing along the narrow passage in single file, our backs to the cliff.

"Good thing we waited for low tide," said Tanuu. "This path would be—ARGH!"

A wave broke against the cliff, Tanuu catching the worst of the spray.

Annith wiped salt from her eyes. "More of those will be coming."

Water bubbled out of several fissures in the cliff. I followed a deep one with my eyes, upwards until I couldn't see it anymore. It seemed likely that one of these fissures could open to a cave—but how would we get to it? Would we need to scale the cliff, or lower ourselves from the top?

Tanuu followed my gaze, and then poked his fire iron into the gap. It went in halfway before hitting solid rock. "Nope."

"Look out!" said Blacktail.

I whirled around with my crossbow ready. She'd crouched, iron dagger over her head like a harpoon. I followed her gaze with my weapon, but the water was empty.

"I saw hair," she said, breathless. "Light. Reddish."

"Sure it wasn't seaweed?" said Tanuu.

Blacktail snarled like a dog. "Yes, I'm sure."

"She probably sees our iron," said Annith.

We stayed facing the water for a minute, weapons up. Nothing surfaced.

Blacktail stood. "Let's keep going. I don't like this. We're trapped between a rock and a dead place."

We continued in silence, checking the water for threats and the cliff face for crevices. As Annith predicted, more waves soaked us as we edged along, until we were drenched and shivering.

Two persistent bald eagles followed, making silent circles.

I stopped as a gap wide enough to fit my foot opened in the stone face. It continued above my head.

"Don't you dare," said Tanuu, when I hooked my fingers and a toe inside it.

I squinted upwards. "I'm just checking. I don't think I'm that good a climber, anyway."

I traced the fissure with my eyes. It stayed the same width, and might have even tapered part way up the face.

"Keep moving," said Blacktail, a crushing grip on her dagger as she scanned the waves.

Cold, wet, and getting moody, I conceded.

We kept shuffling across the narrow strip of rock, waves reaching for our legs in a rhythm. Nobody spoke. My nerves pulled taut as I wondered if the tide would rise before we found dry land again.

After another long while, the cliff lost elevation. We all sped up.

We rounded the next corner to find ourselves facing a mound of solid, black rock.

Tanuu raised the fire iron in celebration. "Skaaw!"

I breathed a sigh of relief. We raced towards it and scrambled up without hesitation, eager to put distance between us and the water.

From the top of the lava swell, I scanned the beach. Skaaw was smaller than I'd expected—maybe the size of a school gym. The hardened lava descended sporadically from tree line to water, chiselled by a million years of tides and earthquakes. Every surface had ripples and holes, preserving the exact moment when the lava had frozen mid-flow.

"Nice place for a mermaid to chill out," said Blacktail.

She was right. Rock pools were everywhere. The shelves of lava might as well have been benches and picnic tables.

"Stick together," I said. "I don't like this any better than the cliff."

We advanced slowly over the uneven footing. Every wave sounded like a mermaid rising from the water.

I kept track of the blind spots. Rock pool to the left. A drop-off to the right. A thick column ahead.

I motioned for Annith and Tanuu to cover Blacktail and me while we cleared the column. We rounded it at a wide angle like we were trained, finding only empty lava rock at the end of our crossbows. Without a word, we continued.

Two pools lay ahead, linked together by an hourglass pinch point. I leaned over, crossbow ready. Urchins, crabs, and seaweed speckled the bottom. No caves, no mermaids. We stepped across the pinch point and kept going.

If we did encounter a mermaid, our only option would be to fight. Trying to run over the ripples and holes would guarantee someone falling.

We peered down a crevice. Green algae wallpapered the sides. A stream at the bottom pulsed with each wave. We hopped over.

Then the lava rock plummeted, ending in a pool too deep to see the bottom. A wave exploded against the back, sending a wide spray.

As it retreated, the pool drained to reveal a large hole.

I stepped towards it, using the ripples in the rock as a ladder.

Tanuu grabbed my arm. "What are you doing?"

The next wave came, the pool filled, another spray erupted.

I pointed with my crossbow. "Watch."

The swell retreated, and the cave opened up.

"Oh my gosh, don't tell me you're going to jump in there," said Annith.

Another wave exploded against the rock. The spray rose high over our heads, like the spout of a whale. The tide was coming in.

I hesitated, shivering. It had been several hours since we left, and every part of me was sore. A morning spent scrubbing the house wasn't helping.

"Let's take a break," said Annith.

"Not until I've checked this area," I said.

"Meela, this beach is too alive with sea gunk," said Blacktail. "The water must come all the way up at high tide."

"So?"

"So Adaro could easily get to anything on this beach. Including that hole."

I frowned. She was right. If the Host was here, Adaro had no reason to make me get it for him.

I followed Annith's eyes past the pool, where the lava rock dropped off to a pebbled beach. The gap was as wide as a street and backed onto a heavenly patch of sand.

"Come on," she said. "We're all tired. Continuing like this could be dangerous."

I glanced at the lava behind us, disheartened. What were we missing?

Annith led us as far from the water as we could manage. We slumped down, leaning against a pile of driftwood. Sand clung to our wet clothes.

"My arms are dying," said Annith, massaging her biceps.

Blacktail held out her dagger. "Trade me."

"You're the best," said Annith, wincing as she lifted an arm to take it.

Tanuu rummaged in his backpack and pulled out a tin of jerky. "Don't ask what kind it is."

I grabbed a piece of the dark red meat, mouth watering.

Mystery meat was nothing new. Without the ability to fish, wild game had been over-hunted. Most families supplemented their diets with any meat they could find: birds, rodents, the occasional bear, even raccoons.

"Mm, cats," said Blacktail.

"Kittens, actually," said Tanuu. "Fluffy white ones."

"You guys are awful," said Annith through a mouthful.

As I scarfed down a fifth piece, I took in the patch of beach. The tide crept up the pebbles. The driftwood at our backs created a border between sand and earth. Beyond it, the earth sloped upwards like the trough of an ancient mudslide.

Ravendust bushes sprang from the patchy grass in clusters. Beside us, two of the tar-black bushes even grew on the beach, having been pushed away from the crowded earth.

That, I thought, was the mark of a relentless plant: so deeply rooted that it would grow through rock and sand.

The black lava rose to our left and right. Beyond Skaaw Beach, the cliff continued.

"Let's go a little longer," I said. "We can cut back through the forest at the next break in the cliff."

"What if there isn't another break for ages?" said Annith. "We could be in the middle of nowhere when the tide comes in."

She had a point. With the tide advancing, we risked drowning—or worse.

What, then? Did we give up and go home? The idea irritated me. We'd spent the whole day searching and hadn't found any indication that the goddess Eriana had been more than a made-up story.

Seeing my expression, Annith climbed onto the lava rock and squinted at the beach ahead. "I mean, we could keep …"

She didn't bother finishing the sentence.

Blacktail stood. "The waves are too violent. Look at all the white. Anyway, we're searching too close to the water. It has to be somewhere Adaro can't reach."

Annith turned to the bank behind us. "Maybe we should check a bit higher."

Before I could answer, she began to climb the slope. Blacktail followed slowly, poking the fire iron into the sand at regular intervals as though checking for a trapdoor.

I smiled in spite of my exasperation. At least they were willing to keep searching. The Massacre must have given us all the same relentless stamina.

"Sure," I said. "Tanuu, go ahead of me."

He didn't answer.

"Tanuu?"

I turned.

Tanuu was at the shoreline, on his knees.

He was face-to-face with a young woman.

She was naked, strawberry hair combed away from her face, dripping down her back. The waves concealed her lower body. Soft freckles swept across her cheeks and the bridge of her small nose, adding youthful innocence to the otherwise mature and elegant face. Her white skin was too smooth, parted lips too full, vibrant eyes too large, too captivating.

The mermaid's hand came to rest on the back of Tanuu's neck.

I shrieked. "Tanuu! Stop!"

He didn't hear me, or at least didn't acknowledge that he had.

I snatched up my crossbow in the same moment as the mermaid's skin rippled into the texture and colour of rotting seaweed. Her ears sprouted longer, bulbous. Webs grew between the fingers behind Tanuu's head.

I raised the crossbow—but Tanuu blocked the line between the mermaid and me. I couldn't shoot.

The demon's eyes burst crimson, as though filling with blood. She bared a row of long, pointed teeth.

Tanuu seized up. His cry of terror echoed off the surrounding cliffs.

I ran forwards.

Blacktail was already there. She raised the fire iron over her head and brought it down hard. The demon reached up to defend herself, catching the fire iron in a webbed fist. It sizzled on contact. She howled in pain.

I reached for Tanuu—but an irregular wave lapped beside me. I spun.

A second demon lunged from the water, snarling. I fired. The bolt shot through her forehead.

I grabbed Tanuu by the arm, hauling him away. Annith appeared beside me to help, having leapt down from the bank.

Blacktail yanked the fire iron out of the demon's grip. The hook sliced her webbed hand with a spray of blood.

Tanuu stumbled, gaping at the demon that had been a beautiful woman a moment ago. I kept a firm grip, dragging his dead weight further from the water.

The demon lunged for Blacktail's legs. Before she could bring her to her knees, the iron came down hard on the top of her head. She fell sideways, and Blacktail struck again, putting the weight of her body into the swing.

After five years of military training, her aim was true and her strength impressive. I winced as the hook met the demon's face. Blood spilled onto the rocks. The demon spun at the impact, keeling into the water.

She lay motionless. A wave carried her tail onto the shore, where it fluttered in the breeze.

Annith and I let go of Tanuu part way up the beach. He fell into the pebbles.

A moment passed where we all stared at the two mermaids, panting. In death, their skin faded to a human tone.

"You're not the only one with a good swing," said Blacktail, straightening up.

Tanuu gawked at her, the distant look in his eyes clearing. "That ... that girl was a sea demon!"

I pulled him to his feet by his armpits. "Caught on, have you?"

As we retreated, Tanuu seemed to have lost the ability to hold his jaw closed. He kept stumbling as he looked over his shoulder to his attacker's corpse, and then to Blacktail, and then back to the mermaid.

Blacktail wiped the fire iron clean in the grass.

Nobody said anything for a long time. My heart pounded. I thought I might be sick. For those few seconds, the Massacre had come surging back. My adrenaline kicked in so fiercely that my arms and legs trembled.

Annith and Blacktail's eyes were wide and glazed, their lips ashen. Annith's frizzy hair was plastered to her dirt-smudged face, reminding me of the way she'd looked on the Massacre.

I drew a long, slow breath, trying to calm my heart.

Tanuu had nearly been killed carrying out my plan. What had I been thinking, letting him come to the beach? I should have forced him to stay back, or snuck away—anything to stop him from putting himself in so much danger.

On top of that, I'd killed another mermaid. I'd pulled the trigger without thinking, as easily as I had on the early days of the Massacre.

As much as I hoped to think I'd changed, I was still the killer my people had trained me to be.

"Look," said Tanuu, struggling to breathe. "This is a terrible idea."

"I tried to tell you that," said Blacktail.

"Not just for me. For all of us. Those sea demons … I mean, they're …"

He glanced at the water, looking like he might be sick. The dead mermaids lay half-submerged on the shoreline, rocking in the waves. Behind his horrified expression, he was obviously working out what we'd faced on the Massacre for an entire month.

I bent double, rubbing sweat and salt from my face. "What else are we supposed to do?" I said, muffled by my hands.

"Something that doesn't involve getting eaten by a monster while we hunt for a cave that may or may not exist."

"You're sure we can trust … that demon king?" said Annith, a bit too hesitantly.

I narrowed my eyes at her. "They're not monsters. They're predators. Just like humans."

"Whatever they are, they've got a taste for human blood," said Tanuu.

"It's not like that. They're attacking us because—"

"Because Adaro told them to, I know. But you're doing what he asked. You're looking for the Host. Shouldn't he cool it with the attacks now?"

I huffed. "He wants us to know he's still in control."

They turned their gazes in unison, as though looking across to Adaro's kingdom. I couldn't tell if they were unconvinced, or uneasy about Adaro.

Blacktail made an abrupt movement. I reached for my crossbow as she grabbed the fire iron with one hand and flung the other across Tanuu's chest.

A head poked out of the waves. She'd already transformed into a demon. She floated towards the shore, keeping her deep red eyes on us. I kept my grip on my crossbow but didn't raise it.

The demon wrapped her long, webbed fingers around the first mermaid's hair and pulled her into the water. The sound of the body dragging across the rocks rose over the wind and waves. Then she did the same with the other body.

A swell engulfed them, and they vanished.

I didn't loosen my grip on the crossbow.

A wave smashed against the lava rock on our left. The spray hit me a moment later, clinging to my already cold face.

"Let's climb out of here," I said.

Annith pointed the dagger at Tanuu. "Gentlemen first."

He opened his mouth to protest, but Blacktail gave him a shove with the fire iron. "Go."

We clambered up the earthy slope, using Ravendust weeds as grips. The bank flattened into a field of waist-high grass, pricklebushes, and scattered boulders. Coal-black leaves poked out of the otherwise vibrant greenery, so the field appeared freckled.

We scanned our surroundings. I vaguely knew the way home. But was home where we needed to go?

I licked my dry lips, tasting salt after being on the beach for so many hours. Even this short distance from the water, the air felt thinner, less sticky. My entire body ached, now that I let myself relax. The others must have been exhausted, too. I should have let us stop sooner.

"You hit up the school library, too, right?" said Tanuu.

"We searched about a million books," I said, my tone more waspish than intended.

"Have you talked to anyone?"

"No one supports us. And I don't trust them."

"Come on. Forget the Massacre Committee. Everyone else loves you."

I snorted.

"It's true!"

I started across the field, stepping high through the long grass and hidden stones. The others followed.

"We could try talking to elders," said Annith carefully. "Or teachers."

"You don't have to tell them it's about the Host," said Tanuu. "Just ask about our history. You know all the good stuff's been passed verbally."

I watched my feet. There were probably people who had more information than we'd been able to find in our research. But could we approach any of them?

"Ask the training master," said Tanuu.

When Annith and I let out cries of disgust, he added, "Anyo, I mean! He's teaching at the elementary school now."

Anyo, an elementary school teacher? I couldn't picture him teaching kids how to multiply.

"He does know a lot of history," said Blacktail. "Bet he'd be happy to share it."

I slashed long blades of grass out of my way with the crossbow. I was still angry with Anyo for not defending us at that disastrous meeting.

"Meela, you gotta trust some people," said Tanuu. "We're all a part of the same fight."

If we were all on the same side, why did I feel so alienated because of what I wanted? My people might have wanted freedom, but they wanted to kill mermaids to get it.

I considered Tanuu's words. Of anyone who might be able to tell us our island's history, Anyo was probably the one I trusted most.

"He wasn't necessarily against us finding the Host," said Annith, watching me. "He could've been quiet because of the others. He might even support our search for the legend, now that he's been sacked."

I didn't know if he'd go as far as supporting us, but I could hardly imagine him ratting us out to the committee. Besides, after what I'd just seen, blindly searching for the Host was a much bigger risk than simply going to Anyo for information.

Sighing, I checked the position of the sun. Behind the patchy clouds, it sat low on the horizon. School would have let out long ago.

I scanned our attire. We were wet, filthy, and miserable looking. Blacktail's clothes were splattered with blood. Not to mention our weapons. Even if Anyo was still there, we couldn't go to a schoolyard like this.

"Tomorrow," I said. "After the kids go home, we'll talk to Anyo."

CHAPTER EIGHT
Lesser Evils

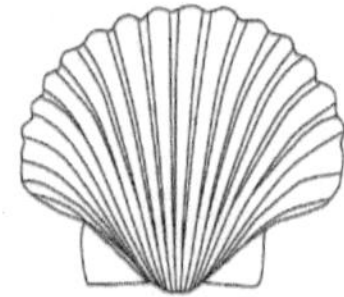

A blanket of hammerhead sharks darkened the world above. They came from the west, a tight cluster of at least a hundred.

The baitball and the tuna scattered. A pair of feeding dolphins shot away.

I yanked my weapon from Spio's bag.

It wasn't the presence of the sharks that scared me, but the way they moved. They bumped into each other, moving too fast, too erratic. Rather than swarm the easy meal, the sharks had pushed straight through.

"They're fleeing something," I said.

Spio let the half-gutted tuna float away and pulled out his own Iron Hook of Doom.

"Smells like merpeople."

My lips prickled. My teeth had lengthened, cutting into them. Ready to fight, my body transformed without my will. I gripped my weapon with both hands.

A few mermen up, Officer Strymon drew himself closer to the shoal. He scanned the line. "Enemies on all sides, soldiers!"

He'd barely drawn his longblade when a war cry sounded. The current changed at my tail.

Instinctively, I bared my teeth and rounded on the threat.

An army surged from below. Hostility closed around us, thick and suffocating.

They were going to pinch us between them and the sharks.

"Sideways," I shouted to Spio.

We spun, but the opposing army already directed the sharks back, surrounding us. The predators formed a wall, trapping us inside the swirling ring.

The Battle for Eriana Kwai flooded back to me, bringing to life my every nightmare. This wasn't how I was supposed to die—half a world away from everyone I loved, fighting for a cause I didn't believe in.

Sharks and adrenaline-fueled mermen wreaked havoc on my senses. I didn't know where to turn. Everything moved at blinding speed. I was used to fighting against the predictable, slow pace of a human.

Ripples grazed my skin from below. A merman with dreadlocked black hair shot towards me.

Spio dove between us. "I'm on it!"

He swung hard. The hook sliced the merman's chest, spilling a cloud of blood.

"Weapons up, Lysi. This fight's gonna be *off the hook*."

Yelps rose over the rushing current as more soldiers closed in. They resembled us in appearance and weaponry, except for the dishevelment they all shared. They must have travelled an entire tidecycle to get here. Where had they come from?

A tiny mermaid with a dagger in each hand darted around Spio. He retaliated with disorienting speed.

Mermaids?

This wasn't one of Adaro's armies, divided by gender. This was the side I should have been fighting on. Could I join them? Would they know I was an outsider?

My hope vanished as someone charged me from behind. I whirled. A merman swung a mace at my head and I curved out of range. He struck again, tireless, covered in scars and apparently fearless about acquiring more.

I was faster than him, but I could only retreat for so long. Already the sharks were at my back. I had to act.

Holding my weapon with both hands, I swung hard. The hook grazed his stomach. It was a weak attack, but I had the advantage of iron. A line of blood seeped from his flesh, below an existing scar that stretched across his chest.

The merman snarled. He aimed for my head and I somersaulted backwards. I came back with another two-handed swing, hitting his stomach in the same place, cutting deep. He spluttered, blood clouding in front of him.

I shoved him away. He slumped over.

Panic squeezed my lungs. I hadn't meant to kill him. Had I? Did I have a choice?

Spio appeared next to me. He watched my victim sink and then shouted over the din, "That guy really had an *iron stomach.*"

I turned to him, numb.

His expression flickered. "It's all right, buddy. Our guys are good. We'll win this."

"Spio, we're not winning anything, here."

Something changed in his aura, but I didn't have time to decide what. His nostrils flared as he focused on something behind me.

I glanced back. The sun had set, darkness stripping the world of colour. Between the soldiers and whirling bubbles,

Officer Strymon's glare fixed on us, eyes blending with the bloody water. The illusion of his eyeless skull sent a ripple of unease through me. Had he heard me?

A mermaid descended on him and he turned, swinging his longblade.

"We can talk about this later," said Spio. "This fight's getting messy, and it's time to *iron out the kinks!*"

He sped away, twirling his weapon. I gaped after him.

Clouds of blood spilled in all directions. It clung to my skin, dirty, thick, warm. It was impossible to move without tasting it.

The spinner dolphins shot past, cackling. They wore the assault vests. Sure enough, anyone in their path dove out of the way.

A body crashed into me, throwing me backwards. I stopped myself before I hit the circling hammerheads—but not before a tooth sliced my shoulder, drawing a stinging line of blood. My temper rose.

A bony mermaid with patches missing from her blond hair closed in, raising a slate dagger. I gritted my teeth and shot towards her.

She realised what the hook was made of too late. The iron met her sternum. Her mouth opened and bubbles exploded from it. She must have screamed, but the world was too loud for me to hear it.

I pushed myself away from the sharks, wiping my shoulder clean. The animals were becoming more agitated. I caught their desperate urge to join what they must have thought was a feeding frenzy. Some tried to break the circle, chasing whatever prey was bleeding freely, only to be shoved back by a swinging tail or weapon.

An empty pocket had opened in the centre of the ring. I detected a huge presence, wild, out of control.

The great white had been injured, and she was angry.

Something sharp grazed the side of my neck. I spun and found my assailant clutching a knife. I retaliated hard. The hook caught him in the arm.

Bubbles left his mouth. He reached for his seared flesh, eyes locking onto the iron that did it.

In his moment of hesitation, I roared and swung again, knocking him into the wall of sharks.

They erupted. No anger, no excitement, only bare instinct to attack.

The merman's scream carried as unimaginable force clamped on his arm, tearing through at the elbow. Another bit his waist. His weapon fell from his grip and sank.

I turned away. My anger gave way to panic. I needed air. Why was I doing this? I was letting the surrounding aggression become my own. Even the sharks seeped into my senses.

Something tightened around my hair and pulled me down. I shrieked, twisting to find a mermaid swinging a club at my head. I lifted an arm to block it. The club hit my wrist and my weapon fell from my grip.

"No!"

It disappeared in the chaos below.

The mermaid released me, winding back for a two-handed blow. She was muscled, tough, her head shaven almost to the scalp—maybe to avoid whatever parasite had eaten the last mermaid's hair.

I shoved her away with my tail, keeping myself out of reach.

A struggle above grazed my skin. Coho struck a fatal blow to a merman, who dropped a conch shell. I lunged for it.

My opponent shot towards me. I seized the shell, flipped over, and drove into her.

A shark darted by our heads, snapping at a cloud of blood. We flinched. Several sharks had abandoned the circle, diving inwards to feed on the corpses. Our own military animals fought back, chasing them outwards—partly training, mostly instinct.

The mermaid tensed to strike. I swiped the shell at her face from close range, but didn't put enough strength into it. It slid across her flesh without a mark.

I pushed her away before she could swing at me.

Her eyebrows pulled together, like she sensed my reluctance. The expression softened her face. She must have been no older than me.

A shark blasted between us. We recoiled from its swinging head.

Without taking my eyes off the mermaid, I cast my senses around. Hammerheads thrashed among the bodies, feeding, snapping at anything. Some fled.

The mermaid seemed to consider striking again, but her focus was elsewhere. She glanced over her shoulder.

I considered chasing my iron hook. If I swam fast enough, could I catch it?

I stayed put. The suffocating depths were uncomfortable even by day. Now, the deep-sea creatures would be rising for the night. I was in no state to fend off overlarge teeth and a hinged jaw.

In front of me, terror rose from the mermaid like a wall of ice. The red drained from her eyes, her skin paled, her teeth retracted. She spun around, searching.

Her army was gone. Had they retreated?

No. They'd been killed. Bodies floated around us, the smell of death thick.

Before the mermaid could react, two officers seized her by the arms. Someone shoved me out of the way. Strymon appeared between us.

"If you have a moment, darling," he said to the mermaid, "I have a few things to ask you."

The mermaid's green eyes widened.

Nearby, mermen shouted to get the animals under control. The spinner dolphins circled at top speed, cackling.

"Where's the mako?" someone shouted.

"Left with the shoal," said someone else.

At least ten soldiers closed on the great white, who wove between the corpses, tearing off chunks of flesh with violent jerking motions. Blood clouded from a long gash in her side.

The billfish fed, too, driven into a frenzy.

"Are there more where you came from?" said Strymon.

The mermaid turned her head, jaw tight. Strymon's dark gaze flicked over her shaven scalp. He didn't mask his disgust.

"You must understand, darling, that this attack has left us a few soldiers short. Of course, we didn't lose as many as you did"—he chuckled, waving a hand—"but His Majesty will be displeased if we swim into the same net twice."

Still, the mermaid said nothing. Strymon's aura darkened, though the faint, insincere smile remained on his face.

I lingered behind them, suspended. Nobody else seemed to notice or care about this interrogation. Soldiers breached, tended their wounds, and rounded up the scattered animals and supplies. The commander wove through the flurry, shouting at everyone to gather the assets and move away from the bodies.

Strymon exhaled dramatically. As though given no choice, he pressed the argillite blade against the mermaid's throat hard enough to draw blood.

"You can be certain that whether or not you tell me, we will find the others. When that happens, we will deliver the same treatment as we did today."

He pushed harder, until blood swirled around her pale face.

"So you can make our job easier in exchange for your life, or you can die here, knowing we will still find—"

"Medusa's army has no limits," said the mermaid.

Strymon eased up on the blade. "Where are they stationed? Are there more coming towards us?"

The mermaid's gaze flicked to me, and then back to Strymon.

No one could help her, and she knew it. Her fear dissipated as she surrendered to her fate. Resolve took its place.

She snarled. "Queen Medusa will always be the rightful ruler of the seas. Your king will pay for all he has done."

There was a terrible pause. I felt Strymon's decision before he acted. I looked away, but it wasn't enough to stop me from feeling the stab of the blade.

The soldiers holding the mermaid's arms let go. I smelled the blood, felt the life leave her body.

"Fall in line and wait for the commander's instruction," shouted Strymon.

I turned and collided with Coho.

"You okay?" he said.

I shook my head once. I needed the surface. Without hesitating, I shot upwards and broke into the hot night air.

I'd killed someone. More than one. I'd never killed a merman or mermaid before, and I hadn't planned on it. Then, maybe worse, I'd done nothing to stop that mermaid from getting murdered. She should have been my ally and yet I had done nothing to protect her.

Coho and Spio surfaced.

Spio had an Iron Hook of Doom in each hand. He passed one to me, apparently not caring that I'd nearly lost his precious weapon a moment ago.

I tried to thank him, but couldn't form words. I took a deep breath.

"Either of you hurt?" said Coho.

I shook my head.

Spio grimaced. "Bruised ribs, I think."

"This is bad," said Coho.

"Don't worry, I can still fight. You haven't lost your champion."

Coho ignored him. "The Atlantic army made it a lot further north than we thought. Either we were given a wrong tip, or they've got secret reserves hidden around here."

"What do we do?" I said, secretly hoping we'd have to turn around.

"We get in line and wait for orders."

A heavy silence fell between us. At my tail, ripples pulsed from the feeding hammerheads. Fins skimmed the surface as more sharks joined in. No doubt they'd smelled the bloodshed from a league away.

Coho and Spio submerged. I took a long, slow breath, and followed.

Beneath the surface, soldiers convened in an enormous, perfectly spaced grid. I copied Spio in positioning myself, treading upright.

The mood had darkened since the attack.

The commander rose higher than the grid and faced us. He was flanked by ten officers, whose hair glistened with emeralds.

"We are stopping sooner than planned, but we must consider our strategy," said the commander. "I will consult the king as soon as we are able to locate an acoustic channel. In the meantime, we will spend the night at a reef half a league east."

He glanced to his officers, and then back to the army.

"Soldiers, you fought bravely. This has been a war of many successes, but also of many sacrifices. Keep up your unwavering courage and remember whom you fight for. The opposition we met today, and those we will meet in the coming days, are resisting the rightful king. They are damaging the potential for a prosperous tomorrow—a worldwide Utopia. Remember this as you swing your weapons, and it will be impossible for them to take us down."

He glanced to Strymon, who floated closest to him. Strymon smiled.

"For the king," said the commander.

"For the king," said the army around me. The sound rippled like the moan of a whale.

We followed the officers towards the reef. Nobody spoke. The words "rightful king" and "worldwide Utopia" lingered in my head.

The reef was a lumpy, shallow plateau that protruded from the water in a few places. It might not have been an ideal place to rest, but to me, it was perfect.

At my request, Spio and I moved to the furthest edge possible, away from everyone else. I perched with my tail in the water and my upper body in the open air, leaving me free to breathe without growing too warm in the tropical breeze. My tail tingled when I sat down, every muscle having been worked past the point of exhaustion.

Thousands of stars shone in the clear sky. The soldiers shuffled around noisily, grabbing food, finding a place to nap, rehashing the fight with excessive bicep-flexing.

Spio told me to rest, since I looked terrible and had obviously not slept in several tidecycles.

But even with Spio on lookout, my body wouldn't let me drift off. Not in such unfamiliar surroundings. Plus, even though I trusted Spio, I wouldn't have put it past him to find sudden inspiration for a new weapon and leave me to go find a narwhal horn.

Waves whispered against the rocks, pushing my tail back and forth. A pair of seagulls squawked overhead. The air felt thicker than I was used to, wrapping around me like a blanket.

It all should have sung me to sleep. But I lay staring at the reflection of the moon on the water.

After a while, I rolled over. Spio was sitting up, gazing at the black horizon.

"Spio?"

He turned.

"You remember that friend I told you about? The one I had as a kid before ..." I motioned to the scar on my waist.

"You mean that human girl from Eriana Kwai?" he said.

I sighed. So much for subtlety. "Yeah. Her."

He'd known about Meela for years. He also knew her father had been the one to give me the iron scar.

Spio listened while I told him about seeing Meela aboard the ship we were sent to attack. I didn't know why I needed to tell him so badly. Maybe I wanted to explain why I was here. He never would have asked me outright.

"She's the same girl," I said. "I mean, she's different, older, but that compassionate little girl is still there. The one who cut me free of the fishing net the day we met. The one who moved a starfish once because she didn't want it to dry out in the sun."

I smiled to myself. "It was easy for me to remember why we were so close. I remember being afraid she would get sick of me and stop coming to see me—but she never did. She kept coming back."

"As kids, you mean?"

"As kids … and on the ship. In battle. She came to see me in secret."

"You miss her," said Spio, in a tone so casual he might have been pointing out a halibut.

I stared at my hands, feeling myself blush. I must have given more away in my mood than I intended.

"I love her."

He grinned. "Ah, so Adaro saw you talking to Meela and got jealous. He couldn't accept that your heart belonged to someone else. Not to mention the *someone else* wasn't even a merman. Or a man by any definition."

I shoved him. "Ew! No, the girls realised what was going on. Adaro decided he could use me as leverage, to get Meela to do what he wanted."

"So he threw you behind jellies as a threat to Meela? What a jerk."

I cringed and glanced around, as though dodging an iron bolt. "Shh!"

He lowered his voice. "Seriously. That guy can go bathe in whale turds."

"Don't say stuff like that," I whispered, not feeling the humour.

Though we were isolated on the outskirts of the reef, a few mermen were in hearing distance. For all I knew, someone was listening.

"You know he screens former humans?" whispered Spio. "Coho had to take a test to prove he'd left his human life behind and was loyal to merpeople. Like his past is criminal. It worked out, but I don't know how it would've ended up if he didn't get hitched to Ephyra."

"Coho used to be human?"

"Yeah. Ephyra saw him and wanted to keep him."

I wrinkled my nose. "You make it sound like she wanted a pet."

Spio shrugged, as if to say, 'Your words, not mine.'

"Who's Ephyra?"

"She works in government. Minister of, I don't know, telling Adaro he looks pretty or something. I met her once. She reminds me of what you would look like if you were ten years older and had dark hair. And darker skin. And bigger—"

"So she looks nothing like me."

"Not really."

Spio studied me for a moment.

"What?"

He glanced around. "There's something you should know. I think. Or maybe you don't want—well, I think you should know it. If you want. But you don't have to. But if I tell you then you're kind of doomed, anyway."

I waited, not understanding in the slightest what he was on about.

Without warning, he slid into the water. I stared at the ripples he left behind. He moved away from the reef.

He must have decided we weren't far enough away from everyone. I slid in after him.

We surfaced far from the others, beside a rocky protrusion so small we had to fight a pelican for it.

Spio propped his arms on the rock. I did the same across from him. Waves hissed rhythmically against it.

"I get the drift you don't really want to be here," said Spio. "You want to be back home with that human."

I said nothing.

"I want to help you get home, buddy."

I sighed in relief. "Spio, thank you."

"But we need the right moment," he said. "That moment, in my expert opinion, is one where you don't have a chance of getting caught and executed for breaking oath."

"That's reasonable."

"A few of us in the unit—we have a plan."

"You want to escape?" I whispered. "How many of you?"

He shook his head. "It's more than just escaping I'm talking about. We all agree Adaro's been a bit of a ..."

Tyrant, I thought, not daring to say it aloud.

"Lumpsucker," said Spio. "Everything he's done has been a disgrace to merpeople."

I glanced around, nervous. The army was well out of sight, but I still heard the distant hum of conversation.

"A lot of guys feel the same," said Spio.

"They do?"

"Lysi, it doesn't take a whole lot of goop in your skull to see the number of deaths Adaro's causing. Between the Battle for Eriana Kwai and the expansion across the Pacific, we're getting picked off like krill."

"Not to mention the humans who get in his way."

"See, you get it. A lot of soldiers talk all wise and righteous, but no one has the guts to do anything about it."

"What about the other cities?" I said. "The Atlantic Queen? Soon his army will be big enough to match hers. Someone must be noticing."

"They don't give a flying flatfish. I think they aren't expecting Adaro to get that far. Think about it: the Atlantic is the biggest, oldest kingdom in history. Do you really think Adaro has a chance of taking it?"

"At this rate, yes."

"That's what we thought," said Spio. "We're a tidecycle away from a total clusterf—"

Beneath our tails, something moved. We froze, feeling the ripples. It was small. Too small to be anything. The way it flapped about, it was probably a squid.

Spio continued, dropping his voice lower. "We've decided we're not happy doing his battles, helping him take over the seas."

My pulse quickened. If others wanted Adaro ousted from the throne, maybe it was possible.

"You know the first thing he'll do once he's king of the seas?" said Spio. "He's gonna push humans out of the water for good, and we're gonna have the wrath of the President of the United freaking States of America dropping iron on us like snow."

He was right. Adaro might have been keeping away from open conflict with the rest of the humans for now—I thought of his truce with the Aleut people near my home—but those peace treaties wouldn't be forever. He would declare war on humans as soon as he was ready. As soon as he secured the oceans.

"We're stopping him before it's too late," said Spio.

"But how can anyone stop him? No one has power over the king."

"We already have a plan."

Spio dropped his voice so low, I wasn't sure he even spoke. I had to lean so close that he could have bitten my ear.

"We're gonna assassinate him, Lysi."

I leaned back to see his face properly.

He stared back, dead serious. Moonlight glinted off his dark eyes. Replacing Adaro with a new king or queen was one thing, but killing him?

I sank lower into the waves, shaking my head. This wasn't a choice I wanted to make.

"Spio, what about the oath? We swore total obedience—"

"The oath!" he said. "That doesn't matter anymore. Our duty as soldiers isn't to Adaro. It's to merpeople. And the enemy of merpeople is the one waging war across the globe. King Adaro is more than just the enemy of the humans. He's our enemy, too."

A wave broke against the rock and sprayed over us.

I exhaled slowly. "You surprise me, sometimes."

"I stole that speech from Pontus."

Spio tilted his head back, basking in the tropical air. The night was too silent and peaceful for what raged inside me.

He was talking about life-or-death.

But when had I ever not been in that territory? I risked death every day fighting a war I didn't believe in. Now I had a chance to risk my life for a cause I did believe in.

This was more than I was ready for. I just wanted to go home. I wanted to work with Meela on the plan we already had, not join forces with a bunch of guys I didn't know or trust.

"Until that lumpsucker's dead, any attempt to escape is gonna get you killed," said Spio. "You saw the way the officers are."

I glanced back towards the army. Maybe this was the best way home. With Adaro dead, I would have no obstacles. Plus, I wouldn't have to worry about Meela. She would be safe from him, and so would her people. That was all she wanted.

"Of course, I gotta take this up with the guys," said Spio. "They won't be happy I told you. We agreed not to recruit others."

"Why not?"

"It's more likely someone will betray us or let something slip."

I frowned. I hadn't even met these guys and already they didn't want me around.

"As far as they know," he said, "you're a pretty face who got stuck here because you already did something stupid."

"These guys made it clear they don't think I'm a pretty face." And, if I admitted it to myself, I had noticed a lot of sidelong glances, sneers, and whispers.

Spio waved a hand. "They don't know how to react to you."

"Am I that much of a freak?"

"A freak? No. But you aren't exactly …"

"Normal?"

"Conventional."

I raised my eyebrows.

"Lysi, any other mermaid, she sees a sailor, and she turns on the charm and lures him into the water. Just because. You'd rather get him in the water by tripping him and watching him do a bellyflop."

I grinned. "That was pretty great, wasn't it?"

"It was awesome. I still have that guy's shoe at home."

"He had it coming."

Spio pointed at me. "You see what I mean, though? You're different. Some find it weird."

I realised I'd been trying to dislodge a live shrimp that had gotten stuck in my hair. I dropped my hand. "Do you think I'm weird?"

Spio clapped me on the shoulder and looked me dead in the eye. "Would we be friends if I didn't?"

I smiled.

"So you're in," he said, more statement than question.

I bit my lip. "Spio, this is high treason."

He shrugged. "Which evil is bigger, Lysi? Doing away with him, or letting him live?"

CHAPTER NINE
Eriana the Mortal

Memories of elementary school flooded back as we crossed the schoolyard.

"That's where I shoved Dani in the mud," I said with a dreamy sigh.

Tanuu squeezed my shoulders. "That's my girl!"

The mud puddle, affectionately called the Eriana Trench, was smaller than I remembered, but still big enough that I understood why kids got in trouble for trying to wade into the middle.

"I bet there's a solid layer of paper on the bottom," said Annith. "All those years of paper-ship battles."

"Kids always chucked my shoes in there," said Blacktail.

Tanuu, Annith, and I turned to her.

"They did?" I said. "Why?"

Blacktail shrugged.

"That's just mean!" said Tanuu.

"Kids are mean when you've got big ears and don't talk much."

"You shoulda been my friend," said Tanuu. "I would've put them in their place."

Blacktail laughed. "Right. You never would've been my friend."

"Yes I would have!"

"You were too cool, with your soccer and your little group of boys. Did you even know I existed?"

Tanuu rushed forwards to hold the door open for us. "Yes. You were the quiet girl who was good at drawing."

Blacktail raised an eyebrow at him.

"You can draw?" I said.

She walked past him. "We still would never have been friends. And stop being so nice. I only saved you because you looked so pathetic kneeling in front of that mermaid."

Annith and I giggled.

"Did you see her?" said Tanuu defensively. "I mean, she was ..."

He glanced at me with a guilty expression.

I clapped him on the arm as I passed him. "Out of your league?"

Inside the school, everything was definitely smaller than I remembered. The hallways were narrow, the art on the walls barely came up to my chest, and inside the classrooms, the desks were so tiny I wondered how I ever fit in one.

The place smelled like crayons. As we searched for the grade seven classroom, our whispers and scuffing shoes echoed in the vacant hallways.

We knocked on the open door. Anyo lifted his heavy eyes from a pile of papers, his forehead deeply lined. Then he seemed to notice who was standing there and his face softened.

"Ladies! Come in."

We entered, Tanuu awkwardly bringing up the rear.

I suddenly regretted being angry with Anyo. Of course he would always be happy to see us, his trainees and his legacy—like a proud uncle.

I scanned the classroom. The desks had been arranged in groups of four. Some kids had taped pictures to the tops. On the right wall, the blackboard had algebra questions across one side, and 'Clean-up Duty' with a few names at the bottom. The wall behind us displayed the students' drawings of the circulatory system.

In the corner, a bookshelf overflowed with chapter books, including some in English, and textbooks on the world wars, animal habitats, the human body, and natural disasters. A poster of the earth's crust had been taped above a dozen dioramas of earthquakes and volcanoes. Some had clearly been thrown together last minute, while others were clearly assisted by overachieving parents. I thought being a teacher looked kind of fun.

We stood across from Anyo, not sure where to sit.

"Come to learn from a retired training master?" he said, bitterness clipping his voice.

He drew an X on the homework he was marking with enough force to rip a hole in the page.

"These kids are lucky," I said.

Anyo snatched another piece of homework from the stack. "They don't care."

"Come on, a former training master for a teacher?"

He hesitated, and then grumbled, "I guess I haven't had problems with kids stepping out of line. Probably scared to."

"They want to learn from you," said Annith.

He made a violent checkmark.

"Is that why you're here? To learn from me? Well, kids, will it be math or science?"

"Actually," said Annith, "we were hoping you could teach us a bit of history."

Anyo's pen faltered. The tip hovered over the page, so he wasn't writing anything but also wasn't looking at us.

"Trying to catch up on the high school you missed during training?"

His tone made it clear he was grasping. He knew where this conversation was headed.

I followed his eyes to the filing cabinet beside the desk. The bottom drawer gaped open, full of paper and books.

"We hoped you could tell us about Eriana herself," I said. "We know she was born mortal, but stories all tell of her as a goddess, not a human."

Anyo turned back to his marking. "The story of Eriana is more myth than fact. We don't teach it anymore."

"At all? What about our culture?" I said, voice raising an octave.

My own agenda aside, the idea that the school board had taken out such an important part of Eriana culture horrified me. Even when I'd been in elementary school, our education on the goddess Eriana was limited to a single picture book in grade two.

"They can't do that," said Blacktail. "Even if it is myth, it's still part of our history."

Anyo shrugged. "It's the board's decision, not mine. If you want to take it up with them, I can give you contact information."

I crossed my arms. "Who was Eriana as a human? Where did she come from, before she discovered this island?"

Anyo looked at the filing cabinet again, and then out the window, and then back to the pile of homework on his desk. Finally, he met my eyes.

"I don't know anything about the Host."

"This isn't about the Host," said Annith, but I waved a hand.

"We didn't expect you'd know anything about that. We just want to learn more about Eriana. Anything you can tell us."

He stared at us, rubbing a calloused hand over his mouth. The clock behind him filled the silence, ticking loudly.

"I've never heard of anything called the Host of Eriana," he said.

"That doesn't mean it doesn't exist," said Blacktail.

"Maybe you know it, just not by name," said Tanuu.

"What if it is real?" said Annith.

Anyo took in our determined expressions, probably noting the way we leaned towards him, hanging on his every word. He seemed to be having an internal struggle. I said nothing.

"Adette is in training," he said.

It had crossed my mind that Anyo's daughter was now outside his control, a generic member of the new training program.

"I don't trust Mujihi's training methods," he said. "So I can't pretend the prospect of ending the Massacres doesn't interest me."

"We want to help Adette," I said. "We want to help all the trainees."

His expression revealed nothing. He ran a hand across his scalp. Absently, he traced his fingers along the scar he'd gotten from his days as a Massacre warrior.

Yes, I thought, *we want to avoid more injuries like that one.*

He caught my eye, seemed to realise what he was doing, and sighed. "I can tell you the story of who Eriana was as a mortal. But I don't think it will help."

He motioned for us to sit. We pulled chairs out from the tiny desks and sat down while he opened the second drawer of the filing cabinet. He produced an ancient, barely held-together book and placed it in the centre of the desk.

Annith, Blacktail, Tanuu, and I leaned closer. The leather cover had a familiar emblem: a sea lion, teeth bared in pursuit of prey. It was our national animal—though it hadn't had much presence since the mermaids invaded. At some point in the last thirty years, someone had chosen the northern saw-whet owl to grace our flag instead—an animal of the sky, not the sea.

"I dug this up after you talked to the Massacre Committee," said Anyo. "My family's had this book for generations. Have you come across anything like it?"

Annith and I shook our heads.

"It's only pictures, mind you. The stories have been passed orally."

He opened it, revealing soft, uneven pages of animal skin parchment. It had a musty odour, like it had been forgotten about in a shed for a few decades. The first page was a colour sketch of a young couple holding a newborn baby, bundled in thick grey and brown furs.

"The discovery of our land is, of course, said to be the work of one woman named Eriana. Her exact birthplace is unknown. Most historians believe she came from up north, but she might have sailed here from further away, like Russia or Japan."

"Where do you think she came from?" said Blacktail.

"Given the legend and proximity, I think she came from what we now know as Alaska."

He flipped the page to a child standing in the snow, hair blowing around her face, encircled by half a dozen bald eagles.

"Eriana's people called her a charmer of animals, because from an early age she spoke to them in ways no other human could. She grew up playing with wild hares, pouncing in the snow with foxes, running with herds of caribou. She was known for calling families of eagles to fly circles around her, simply for the joy of feeling their wings. But her skill proved useful, too. If a pack of wolves wandered too close to her people, she could guide them away without evoking so much as a growl."

Anyo flipped to a young woman standing before a herd of caribou, surrounded by a world of snow.

"One year, a rough winter hit Eriana's people. With it came a terrible spell of hunger. They begged her to summon wild animals to sacrifice themselves for food. Driven by hunger, Eriana complied. She called a herd of caribou and made them wait until, one by one, her people had slain and eaten them all."

The next page showed a group of faceless people huddled against a whirling blizzard.

"But the Gaela did not approve. She had given Eriana this gift of speaking to animals, and was furious that Eriana had cheated the natural order of the animal kingdom. Eriana's gift, said the Gaela, was meant to bring peace between the species, not deceive innocent creatures. So she sent the Aanil Uusha to punish Eriana."

Anyo pointed at the blizzard, and I looked again. The face of Death himself could be seen in the lines of the whirling storm.

"That night, the Aanil Uusha swept over Eriana's people in the form of an ice storm. Eriana tried to plea with him, but

Death was merciless. He took the lives of her entire tribe. He was about to turn on Eriana herself …"

He stared at the page for several seconds.

"But?" I said.

"The Aanil Uusha thought it would be a better punishment to leave Eriana and let her live her life in guilt. At least, that was how my mother told the tale. This is where the legend diverges. My father said Eriana and Death made a bargain, resulting in his agreement to give Eriana her life."

"What kind of bargain?" I said.

Anyo shook his head. "My father didn't know. That's why I was always told my mother's version."

I glanced to Annith. So there was a hole in the legend.

"No one really knows why Eriana survived, then," said Annith.

"There is some uncertainty about how she escaped the ice storm," said Anyo.

He turned to the next drawing: Eriana on a warship, crashing through stormy seas.

"As it's told, the Aanil Uusha built a ship from the bones of her people and the caribou, allowing her to sail away from her barren homeland. She landed on our shores. For the rest of her life, Eriana would fulfill a duty to protect the animals of our island, fending off anyone who dared approach."

Anyo sat back. "That ship is now said to lie in the middle of our forest."

"The Enticer," said Tanuu.

Anyo nodded.

"The library books said Eriana guarded the island with her warship," I said. "But the ship can't be the Host, can it? Don't you think she would've had something more powerful and, well, scary?"

"Ah," said Anyo. "That leads me to the reason I dug this book out in the first place." He pushed the ancient book towards me. "Have a closer look at that drawing."

I leaned in.

"There's a pair of eyes in the water," said Blacktail at once.

She was right. Beneath the ship, something irregular was sketched into the wavy lines representing the stormy ocean. Angry, enormous eyes. They could have been overlooked as swirls in the water, but once I accepted them as a pair of eyes, I couldn't unsee them.

Nothing indicated who, or what, they belonged to.

"Do you think her pet is a sea demon?" said Tanuu. "Maybe the Host is an ancient mermaid deity."

I chewed my lip, staring closer. Each eye was larger than Eriana's head.

"I don't think so," I said. "Adaro would never call a mermaid the pet of a human."

"Besides, look at the colours," said Blacktail, pointing. "A sea demon's eyes are red. These have been drawn to match the colour of the water."

I looked to Anyo, who shrugged.

"As a boy, I remember asking my father about those eyes beneath the ship. He told me it represented the angry sea. Now I wonder if it's something more—something that fills the gap in the legend."

I rocked in my chair, thinking. How much could that story be trusted? Were we supposed to interpret it metaphorically?

Whatever I thought about the gods of Earth and Death punishing Eriana, the fact was that Eriana had escaped an ice storm that killed everyone else. How? Did it have to do with the Host?

"Why is it called the Enticer?" I said.

Anyo rubbed a hand across his scalp. "I assumed Eriana used it to entice fish while she was hunting."

I frowned. "That doesn't make sense. I thought her duty was to protect animals, not hunt them."

"Then maybe she used it to call them to her for other reasons."

I let it drop. The story had gaps, but it also answered several questions.

"Thanks for showing this to us, Anyo."

He snapped it shut. "That's what I know. Like I said, I'm not sure it helps."

It did help. A glance at the others told me they felt the same. Their eyes were wide, excited.

We had a starting point: the legend of the Host of Eriana had to do with the ancient ship at the Safe Training Base.

"But how does the story end?" said Annith. "How did Eriana become a goddess?"

"When Eriana died, after a life of servitude to this island, it's said the Gaela forgave her. Eriana ascended to the stars to become a goddess, where she remains protector of our island to this day."

"Some protector," said Tanuu, looking up as if addressing the sky. "You could maybe help us out with these sea demons, eh?"

I smacked him on the arm. "Don't be disrespectful."

Annith was still focused on the book. "Do you mind if we take this?"

Anyo hesitated. "I'd rather keep the world's only copy in my possession."

"Oh. What other stories are in there?"

"Nothing more on the topic of Eriana herself."

"Why haven't these stories been shared more widely?" said Blacktail.

"Perhaps with more recent history to teach, and under the influences from other nations, the school system has considered legends this old to be irrelevant."

"But it's our history," said Annith. "We need to keep telling it so we don't lose it."

"I've told the stories to Adette," said Anyo. "She's known them her whole life."

No one said anything, but I knew what Annith was thinking. Did anyone else on Eriana Kwai know all these stories? What if Adette died on the Massacre? What if something happened to Anyo?

"You should get the stories written down somewhere," said Annith timidly. "In case … I mean, it would be tragic if our history was …"

A pained expression overcame Anyo's face.

"Adette won't have to go on the Massacre," I said. "We'll find the Host."

My confidence must have rang through the room, because the others sat up taller.

"You have a kind heart, Metlaa Gaela," said Anyo. "Never let this unfair world take that away from you."

I gave an almost-smile, not sure what to say.

He checked the clock on the wall and stood.

"I wish you luck. For now, all we can do is hope Mujihi proves to be a more effective training master than I ever was."

"He won't be," said Annith, Blacktail, and I together.

Anyo turned to slip the book into his bag, and I thought I saw him hide a smile.

"Before I left, I added a mind and body component to the program," he said, "for more, ah … mental preparation and soundness. I've come to realise such training is woefully lacking."

"How's it going over?" I said.

His expression sank into a deep frown. "I don't think the program is following through with it, given that last year's top combat student is head of training."

I jumped up so fast, my chair tipped over with a loud clatter.

"He put—head of training?"

Annith and Blacktail caught on at the same moment, gasping in outrage.

"You haven't heard?" said Anyo dispassionately. "Yes, Dani was just appointed. I tried to put you in there with her, Metlaa Gaela, but Mujihi has already chosen his other assistant teachers for the program."

"Texas, no doubt," I said, not bothering to hide my venom.

Anyo shouldered his bag. "You must admit she showed exceptional skill with a range of weapons. Combined with her leadership skills, she could make an excellent teacher."

I gaped at him. On the Massacre, Dani had managed to create nothing short of a cult. Those who'd never experienced the worst of Dani called it 'leadership skills'.

"You honestly think that?" I said.

Anyo's eyes flicked past me. "Ah, speaking of … We were just talking about you."

I whirled around to see Dani in the doorway, her wicked expression darkened by black-lined eyes.

"All good things, I'm sure," said Dani, casting an appraising glance around the room as she sauntered in.

"We're on our way out," I said. "Sorry to have missed your visit."

Dani made a sympathetic sound. "We'll catch up later."

She straddled the chair I'd just been sitting on, facing Anyo, and motioned that he should sit back down. He obliged, dropping his bag.

Annith closed the door behind us with a little too much force.

The moment we were outside, Blacktail whispered, "What was she doing there?"

Annith and I said nothing.

"She was probably going to ask for advice about the training program," said Tanuu lightly.

The rest of us shared an uneasy look.

"You don't know Dani," I said.

"What, you think she was eavesdropping?"

I didn't respond.

"She really won't want the Massacres to end now," said Annith. "She's in a position of power over like, a hundred girls."

The idea sickened me. If the potential for glory hadn't driven her mad enough on the Massacre, it would now. The success of every future Massacre could come back to her training methods.

What would she accomplish as head of an entire training school? Her captaincy on the Massacre had been a gradual climb to power because she'd met opposition from me and other crewmembers. Now, every one of these trainees would be desperate to prove her worth in training, and do anything to make Dani like her.

Tanuu cracked his knuckles. "Let's do this thing quick, before she can go all crazy on those trainees. Let's go to the Enticer."

"We can't go right now," I said. "Mujihi is probably still there. I don't like the idea of asking him if he minds if we have a poke around the training base."

"When do we go, then?" said Annith.

I thought for a minute. "We'll want daylight, which means we'll need to go when the trainees are on a rest day."

But would the trainees even have rest days? I felt like the word 'rest' was not in Dani's vocabulary.

"Tomorrow's Sunday," said Blacktail.

"What if Dani shows up again while we're there?" said Annith.

"We won't be stealing anything this time," said Tanuu. "There's nothing to get us in trouble for. It's not like the training area's outta bounds."

"You weren't there when Mujihi was yelling at us," I said.

Annith grimaced.

"Sounds like we need to get him and Dani out of the way," said Blacktail.

We pondered this as we walked down the dirt road. That was exactly what we needed.

"What if we told Dani she got some *Heroes of Eriana Kwai* award, and she has to go to the other side of the island to pick it up?" said Tanuu.

I laughed. "She's a lot of things, but stupid isn't one of them."

"We could set her house on fire," said Blacktail dryly.

"I've got one," said Annith. "Rik can have them in for an interview about the new training program."

I gasped. Of course. Rik was an intern at the news station. An interview with the new training master and head of training would undoubtedly be newsworthy.

"Annith, you're a genius!" I said. "Think Rik will be up for it?"

"He's already talked about doing it. He hasn't yet because I threatened to dump him if he gave Dani any limelight."

We arrived at the fork in the road and stopped. Something like excitement passed between us. Whatever Anyo had said about the story being a myth, we now had more direction than ever before.

"That's our plan?" I said. "Get Dani and Mujihi away from the training base, then have a look around the Enticer?"

The others nodded.

"It's a start," said Tanuu.

"I'll get Rik to do it tomorrow while the trainees are off," said Annith. "It's our best shot at being discreet."

With a wave goodbye, Blacktail and Tanuu set off one way towards their houses, while Annith and I left in the opposite direction.

We didn't speak for several minutes. I ran through everything Anyo had told us, replaying the story in my mind so I wouldn't forget any of it. I lingered on Eriana's escape from the Aanil Uusha. I didn't think it came down to punishment, forcing her to live the rest of her life in guilt. Did I believe she made a bargain with Death? What had she offered in return? And what did those eyes in the water belong to?

I considered the end of the legend, how Eriana had ascended to the stars to protect our island as a goddess. Tanuu was partly right in accusing her of not protecting us. I recalled what King Adaro had said about the legend, how Eriana's Host was apparently bound with its master's soul. Did this mean Eriana's soul was literally trapped inside her pet as a further punishment? Or was this all a metaphor, and Eriana's body was buried in a cave somewhere next to her pet wolf?

"Is everything all right with you and Tanuu?" said Annith, jolting me out of my thoughts.

"Oh," I said, and hesitated for way too long before saying, "Yes. We're fine."

"No you're not."

I brushed my hand along the tall grass on the side of the road, the soft ends tickling my palm.

"I just need space," I said, spewing the same lie I'd been telling Tanuu. "The Massacre was draining and I need some time to myself."

"Uh huh." Her flat tone suggested she knew I was lying but also wasn't about to pry.

I glanced around, checking we were alone. The empty dirt road extended out of sight, sloping in an uphill climb. Dense grass, bush, and trees pressed in on either side, obnoxious with birdsong.

I let my hand graze a Ravendust bush, which stained my palm black. I wiped it on my jeans. "I don't think I'm in love with him."

I expected the words to hang in space. But without any note of surprise or judgment, Annith said, "Don't feel bad, Meela. It happens. It's okay to fall out of love with someone."

Falling out of love might have been a loose definition of what had happened. Now that I knew what love felt like, I wasn't sure if I'd been in love with Tanuu in the first place.

"I don't know if I can tell him," I said, my throat tightening. "I can't do that to him."

"You still care about him."

"Exactly. It's like, I love him, but I'm not *in* love with him. Does that make sense?"

"Yes."

I let out a breath. I should've talked to her about this ages ago.

We stopped at the place where we had to part ways.

"Are you going to break up with him?" she said.

I dug my toe into a groove in the dirt road, avoiding her eyes. "Can't I be distant with him until he gets the point and moves on?"

Annith half-laughed. "I thought you said persistence was his most endearing quality."

I made an indistinct grunt.

"You can't try and subtly wean him off you," said Annith. "That'll draw out the pain. He'll spend every day dragging behind you, hoping you're going through a phase and will come back to him."

I sighed. Annith threw her arms around me in a rib-crushing hug.

"One day you'll find someone to sweep you off your feet," she said into my hair.

I hugged her back.

In a perfect world, I would tell her I'd fallen in love years ago. I'd tell her love looked like sapphire blue eyes and coppery blonde hair and smooth, ivory skin. But I couldn't. Not in this world.

The thought of Lysi tightened my chest, a pang of dread and urgency. Every second that passed, she was somewhere far away, waiting for me to free the Host.

I needed to hurry.

I wondered where Adaro had taken her—if he had her imprisoned, enslaved, or tortured. I wondered where she was at that moment. I hoped, with every fibre of my existence, that she wasn't suffering.

CHAPTER TEN
Fit for a King

I convinced Spio to swallow as many glowing copepods as he could before puking. I wanted to see if it would make his skin glow. He didn't get so much as a blue ear.

The cool part was seeing a few hundred of them erupt from his mouth when he did vomit. A few onlookers applauded.

We were travelling southwards again. After the hammerhead attack, the commander decided we would continue as planned, but take an alternate path in case the Atlantic army was waiting to ambush us along the main current.

Unfortunately, the path was inside a canyon—a barren world with little daylight. I relied on vibrations to guide me, feeling the steady current of the surrounding army, the occasional fish—transparent and creepy at this depth—but little else. No mammal in its right mind travelled this low.

Breaching happened in regimented shifts, and we had to hold our breaths for longer than was comfortable.

Other than not being attacked, the only good thing about the canyon was its cooler climate.

Onlookers abruptly stopped clapping as Officer Strymon drifted over. Spio and I fell silent, as though the swarm of copepods we'd left behind was nothing unusual.

He lingered beside us, darkness masking him from view.

"Those of you I have indicated are free to breach," he said.

The group behind us broke towards the surface. Strymon began to move on.

"What about us?" I said.

It had been nearly a quarter-tide. With the depth adding pressure to my lungs, I desperately needed air.

"You have just gone for breath, darling. His Majesty's army is no place for greed."

"We haven't!"

He ignored me, turning away.

"You can't skip us," I said.

His smug aura challenged me to watch him do just that.

"Officer," said Spio. "If two of your soldiers black out in the middle of a canyon—"

"Silence!"

Ripples told me Strymon had dropped a hand to his longblade.

I clenched my fists, wanting to argue but knowing that would be stupid. After a moment, Strymon continued along the line.

The blackness seemed to thicken around us.

"Spio," I whispered, panicked. "I need air."

We would get in trouble for breaching out of order. Was that Strymon's plan? It was either that or pass out and get carried to the surface.

"Hey," whispered the merman in front of us.

He held something out—plant-based, flat, the size of my palm.

"Kelp buoys," he whispered. "I brought a couple in case of emergencies. It'll make your head spin like an otter, but there's enough oxygen to get you by a little longer."

I said nothing, feeling him out. He seemed genuine. He waited for one of us to take the buoy.

"You are a noble and wise specimen," said Spio, accepting the offer.

The merman reached into his bag for a second.

I hesitated to take it. I'd never heard of inhaling kelp buoys. Was he trying to dupe us? Poison us?

"What's your name?" said Spio.

"Anthias."

"Spio. Pleased to meet ya. This is Lysi. She doesn't get out much."

I stuck out my tongue and took the kelp buoy from Anthias' outstretched hand.

"There's no air in here," I said, turning it over.

"It's compressed because we're so deep," said Anthias. "You need to suck on it. Trust me, it works."

I heard Spio inhale from his. "This tastes like a fart."

A short while later, we passed over a shipwreck. It was invisible to the eye and ear, but noticeable in the impurity bleeding from it like a carcass. The presence of that much iron grated my skin and stung my scar like a fresh burn.

As usual, I let the pain remind me why I hated Adaro.

His fault, I thought. *His fault we're at war. His fault humans think we're monsters. His fault I'm not with Meela right now.*

I'd wanted an update from Spio on the treason plan. But the chance for that wouldn't come on a trip like this. The further we travelled, the more convinced I became that this was my way home. How soon after the plan was executed would I be able to take off to Eriana Kwai?

My eyelids fluttered. My muscles had become distinctly sluggish since inhaling the buoy.

"Ssspio," I said, my tongue not responding. "I need … mph …"

He mumbled something I couldn't understand.

"Guys," said someone in front of us.

I grinned. It was that nice merman. What was his name?

"We're surfacing," he said. "Think you can make it?"

I nodded. Or, I thought I did.

"Guys?"

"Lysi," said Spio. "I can't … I can't see."

I blinked, realising I couldn't see, either.

"None of us can," said the nice merman. "We're in a canyon."

Surfacing was a long, slow process. We had to do it in stages to give our bodies time to decompress. My eyes stung as they adjusted to the sunlight.

I didn't remember breaking the surface, but I found myself coughing and rubbing water from my eyes. I slowed my breathing, letting sense trickle back into my brain.

The sun dipped low on the horizon. A lost timber raft floated in the high swells, overgrown with barnacles and teeming with life. Colourful fish plucked at the weeds, while the edible ones darted away once they realised they were under attack. Already, the mermen around me were feeding, digging fish out of hiding places and tearing edible weeds off in chunks.

Spio leaned close and said in an undertone, "Meet in the turtle's lair when dusk reaches the apex."

I stared at him.

"The floating piece of junk way over there. Sunset."

"Got it."

He dove. I drifted to the raft, too exhausted to eat.

Finally, I would get to hear about this plan. My insides churned as I wondered about the other guys involved. Would they trust me? Would I have to prove how much I hated Adaro?

I pulled myself onto the logs and rolled onto my back. I let the tropical air bathe me, for once comfortable in the heat. I thought I might catch a few moments of blissful rest before meeting Spio.

Eyes closed, I sunk into the raft, the weight of my body pulling me down, ready to sleep for days …

"Hey," said a voice.

I opened my eyes.

An unfamiliar merman floated next to me, arms locked over the logs. His face was close enough that I felt his breath. I leaned back.

His wavy black hair fell across his defined face, hiding one eye in a strategically mysterious way.

"Yes?" I said. I couldn't stop my voice from sounding unenthused.

"I wanted to introduce myself," he said in a low, rumbling voice. "I'm Axius."

"Um, hi. I'm—"

"Lysi, I know. You're the glimmer of beauty in this male-infested place."

I stared. He readjusted his arms in an awkward way that made me wonder if his biceps were flexing that much on purpose.

"Being here alone can be tough," he said. "A lot of guys have at least one brother with them. I've got all sisters. Five of them. They're all in reserve for the Battle for Eriana Kwai."

I nodded. This guy projected so much confidence that I had the urge to swat it away, like a fly buzzing in my face.

"I know what you're thinking," he said. "A lot of girls ask me how I managed being the only male. Sure, it was tough, but the experience has given me a deep understanding of femininity. Are your siblings still in training, Lysi?"

"Er, no. My brother's fighting in the Battle for India."

He waited.

"That's it," I said.

His eyes widened. "Sorry, I didn't—"

"My parents haven't died. They just didn't want more kids."

"Oh."

I'd grown used to it. Families rarely had only two children. Spio was the oldest of twelve. My parents said they'd stopped after me because they felt complete after my brother and I were born. As I grew older, I came to suspect they just didn't want to bring more children into Adaro's kingdom.

"Puts you in a good place for inheritance, right?" said Axius. "Only two of you. Mind you, my mother's one of the wealthiest mermaids in Utopia, so even with five sisters I still get my fair share. With my career plans, someday I'll own the estate."

He flashed me his fangs. I couldn't bring myself to smile back. What did he want me to say? Congratulations? Marry me?

"If you need someone to talk to, Lysi—"

"Give it a rest, Ax," someone shouted from the other end of the timber raft.

A few heads turned. A merman with a ponytail was grinning at us, pointed teeth glinting in the sunlight.

"What?" said Axius.

"You're wasting your time," said ponytail. "It's obvious she's taken."

Axius took sudden interest in catching a fish beside him. It was tiny, bright orange with white stripes. Too colourful to be worth eating.

"Are you?" he said.

"I—well, I'm—"

I snatched a sardine from the water and downed it without chewing. I considered whether it'd be in my best interest if all the guys assumed I had a huge, vicious boyfriend who could beat them into blobs of algae.

"Is it that dorky guy?" said Axius.

"Who?"

Next to us, a tangle of seaweed popped out of the water.

Not seaweed—Spio's head.

"Don't try and swim under the raft," he said, plucking weeds from his hair. "I lost my hat to a bladderwrack."

He saw my expression, then spotted Axius.

"What's up, Ax?"

Axius looked back and forth between us.

Spio must have sensed the awkwardness, because he pulled himself up next to me and threw an arm across my shoulders.

"This guy bothering you, sugarkelp?"

"No!" said Axius. "I was just introducing myself."

"I hope that was all," said Spio casually, "because I'd hate to have to fight you."

I turned my head into Spio's shoulder to stifle a laugh.

Axius cleared his throat. "Like I was saying, Lysi. If you need a friend …"

"Thanks," I said. "Nice meeting you."

"I'll let you get to it, then." He slapped the raft like we'd just come to an agreement, then submerged.

Following a moment of palpable silence, Spio removed his arm from my shoulder.

"Back in a bit. I gotta get my hat back before the fish turn it into a vacation home."

He disappeared with a slop of water against the raft, leaving me alone. The grin slipped off my face.

Across the raft, ponytail still stared. I turned my back to him and his friends, lying down.

The pink hues of the setting sun might have been beautiful, if I didn't know that the world beneath was so vacant. The view in every direction was nothing but sky and ocean. Not even a shadow of land rose in the distance.

The emptiness seeped into my mood. I closed my eyes, thinking of home. When I opened them again, the sun had long set.

I sat up with a start. For a moment, the rising and falling of the raft made me think I was back in the Battle for Eriana Kwai, hiding behind the helm of Meela's ship.

Then I felt the presence of an army of mermen around me.

Then I remembered Spio telling me to meet him.

I cursed, wondering why he hadn't come to get me.

"Relax. You haven't missed anything," said Spio.

His face appeared in front of mine. He was wearing his leather cap again.

"Mph." I rubbed away the clump of weeds stuck to my cheek. "How'd it get dark so fast?"

He slipped off the raft and submerged. I followed.

"We're in the tropics," he said. "Twilight is ultra short near the equator. Didn't you learn anything in school?"

"I learned how to deliver a perfect sideswipe. Want me to demonstrate?"

He dove deeper. We swam downwards first so no one would feel where we were headed, then turned towards the floating junk. Glowing copepods, shrimp, sea slugs, and comb jellies had risen for the night, giving the illusion that we were gliding through the starry sky.

We travelled far enough away from the group that they wouldn't hear us as long as we spoke quietly. The first to arrive, Spio and I investigated the junk raft. Weeds and slime covered so much of it that it took us a moment to ensure it was safe.

"I'm feeling nothing but rubber and plastic," I said.

Without hesitating, Spio flung himself aboard. It rippled like a gelatinous blob, creaking as bits of litter scraped against each other.

Fish tickled my skin as they darted past me, having been ejected from their beds. I pulled myself up next to Spio.

"Ooh." I wiggled deeper into the cushiony slime. "I might sleep here tonight."

A merman poked out of the water beside us.

"What's this? Secret meeting?" he said.

"No," I said, at the same time as Spio said, "Yes."

Spio turned to me. "He's referring to our secret plan. Code *Murder.*"

I rubbed my hands down my face.

"And by *murder,*" said Spio, "I mean—"

"All right!"

He flashed a grin. "Lysi, this is Pontus. He's in on it."

"I'm more than *in on it,*" said Pontus. "I basically initiated this whole thing."

Spio raised his hands. "Let's not start giving credit. But if we were to, we all know this was my idea."

The raft rippled as Pontus hoisted himself up.

A merman with a wispy brown beard and a scar blinding his left eye surfaced next.

"Ahoy!" he said.

"This one thinks he's a pirate," said Spio.

"Except I lost my eyepatch again," said the merman.

I couldn't tell if he was being serious.

"We call him Nobeard," said Spio. "Because he doesn't have enough scruff to earn him the name Blackbeard."

The merman gave off some disgruntlement at this. I guessed he'd tried to avoid the nickname without success.

Then the hugest merman of all of them emerged, with arms the size of baby dolphins. I couldn't understand why everyone greeted him as 'Junior', until he introduced himself as Pontus' younger brother.

The next merman who surfaced brought me a small sense of relief.

Coho scanned the group, lingering on me. I gave him a small wave. He returned an uncertain nod. I dropped my hand, wishing I hadn't bothered.

"Guys, meet our new member: Lysi," said Pontus.

They all stared. I counted six of us gathered on the junk raft. Waves lapped against rubber and plastic, the only sound besides the low, indistinct murmur from the army.

"Thought we agreed not to recruit," said Nobeard.

"We did," said Pontus, "but Spio opened his fat mouth, and now she knows too much."

I dropped my gaze to the slimy net at my tail.

"Spio told us all about you, Lysi," said Junior.

Uh oh.

"None of the bad stuff," said Spio. "I didn't say anything about our time at summer school—"

"Thanks, Spio," I said.

"The commander is skipping this one," said Pontus, "so I'll get started."

I shot Spio a questioning look.

"The commander is our ally," said Pontus, catching my surprise. "He's a key component of the plan. But he attends select meetings so as not to draw suspicion. I'll follow up with him one-on-one."

I nodded.

"I'll go over our rules, Lysi," said Pontus, in a tone that dared me to break any of them. "First, at risk of being overheard, we meet above surface, and only above. Second, in case we are overheard, we don't refer to our target by name. Third, we do not discuss our plans outside meetings. Fourth, we aren't even friendly with each other outside meetings, except for Junior and me. You and Spio can keep doing your thing, too. But that's it. No one needs reason to believe we're meeting at all, never mind what we're meeting about. All right?"

"Got it."

"Now, the plan. You are probably aware the target has some kind of guard on him at all times. No matter how skilled the assassin, it will be impossible to just swim up and kill him. The hit needs to come from afar, and it needs to be guaranteed lethal."

"Iron?" I said.

"More or less."

"I wanted to make a big-ass Iron Hook of Doom," said Spio. "With an anchor from a cruise ship, you know? We'd squash the guy like a jelly."

"Your ideas never cease to amaze me, Spio," I said.

"Wait until you hear about this plan. He's gonna end up like a pile of sand."

"What?"

"We're blowing him up—"

"The idea," said Pontus, "is to detonate a moored mine located a league west of the Moonless City. The explosion will kill the target instantly, whether from the force of the blast or from the iron shrapnel itself."

The auras around me were calm, determined. They had discussed this enough that the idea no longer scared them.

An approaching flock of gulls chattered obnoxiously, wings glinting in the moonlight. I imagined the water beneath them erupting in a sudden explosion from a mine. It would be effective, all right.

"Everything's set and we're waiting to hear when the target will next visit the Moonless City," said Pontus, speaking to the group, now. "It could be sooner than we anticipated. The commander is sending a message tonight on a nearby acoustic channel to report the hammerhead attack. With luck, the target will come this way immediately, along with the chief administrator, secretary, adjutant general, director of foreign relations, and probably a few bodyguards."

"We're killing all of them?" I said.

I sensed a strong air of indifference.

"The director of foreign relations also deals with human relations," said Spio. "She's the reason my brother-in-law got chucked in prison."

"Prison?"

"Former human. He didn't pass the screening."

I narrowed my eyes. "All right. So we're blowing up a few of them."

Spio gave a fist pump.

"How are we going to make sure he passes the mine on the way to the city?" I said.

"My wife is taking care of that," said Coho. "She's minister of communications."

Pontus nodded. "Ephyra will say she received information that there's an Atlantic army waiting to ambush them on the main current. She'll advise him to take an alternate route that happens to run past the explosive."

"Sounds believable, given what just happened," I said.

"As for us," said Pontus, "the commander's going to send us to the Moonless City as a private detachment on the same day."

I straightened. Finally, my chance. I'd be returning north under official orders.

"We have our hiding positions worked out, Lysi," said Pontus. "We'll be far out of the way when the explosion happens. Once the target is dead, half of us will come back here to tell the commander it's done. He'll bring the troops home. The other half of us will take off to Utopia and seize power until the commander arrives. We're instating him temporary king until we have a proper election."

"We took a vote and decided we liked democracy," said Spio.

I imagined being at the front of the movement in Utopia when Adaro's rule blew to pieces. The prospect excited me.

Even more, being in Utopia would mean an easier escape to Eriana Kwai. I would be able to tell Meela she could stop searching for the Host. And I had to do that as soon as possible. If I knew Meela, she would be risking her life trying to find it.

I picked at the soggy fishing net beneath my tail. Meela didn't deserve this. I had to get back to her and make sure she was safe.

"Who goes to Utopia when it's done, and who comes back here?" I said.

"You'll be coming back here to notify the commander," said Pontus. "Along with me and Junior. That way, the numbers are even."

His tone was final. My heart sank.

The others must have felt it, because Nobeard said, "Love, we all want to go back to Utopia."

I considered whether I'd be able to bolt, anyway. I didn't owe these guys anything. We had a job to do, and after that, I had my own agenda.

Still, could I bring myself to abandon them?

"Lysi can take my place," said Spio. "I'll come back here."

"No," I said. "I don't want you to—"

"It's fine, Lysi."

"But—"

"I'm not giving you a choice."

I felt him out. He was serious. A true friend, he wanted me to go to Utopia in his stead.

"Thanks," I whispered.

"That's the plan, then," said Pontus. "We'll know more when the commander gets back with news from home."

I nodded.

"Let's raise a toast," said Nobeard.

"Excuse me?" I said.

"Nobeard brought rum," said Spio.

I smiled. Of course he did.

With a flourish, Nobeard produced a partially drained glass bottle.

"Just take it easy, Spio," I said, thinking of the time he drank a whole bottle of something he found in a shipwreck and puked for two days.

He waved a hand. "It's healthy to flush out the system with toxic waste once in awhile."

"Where'd you get it?" I said.

"My dad's a former landlubber," said Nobeard.

I sensed a trend.

"Do all of you have some kind of connection with humans?"

"Clever," said Pontus. He took a gulp.

"Some of us more directly than others," said Coho. "But the new laws don't bode well for any of us."

He seemed open to the topic, so I indulged my curiosity. "When did you become a merman?"

"Years ago," said Coho.

The guys let out a collective groan.

"What?" I said.

"Gather 'round, lassies," said Nobeard, "for the most romantic tale in all of—ouch!"

Coho punched him in the shoulder.

"All right, all right," said Nobeard. "Enlighten her."

"Did she lure you?" I said.

"She didn't have to," said Coho. "I knew right away that she was the most beautiful thing I'd ever seen."

"Well, obviously—" I began, but Spio jabbed me in the ribs.

I'd wanted to say that wasn't how it worked. Of course he thought she was irresistible at first sight. That was the mermaid allure.

I'd always wondered about the feelings of a lured man. Did Coho truly love Ephyra, or did the allure always pull him towards her? Did it matter, if he was happy?

"Ephyra and her girls were supposed to kill me and my crew," said Coho. "I was the last survivor, and the other mermaids were waiting for Ephyra to finish me off so they could go home. But she didn't. We locked eyes ... and she couldn't bring herself to kill me. She changed me into a merman instead."

"She kissed you?"

"How else would she do it?" said Spio.

"Just clarifying."

The rum made its way to me. I took a small gulp, forcing myself not to project disgust.

"She didn't care what the other girls thought," said Coho. "She did it right there in front of them. I went with her into the sea, and we've been together ever since. We have five kids. She's due for our sixth in a few months."

"I didn't know you were having another guppy!" Junior raised the bottle of rum. "Congrats, bud."

The other guys clapped Coho on the back, congratulating him.

"That's what's important," said Junior. "Family. When this is all over, I'm going to settle down and have a few little ones."

"I think you need a girlfriend, first," said Spio.

The guys burst out laughing.

Junior scowled. "Not like any of you cods have girls back home!"

"I'm working on it," said Nobeard with a roguish wink.

"What about you, Lysi?" said Coho. "You're not fooling anyone with this guy."

He jabbed a thumb towards Spio.

"Because I'm so far out of her depth, I know," said Spio.

"Anyone back home?" said Coho.

I poked at a plastic bottle beside me.

"Um, yes," I said. "Sort of. Before I got taken away from … from everything."

"Sounds tragic," said Spio. "Tell us about this guy."

I narrowed my eyes, trying to decide whether he was being thick or playing with me. His mouth twisted at the corners.

"She's a girl," I said to the group.

The guys erupted in a chorus of "whoa!" and "right on!"

"How'd you meet?" said Pontus.

I hesitated. Then I realised I had no reason to. These guys would be the last to judge me for having feelings for a human.

They must have sensed the truth by my silence.

Nobeard made a triumphant sound. "Ship or shore?"

"Ship. I mean, shore, at first … the ship came later."

"Besides having legs, what does she look like?" said Coho, handing me the rum.

"Um, she's got green eyes, and dark hair, and …"

And soft, warm skin that smells as sweet as the forest.

I blushed and took a large gulp of rum.

"You haven't turned her yet?" said Junior. "Why not?"

"Oh," I said. "I don't want that to be my decision."

"What do you mean?"

"I like her the way she is."

The guys fell silent. Then Nobeard said, "You're not like other mermaids, are you?"

They chuckled.

"She's a rebel," said Pontus, "like us."

He clapped me on the back. I couldn't help smiling.

"Oh, a party!" said a voice. "Or, perhaps, am I interrupting an important meeting?"

We whirled to see Strymon floating beside our island of junk. He wore that benign smile, but his mood prickled beneath my skin.

I hadn't heard him surface. How long had he been there?

The ensuing *plop* must have been someone dropping the bottle of rum into the ocean. The human indulgence would surely be forbidden.

"Good evening, Officer," said Pontus, suddenly professional.

Strymon scanned the raft—our guilty auras. I tried to breathe into a mood more passive and relaxed.

"Is there a reason I am finding you so far from the others?"

"Sir, the raft was noisy and crowded," said Pontus. "A few of us gathered over here to try and get a proper—"

"You are aware that you have been ordered to stay together."

"Yes, Officer," said Junior. "We thought this was a sufficiently short distance."

Strymon studied us for so long that the aloofness around me waned. His expression turned to stone.

"You are far enough that you cannot be seen, heard, or felt from the raft. Why, I wonder, would you want that?"

Pontus shifted. "We didn't mean—"

"You will return immediately."

We answered with a chorus of 'yes, sir's.

Before anyone reached the water, Strymon said, "I expected better from a veteran of Eriana Kwai."

I turned to him.

"I believe the rest of the army would, too. It is logical, then, that you serve a punishment for your disobedience."

I opened and closed my mouth.

"Everyone will need a good meal after that journey. You will gather food in time for daybreak."

"For the entire army?" I squeaked.

Where was I supposed to find that much food? Around us in every direction, the horizon was black and empty. Beneath the surface would be no different. I'd have to weed the raft and dig out any edible fish using it as a haven.

"Come on, dude," said Spio. "There isn't even a reef around here to—"

"And you," said Strymon, "can spend dawn assisting the trainers in delousing the great white. Does anyone else care to volunteer their service?"

The other guys stayed quiet.

"If I find any of you wandering again, I will report your actions."

Strymon submerged. Waves lapped against the plastic and rubber.

"And that's why we don't meet much," Pontus mumbled.

I turned for a last look at the floating pile of garbage, our short-lived haven.

I couldn't help feeling like Strymon held a grudge against me, in particular.

Of course he does, I thought. *He knows you're here because you did something to disobey the king.*

My first encounter with him couldn't have helped matters.

I leaned into Spio and whispered, "It doesn't matter if he reports us to the commander, does it?"

"He's got other channels of communication," whispered Coho on my other side. "It's not the commander we should be worried about."

CHAPTER ELEVEN
Eriana's Bargain

We set out for the Enticer early the next day—a Sunday. The trainees had the day off, and Dani and her father were scheduled to gloat to Rik about their training program for at least an hour. That would, theoretically, give us plenty of time to search the area.

Tanuu brought his fire iron, claiming it saved his life and he wasn't about to put it out to pasture yet.

We stopped in the clearing where the ship waited, ancient and crumbling as always. The training area hadn't changed in years—apart from the blackened remains of the fire pit Annith had tripped over.

"Let's look around a bit," I said.

I ignored the nagging doubt that we wouldn't find anything. The area had been so overused throughout the years that the dirt had been trampled into near clay. Even ferns and grass didn't grow. The ship's deck sagged in the middle, the railing chipped and battered. Anything worth discovering would have been discovered long ago.

Or maybe it was just that no one had been searching in the right place.

Under a blanket of low clouds and towering cedars, a chill settled in the woods. A raven cackled at us from the edge of the clearing. I glanced sideways at it, feeling watched. Ravens were too smart, infamous for learning pesky behaviours like stealing.

We started around the outskirts of the ship, pushing leaves and twigs out of the way to check for anything strange where the hull met the dirt. The ship seemed to have sailed right through the earth before settling in its place.

Turning up nothing, we split up. I stomped on the dirt around the clearing, listening for hollowness that might indicate a trapdoor. Tanuu knocked on the surrounding trees. Annith crawled around the deck on all fours. Blacktail stood on the ship's railing and surveyed the ground from above.

Tanuu glanced up at Blacktail, laughing. "Do the leaves on the ground spell the location of the Host?"

Blacktail pulled a face and jumped down. "Have the trees whispered their secrets to you?"

"Not yet," said Tanuu, "but I did piss off a squirrel."

I zigzagged across the entire clearing until my legs hurt from stomping and I was certain only worms lived beneath our feet.

The raven cackled again.

I stopped at the cabins and stared around, hands on my hips. A pile of stuff sat outside the door of the nearest cabin. It seemed to be a heap of black barbed wire, except …

I stepped closer. My heart skipped a beat. The wire was all connected. This was a huge, iron, barbed net.

Dani had been fond of using fishing nets to trap mermaids on the Massacre. This must have been one of the new weapons they were trying out. It would roast the mermaids alive. It would split their flesh and drown them and burn them all at once. A victory for the girls, maybe, but I couldn't let that happen. If other mermaids were at all like Lysi, they didn't deserve this.

"Meela," said Annith, "have you ever looked closely at these carvings?"

My brain stalled. I couldn't take my eyes off the net.

"Meela?" Her boots thumped across the deck.

"Yeah?" I peeled my eyes away. "Did you find something?"

"Carvings. Come look."

With a last glance at the iron torture device, I turned my back and returned to the Enticer. If we could find the Host, I wouldn't need to worry about that net.

I hopped onto the deck. Annith crouched at the helm, face pressed close to the wheel.

I knew the ship was covered in detailed engravings, but admittedly, I'd never taken the time to study them.

Annith pointed to one in particular: familiar wavy lines, and two eyes that could have been mistaken for swirls in the water. To the left, the wavy lines broadened and coiled around a cluster of human faces. To the right, the lines disappeared altogether, replaced by a forest.

I crouched, tracing my fingers around the wheel's perimeter. The wooden handles glistened from being touched so often, and smelled of sweat. I identified a few animals and birds in the carvings, but found I couldn't decipher most. The art was symmetrical, with the same carvings on opposite ends of the wheel.

"I'm wondering how true the legend is," said Annith. "Like, this looks like wood to me, but the ship is supposed to be made from the bones of Eriana's people."

I yanked my hand away. She was right, though. It was clearly not made of bone, and likely human labour had pieced it together, not divine magic.

Tanuu climbed up next to us. "I betcha some parts are more literal than others. The ice storm was probably told as it happened."

"What about the Host?" I said. "Was Eriana's soul supposedly bound to a stupid seagull that died a few years later?"

I hoped the others would refute that idea. *Of course not! That's the truest part! The story is literal and we're totally on the right track!*

No one volunteered anything.

Then Blacktail said, "Here's something."

She was looking at the ship's mast, arms crossed.

We gathered around it.

A single carving ran down the length of it: a long, curving pattern about a hand's width, beginning at eye level and disappearing beneath the wooden planks at our feet.

For a long time, the four of us stared at the carving without speaking. I'd noticed it before during training, but hadn't thought anything of it. Now ... the blood seemed to drain from my head. Annith sucked in a breath. Realising I'd stopped breathing, too, I inhaled slowly, letting my thoughts fall into place.

At eye level, engraved in the ancient wooden mast, was the head of a serpent. Its forked tongue curved from open jaws, its eye angled in an expression of anger.

"Uh ..." I said.

I dashed back to the wheel. The eyes in the water were the same shape.

I returned to the mast. The serpent's body curved down the wood. I followed it until I was kneeling and the engraving disappeared beneath the planks.

"It's pointing us below deck," said Tanuu.

I looked up at him.

"I was afraid of this," he said. "We gotta crack open the hull."

This had to be it. Snakes didn't exist on Eriana Kwai. Why else would one be carved into the mast?

I glanced around the deck, an odd dizziness in my head. If there had ever been a door leading into the hull, it had long been boarded up.

A flashlight appeared in front of my nose.

"Hold this," said Tanuu. "I'm gonna pull up the boards, all right?"

Numbly, I accepted the flashlight and stood.

Tanuu used the fire iron to pry up the refurbished planks, taking care not to break any. They came away loudly, cracking through the silent forest.

"We're vandalising a historic site," said Annith in a high voice.

"We'll put them back," said Tanuu. "Besides, can't be much worse than what the trainees have put it through."

Still, I couldn't help feeling guilty as I helped pile the wood.

Once the hole was big enough to fit through, Blacktail peered in.

"Think anything's down there?"

Tanuu leaned closer and whispered in her ear. "Scared?"

She shot him a glare. "Care to go first?"

"Of course," he said. "I'm here as gallant protector of you fine ladies."

He made to jump into the pit but Blacktail grabbed his arm and scoffed. "Don't be stupid."

Clicking on the flashlight, I peered in beside them.

The pale beam of light revealed wet clay—a decent landing, but surprisingly far down. The ground beneath the hull had been dug into a pit.

"There's the cave you were looking for," said Annith.

She stayed back from the hole, averting her gaze from the height.

I'd always assumed nothing existed beneath the ship but rot and worms. The Host wouldn't be here, would it? Had we been training for battle on top of a giant snake all these years?

"Let's lower ourselves in," said Tanuu, holding up a coil of rope.

"Where'd you get that?" I said.

Tanuu shrugged and pointed across the deck. "It was laying there. They must've used it in a training drill."

He tied one end to the mast with a complicated knot and chucked the coil into the hole. It hit the bottom with a *splat*.

"Let's have that fire iron, just in case," I said.

"We going in?" said Tanuu, handing it over.

Flashlight in my belt, weapon ready, I sat down and dangled my legs inside the pit.

Tanuu made to grab my arm. "You're not going fir—"

I scooted forwards and seized the rope before he could touch me.

I hit the ground and my knees buckled, but I kept my grip on the iron, ready to swing at anything that moved.

"Dammit, Meela!" said Tanuu, a note of panic in his voice. "Move over. I'm coming down."

I rolled to the side, iron still ready, as Tanuu crumpled beside me.

The pit was damp and warm, a greenhouse of earthy smell. Up to shoulder height, the sides were a combination of layered earth and pieces of rotting hull. Tree roots sprouted towards us like fingers. Above ground level, slivers of daylight peeked through cracks in the boards.

"Ready for us?" said Blacktail.

"Someone needs to stay at the top," I said, "so we don't get stuck down here."

Above, Blacktail glanced back to Annith, who lingered out of sight.

"I'll stay," said Annith. "I'm not great with … climbing."

"Sounds fair," said Blacktail.

She dropped into the hole without using the rope, landing catlike next to Tanuu and me.

"Not much down here," I said, shining the light around more carefully.

I checked the ground, easing my fear that I'd crunch on some human skull or a writhing mass of worms. I found broken wood, nails, plastic, a lost mitten, a murky puddle. We might have landed in a garbage pit.

Stepping slowly, I lifted the light to the walls of the hull. Tanuu followed, running his hands along the grimy surfaces.

We searched the area thoroughly, testing for trapdoors, feeling for irregularities, combing for anything odd among the debris. I examined a clay bowl that looked like it might belong in a museum, wondering if the ship had living quarters at one time.

"Meela," said Blacktail, and the note of urgency in her voice made me whirl around with the weapon ready.

She pointed at a wooden cylinder in front of her, which must have been the rest of the mast. Faintly lit from the daylight above, it ran from the deck down into the clay at our feet, where it splintered.

"Look at the bottom of the carving."

I shone the flashlight on it. The carving of the serpent continued downwards. It ended at my waist in that open-jawed, fork-tongued head.

"What am I looking—?"

I gasped.

"What?" said Annith.

"The head," I said. "It's at the bottom, too."

Annith made an indiscernible noise of surprise. Tanuu came to see for himself.

"Sisiutl," he said.

"Bless you," said Blacktail.

Tanuu shoved her. "The two-headed serpent. The symbol of invincibility."

I shrugged. I hadn't heard the name before.

"Come on! The legend's from all over the Pacific Northwest." He leaned closer to it and added breathlessly, "Cool."

"Not cool!" I said. "Don't you know what this means?"

The possible manifestations of this thing played across my mind. Was the art accurate, or did it take liberties, like with ravens and bears and elk? How much power were we up against?

Tanuu frowned, staring at the engraving. "I've seen this somewhere."

"Where?" said Blacktail.

He continued to stare, until his frown deepened so much that his eyebrows became one.

"I'm not sure."

"What else is down there?" said Annith.

I shone the flashlight back on the ground. "Bugs. Litter. Some stuff people dropped. I think there used to be a cabin and a galley down here."

I kicked bits of wood around half-heartedly. My boot clinked against something.

I bent down. The flashlight illuminated something pale.

It was a dagger. The whole thing was beige, from hilt to blade.

"That's a bone dagger," said Tanuu quietly.

I nearly dropped it. "*Bone?* Like, part of a body?"

"An animal, I bet, but yeah."

"I've never seen one of those," said Blacktail, her voice also hushed.

I pushed a finger against the blade, the edge about as sharp as a butter knife.

"Me neither."

Designs were engraved into the hilt. I held the dagger horizontally to study them: at the top of the hilt, a large tree; at the bottom, a clump of smaller trees. An irregularly shaped hole opened between them.

On the reverse was a fanged animal head, jaws parted, with a long, narrow eye. Based on its similarities to the carving on the mast, I took it to be the head of a serpent.

"We're borrowing this," I said, stuffing it in my belt.

Outside, the raven cackled with more volume than ever. Annith cursed, making the three of us jump.

"Turn the light off!" she said.

Before we could ask why, she chucked the pile of boards roughly over the hole in the deck, plunging us further into darkness. I clicked off the flashlight.

"Are you looking for someone?" said Annith pleasantly.

I froze. Tanuu and Blacktail seemed to have stopped breathing.

Annith's boots thumped across the deck, moving further away from the hole.

A girl's voice answered from the ground, alarmingly close. "I was hoping Dani would be here. I wanted to do some extra practice."

"Oh," said Annith, still cheerful. "Dani's not here. Besides, you should give your muscles a break."

The girl must have shown apprehension, because Annith added, "Recovery time's important. By the time May comes around, you'll be at optimal fitness."

"But I haven't got until May, and my aim isn't as good as the others, so I think I would be better off practicing today instead of resting."

There was a heavy silence.

"What do you mean, you haven't got until May?" said Annith, all lightness gone.

"We're leaving next week."

The blood drained from my face.

"They haven't made another ship yet," said Annith.

"They patched up the last one."

"The Bloodhound?"

"It's not Bloodhound anymore. It's Vindicti."

Another heavy silence. Without daring to move my feet, I leaned over and tried to peer through a hole in the wood. The girl had stopped a few paces away. I stooped, angling my gaze upwards until I could see her face. I recognised her large eyes and thick, messy hair, as I'd seen her around the training base. She had an irritated-looking injury on the side of her neck, and scratches across her sallow face.

"Why are they sending you out so soon?"

"They thought it'd be better to surprise the demons, since they're probably still picking themselves up from …" The girl hesitated. "If Dani's not here, I think I'll go."

Annith didn't argue.

Shortly after the girl disappeared from my sight, her footsteps stopped.

"Is it scary out there?" she said, so quietly I had to hold my breath to hear.

Yes, I thought, *you'll live every second of every day wondering when it will be your turn to be impaled, or drowned, or eaten, or strangled, or—*

"It's only scary if you forget the reason you're there," said Annith. "Remember who you're fighting for, and you'll be all right."

A few more seconds passed.

"You'll be all right," said Annith again.

The girl made an indiscernible noise. It seemed an eternity before she left.

Annith crossed the deck and slid the planks away.

Her face appeared against the grey sky, eyes wide.

"They can't," I said at once. "The Massacres are in May. They've always been in May."

"They've also always had male warriors," said Blacktail. "Breaking traditions is the trend lately."

"But May has the most hours of daylight! This'll put the girls at a disadvantage. They haven't even had enough training," I said, arguing with no one.

I thought of Adaro, and how he began sending out all his warriors at the end of our Massacre, even the ones who had just started training. He wanted more warriors attacking us, no matter what the cost. Now we were doing the same.

And the iron nets. What'll happen when they go out with those iron nets?

No one had words of reassurance. Adaro had threatened to destroy us if he found another of our ships over his city. He would view an early Massacre as a betrayal from me.

"This war is out of hand," I said.

Blacktail made a small noise. She looked as solemn as ever, with the daylight from above accentuating the pockets under her eyes.

Tanuu stepped towards the dangling rope. "I guess we'd better hurry up and find this serpent."

"Where?" I said bitterly.

Tanuu's eyes darted around as he considered. Blacktail chewed her lip.

Yes, that was our starting point, but we were no closer to finding the Host. Would we even be able to do it in time? I felt like that iron net had been dropped on top of me.

I pulled the bone dagger from my belt and turned it over. It must be significant, somehow. I even felt a strange sense of familiarity looking at it. I poked my fingers through the hole in the hilt, wondering about the design. Was something supposed to be here? A precious stone, or maybe something that decayed and fell out over time?

"What are you smirking at?" said Blacktail.

She was looking at Tanuu, whose smile tugged at the corner of his lips.

"I remember where I've seen the two-headed snake."

"Where?" said Blacktail and I together.

"The totem poles by the old docks. The biggest one has a serpent head at the top, and another upside down at the bottom."

Blacktail gasped. "It does!"

Tanuu shook his head in disbelief, staring at the engraving on the mast. "We're looking for history. The totem poles have our history carved into them. Why didn't any of us think of it?"

"Probably because that area's been blocked off our entire lives," I said dryly.

I'd seen them from a distance once as a child, back when Nilus was alive. He promised to take me to see them up close when he returned from the Massacre—after he'd killed all the sea demons for me.

"We should get out of here, anyway," said Blacktail, grabbing the rope. "The devil and his spawn could be back any minute."

Tanuu crouched and patted his shoulder. "You girls go first. I'll give you a boost."

"I am not getting on your shoulders," said Blacktail. "I'll crush you."

"The only thing you're crushing right now is my masculinity."

"Oh, come on. I spent five years in Anyo bootcamp. I weigh more than you think."

"Just shut up and climb."

She sighed. "You can give me a boost with your knee."

He knelt so she could use his thigh as a step. He pushed her up.

"Oy! Watch your hands," she yelled, sounding affronted.

"Sorry! Sorry! I meant to push your leg!"

I smirked. Above, Annith turned her face to hide a giggle.

"Next," said Tanuu.

"I'm not getting on your shoulders, either," I said.

Tanuu sighed dramatically. After a brief argument, I put as little weight as I could on his thigh, using my arms to pull myself up the rope.

Annith grabbed my armpits, and then my swinging leg, and helped heave me up.

Tanuu climbed the rope easily enough, and we pieced the deck back together. We stamped the boards down, making sure to leave no cracks.

With the fire iron over Tanuu's shoulder and the mysterious bone dagger in my belt, we left the Enticer.

The totem poles had once been the main port of entry for tourists. For the last thirty years, the area had been abandoned and roped off to discourage anyone from venturing near the water.

The welcome sign hung intact, faded and grimy, with bird droppings running down the sides.

We hope you enjoyed your time on Eriana Kwai. The message was written in multiple languages, welcoming people from all over the world.

I scowled.

As we crossed the gravel that was once a parking lot, the wind picked up, moaning in my ears and making it difficult to hear anything else.

I folded my arms against the cold. Without the canopy of trees to protect us, a sticky mist clung to my face and hair.

Cedar logs marked the edge of the parking lot. The cultural centre crumbled beyond that, a lawn out front that had not been mowed in three decades. A faded 'Closed' sign hung on the door.

"What's in there?" I said.

The window was opaque from grime, with a rock-sized hole in the middle. I peered through but saw only darkness.

"Museum, dining hall, art gallery ..." said Tanuu. "Probably a few rats."

"Museum?" said Annith. "Do you think it has information about Eriana?"

"It's aimed at tourists, so you'll be more likely to find a miniature replica of the totem poles so people can take funny pictures."

We continued on, stepping over a line of rope to get to the totem poles. They stood at the edge of the grass, before the earth turned to pebbles and dead seaweed. The tide was halfway in—far enough that we wouldn't be splashed by waves, but close enough to pose a threat.

I scanned the shoreline as Tanuu led the way. The horizon was grey, the world below desolate. A seagull cried from a droppings-strewn buoy, barely audible over the wind.

Blacktail gripped her dagger, eyes glued to the crashing waves.

"Don't trust your ears," she said. "Keep an eye on the shoreline."

Tanuu stopped in front of the largest totem pole. One serpent towered over us, another one upside down at our feet, with several animal figures locked between the two heads. The poles might once have been painted in rich, deep hues, but now they were faded and chipped.

We combed the area the same way we had done the Enticer.

I knocked on the poles as Tanuu had done with the trees, but I wasn't sure what to listen for.

"Hey Tanuu?" I pressed my ear against what happened to be the side of a raven's head. "This one sounds different when I knock on it. Is that because it's bigger?"

"Ah," he said wisely. "That's because this particular one was carved on a Tuesday afternoon."

I straightened, eyeing him.

"Let's see," he said, jabbing me in the ribs.

He pressed his ear against the raven.

"Wow, the totem looks just like you," said Blacktail.

He pulled away and studied the figure. "You mean my large and manly nose? Or is it the dark and mysterious eyes?"

She pulled a face.

Tanuu clapped a hand over the beak. "You know what, Meela? You're onto something. This one's hollow."

I grinned.

"The question is, how do we see inside?" he said.

The four of us circled the pole, pushing and pulling different pieces, trying to see if anything opened.

"Wait a minute," said Annith.

She backed up a few paces, eyes fixed on the topmost serpent. Her mouth fell open.

"What?" I backed up to stand next to her.

"Look at the way it's carved. The serpent's tongue. The bear's open mouth. The raven's beak. The horns of—whatever that thing is."

"A deer," offered Tanuu.

"Sure. Well, I think we have to climb it."

I gasped. "Annith, you're right. Every totem has something to step on."

I placed my foot on the snake's curled tongue and my hands on the raven's beak.

"Hold up," said Tanuu. "I don't know if that's a good idea."

Already off the ground, I looked down at him. "Why not?"

"It's windy and you're about to climb a slippery wooden pole."

I stepped one higher into the bear's open mouth. We'd trained climbing masts for years. I wasn't afraid of falling.

"Meela, stop," said Tanuu. "Let me do it."

I stepped on the raven's beak.

"No, I should climb it," said Blacktail. "I'm the smallest. You can catch me if I fall."

"With what?" said Annith. "We should get a tarp or a blanket. This isn't safe."

"Good idea," said Tanuu. "We can …"

He sighed. I was already half way.

I kept my eyes on my hands, knowing my legs would betray me if I looked down.

A gust of wind pushed me away from the pole. I tightened my grip. I didn't stop until coming face-to-face with the angry eye of the serpent.

Clutching its forked tongue with both hands, I could see further down the beach than before. The only life besides us was a bald eagle fighting three crows a short distance away.

Feeling around the pole with one hand, I traced my fingers along the creature's mane of horns, fumbled down the back and around the sides, and pushed against the wood.

"There's nothing," I muttered, feeling around the back of the head one more time. "I'm coming down!"

Then the wood shifted. I pushed harder. It was loose.

"Ha!"

I shuffled around the pole, using the short wings of a saw-whet owl as a foothold.

A voice yelled at me from below, but I couldn't make out the words over the wind.

"What?"

Regrettably, I looked down. My stomach squirmed, and I reflexively pressed my body against the pole.

"Did you find something?" yelled Annith.

"Maybe. The wood here is loose."

She yelled something back, but it was lost in the wind.

A rectangular panel had been cut into the pole. I dug my nails into the crack and worked my fingers around it. It slid to the left. I kept pulling until it opened enough that I could peek inside.

The totem pole was hollow, but I saw only the other side of the trunk.

My body trembled from some combination of exhilaration, the cold mist, and my straining muscles.

I stuck an arm in and felt around, trailing my hand along the rough insides. Something rolled beneath my palm. I ran my fingers across it. Twine.

I pulled, feeling the weight of something dangling at the other end.

Excitement bubbled in my stomach.

"Someone really wanted to keep this hidden!"

I used my teeth to hold the twine while I pulled it up, bit by bit, until I reached the end.

"It's parchment," I said, more to myself.

Several pages of tan animal skin parchment had been tied to the end. I slid the roll from the loop and stuffed it down my shirt for safekeeping, then fitted the door back in place.

I climbed down, moving slowly. My arms and legs were trembling.

At the bottom, the others gathered around and watched as I unfurled the parchment.

"It's in the old language," said Blacktail. "Tanuu, you're the only one who went to high school."

Tanuu took the stack of papers with a flourish. "I see you require my intellectual prowess."

"So you're more than just a good swing, then?"

He smirked.

As we watched in rapt silence, Tanuu scanned the first page, turned it over to check the blank reverse, and then riffled through the remaining pages.

"Give me a minute. They're out of order."

"Let's do this away from the water," I said.

We retreated to the cultural centre and sat on the front step while Tanuu sorted the pages. While the overhang blocked the wind, it did little to stop us getting wet, with mist drifting up our sleeves and down our backs from all directions.

I studied Tanuu's face for a reaction, forcing myself to be patient and let him think. His eyebrows stayed pinched in concentration.

Finally, he stopped shuffling pages. He stared at the words a moment longer.

"Hurry up!" I said.

He glanced up, cleared his throat, and read, "The day a bargain was made between Eriana and the Aanil Uusha, chaos befell the Gaela's earth."

My heart beat faster. This was it. The story did involve a bargain.

"While history must be preserved, this knowledge is best left guarded by the spirits of the island. This is a chance for you, reader, to withdraw from these pages and trust the spirits with their secrets. This is the story of Eriana's Crypt."

CHAPTER TWELVE
The Mine

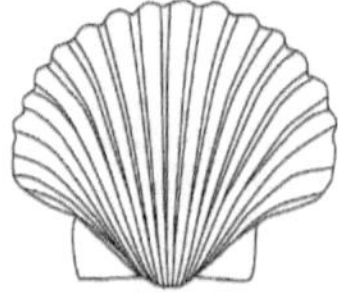

I couldn't bear the thought of the army watching me hunt for them like some fish wench, so I gathered food while everyone slept.

With each fish I caught and beheaded, I pretended it was Strymon.

I formed a pile of tiny corpses on the raft.

For a half-tide, the world was peaceful. Gentle snoring and lapping water whispered in my ears. Then the waves glimmered as the first rays peeked over the horizon. Fish dashed about, hunting for breakfast. Too soon, activity stirred on the raft, and I hadn't slept all night.

I tossed my armful onto the pile and submerged before anyone could bother me.

I pushed myself into a tangle of weeds to get at the fish inside. Kelp wrapped around my neck and arms like a noose.

Sensing some kind of activity, I pried away a log to reveal a sardine haven.

"No one hides from the fish wench."

I'd just stuffed one in my mouth when Axius appeared next to me.

"Morning, beautiful," he said, drifting closer than necessary.

That sense of confidence wafted at me like a cloud of whale pee.

I untangled myself from the weeds with little grace.

"I wanted to apologise," he said in that low, suave voice. "I didn't mean to threaten your relationship with that other guy."

"Sure," I said, trying to keep feelers on the scattering sardines.

"It's just, you really caught my attention."

I picked a bone from my teeth.

"Lysi, I've felt something special since you came here. Like you and I were meant to—"

His words dissolved as I surfaced to add more catches to the pile. It had gotten significantly smaller in that short time. Mermen pulled themselves over as they awoke. They saw me rise with fresh catches, but I ducked back under before they could say anything.

" ... usually the centre of attention when I go out," said Axius. "Maybe partly my looks—I definitely got my mother's hair and my father's strength."

I scanned the overhead raft. The sardines had vanished. I resorted to picking clumps of sea lettuce. When I rose to add them to the pile, everything I'd caught so far had gone. A group of guys hovered nearby. I bit my tongue so as not to snap at them.

I dove to find Axius talking about his parents' estate, how it was actually an ice castle or something.

Eventually, I turned to him.

"… should be making enough to buy my own business centre out west," he said.

"Axius, I'm really not interested. Also you're scaring away my fish."

He carefully pushed a lock of hair across his eyes. "All right. I can take a hint."

I raised my eyebrows.

"I'm here if you change your mind," he said. "Where we take this passionate adventure is up to you."

I tried not to pucker my face. *Passionate adventure?*

"Thanks—"

"But I think if you give this a chance," he said, drifting closer. "You'll find something special between us."

I squinted at him. Maybe if I hid on the other side of the raft for a while I could lose him. I swam purposefully in that direction, irritated when he followed.

"Are you and that guy engaged?"

I considered lying, and then thought he might ask why my hair wasn't jewelled to mark the engagement, and then wondered if it would make a difference for him either way, and by that time my hesitation told him the answer.

"Lysi, a pull of the universe made Adaro send you here, and that same pull made him send me here. I think it's f—"

"No. Do not say *fate*. Everyone gets drafted. Nothing magical brought us together."

I stopped, realising we'd swum the entire perimeter of the raft. Above us, a mackerel pushed its nose into the weeds, trying to get at a sardine.

"Not much of a romantic, are you?" said Axius.

I closed my eyes, willing myself to stay calm.

"I promise I'll be a better boyfriend than that weird geek."

I rounded on him.

"Axius, I swear, if you don't shut up and leave me alone I'm going to punch you in the face."

He faltered. My eyes had filled with blood.

"Am I bothering you?" he said, deflating, as though realising there might be a chance I wasn't interested in him.

Someone slid into the water behind Axius. Junior caught my eye and nodded in the direction of the floating junk that had been our meeting place.

I smiled a little, and regretted this at once, because Axius seemed to take it as a sign that I'd fallen in love with him. He made to grab my hand, but I casually pulled it back to scratch my nose.

"When this is all over, Lysi, I'd like to introduce you to my parents. My mom has a great place up in the Bering. You'd love it. We've got dolphins. I could teach you sports."

Junior dove and disappeared.

"What?" I said.

Overhead, the mackerel kept burrowing into the raft.

"For real! You can see them when you come stay with me."

I didn't have time for this. The guys would meet without me. I needed to get rid of this suckerfish.

"No," I said. "I'm not coming to stay at your weird … dolphin ranch."

"Why not?"

Abruptly, I snatched the mackerel from overhead and bit it behind the skull, killing it.

"Look, I'm supposed to be gathering food. Can you take this up for me?"

He hesitated, and then gave a lopsided smile that was probably supposed to be charming.

"Anything you want, beautiful."

He drifted upwards—apparently too cool to swim normally. The moment he breached, I dove.

"How about you be the fish wench for a while," I mumbled.

I shot away at top speed, finding a favourable current at a deeper swim.

I hoped the guys had waited for me. What were we meeting about? More planning?

The bottom was fathoms away, leaving me in emptiness. The timber raft grazed my skin as a single, faint energy. Something else moved far below. I couldn't tell what it was. Maybe a giant squid, but I couldn't be sure.

Some distance ahead, deeper still, a smaller body moved. I felt it out for a moment before deciding it was Spio. I dove to catch up.

My lungs tightened with the pressure. I normally didn't have cause to dive this far, and here was the second time in two days. Blackness pressed in from below. Looking at it made my stomach churn like I'd swallowed a school of guppies.

"How was the great white?" I whispered as I caught up to Spio.

"A bit frisky, but you know how sharks are. It was just a matter of nimble spearwork and keeping her mouth occupied."

We stopped in front of Coho, Pontus, Junior, and Nobeard. They were suspended in the middle of the twilight layer.

It must have been too risky to meet anywhere else with Strymon lurking around.

Pontus carried a chert longblade, but the others were empty-handed. Spio wore his favourite hat. Nobeard had found his eyepatch—or he had made a new one.

"How's your boyfriend?" said Junior.

I groaned.

The guys burst into muffled laughter.

"I'll gladly defend your honour next time," said Coho, cracking his knuckles.

I smiled, feeling a rush of fondness for these guys. My brother would have made the same offer.

"Show him your demon side, Lysi," said Spio. "Remember that time you scared the flippers off that scuba diver? He would've killed us with that blowhole thing if you didn't bust the fangs out."

"I think you and I remember that story differently."

Something approached from the side. We turned, listening. A merman.

We stayed frozen, not daring to move.

The commander appeared. I relaxed a little, though he projected a grave aura.

"The target is on his way," he said at once, keeping his voice hushed. "He is taking the planned route and will be passing the mine this afternoon."

No one said anything. I glanced to Spio, my pulse quickening.

"I presumed I would receive more warning than this, but can you all be ready to go immediately?"

"Yes, sir," said Pontus.

"Follow the long currents in the open. Pontus knows where to switch and where to break for the shallows. Pontus, you will share the directions with the others in case something happens?"

"Yes, sir."

"Coho, remember to arc the shot. From that distance, the impact will be light, but it will be enough to detonate the mine. I trust your aim."

Coho nodded.

"Hide among the coral until the explosion happens," said the commander to the rest of us. "Once you have confirmed the target is dead, split up as planned."

He paused. I caught a fiery determination that hadn't been there on our first encounter at the Moonless City. At once, it made his aura seem years younger, yet I somehow knew he'd fought a lifetime of battles for King Adaro.

"There is something we all need to understand about this plan," he said. "I know we are all eager to bring a new, free regime to the North Pacific, but this is not the time for heroics. If anything goes awry, your priority is to keep yourself safe and hidden. We must keep our identities secret so we can try again, and again, and again. If you attempt to help a comrade instead of fleeing, you risk being revealed and tried for treason. Understand?"

The guys nodded. I hesitated, but nodded, too. So if anything went wrong, we were supposed to save our own tails. The thought wasn't comforting, but I supposed it made sense; we had to be able to try again. We owed that to everyone we were doing this for.

"Retrieve your weapons and anything you need for the journey. Meet northwest of the raft, just out of range. Leave immediately. Do not linger. Do not let anyone see you."

When no one said anything more, the commander turned and vanished.

A mixture of unease and excitement permeated the group. I couldn't tell who was feeling what. My own emotions rampaged. I felt mostly terror. This had all happened so quickly. In a matter of days, I'd gone from alone and imprisoned, to part of a band of rebels.

We separated so we could return to the raft from different angles. I rose slowly, depressurising. It was just enough time to let me spiral into a full-blown panic.

I was going on a mission to murder the king. What if we failed? What if we succeeded? This would be a complete upheaval. Would Adaro still have loyal followers after he was dead?

At the surface, I grabbed my one possession: my Iron Hook of Doom. I'd kept it inside a tire for the night.

I turned to find myself nose-to-nose with Axius.

I groaned.

"There you are," he said. "Sorry I lost you back there. I can't keep up with that streamlined little body of yours."

I wrinkled my nose, wishing I'd never hear the words 'streamlined little body' again.

He seemed to have groomed his hair in the time since I'd ditched him. It fluttered across his face like a blanket of silk.

"Listen, I know you have your reservations, but I feel like you're the perfect girl for me."

"Ax, you don't even know me."

He motioned to my body. "Well, physically, you're like, bang on."

"Ew."

"I like your stylish carelessness with your hair and makeup. You've got more to offer—like being clever, and feisty, and great to talk to."

I leaned around him, searching for the others.

"I mean, you're the shy type," he said, "and that's okay. I like that. You're a great listener."

Activity stirred on all sides. When I concentrated, I sensed a couple of bodies moving northwest.

"Why do you have your weapon?" said Axius. "Are you going somewhere?"

"No," I said, a bit too quickly.

His eyes widened. He waited for me to continue, for once, more interested in listening than talking.

"I need to take this for inspection," I said.

"Oh, thanks for reminding me. I'll go with you. I need to get a replacement. Broke mine in half during the battle."

He drifted closer, waiting for me to lead the way. This guy was worse than a parasite.

"Do you, uh, have the pieces?" I said.

"Part of the handle. You should see it—"

"Good," I said. "They won't give you a new one without proof that the other is destroyed. Otherwise they think you're hoarding."

"Since when?"

I shrugged. "Don't ask me. I'm relaying what they told me when I arrived."

"You're a smart girl, Lys—"

"I'll wait here while you go get it."

His face seemed to melt into childish delight at the prospect of my waiting for him. I almost pitied him. Almost.

"I was thinking—"

"Go!"

He smiled, and then drifted upwards. Once again, the moment his head broke the surface, I took off.

He was not the sharpest tooth.

I veered left, and then stopped. Strymon and the commander were two fathoms away, talking in low voices.

"You will trust that each of my plans has a purpose, Strymon."

"Of course, sir. But as First Officer, it is my duty to know these plans and help advise."

"And as commander, I try to avoid placing all my eggs in one reef."

Something glinted in the corner of my eye. Spio disappeared behind the raft with what must have been the most conspicuous weapon I'd ever seen. The long, bone handle led to a three-pronged iron tip. The middle prong, the largest, had been wrought to hold a blue stone that was so pure it seemed to glow.

Strymon glanced over, then back to the commander.

"Sir, it is the king's order to keep the unit whole. Any division weakens our—"

"Did it occur to you that I might have received separate instructions?"

"In the interest of unity, sir, I would expect further instructions to be shared with the officers."

"Not if the king has reason to distrust certain officers."

Strymon recoiled. "Sir, I … you know I have only …"

I dove below the hanging weeds, taking a direct line to our meeting place. I pushed down any uneasiness, deciding I wouldn't tell the guys about what I'd overheard. The commander could deal with Strymon. We didn't need more stress looming over us.

They were waiting. Coho fixed a wooden crossbow across his back.

"Sorry," I mumbled.

"Boyfriend troubles?" said Junior.

I shot him a glare. He raised his hands in mock surrender.

"Let's go," said Pontus, with a hint of urgency.

We swam hard and fast.

The blue stone from Spio's weapon glinted in the light. I scanned it from iron tip to bone handle.

"Spio, that weapon is gorgeous."

"The Trident of Terror," he said, holding it out.

"How long did it take you to make?"

"It's been my working project for a few tidecycles. A special weapon for a special occasion."

For the first several leagues, we brushed the surface as we travelled, breaching as we pleased. In such a small group, it was easier to keep our senses tuned ahead for danger. Then we heard the long, ghostly moan of a pod of grey whales. In one motion, without discussing it, we dove deeper. We swam along the lip of the canyon we'd followed on the way south.

I kept my weapon on the opposite side of my scar, trying to avoid the sting of holding the iron too close. Still, as we passed over that unseen shipwreck, my skin prickled and my scar burned.

I clenched my jaw.

Adaro's fault, I thought. *His fault you're here. His fault you're not with Meela.*

Some time later, we broke away from the canyon and veered east. We followed a stronger current into emptiness so vast I couldn't sense the bottom. This was the most direct path, but not a comfortable one. Food was nonexistent, and we faced the possibility of encountering a whale or a shark.

We surfaced for breath after another quarter-tide, and then dove again. By that time, the hook weighed heavy on my arm, but I wasn't willing to put it away.

The only time anyone spoke was to go over the details of the plan—like repeating it a million times would help it go smoothly.

"Let's go over our hiding places again," said Junior. "We can map out the exact crevices."

"Would you stop, please?" I said. "You're making me nervous."

"It's a law of the mind. Practicing something in your head is as effective as practicing in real life."

"Since when have you been into Vassana?" said Pontus.

Junior projected embarrassment and mumbled something about self-improvement.

"Amathia is really into that," said Spio. "She's always talking about attracting what you want by sending messages to the universe."

"Who's Amathia?" I said.

"A girl back home. She's not my girlfriend. Yet. But I'm working on it by sending messages to the universe."

"Is it working?"

"I think so. Yesterday I saw a chunk of moss shaped like boobs. I think it's her, sending messages back."

"Right on!" said Nobeard.

I pursed my lips.

The current changed. Activity ahead. The others didn't notice, so I shot to the front and extended a hand to stop Pontus.

"Wait."

Chaos stirred in the distance.

"Feeding frenzy?" said Pontus.

"No. It's too spread out. Listen."

The glopping current clouded the sound, making it hard to identify. It was close, yet carried a league into the distance.

"I don't smell blood," said Coho.

He was right. It wasn't a frenzy.

"Let's go slow," said Pontus.

Instinctively, we clustered together. We moved at half the speed as before, keeping silent and using minimal movement so we could feel the current.

Their controlled, precise movements revealed what they were—or who they were. The murmur of voices followed. They were deep, distorted.

We slowed our pace even more.

Their presence blended, hard to distinguish. But the mood was clear, floating on the current like plankton.

It was despair.

We stopped.

Shapes of mermen, mermaids, and children materialised. They formed a line moving northwest, crossing our path at an angle and stretching farther ahead than I could sense. Ropes tethered them together—though that wouldn't hold them if they really wanted to escape. What held them were the armed soldiers patrolling the lengths, keeping them from drifting sideways or downwards.

We sank a little. In the open water, there was a chance they'd sense us.

The merpeople in line were not from Utopia, or anywhere up north. Their tails were more colourful than ours, shades of blue and pink and yellow, like the reefs I'd seen in these latitudes. Something glimmered in their faces, ears, and collarbones. I thought they might have been gems.

Their hair was bunched and braided in a way that reminded me of snakes. It drifted wildly, some braids apparently supported by kelp buoys because they floated weightlessly. Others had glinting gems braided into the ends.

Even the shape of these merpeople was slightly different—longer, slimmer.

Where had they come from?

A commotion caught my attention. A mermaid with a vibrant green and yellow tail was fighting a guard. Her cheekbones glimmered as sunlight caught the row of gems embedded in her skin. Her eyes blazed red. She yanked at her ropes so those closest were jerked forwards. The noise and turbulence of their struggle blasted through the empty water.

"He is too young to fight," she shouted. "Please, let him stay."

It took me a moment to understand her accent. The dialect was different—lower, more pronounced.

"He's old enough to work in the camp," said the guard.

He looked and spoke like us. The guards had come from up north.

Two others appeared at his side. They shoved the mermaid back in line.

"Then let me stay with him," said the merman behind her. "I'll do better in labour than on the front."

A smaller, more tender aura existed somewhere between them. A child.

"You'll go where you are assigned," said the guard.

"If you think I am going to do battle for that scum you call a king," said the mermaid, "you are sorely—"

The guard struck her across the face. She collided with her husband and child, creating a ripple several prisoners down the line.

My heartbeat sped up. I tried to calm it before I became desperate for breath.

This line must have been all merpeople under Queen Evagore's rule—or, at least, they were at one time. Now they were being rounded up and sent to the labour camp, or straight to the battlefront.

I wondered what Adaro was making them do at the camp, and if Katus and Ladon had been truthful in telling me about the conditions. Then a terrifying thought occurred to me: Would similar round-ups be happening back home?

The dread tightening around me told me the guys were wondering the same.

"Evagore was ripped from her throne!" said the mermaid, disentangling herself.

"Enough!" said the guard.

"Adaro will meet the fate he deserves. The queen will return to her kingdom—"

A dark, stone blade flashed between them. Before I understood what had happened, blood poured from the mermaid's throat and clouded around her face. Then the boy was screaming, and the father grabbed him before he could lunge forwards.

"No! Mom!"

The scuffle died quickly, as those nearest fell back.

"Finally!" said a voice behind us, so near and with such volume that I startled into demon mode.

We whirled around, weapons raised.

"Whoa, guys, it's just me," said Axius.

No. No, no, absolutely no.

I spun back around, facing the line of prisoners. The nearest guard had turned in our direction.

Though I couldn't see his expression, I could make his shape out in the water.

And if we could see them, they could see us.

I grabbed Axius by his perfectly combed locks.

"*Dive*," I said through clenched teeth.

No one hesitated. We shot downwards, hurtling away from the scene. I dragged Axius along, forcing him to keep up, before throwing him away from me.

We swam at top speed until we reached twilight level, then kept going until there was barely enough light to see.

How had he followed us? I cursed myself. We'd all been too focused on what lay ahead to pay attention to what was going on behind.

Pontus stopped. He whirled around and grabbed Axius by the throat. "Everyone shut up."

More than ever, I felt the predator in him.

We held position, weapons raised. Anger bubbled inside me. We stayed quiet for a long while, listening, feeling, watching the world above.

Nobody had followed.

Pontus turned back to Axius and snarled. "What are you doing here?"

His hand was clasped so tightly around Axius' neck that I wondered if he would break it.

"I lost Lysi back at the raft," said Axius, voice strangled. "I searched for a while, then heard the First Officer say something about a few guys and the girl leaving, so …"

"You followed me?" I said, voice escalating to the pitch of a dolphin.

Pontus released his grip on Axius' throat, stunned.

"Oceans couldn't keep us apart, Lysi."

"What the crap is that supposed to mean?" I said.

Axius massaged his throat. "I followed your scent."

I stared at him, shaking with anger. Spio snatched the hook from my hands just before I slammed into Axius and started punching him in the chest.

"That - is - so - creepy!"

Axius raised his arms to fend me off.

Coho drifted closer. "If he was able to follow our scent, who's to say someone else didn't follow his?"

I stopped punching. We all looked at Coho, and then Axius.

"Did anyone tail you?" said Nobeard, aiming his mace at Axius' throat.

Axius squeaked.

"Answer him!" I said.

"I don't think so," he said in a small voice.

Coho turned to us. "What do we do with him?"

"Ever heard of keelhauling?" said Nobeard, mace still raised.

"Oh! The Trident of Terror can have its inaugural stabbing," said Spio.

"We aren't killing him," said Pontus. "We'll send him back."

"We can't send him back," said Junior. "He probably overheard everything."

Nobeard jabbed Axius in the throat. "Did you?"

"Yes." Axius pushed the weapon away. "Everything. And now I know …"

His eyes found mine, dim red orbs in the blackness.

"You aren't really going out with Spio."

Something incoherent burst from my mouth, like a muffled scream and eight different swear words. I wrapped my fists in my hair.

My frustration reached beyond his relentlessness. I couldn't believe our plan was at risk because of him. Because of me. I was already the spotted fish in this group. Now Axius had to force himself between them and me. The others probably wished they hadn't let me come.

Axius turned back to the guys. "I know you're going to kill someone at the mine. I'm assuming it's someone important, or this mission wouldn't be a secret."

"Wait," said Pontus. "You don't know who our target is?"

Axius didn't respond.

The blanket of stress dissipated a little. Nobeard lowered his weapon.

"Lysi," said Axius, "if you let me come with you, there's something important you should know about the mine."

I bared my teeth. "Liar."

But he wasn't. I wanted to send my fist through that air of bald earnestness.

"I've been to the Moonless City before," he said. "My mother took us all—"

"I don't care about your family vacation! Tell me what you know about the mine, Ax."

"Not until you agree to let me come with you."

I glowered at him.

"Cover your ears and hum," said Pontus. "Don't stop until we let you, or you're dead."

Unrattled, Axius did as he was told.

The rest of us grouped together.

"You think he's serious?" said Spio.

"He is," I said.

"We should let him come. He could be useful," said Pontus.

"That grog-for-brains will wreck our plan," said Nobeard.

"It's not like we can send him back. He might blab," said Junior.

"Or Strymon could interrogate him," said Pontus.

"So what do we do? He's a risk either way," said Coho.

"I say we send him home," I said.

"Of course you do," said Junior.

"No, listen." I dropped my voice to barely a whisper. "His family is well-off under Adaro's reign. I haven't had any indication from him that he'd want to … you know."

I glanced at Axius. He was still humming tunelessly, hands over his ears, looking like a complete cod.

"He's not going to be into the plan," I said.

"But what about whatever he knows about the mine?" said Coho.

"We'll beat it out of him."

Coho laughed.

I shrugged. I was being serious.

"He's still our ally. We're not going to beat him into a blob of algae," said Pontus with an air of amusement.

"If we send him back, we could try bribing him into silence," said Coho.

"With what?" I said.

There was a pause. All eyes landed on me. I backed away.

"Nope."

"Just tell him you'll go out with him," said Junior. "You don't actually have to do it."

"Yeah," said Spio. "Where are you going to go for a date, anyway?"

I scowled. He wasn't supposed to side with them.

I considered our options. We could let him come with us, or we could send him back and do our best to ensure his silence—which might not work anyway, knowing Strymon's determination. As far as I was concerned, this was a lose-lose situation.

I snarled.

"Fine, he can come. But you understand he absolutely cannot know who our target is?"

Pontus shrugged. "He might be into it."

"No. He won't."

I tried to read each of them, hoping they believed me. I caught Spio's eye. He nodded.

They all turned to Axius.

"Also, you fish faces have to keep him away from me," I said.

"Deal," said Junior.

"Aye, aye," said Nobeard.

"My pleasure," said Coho, rubbing his knuckles.

Spio returned the Iron Hook of Doom to me.

Pontus waved Axius over, who stopped humming and let go of his ears. He seemed much too pleased for a guy who'd just ticked off a group of armed outlaws.

"We've decided you can come," said Pontus.

Axius' face melted into a stupid smile, like he was sinking into a pleasant dream.

I clenched my teeth. "Now, tell us what you know about the mine."

He motioned behind us.

"You're swimming past it. It's a league that way."

We all turned to face the direction he was pointing. How could that be? We were still in open water.

Axius' grin faded at our expressions.

Pontus shook his head. "I was given directions from the— from someone who knows what he's talking about. He said to keep following the currents until we feel the shallows."

"These are the shallows," said Axius. "A league that way, you'll find a cliff face. The mine's on top of it."

I waited for Pontus to argue, but he didn't. He looked down, plainly listening for the bottom.

If I strained my ears, I heard a handful of bottom-dwellers snapping and grunting.

Pontus clenched his fists. "He said the shallows. I asked him what to listen for. He told me …"

But it made sense. This was probably it. In the middle of the open water, the shallows would still be quite deep.

Spio placed a hand on Pontus' shoulder. "It's all right, dude. The mistake belongs to all of us."

Pontus shrugged away. "It's not a mistake. I would have noticed."

"Either way, we should get moving," said Junior.

Pontus glared, but turned and led the way.

Junior and Nobeard immediately flanked Axius. Spio and Coho fell into place beside me.

After a moment, Junior said, "Keep low, brother. We don't want to run into the line of prisoners again."

Pontus gave no reply, but obeyed.

We swam southeast at breakneck pace. Gradually, the bottom rose beneath us. A cliff loomed ahead. We climbed to meet it.

The comfort of solid land would have been a relief, except that prickly feeling returned, like the water around us was tainted.

Though the mine would be decades old, with fish and greenery treating it like nothing more than a floating rock, the metallic, manmade scent was there.

Pontus slowed atop the cliff, scanning the world ahead. We caught up.

"There," I said, pointing my weapon to the right.

The spherical mine was barely visible through the blue, a shadow suspended in nothingness. The wire tethering it to the sandy floor had grown fuzzy with weeds.

We watched it for a moment, as though waiting for it to move. No one spoke.

Until now, I hadn't known what to expect. I'd wondered whether the blast would be fatal. I'd wondered how Coho was going to detonate it. I'd even wondered if the mine had somehow exploded already and we would arrive to find a crater and a cloud of debris.

The hovering shadow and its toxic aura drowned any doubts. We were in the presence of something more destructive than any of us had experienced.

The gloom thickened as we drew nearer. Ripples spread from little fish darting around the iron horns. It made me queasy. This explosion could end our own lives along with our target's.

"I'm going to find my angle," said Coho, motioning with his crossbow.

His voice carried in the smothering silence, sharp and resounding.

He separated from us. The rest of us continued over the empty sand.

"There should be a bunch of coral coming up," said Pontus. "We'll hide in the divots."

Axius darted forwards to fill the gap beside me.

"So how long until your target gets here?"

"Don't know," I said.

Below, sand turned to boulders and coral. A rainbow of reef fish darted around as we passed over them.

"You tired?" said Axius.

"A bit."

Even with the reef fish, the coral wasn't as active as it should have been. Intermittent crackling and pale colouring remained in what should have been a vivid landscape. I wondered if the bare sand and rock beneath the mine was once a reef.

"You've had a long journey," said Axius in a pitying tone.

"We all have."

So far, nothing suited as a hiding place. At the sparse edge of the reef, every clump of rock was too shallow.

Ducking behind a boulder wouldn't be enough. I pushed further from the mine.

Fish darted inside the coral and disappeared from sight, sound, and feel. Prime predator protection. Borrowing their homes would have worked, if we could fit.

"Let me catch your dinner tonight," said Axius.

"I'm not hungry."

"Just a snack, then."

"No, thanks."

"Too late."

I glanced over. He held out a dead anchovy. I raised my eyebrows. Had he been carrying that with him?

"Guys should do the hunting once in a while," he said, as if this was some noble gesture.

I didn't take it. My stomach was too knotted for food.

I turned my attention back to the floor. Most crevices weren't big enough. The rest were too big, and wouldn't be snug enough to protect any of us from the blast.

Something foreign darted by, sending squiggly ripples across my stomach. I recoiled. An eel disappeared between two rocks. Everything here was strange and unfamiliar. What kind of fish had dark and white stripes like that?

Maybe Spio would know its name. I glanced around, wondering where he'd gone off to.

"Most girls think it's sweet when I catch their dinner," said Axius.

Though I couldn't see Spio and Nobeard, I sensed them darting around across the way. They obviously hadn't found a hiding spot, either.

Fear crept over me. What if we couldn't find a place? What if Coho couldn't find somewhere close enough to shoot from?

I peeked behind a cluster of dead coral. Pathetic.

"I'm not impressed, here," said Axius.

I closed my eyes, reminding myself that it was rude to punch others in the face.

"What's wrong?"

"I caught your dinner. I poured my heart out to you. I'd expect you to take my hand, kiss me on the cheek—show me you care, you know?"

I stared at him for a long moment.

"You caught me an anchovy. After I said I didn't want it."

He opened his mouth to say more, but Junior and Pontus swam over.

"Hey, guys!" I said, a little too excitedly.

"We should breach," said Junior. "He'll be here soon."

I glanced to the surface. "Have you found a place—?"

Spio appeared next to them. "Better do it quickly. I feel them coming."

I exhaled in surprise. Spio turned northwards.

We froze, listening, feeling.

The sting of iron bled from the mine and clouded my senses. I pushed past it.

Over the chattering fish and snapping shrimp, a larger, deeper oscillation carried. They made no sound, but the rhythm of their tails was distinct. Controlled, precise movements grazed my skin.

Was it Adaro's crew, or another group of travellers? I caught myself hoping it wasn't Adaro. We'd been trekking all day, but in that time, I still hadn't mentally prepared myself.

"Hide," whispered Pontus.

We scattered. Panic struck me from every direction, blooming across our group like algae.

Axius tried to tail me, but Spio tugged him away. Pontus, Junior, and Nobeard shot in the other direction.

I brushed close to the rocks, searching frantically. I passed boulders, flecks of coral, and swaying anemones, none of it useful.

A few fathoms ahead, Spio disappeared behind a dead ledge of coral, forcing Axius down with him.

Good. Hopefully he'd keep Axius hidden so that cod wouldn't see what was happening until it was too late.

But where would I hide?

The group was close enough to distinguish. At least twenty of them. I glanced over. A dark shadow closed in.

I was out of time. Would Spio and Axius have room for me? I'd have to try and squeeze in.

I streaked towards them.

As I swam over the next cluster of boulders, I stopped short. They formed a tight semicircle. The middle one slanted inwards over a rut in the sand, providing a small cave that faced away from the mine. I would fit if I curled my tail in front of me.

I dropped and wedged myself inside.

I kept as still as the rocks, listening, trying to feel beyond the sting of iron. My wake dissipated.

Mostly males, but at least two females.

Something moved to my right. Coho. I leaned out of my hiding place. He was in the open, unloaded crossbow in hand. He seemed to be searching for somewhere to hide. Why wasn't he preparing to shoot?

I waved my tail.

The current caught his attention. He darted over. I moved my weapon so we could both fit, stabbing it into the sand.

Coho squeezed into the tiny cave beside me.

I jabbed him in the ribs and raised my eyebrows.

He shook his head, pointing over our shoulders.

Was this a false alarm?

In such close contact, Coho's fear seeped into me, making my heart pound faster.

I leaned over, barely enough to see past the rocks.

My eyes found Adaro. His tangled hair flowed behind him, matted around the six-pronged crown on his head. The others surrounded him, keeping him safely in the centre as they travelled.

Yes, even a skilled assassin would have a tough time shooting iron through his heart. This was the only way. We had to take them all out at once.

Guards made up the outer ring, each carrying an argillite longblade. My jaw tightened when I saw Katus and Ladon. Those flanking Adaro inside the ring were adorned with jewels and didn't carry any weapons. They must have been the ones the guys had mentioned—chief administrator, secretary, and whoever else.

My eyes locked onto a mermaid, curvy and tan-skinned, with immaculately groomed black hair, a headband of white pearls, and red lipstick. She turned her perfectly shadowed eyes in our direction.

I leaned back.

Coho's racing pulse told me everything.

"Ephyra?" I mouthed.

He nodded.

She swam within arm's length of the king, protected by the ring of guards. If the blast killed Adaro, it would kill her, too.

I worried the entourage would feel my pounding heart the same way I felt Coho's. I kept as still as the rocks, not even daring to exhale.

Their presence grew stronger. They were close to the mine.

We were going to miss our chance. But how could Coho shoot when his wife and unborn child were beside our target?

At the thought of his children, I grabbed Coho by the wrist, as though to stop him from pulling the trigger.

What could we do? Could I make a diversion to give Ephyra a chance to flee? Would she take the opportunity if I did?

The combination of panic, the iron-tainted water, and a desperate need for oxygen sent a wave of dizziness to my head.

They drew level with the mine.

A disturbance pushed the water in front of us. I straightened, listening.

Coho didn't seem to feel it. His head was turned, facing the back of our cave as though he could see through it.

Something pulsed again.

It was a mermaid. She moved with fluid silence, and then I lost her.

I kept staring.

A moment later, the tiniest hint of a vibration. I barely saw her through the blue, but felt her gaze. She stared at Coho and me, motionless.

Something was different about her. The current around her body revealed a longer, leaner frame. Her hair reminded me of living snakes. Something glinted from her cheek—a gemstone.

As faintly as the gurgling current, I heard a whisper. I strained my ears to understand.

"*Para la reina.*"

Para what?

She'd said it in a human dialect. I didn't know any human languages other than Eriana.

I sat frozen, my pounding pulse the only difference between the rocks and me.

Who was she? Why was she also hiding?

A stronger disturbance brushed my skin, coming from the side. In an instant, the mermaid disappeared.

I glanced over. Spio and Axius were visible from here, ducking beneath the ledge of coral.

Axius was struggling.

Coho noticed, too. He leaned forwards, his dread palpable.

Spio fought back, forcing Axius beneath the coral.

He had realised who our target was.

Ladon's voice cut through the pressing silence. "Do you feel—?"

"Oh, my necklace!"

A mermaid. They were so close that I felt the vibration from her moving lips. Was that Ephyra?

"Sorry," she said. "I see it. One moment."

"You weren't wearing a necklace," said another mermaid.

"I was. It fell off back there. Excuse me, please."

The water pulsed. She'd moved away.

The way our cave blocked the current made it hard to tell exactly where she was. But this was it. Coho had to act.

He loaded a dart into his crossbow and leaned forwards.

"Your Majesty!"

The shout came from beside us. Axius.

Coho froze.

Adaro's group stopped. The changing current glopped in my ears.

Coho leaned around the rocks.

Axius shouted again, voice cracking with hysteria. "Sir! Move—away from—"

His words broke. Spio pinned him between the coral and his Trident of Terror. I smelled flesh searing beneath iron.

"Treason!" shouted Axius. "Get away from the m—"

Spio stabbed Axius through the chest. Axius spluttered, his last breath leaving him in a large bubble. It rose like a beacon from where Spio was hiding.

"Shoot!" I said to Coho. "Now!"

Adrenaline turned my words into a shriek.

I peered around the boulder. The group was focused on Spio's hiding spot—except for the brown-haired mermaid at Adaro's tail, who turned her head. Her green eyes found mine.

In the next heartbeat, everything happened at once.

The nearest guard charged straight for Spio. Ephyra's tail flipped up as she disappeared over the cliff. Katus and Ladon seized Adaro by the arms, pulling him backwards.

Coho squeezed the trigger.

CHAPTER THIRTEEN
Family Crest

Mist dampened our skin and clothes as we huddled on the front step of the cultural centre, waiting for Tanuu to continue reading the pages. He scanned our faces. We must have shown desperation, because he hastened on.

"For millennia, the waters of the Pacific were ruled by one beast. Sisiutl, leviathan, the two-headed snake—she is one creature with many names, her malevolent presence scattered throughout ancient history."

"Leviathan," said Annith. "I've heard of it. Isn't it supposed to have seven heads?"

"One head," said Blacktail. "It's supposed to be like a gigantic alligator."

"Sisiutl has three," said Tanuu. "The middle one's human."

"Apparently, it has two," I said impatiently. "Keep reading."

Tanuu returned to the page. "Not earth, air, fire, or water can wound the leviathan. Neither iron nor bronze, weapon nor poison. Her double coat of armour is impenetrable; the shields cannot be parted. She is spared from blindness by the presence of two heads, neither weaker than the other. The mouths are lined with venomous teeth, their bite strong enough to crush stone. This is a creature with no equal, and so she lives without fear."

"She's indestructible!" said Annith.

Some mixture of awe and terror roiled in my stomach. This serpent was a living, breathing weapon.

"As man settled near the ocean to raise his sons and daughters, the leviathan's presence threatened life above all other forces. None could vanquish her or predict when her wrath would fall upon the town. Yet if man was to prosper, someone would need to tame the untameable. Then, a child was born with an unprecedented gift."

"Eriana," said Blacktail.

"Eriana. The child possessed a connection with the spirits of animals, which grew stronger as Eriana grew older. She lived under the protection of the Gaela, who saw value in her skill and sought to protect the girl from Death. But Eriana betrayed the Gaela. She abused her gift, which struck imbalance upon the Gaela's earth."

"That's the snowstorm," said Annith. "When she killed all those caribou."

I shushed her. The three of us had leaned closer to Tanuu.

"Angry, the Gaela sent the Aanil Uusha to punish Eriana. The Aanil Uusha went to earth, but with his own plan. He had long felt cheated by the two-headed serpent. The beast destroyed villages and killed its inhabitants before Death was ready to claim them. Even the Aanil Uusha could not take the life of the leviathan—but in Eriana, he saw the chance to control it."

Tanuu turned the page. The animal skin made no sound beneath the wind.

I checked compulsively over my shoulder to make sure nothing but waves advanced on the beach. The mist had thickened, shielding my view of the shoreline.

"The Aanil Uusha made a deal with Eriana. To spare her own life, Eriana agreed to wrest control of the indestructible serpent. She followed its wake in a ship made from the bones of nature's victims. The beast churned the ocean like a maelstrom, but Eriana's ship, supported by the spirits of a thousand people and animals, endured.

"She caught up to the leviathan. As the creature reared an enormous head, preparing to strike from both sky and sea, Eriana shouted a simple command: *Stop*. The leviathan, for the first time in existence, ceased her attack. She closed her jaw and raised her other head. Four eyes as blue as the sea met Eriana's. *Follow me*, she said, and turned her ship homewards. The leviathan obeyed."

"I knew it," I said. "She's the only—"

It was their turn to shush me.

"For three decades," Tanuu read on, "Eriana lived alone on an island in the Pacific. She guided the serpent in a benign existence, using the beast to turn people away from her home.

"But the loneliness became too much to bear, so Eriana permitted select ships to disembark on her island. She began life anew with another family, eventually marrying and bearing three children.

"But attempts to access the island continued, once the world learned of the two-headed serpent. Sailors came from afar to see the beast, to capture or to fight it, and made their home on Eriana Kwai.

"In time, Eriana was fatally wounded in battle. Knowing she would soon die, she prayed to the Gaela for an indefinite resting place for the serpent, a crypt beneath the island where none would find it. The Gaela answered her prayer and created Eriana's Crypt. The crypt can be entered only by a fissure in the crust of the earth."

"A fissure!" I said. "We have to find a fissure—"

Annith clapped a hand over my mouth.

"As Eriana guided the serpent to her crypt, a bush with leaves of coal grew where each drop of its venom fell.

"But the Aanil Uusha was afraid to lose the only one who could control the leviathan. He did not permit Eriana's soul to ascend to the stars as a goddess, as the Gaela had intended. Instead, he bound her soul to the serpent. Host to her soul, the otherwise untameable beast could still be controlled by a mortal as long as the spirit of Eriana was a part of it.

"He granted Eriana the ability to leave the crypt by blood alone. To awaken her, a drop of mortal blood from a descendant of Eriana must be fed to the leviathan's sleeping jaws. By ..."

Tanuu shuffled the pages, not looking at us. He mumbled to himself, re-checking the pages and their empty reverse sides. His frown deepened with each passing second.

"What's wrong?" said Annith and I together.

"One's missing," said Blacktail.

Tanuu looked up at her, eyebrows knitted. "Yeah."

I stood. Had I dropped a page? Or had one slipped out long ago, and was now lying on the ground inside the totem?

"I have a page left," said Tanuu, "but the sentences don't match up."

"Read it anyway," I said.

"… gains control of the leviathan until death. Control is passed by blood: either to a descendant of one who is in control of the serpent, or one who takes the controller's life. So it will go, until the leviathan ceases to exist and Eriana's soul is free to ascend to the stars as the Gaela intended."

He placed the pages on his lap with rigid calmness.

I spun towards the totem poles, but the wind had blown in a blanket of fog and I could no longer see them. My heart pounded. This legend was real—and serious enough that someone had hidden the written evidence. The missing page hardly concerned me. We had the information we needed. The Host was in a crypt somewhere on this island, and we knew how to free it. We needed the blood of Eriana's descendant. I could do it.

But according to these pages, the Host of Eriana's soul was the most dangerous, powerful creature to ever live.

The gravity of the situation washed over us for a long moment. I crossed my arms. A chill had set in, and the fog brought with it the sharp scent of the ocean. If not for the solid ground beneath my feet, I might have felt like I was back aboard the Bloodhound.

We were meddling in something much bigger than the fate of Eriana Kwai.

No matter what was happening with the Massacres, I couldn't unleash something this dangerous.

"This isn't worth it," I said.

They looked up. All three bore wide, unfocused gazes that said their minds were reeling as much as mine.

"We can't wake a leviathan," I said. "*The* leviathan. This legend is beyond us."

Tanuu stood. "That's more reason to do it. If we don't find the Host, anyone else could."

"So let's burn the pages," said Annith. "I'm with Meela. Let's make sure no one ever stumbles on it."

"It's the serpent we gotta destroy, not the pages," said Tanuu. "And what about the crypt? Someone could still come across that."

"No one has, yet," said Blacktail.

"That's not to say they never will," said Tanuu.

We stared at each other, the three of us against Tanuu. How was it that he was so willing to press on? Maybe the Massacre had exhausted the supply of hope in us girls.

He did have a point: even if we destroyed evidence of the legend, the leviathan still existed somewhere, waiting to be found.

Still, we had no place being the ones who discovered it.

"How old are these totem poles?" I said.

Tanuu shrugged. "Couple hundred years, maybe."

"This legend is thousands of years old. That means someone found these pages since then, and deemed it dangerous enough *not to pursue it*. They hid it. They didn't want anyone to know about it."

"They hid it, but they didn't destroy it," he said. "Maybe they were too scared to pursue it."

"And you're not scared? *Nothing can wound the leviathan ... venomous teeth ...*"

"*Until the leviathan ceases to exist*. That means it must be possible to kill it."

"That's probably a metaphor for eternity."

Tanuu's eyebrows pulled down. He leaned against the wall, the stack of parchment in his fist.

"We keep calling the leviathan *it*," he said, "like some soulless thing. But she's not a thing. She's the spirit of Eriana. She's a part of our people, our history, and she's trapped inside Sisiutl. If you ask me, she needs us."

I searched his face. His dark eyes met mine, pleading. He believed it. He believed the goddess of our people was prevented from ascending to the stars to watch over us.

Did I? Was the spirit of Eriana real, bound inside the leviathan and stuck in her crypt forever?

If that was true, she did need us. Only her descendants could wake the leviathan. But even then, the legend said Eriana could not ascend to the stars as the Gaela intended until the leviathan ceased to exist. When would that be? How was the death of the indestructible even possible?

"I don't think we stumbled on this legend randomly," said Tanuu. "I think it's our destiny to use our blood to wake her up. To free Eriana."

I rolled my eyes. I'd heard enough about my destiny for one lifetime: my destiny to go on the Massacre, to slaughter mermaids, to avenge my brother, to ally with murderers like Dani. I didn't believe in destiny anymore.

"Meela," said Tanuu. "Remember who you're doing this for."

I turned away so he wouldn't see my grimace. He was referring to our families, of course, and our people, and all those we'd lost on the Massacres. We needed freedom from Adaro more than ever.

So did Lysi. So did all the merpeople.

Yes, this legend was bigger than us. But so was this problem. Could we fight the most powerful king of the seas with the most powerful beast ever to live? Should we?

Annith and Blacktail had said nothing. Were they considering the idea, too?

"Say I used my blood to do it," I said. "The leviathan wakes up. I have control. Then Adaro gets here with Lys— with his army … I command the leviathan to kill him, right?"

I crossed my arms, hunching against the cold. I glanced to Annith, but she had looked away.

"Then," said Tanuu, "we make sure it stays under your control until we figure out how to destroy it."

I considered him. His face was set. I felt a rush of fondness for him, for believing in this for me.

"Do you think Adaro knows the part about passing control of the Host by murder?" said Blacktail.

"Like, does he intend to kill Meela after she frees it?" said Annith.

I thought I knew enough about Adaro to guess the answer.

"We're talking like Meela's gonna use her blood to free it," said Tanuu. "You're sure you're a descendant, then?"

"Aren't I? Aren't we all?"

Tanuu shook his head. "My ancestors came from Haida Gwaii, ages back."

Annith and Blacktail appeared as unsure as I was. My parents and grandparents had been born here, and as far back as I knew, their parents' parents had been born here.

"We still don't know where the crypt is," said Annith. "Once we find out whose blood to use, where do we go?"

"The word *crypt* makes me think of a burial ground," said Tanuu. "Maybe it's beneath the graveyard."

Annith pulled a face. "I am *not* digging around the graveyard, thank you very much."

"I doubt it's there," said Blacktail. "Eriana guided the serpent to a fissure in the crust of the earth. We shouldn't start digging randomly."

"What if the fissure got covered, or built over top of?" said Annith.

My heart fluttered. The girls were talking like we were going to do this.

"The story mentioned a bush with leaves of coal," I said. "That's Ravendust, isn't it? It said the plant grew from the leviathan's venom while it crossed over the land."

"It must have slithered all over the place," said Annith, "because those bushes grow everywhere."

"Are they, though? Are they everywhere, or do they actually form a line from the water to a destination?"

No one answered.

"We won't know until we try and follow them," I said.

"From where? Which direction?" said Annith.

"Skaaw beach," said Blacktail. "Where Tanuu got attacked by that sea demon. Remember the gap in the lava flow? The bank we climbed up?"

"Oh!" said Annith.

I stared in that direction, my line of sight stopped short from the fog. When I thought about it, the lava rock had been parted, like something huge had broken through.

"Remember all the Ravendust that grew between it?" said Blacktail.

I thought of the black leaves poking up in the meadow. Was I remembering wrong, or did they form a vague, freckly line across the grass?

I looked to each of them, finding unmistakable excitement gleaming in their eyes. A smile tugged at my lips, and I let it.

"One of us is bound to be a descendant, don't you think?"

"If not, we'll ambush someone who is," said Tanuu.

"What, and steal their blood?" said Blacktail.

Tanuu grinned mischievously.

"Zey vill call us"—he raised an arm across the lower half of his face—"ze vampires of Eriana Kwai."

"Genius," said Blacktail. "Keep the ideas coming."

"I'll ask my parents about my ancestry," I said. "Blacktail, Annith, you do the same."

Something with claws scurried across the other side of the door Annith was leaning against. She screamed, leaping to her feet.

I glanced around, again failing to see the shoreline through the fog.

"Yeah, let's get away from here," said Blacktail, reading my thoughts.

Tanuu stuffed the parchment inside his jacket. "Okay if I take this?"

I shrugged. "You're the only one who can read it."

"I'll keep it safe. I wanna re-read it a few times and see if I get anything more out of it."

As we made for the road, I imagined myself controlling the leviathan. How would it feel to have power over the most fearsome creature to ever exist? I could make it do whatever I wanted. I could kill Adaro, and then ensure no one ever threatened my people again.

It would be like when Eriana originally had the serpent under her control. We'd be invincible.

I glanced to the others. They were lost in their own thoughts, watching their feet—all with slight grins.

I grinned, too. With my friends at my side, I finally felt like we were gaining ground. We knew what the Host was and how to free it—and if the Ravendust bushes didn't let me down, we'd soon know where it was hiding.

If Eriana's Host was ever meant to be freed, we were going to be the ones to do it.

From the kitchen table, I watched my mother pull a casserole dish from the oven. She placed it on a vaguely circular hot pad I'd knitted in grade five. Her lips puckered in concentration as she sprinkled spices over it.

I was trying to think of the best way to ask about my ancestry without letting my parents know this was about the Host. Could I ask out of nowhere? Would they wonder where my sudden curiosity came from?

My father lay sprawled on the couch, reading some newspaper comics that must not have been very funny, because his expression was blank.

Maybe I could try and segue into it. But how?

My mother glanced at me, seeming to feel my stare.

"Hi," she said.

"Hi."

She tasted a piece of whatever was in the dish and glanced back at me.

"Hungry?"

"Smells good," I said.

I couldn't think of an appropriate segue. Maybe it would be best to jump into the question.

My father seemed to detect the weird silence. He lifted his eyes from the newspaper.

"I was thinking about … our family," I said to both of them. "Tanuu was talking about his grandparents yesterday and I thought … I never got to meet mine."

"You would've liked them," said my father. "Interesting lives. Good people."

"Nilus knew my parents," said my mother. "But only as a child. My mother passed away when he was six. He might not have even remembered …"

She trailed off, shaking her head. I wondered if the memory of both her son and her parents was too much to think about at once.

"Tanuu said his great-great-great-grand-somethings came from Haida Gwaii," I said.

"Most families migrated a couple hundred years back," said my father.

"Did we?"

He rose from the couch, stretching so I heard his spine crack. "I've got a family book somewhere. Let me find it."

He shuffled down the hall. I wanted to tell him I didn't need to see a family book, and I only wanted to know if we were descendants of Eriana, but I held my tongue. That would make it too obvious that I wasn't just asking on a curious whim.

From the kitchen, however, my mother's eyes flicked over me sceptically.

"Anyo said you were asking all sorts of questions the other day. You're not still on about that silly legend, are you?"

I traced my finger along a groove in the wooden table. Why would Anyo tell my parents that? Did my mother read too deeply into our visit at the school, or was Anyo warning my parents about what I was up to?

"Meela ..."

"No," I said. "I was only saying hi to Anyo. That's all."

It pained me to pretend I'd given up because the committee had told me off. But now was not the time for stubbornness.

My mother set three plates on the table and sat across from me. Each had a fair portion of meat and carrots in gravy. My mouth watered. With my mother's garden turning out decent vegetables this summer, dinners since my return had tasted nothing short of fine dining. I'd have to commit this meal to memory and think back to it when we were all living off spruce again in mid-January.

"Speaking of Tanuu's family, I got this meat from them, so you can thank them for tonight's dinner next time you're there."

"I will," I said, digging in. "This looks amazing."

I assumed it was the same mystery meat we'd had at the beach. Bring on the fluffy kittens.

"How is Tanuu, anyway?"

Though my mother's tone was polite, the question irritated me.

I scrutinised her over my plate. "Fine."

"He's such a nice boy. You know he graduated with honours?"

I made an indiscernible noise. He'd mentioned it.

"He's a catch, Meela. Don't let go of him. I can see him being a great father one day."

My fork slipped from my fingers. It clattered onto my plate then to the floor, taking a carrot with it. I stooped to get it.

"Mama, please don't talk to me about this."

I plucked a hair from the fallen carrot before eating it.

"I'm just saying, you're a grown woman. You've dealt with more responsibility than any other girl your age. You deserve to settle down now, and start a life with a man who has a career planned."

"Tanuu doesn't have a career planned. He just graduated."

She raised her eyebrows. "Sure, he does! His mother says he's got a talent for carpentry."

"I bet he does," I mumbled through a mouthful, thinking of how easily he'd pieced the deck of the Enticer back together.

In fact, he'd never mentioned it—but I also hadn't asked.

"Anyway," said my mother. "Now you're done with all that Massacre business, it's time for you to start thinking about your future. You've had five years of warrior training and no time for much else, which is a real shame."

"I've been reading books," I said defensively. "I even read some of Tanuu's textbooks."

"I mean starting a family, Meela."

I paused with my fork halfway to my mouth.

"I don't even want … You know I'm not …"

"You'll be a great mother, Meela."

"Ew, Mama. I can't stand babies. They're annoying and not even cute."

She waved it off. "Don't say that. You'll feel differently when they're your own."

I leaned back, staring at her. How could she bring this up right now? Yes, I'd been through more than most adults I knew, but I was still only eighteen.

"How old were you when you had Nilus?" I said.

"I was your age."

The year my father went on the Massacre. I narrowed my eyes. "Same year you got married, right?"

She hesitated for a fraction of a second. "Right."

Her hesitation told me everything. I made a repulsed face.

"Nice summer wedding, I guess? About five months before Nilus was born?"

"Meela, Nilus was the best thing that happened to me at eighteen."

"I don't care," I said. "I've spent a third of my life in warrior training. I need to live my own life now."

"I wouldn't have a problem with that if *living your own life* meant you were doing something worthwhile. Instead, you choose to spend your days hunting for some silly myth."

I clenched my fists. "I'm trying to stop more of our girls from dying!"

"Use your head, Meela! If we don't send warriors to kill the demons, we're letting them spread like bacteria."

"They're not bacteria," I said. "They want something. Until we use that to our advantage, they'll keep attacking us."

"This is exactly the type of thinking that got you into trouble as a kid. Sea demons don't think like us. They're savages."

I wrapped my fists in my hair, trying not to explode.

"Your mother's right."

I hadn't noticed my father come back. He sat down, placing a cloth-bound book on the table.

"We need to assert our power over the demons," he said. "At the very least, we need to thin the population so they stop eating all our fish."

I didn't know what to say. Nothing seemed to convince them that they were wrong.

"Do you think you're reaching for alternatives to the Massacres for other reasons?" said my mother. "I know as a little girl you felt sorry for the mermaids, and sometimes I wonder if you still—"

I stood. "I'm done. Thanks for dinner."

"Finished already?" said my father, tucking into his meal.

My mother's lips tightened. My father scraped the rest of my plate onto his.

"Can I borrow the book?" I said shortly.

My mother seized it from the table, turning it over as though checking for a hidden message.

"Why the sudden interest?"

I made an exasperated sound and turned on my heel.

They didn't stop me from leaving.

I kicked a clump of dandelions as I walked down the driveway, causing the flowers to pop off and scatter.

"Start a family," I muttered. "They've got a shock coming if that's what they're expecting."

I'd wanted to go back to school and start a career before thinking about any of that stuff. Nobody had talked to me about career plans, but somewhere in the back of my mind I'd always wanted to work with animals. A vet, maybe. I was probably being stupid. A vet needed years of education, and I hadn't even gone to high school.

Between their attitude towards mermaids and my mother's infatuation with Tanuu, how was I ever supposed to tell my parents about Lysi?

Voices carried from around the bend ahead. It sounded like our neighbour, Elaila, and the widow from the Massacre Committee. I pulled my hood over my head and cut through the bush so I wouldn't run into them.

The sun wouldn't set for another four hours. I wandered through the forest, not sure where my feet were taking me. I didn't feel like talking to Annith about this. Besides, she was likely with Rik.

My desire to see Lysi was more painful than ever. I scowled at the enormous trees, not wanting their still, insulating silence, but rather the crashing waves and the cold, salty spray on my face.

I watched my feet. I'd chosen a difficult part of the woods to navigate. Moss-covered logs crossed my path in every direction, slowing me down as I climbed over and sought ways around them. Ferns grew out of every surface—an entire ecosystem sprouting from each fallen tree.

Following an unexplored route, I passed under a rocky outthrust that must have formed in some huge earthquake tens of thousands of years prior. The rock was so splintered and crammed together, the face angled so acutely, it looked like the cliff might fall on me at any moment. A fallen cedar leaned against it, forming a canopy over my head and giving the impression that the tree was the one holding up the rock.

I brushed a hand along the face, poking my fingers into deep cracks where the earth had smashed the rock together. This formation was so close to my home, yet I'd never come across it before. What else had I yet to discover about this place?

Everyone liked to complain that the island wasn't big enough—but now that I was trying to find something, it felt vast and insurmountable. I could spend my whole life combing every bit of this place and never find Eriana's Crypt.

Of course, none of that would matter if I didn't know my ancestry. I would have to sneak my father's book away.

I moved slowly through the dense bush, not caring if I got lost. Several times, I had to backtrack to get around some deep ravine or impassable clump of logs.

Eventually, I came to a well-worn dirt trail. I followed it for a minute to get my bearings, and arrived at a marsh full of skunk cabbage. To my right, a less boggy path would lead me through. This was the route to the training base.

I hesitated, considering whether Dani and her trainees would be there. It was likely, given the Massacre would depart in mere days.

I crossed the marsh with new purpose.

Dani's shouts met my ears before I was anywhere near the Enticer.

"I don't care! You think the sea rats will let you rest because you're out of breath? Get moving!"

I left the path, slowing until my footsteps were silent over the carpet of moss. When I was close enough to see the glade, I stopped, scanning the trees. The spruce to my left had a few solid, low branches. I climbed it. The scaly bark dug into my palms.

"Keep going!" Dani shouted. "*Get - up!*"

I peered into the clearing in time to see her swing something at one of the trainees. The girl scrambled away on hands and knees. Dani's iron prong, apparently the one from the fire pit we'd stumbled on, sliced through the air without making contact.

The girl kept running, joining her classmates. They sprinted back and forth in the clearing, stopping at either end to do a push-up.

Every face looked sweaty, miserable. One girl convulsed at the end of her push-up, as if about to be sick. But without question, these trainees were at the peak of fitness. Their muscles appeared chiselled out of wood. I looked down at my own bicep, which was admittedly impressive, but even from a distance I could tell these kids would knock me flat in a fistfight. Was the new training program really turning out better warriors?

"A demon won't pause to let you stand if you stumble," yelled Dani. "She will catch you and sink her teeth into your flesh. I'm the demon here, and I've got a few more days to prepare you to fight for every second aboard Vindicti."

She swung her iron at a passing runner, who had to leap to avoid being caught in the shins. She landed with a grunt, tripped, swung her arms for balance, and kept moving. Dani's next swing grazed her calf.

"Good. This isn't unlike the weapons you'll be seeing out there. Sea spears. Harpoons. A sea rat might strike face-on, or she might wait until you least expect it, popping out of nowhere to launch a dart into the eyeball of the first girl to lower her guard. She's stronger than you, faster than you, with better vision in the dark and better balance on a careening ship. She will have every advantage, except for one thing: feet. You have your legs, and you can run and jump where a sea rat is stuck to the blood-soaked deck."

She paused, watching the trainees run.

"So use your legs properly!" she shouted, and swung the iron with all her might.

Her victim—the girl who'd been heaving—was too tired to jump, and it caught her hard on the back of the legs. The girl cried out and hit the ground, where she coughed and gasped, unable to stand back up.

Dani descended like an eagle swooping on a salmon. I couldn't take my eyes away.

Then a tall, surly girl burst out of one of the cabins, and Dani turned.

I hadn't seen Texas since we returned from the Massacre. Like many of us, she'd gained a bit of weight back. Next to Dani's bony frame and the overworked girls running laps, her presence was more formidable than ever. She leaned in to discuss something with Dani in voices too low for me to hear.

The girls kept running. The one on the ground took her chance to scramble away.

After a minute, Dani nodded, and Texas skulked back to the cabin. I wondered what subjects Texas taught. My pity for the trainees, if possible, increased.

Dani whirled to face the trainees again. The way she eyed them reminded me of a cat looming over a nest of baby birds.

I regretted coming to watch. Feeling worse, I lowered myself from the tree and landed lightly on the forest floor.

A small scream came from behind me. I spun with my fists raised, but dropped them when I saw Adette standing there, hands thrown over her mouth.

Flattening myself against the tree trunk, I checked over my shoulder to ensure nobody had heard. The girls still ran, Dani still screaming at them.

"What are you doing in the bush?" I whispered.

Adette narrowed her eyes. "What are *you* doing in the bush?"

I opened my mouth, but nothing came out. She had a point.

"I asked you first," I said.

She crossed her arms, flustered.

Though Adette had hit a growth spurt in the last few months, she was still tiny and frail. I tried not to think about how she'd soon be forced to toughen into a warrior like the girls running laps behind me. The question was: how soon? The yearly ritual had crumbled under Mujihi's new program.

"Shouldn't you be in a cabin somewhere with the others?" I whispered, nodding towards the glade.

"Dani's not teaching us until next block. I have Emma right now for First Aid, and she's not as mean if you're late."

"Who?"

"Emma—erm, Blondie."

"Oh. Right. She's teaching, too?"

"Yeah."

Blondie wasn't as bad as Dani or Texas, but she'd still sided with them on the Massacre.

"What about Fern?" I said.

"No. She was supposed to teach Rigging, but Dani didn't want her. Said Fern didn't know what she was doing."

"Figures."

She leaned over to peer around the tree at the older trainees, chewing her lip.

"So why did you skip part of First Aid?"

She hesitated. "I was with Papa. He needed me at home."

"Why? Is something wrong?"

She shook her head, but unconvincingly, with another nervous glance past my shoulder.

When I kept staring, she averted her gaze into the woods beside us, as though contemplating taking off in that direction.

It was then that I noticed a mark on her neck, in the same place as the girl who'd talked to Annith at the Enticer.

It was a burn, barely healed, pink and bubbly.

"What's that on your neck?" I said, jumping forwards.

She clapped a hand over it and looked at me in alarm.

I pulled her hand away. A symbol had been burned into her flesh. Two dots, like eyes, sloping inwards as though angry, and a triangular beak beneath them.

"What is this?" I said through clenched teeth.

She mumbled something.

"What?"

I grabbed her chin and forced her to look at me.

When our eyes met, I saw panic on her face. I dropped my hand.

"We all have them," she said.

"The trainees?"

She nodded once, lips tight.

Heat rushed into my face, like lava bubbling inside a volcano. "Did Dani do this to you?"

Her eyes flicked left and right. Her mouth opened but no sound came out.

"Adette."

"She calls it *branding*. Every trainee gets one, as a mark of her loyalty to her crew and Eriana Kwai."

"And Dani," I said. "It's a mark of your loyalty to Dani."

Adette said nothing.

I thought of the fire pit in the clearing, and the rod lying on the ground—the one now clutched in Dani's bony hand. A branding iron.

"I'm going to talk to the committee," I said. "She can't get away with this."

"No, please don't! My friend Jace told her parents that Dani was being too harsh, and the next day Dani made her run until she barfed."

"But—" I faltered, trying to compose myself, and drew a breath before continuing. "She won't know it was you I was talking to."

"Then she'll punish all of us. Please, Meela."

I ran my hands through my hair. If all went according to my plans, we wouldn't need the training program, anyway.

"Hasn't your father noticed?"

Surely Anyo wouldn't stand for this.

"Yes, but I told him I wanted to do it. Dani has one too, you know. She did it to herself. Twice. She also has a snake head on her wrist."

"I don't care—Wait. What?"

Adette shrugged.

My heart skipped several beats. Why would Dani have branded a snake onto her body? Was it coincidence that I happened to be searching for a leviathan? Or did Dani know something?

Behind us in the clearing, Dani shouted at her trainees. "Twenty more laps and you can stop, girls!"

Adette's eyebrows pulled down in desperation. I nodded once to indicate I wouldn't tell anyone.

"I have to go," she said.

Before I could say another word, she took off into the trees and skirted the edge of the glade. She would enter the cabins from behind, I knew, to avoid the iron rod clutched in Dani's white-knuckled fist.

CHAPTER FOURTEEN
Capital Punishment

I swore the explosion hit me before the dart left Coho's crossbow.

How?

That was all I had time to think before my head cracked against the back of the cave. Torrents surged, slamming me against the rocks, pushing me sideways. It would have carried me away if Coho had not been there to grab me.

Everything was dark, murky. A high-pitched wailing filled my ears. The water stirred too much to feel anything. My flesh stung. My scar seared. Even my tongue hurt from the bitter taste of iron.

All I knew was the rocky cave, and Coho, wrapping his arms around me to stop the current pulling me away.

Terror seeped off of him. Ephyra. Had she made it to safety? She had nothing to cling to, as we did. What if she'd gotten carried away in a whirl of iron debris?

My head throbbed, as though my brain had smashed against the inside of my skull and was now dripping down my spine.

Where were Spio and the others? The blast happened before the guard made it to Spio—but that didn't mean my friend was safe. Had his hiding place been enough? Did he get blasted away?

The sea churned for an eternity. The surface roared as displaced water cascaded back down.

We stayed huddled in the cave, wordless, waiting for the iron to settle.

I pressed my palm over my scar, fruitlessly trying to keep the dirty water from making it burn. I needed to get away from here. Even more, I needed to surface. Between the pain and lack of air, my head spun.

Coho's heartbeat drummed against my skin. Beyond that, my senses were blind. The ringing in my ears wouldn't stop. The world was too murky to see beyond an arm's length. My flesh prickled.

How did the mine detonate? The more I reflected, the more certain I became: the dart had not left the crossbow when the mine exploded. I'd seen Coho's fingers on the trigger.

Did one of the other guys do it—too impatient, or nervous, to wait?

Maybe I'd been confused in all the panic. My perception could have been off. I remembered feeling dizzy moments before.

Slowly, the water calmed.

A face appeared in front of us. I straightened.

Spio.

He looked unharmed, though his face was smudged with green muck and his hair stood on end more than usual. His leather cap had fallen off, or been blasted away.

We exchanged a sense of relief at the sight of each other.

He said something. The words were lost beneath the ringing in my eardrums.

"What?"

My voice was hollow. I shook my head. Pain shot through my skull.

"... going to find the brothers," said Spio.

He sounded distorted, like he was speaking to me from above surface.

"See you back at Utopia, all right?" he said slowly.

I gaped at him. In the chaos surrounding the explosion, I'd forgotten about the rest of the plan. Spio, Pontus, and Junior would need to get moving so they could notify the commander.

"Is Ax dead?" said Coho.

Spio nodded once, jaw tight. He exuded something I'd rarely felt in him before—something dark, serious.

I tried to speak. So many questions raced through my mind but none of them came out.

"Go," said Coho. "Bring our troops home."

Was this victory?

I hadn't exactly planned on a celebration once we detonated the mine, but I had expected to feel some sense of triumph and relief. Instead, I felt only fear.

Feeling like my brain was leaking from the back of my skull, I reached up to check for blood. My hand came away clean.

Before I could verbalise anything, Spio disappeared, leaving a wake of bubbles.

"Wait," I said, but the word hardly came out as a grunt.

I tried to pull myself out of the cave. I was stuck.

I hadn't said a proper goodbye. Anything could happen between now and when we all got back to Utopia.

But he had to go, and this was not the time to linger. I stopped myself from shouting after him. We didn't know who, if anyone, was alive out there.

Coho mirrored my unease.

A glance outside the cave told me my weapon was gone.

Someone appeared on our other side, projecting urgency.

"Abandon the plan," said Nobeard in a low voice.

He rubbed grit from his eyes with trembling fists. He'd lost his eyepatch again.

"Uh, you're a bit late," said Coho.

"I mean telling the commander. He can't mobilise the troops until we're sure the target is dead."

"Of course he's dead," said Coho. "Did you feel the size of the explosion?"

"He wasn't as close as he should have been."

"But they've already left," I said, finding my voice at last. "Spio went to get the brothers."

I sounded hollow to my own ears.

Nobeard turned southwards. "I'm going to stop them."

"No," said Coho, grabbing Nobeard's wrist.

"Mate, I'm not convinced he's dead," whispered Nobeard.

Doubt bled from him so thickly that I wondered the same.

"If he's still alive, where is he?" I whispered.

"Waiting out the rubble, like us."

"Do we try and find him?"

Nobeard turned, listening. "If he's alive and we find him, then what?"

"He won't be alive," said Coho stubbornly. "We can search, but we'll find him in pieces."

He pushed himself out of the cave.

Nobeard extended a hand and pulled me out. We peered over the rocks.

My throat tightened at the devastation. The sand that had once anchored the mine was now a barren, dead crater. The surrounding coral had shattered. I felt no sign of fish, heard no chatter, saw no rainbow of colour.

I'd been too concerned with carrying out the plan to consider what it might do to the world around us.

And then there were the bodies. Corpses floated overhead, sinking gently. Pieces of mermen littered the floor.

The stench of iron wafted, but beneath it, there was blood.

"I need a breath," I said.

"Hold on," said Coho.

He grabbed my arm. Something shifted across the way.

The three of us sank behind the rocks with a soft glop.

Voices rose. At first, the settling current distorted the sound. I strained to hear.

"… you all right?"

Ladon's voice.

Mumbling. Then Katus said, "Where are the others?"

My stomach churned. Katus and Ladon had seized Adaro a moment before the blast. If they were alive …

I had to check. Ignoring Coho's hand on my wrist, I raised myself slightly to see over the rocks. Beyond the brown murk, Katus and Ladon hovered near the edge of the cliff. Even from this distance, I could tell they'd been hit with iron shards. A cloud of blood rose from Ladon's tail. Katus held his arm at an odd angle.

I scanned the corpses, trying to identify the pieces, or any of the bodies falling away into the depths.

"*Find who did this,*" said a slow, menacing voice. "Bring them to me."

I snapped my gaze back to Katus and Ladon. A third shape rose beyond them, using the cliff edge to pull himself up.

My hands tightened into fists. I couldn't fight the webs growing between them, the redness blooming in my vision, the tingling in my transitioning skin.

A shudder ran through me.

He didn't seem to be harmed. Not a puff of blood.

I sank back down, mouth agape. A veil of dread fell over the three of us.

This couldn't be happening.

Spio and the brothers didn't know. They would be well on their way to getting the commander.

"Where is Ismenus?" said Adaro.

Someone swam closer.

"He's over here, sir," said Katus.

"Injured?"

"He's … it's just his tail, sir."

Somewhere near the cliff, someone moaned.

"Leiagore!" said Ladon. "She's here, sir."

A pause while Adaro went to check.

"Repulsive. Put an end to it."

"Yes, sir," said Ladon.

The sound of Ladon's blade driving through flesh carried across the silence. Leiagore didn't scream.

"Where is Ephyra?" said Adaro.

Beside me, Coho's heartbeat quickened. I placed a hand on his shoulder.

"I'll find her," said Katus.

"Please do. If she is alive, I have a few things to ask her. Namely, why she chose to have me detour past this mine the very day it was due to explode."

Rage pulsed from him, palpable even from this distance.

Ripples spread as Katus and Ladon separated.

Numb shock turned to terror. We had nowhere to go. If we moved, they'd feel it. Even if we fled too quickly for them to give chase, they'd see us, and we would be hunted down later for treason.

None of us dared to poke a head up to see what was happening. We curled inside the small cave, barely fitting, keeping as still as the rocks. I tried to push a sense of hope onto Coho, but his despair clouded over me.

The current stirred closer as one of the guys searched the area.

They were going to find us. We had to get away from here.

A shout erupted. I started, sinking deeper into the cave. But it wasn't directed at us. A scream. More shouts, clashing weapons. The current churned.

I glanced to the guys on either side of me. What was going on?

Coho made as though to check, but I grabbed his arm.

"Who are you?" bellowed Adaro.

Silence.

"Answer him!" shouted Katus.

Ripples erupted as he struck someone.

"We are acting in the name of the queen!" said a merman, in that odd dialect.

"The queen," said Adaro quietly. "Are you referring to *the queen* who has not bothered to show up to rule her kingdom?"

The water churned. Several merpeople were struggling. After a moment, it stopped. Someone grunted.

"Now," said Adaro. "Who sent you?"

"No one. We are defending Queen Evagore's rightful kingdom—"

"Who is your leader?"

"No one—"

A thump. Someone grunted in pain.

With each passing heartbeat, urgency pressed in on me. We had to catch up to Spio, Pontus, and Junior. We couldn't let the commander mobilise the troops. What would happen when Adaro found out his army had been ordered to go home the moment after he was presumed dead? He would know there were traitors in his own army.

Adding to my panic, my lungs gave a spasm. I had to get air immediately, or I would pass out. I closed my eyes, trying to slow my pulse.

Adaro paused in his questioning at the same moment I felt ripples coming from the cliff edge.

"Ephyra!" said Ladon.

"Your Majesty," she said. "I cannot tell you how relieved I am—"

"Yikes," said Katus.

"Only a bit of blood," said Ephyra. "The important thing is that His Majesty is alive."

Coho tensed.

"We've caught the traitors who made the attempt on his life," said Ladon.

A pause.

"Of course," said Ephyra. "You are the allied council from the Moonless City."

"Are they?" said Adaro, in a tone laced with venom.

"We are acting—" said one, but Ephyra cut across him.

"Your Majesty, this group gave me false information. They advised me to take this current in the interest of your safety."

"She is a liar!" said a mermaid.

"Silence!"

Ephyra's rage must have come from fear. She was treading over iron with this story. Still, the emotion was convincing, seeming to draw from the attempt on her king's life.

"It is enough that you have made an act of treason," she said. "Do not make this worse by lying to His Majesty's face."

"This fish is not my king."

Another thump.

"You know treason is punishable by death, scum?" said Ephyra.

Adaro said with finality, "Thank you Ephyra."

For a few heartbeats, everyone fell silent. Fear carried towards us from the captured merpeople. I saw in my mind's eye the snarl curling Adaro's lips and the yellowed fangs beneath.

"Kill them," said Adaro.

A scream. Tails beating on rocks, scrambling to get away.

We seized the opportunity. In unison, Coho, Nobeard, and I pushed from our hiding place.

We darted along the bottom, weaving between rocks and debris. I swiped my hands through the sand, stirring up a cloud to mask us from view.

With luck, the chaos of the fight would hide our presence.

We fled as fast as we could. We dove over the cliff and hugged close to the edge. Nobody called after us. Nobody seemed to follow. We kept going. We stayed at top speed long after we'd lost their sound and feel.

A sharp pain stabbed in my chest. I grunted, slowing abruptly.

My head spun.

Air.

I was going to pass out.

The guys must have felt it, because a hand wrapped around either arm, and we shot for the surface.

When we broke, the breath I wheezed in was agony. I coughed, nearly retching, sure I'd passed out for a moment and inhaled seawater. Tears sprung in my eyes.

The guys weren't doing well, either. Nobeard coughed forcefully enough to bring up phlegm, and Coho floated belly up like a dead fish, breathing rapidly.

I did the same, keeping my ears below the surface to listen for threats. I stared blindly upwards, breathing meditatively.

Not a cloud flecked the blue sky.

The sting all over my body subsided. The burn at my waist faded to a dull ache.

We needed to keep going. We had to catch up with the others before they reached the commander.

Soon, I thought. *Just a few more breaths.*

No one spoke. I waited for my pulse to slow.

My thoughts drifted back to the group of merpeople—now undoubtedly dead.

Echoing my thoughts, Nobeard said, "Who were they?"

His voice was weak, briny.

"They weren't from anywhere close to home," I said. "Looked like the Moonless City."

"Didn't get a look at them," said Nobeard.

"You heard their accents, though?" I said.

"Maybe they really were the allied council," said Coho. "Maybe Ephyra wasn't lying."

"What were they doing there?" said Nobeard.

"Trying to kill Adaro," said Coho. "And they almost did."

"We almost did, too," I said. "We might have succeeded if they didn't get in the way."

"It wasn't their fault," said Nobeard. "It was that cod, Axius. If we'd detonated the mine sooner—"

"Then we might have killed Ephyra along with him," said Coho fiercely.

Nobeard said nothing.

"We should get moving," I said.

Coho grunted and rolled over.

We dove, finding a current at a dark, more hidden layer.

Only then did it fully dawn on me that we had not been caught. Adaro and his two remaining guards had no idea of our involvement.

"This is good," I said.

They turned to me, mouths agape.

"Did you hit your head?" said Nobeard.

"She did," said Coho.

Nobeard pulled me towards him and grabbed my head, checking for an injury.

"No, really," I said, pushing away. "That group took the blame. We can try again, and this time, we know we aren't alone."

"We aren't the only ones trying to assassinate the king," said Coho.

"Exactly."

That group had come from a place where others wanted him dead, too—a kingdom whose queen had disappeared.

We travelled in silence then, conserving breath so we could swim at top speed. I spent the whole time dreading what would happen if we didn't catch up to Spio and the brothers. Would the commander announce Adaro's death? Or did he plan to mobilise the army and tell them why later?

After another breach and still no sign of the others, I wondered aloud whether they were in an alternate current and we'd overtaken them.

Coho and Nobeard didn't have an answer.

Maybe the others were swimming just as quickly.

Eventually, the current changed. We slowed, feeling it out. Something huge waited ahead. A pod of whales?

No. The movement was too precise for whales, too controlled for a large school of fish.

It was merpeople. An army of them.

They'd drawn to a halt.

The three of us exchanged a glance.

There was no way that could be our own army. The guys would have had to make it back at the speed of sound.

But as we drew nearer, I heard the commander's voice, deep and distorted at this range.

"… didn't send the message, who did?"

"It's not possible," whispered Coho.

He pushed faster. I streaked after him.

I wanted to shout to the commander to turn around immediately, but held my tongue. That wouldn't be wise with the army and officers so close.

Shapes materialised. The commander faced Pontus, Junior, and Spio. Whatever they were discussing, it prickled me with worry, even from afar.

"Sir," said Pontus, "when you got that message, we weren't even at the Moonless City yet. Think about it."

They turned as we arrived. Spio held my gaze for a moment. He was trying to communicate something, but the surrounding panic buried it.

The soldiers waited a few fathoms away, obedient and dead silent.

We didn't have time to fret about them overhearing.

I pushed myself nose-to-nose with the commander and said in a low voice, "The king is on his way."

"Adaro—the king—coming? I don't understand."

Pontus grabbed my arm. "What do you mean?"

"I mean, the king is alive and well and on his way here," I hissed.

A terrible moment passed between our group, dread thickening like a layer of scum.

"Where is Strymon?" said the commander.

"Don't worry about Strymon," I said. "You have to turn the army around before Adaro gets here."

"I require my officers for that," said the commander shortly.

"Yes, sir," I said, remembering my place.

The commander turned to the army. Those closest to us had picked up on our strained mood and stared openly.

"Turn around," said the commander. "Pass the message along. Tell the officers to come forwards."

They obeyed.

"What happened?" said the commander.

"That's something I'd like to know," said Pontus.

We told the commander about the explosion and the rebel group.

"He executed them for mutiny," said Nobeard.

The commander shook his head. "This does not explain why Officer Strymon told me—"

"Oh, but it does," said Strymon. "You confirmed every suspicion I had."

We turned to find him approaching, a wide grin splitting his square face.

"The king will be interested to see what you have done since—ah, just in time."

He turned his gaze past us. His mood brightened further.

"Good evening, Your Majesty!"

No.

I sank back as Adaro came into view.

Crimson eyes blazing, his fury was so thick it sent a chill down my spine.

"Bring me the commander!" he shouted.

The commander froze. He stared at Adaro with his jaw unhinged, aura paling like someone about to pass out.

Katus, Ladon, and Ephyra flanked the king. As I'd guessed, Adaro looked no more dishevelled than usual, hair matted and little care put into anything other than the crown on his head. Katus and Ladon had grimaces etched on their faces and scars across their bodies from iron shards. Katus carried his longblade awkwardly with his unbroken arm.

Ephyra bore a long gash on her tail. It had stopped bleeding, but the black scarring was distinct against her perfect figure.

My heart sank. She would have a permanent iron scar, like me.

Behind me, Coho's distress was palpable. He wanted to go to her. But the rage pulsing from the merman between them acted as a wall.

"Explain why you have moved my troops," said Adaro.

The commander opened and closed his mouth, wordless.

"Are you aware, Commander, that an attempt was just made on my life?"

Even Strymon didn't know this much. A bubble escaped his lips.

Behind us, the army had been giving the approaching king their rapt attention. Mumbles broke out at his words.

"Yes," said Adaro, lip curling. "And then I arrive here, in the middle of the open, to find that you have mobilised my army."

"I—sir, I had heard that you were dead—I did not know—I thought, without a king, we should—"

"You received a message saying I was dead?" said Adaro, dangerously quiet.

Strymon whirled. His eyes raked over our group. A mixture of terror and fury flowed from him.

The commander spluttered.

"Your Majesty," said Strymon. "If I may. I suspected the commander was involved in a malicious plot."

Adaro made to interrupt him, but grew silent at the officer's accusation.

"The commander dispatched soldiers on a suspicious mission this morning," said Strymon. "Shortly thereafter, I told him we received a cryptic message from the group that said the mission was complete. The commander confirmed my suspicions when he reacted immediately by mobilising the troops."

Adaro turned back to the commander. "*Is - that - so?*"

Rage tore through me. I wanted to rip Strymon to shreds. Spio must have felt it, because he grabbed me by the arm.

The commander had no defense. No one dared speak.

Panic filled me. A tunnel seemed to close around my ears.

Spio's hand tightened on my arm.

It's okay, his energy said.

But it wasn't. True, Strymon had not specified that we were the secret detachment—but what about the commander?

Spio drifted back towards the army, pulling me with him.

He was right: Adaro's focus was on the commander and Strymon. He had no reason to suspect anyone other than the Moonless City group.

The other guys caught on and followed us backwards.

Could we sink deep inside the army? Maybe someone could lie for us, claim we were here the whole time despite what Strymon said.

Good luck finding someone who will lie to the king's face, I thought.

Adaro turned to Katus and Ladon.

"Ensure this fish gets the same treatment our rebel group did."

I caught the meaning before the commander did. I bit my tongue to stop myself from making a sound.

Katus and Ladon didn't hesitate. After years of obeying Adaro, the order to kill was an ordinary assignment.

The commander shouted and tried to bolt. Katus grabbed him by the tail. With a broken arm, he struggled to hold the older merman. But Ladon was fast. He sliced the commander across the tail with the argillite blade, immobilising him. Blood spilled.

A soundless bubble escaped the commander's mouth.

Tears sprang in my eyes. I turned to see Pontus grab his brother by the arm. Junior seemed about to dive in. But we could do nothing. With the king in front of us and his loyal army behind, protecting a traitor would mean the same fate.

Ladon wrapped a fist in the commander's hair and wrenched his head back. Without hesitation, he drew the blade hard across the commander's throat.

Life drained from the merman's eyes. His aura vanished.

As the stench of blood reached my nose, Adaro said, "I commend your actions, Officer Strymon. Or should I say, Commander Strymon."

Junior hissed. The blood drained from my face.

How had this plan gone so awry?

Strymon stuttered his thanks. He turned back to the army, as though to take in everything he'd just inherited.

His eyes fell on us.

We'd reached the army, but still hovered on the outskirts.

"Your Majesty," he said. "Regarding the soldiers involved—"

"I have already dealt with them."

Strymon glanced between the king and us, eyes narrow. "In punishment?"

"I assure you, they will not be able to try again."

Strymon opened his mouth, but no sound came out.

My teeth bit into my lip. I glanced down. My skin had turned into a demon's. I couldn't calm down enough to revert to normal. I couldn't even tell what I was feeling. Was this grief, rage, or terror?

Adaro peered around Strymon to the army. His eyes flicked over the guys and me, and then continued on.

"Most of my guards perished in the blast, Strymon. I require ten of your best soldiers to accompany me on the way back."

"On the way—where are you—are you returning to Utopia already, sir?"

"I am going to the Moonless City. I have business with their government."

"But—"

"Soldiers, Strymon. I do not have much time."

"Yes, Your Majesty."

Strymon faced the army, looked us over again, then turned back to Adaro.

"Sir, are you certain you apprehended all rebels involved in the plot?"

Adaro's mood flared. "The rebels were a part of the Moonless City allied council. Why do you think I am going to the Moonless City?"

Strymon didn't move or reply, his mind obviously reeling.

"Soldiers, Strymon!"

"I—yes, sir. Right away."

When Strymon turned towards us once more, his eyes blazed dangerously. An uneasy feeling rippled over me.

Someone jostled beside me. Coho shot forwards.

"Your Majesty. I request permission to be in your guard."

Adaro considered. "Yes. This is your husband, is it not, Ephyra?"

"Yes, Your Majesty."

"Very well."

"Sir," said Strymon. "I advise …"

He trailed off as Adaro's temper flared.

"I will choose a few more for your guard, sir," said Strymon. "In the meantime, soldier, you should arm yourself with something more lethal than a crossbow."

"Yes," said Adaro, leaning back to size up Coho. "What a poor choice of weapon."

"Yes, sir," said Coho.

He hesitated, holding Ephyra's gaze, and then spun around.

Seizing the opportunity, we followed him into the unit.

Adaro turned back to Strymon. "I presume you will stop over at the military base tonight, now that you are this far north."

"I—yes—certainly," said Strymon, struggling to compose himself.

Spio placed a hand on my arm. Determination bled from him to me.

"Remember what the commander said," he whispered. "If it goes awry."

I shook my head. He'd said to keep our identities hidden, and try again, and again, and again. *We owe it to those we are fighting for.* But all I could think was that he was dead. He had been murdered because we failed to execute the plan.

"Lysi," said Spio. "This was nobody's fault."

"I know," I said, not looking at him.

The weapons hold, made from the ribcage of a whale, travelled in the centre of the unit and was carried on four sides by manta rays.

"Let's make a quick plan," whispered Pontus. "We can use Coho from the inside. He'll be our—"

"Uh, look, guys," said Coho.

Brow furrowed, he didn't meet our eyes. He stared at the enormous grey wings of the nearest manta ray.

"I, uh … I thought Ephyra was killed back there."

At our silence, he continued.

"I knew we were risking our own lives, but I … I didn't know I was risking my family's. I need to take responsibility. If I'm involved, I make it too easy for Ephyra and my kids to become targets."

For a moment, no one said anything. Then Spio squeezed Coho's shoulder.

"I get it, dude. It's okay."

I nodded. "Your family should come first."

The other guys nodded, too. They clapped him on the back.

Coho relaxed.

I was relieved, somehow. One less casualty.

He grabbed a spear—whalebone, double-pronged at one end, serrated blade at the other.

"I'll be wishing for a victory," he said. "But I can't … I'm sorry, I …"

He lingered on the goodbye.

I wanted to hug him, for some reason. In the short time I'd known him, I felt more comfortable around him than I usually felt around others. I wanted to tell him I hoped someday we could hang out, all of us, back in a free Utopia. Maybe I could take the guys to Eriana Kwai and introduce them to Meela.

I didn't say any of this. I settled with a nod, like the others.

"Sir, it was a pleasure doing business with you," said Spio.

"And you," said Coho with a slight grin.

He turned to leave.

"Hey," I said. "Is Ephyra going to be all right? With …"

I motioned to the place on my tail where Ephyra now bore the fresh burn. It had bothered me since I'd seen it.

For most mermaids, when allure meant so much, the unsightliness of an iron scar was worse than any physical pain. And by Ephyra's perfect hair and graceful demeanour, I knew she prided herself on her beauty.

"She'll live with it," said Coho. "She's tough."

I nodded once. For the sake of Coho and their children, I hoped he was right.

"If she needs—I mean—I know what it's like," I said.

"Thanks." His arm jerked towards me, like he almost hugged me, but he turned away. With a final glance at the others, he left.

The rest of us stayed put, hidden deep inside the army. My chest tightened.

Coho was about to be reunited with his wife, and that was what mattered. Wasn't that the motivation for all of us? The desire to be reunited with those we loved?

A jolt of determination shot through me. We had to try again. This was about more than my need to go home. I was doing this for the families who'd been ripped apart by Adaro's reign.

All the mermaids fighting above surface and the mermen fighting below had loved ones. The commander's family would never see him again. He was one victim of countless. All because of Adaro.

I faced the guys. They had already grabbed new weapons. Spio scrubbed his Trident of Terror clean with an urchin.

I sorted through the weapons hold for the sharpest blade I could find.

"So," I said, "how are we going to do this?"

Spio turned over his trident, examining the prongs.

"Don't worry," he said. "I have a plan."

CHAPTER FIFTEEN
Ravendust

In my dream, Lysi had been so vivid, so real, that I opened my eyes wondering why I felt so warm and dry when I had just been on the beach.

Could people experience smell in dreams? I swore it lingered in my nose, that sweet scent of Lysi's breath, like herbs or fruit.

I let myself stay in a daze as I ate breakfast, reliving the feeling of being with her again. But with every bland spoonful of porridge, reality crashed down on me.

I checked the clock. The others would be waiting if I didn't hurry. I stuffed a water bottle, a few carrots, and a sweater in my backpack.

I stepped onto the porch and closed the door without saying goodbye to my parents. A chill had descended between us since I stormed from the house the day before. I supposed

I hadn't helped matters by getting caught snooping for my father's book.

Starting down the driveway, I clung to the comfort of the dream. Lysi and I had been alone on the beach, sitting side-by-side like when we were kids. She told me to stop moving my legs so it would be easier for them to turn into a tail. When nothing happened, she grew frustrated, saying she'd swim away without me if I didn't hurry. Her eyes blazed red, and her teeth grew long and pointed, but I wasn't afraid. I told her to try kissing me to trigger the transformation. Her anger faded, then, and I was left staring into two intoxicating, sapphire blue eyes. I leaned closer—

"Mind if I join you?"

I whirled around to find Tanuu at my shoulder. He threw his arms up in jest, as though to protect his face from my reflexes.

"Stop doing that!" I said.

He dropped his arms, smiling apologetically.

"I thought we were going to meet at the cliff top," I said.

"I know. I thought we could walk together."

"Oh. All right."

I stuffed my hands in my pockets and kept walking, pretending to be oblivious to the way he grabbed for my hand. Wispy clouds drizzled on us, leaving droplets in my hair.

This dream had been blissfully different from usual. I'd dreamt of her a few times since returning from the Massacre. Usually they were violent, nightmarish reminders of that month at sea. They always ended with Lysi lying dead in a pool of blood. The face of her murderer varied among Dani, Adaro, Annith, myself, my father, or even the mysterious shadow of the Host.

This time, I had woken up with my heart pounding for an entirely different reason. It left me with a deep longing, curled on my side, trying desperately to go back to sleep and finish—

"Did you tell your parents yet?" said Tanuu.

I looked at him sharply. "Excuse me?"

"Did you tell them you're gonna use your blood to free the Host?"

"Oh." I forced my mind back to the present, watching my feet as we wandered a deer trail. "They think I'm wasting my time. I don't even know if I'm a descendant."

The bitterness in my voice was thick. I'd wanted an extra day to try again, but with the Massacre departure looming the next day, we had to search for the crypt.

"Man, they still don't believe you?"

I shook my head. "My mother just gets mad when I bring it up."

A fallen hemlock blocked our path. Tanuu hopped over and offered a hand to help me. I accepted out of politeness.

"So they really think the Massacres are a better idea," he said.

"I don't know. I don't get it. Nobody seems to understand that mermaids can think. Everyone's going on like they're an infestation."

"I think they do understand. They're too afraid to admit it. They can't accept that we're not the only intelligent creatures."

We continued in silence for a few minutes, padding over the dirt and twigs until we reached the meadow.

"Wanna come over tonight?" said Tanuu as we traipsed through the grass. "My parents are out. I'll make you dinner. It'd be nice to spend time just the two of us, you think?"

I concentrated extra hard on the grass at my feet. "What are your parents doing?"

"It's cribbage night or something. I dunno. Whatever old people do on a Monday. Does it matter?"

We stopped at the edge of the beach. The lava rock swelled below, dark and sinister. The rising tide crashed through the divots, sending sprays higher than our heads. A cold, salty mist sprinkled my face.

I met Tanuu's hopeful eyes. I thought of Annith's words, and how terrible it was that I kept dragging him along, letting him think I'd come back to him one day.

"Tanuu, I don't think it's a good idea that I come over."

His smile faltered. "Why not?"

I took a breath, opened my mouth, but no sound came out.

My hesitation made his eyes widen in panic.

"No. Meela, I know you've been through a lot, and if you need space, I'll give it to you."

"I know you think I just need time to come around. But that's not it."

He continued to stare at me in horror. I hated myself for drawing this out.

I drew a breath and tried again. "We … We need to break up."

The words sat heavy on my tongue, like a bitter taste.

Tanuu blinked. His face sagged.

He sat on a boulder with a thud. "What did I do wrong?"

"Nothing. It's not—"

"Is it my cooking? I can stop making you dinner."

"No, Tanuu, there's nothing wrong with you."

"Then what is it? I don't get it."

I twisted my fingers in a knot. Would the truth hurt him even more? Or would it be easier for him to accept?

"If you need time to recover from the Massacre," he said, "that's fine. I waited a month while you were away. I can keep waiting. As long as you need."

I shook my head. Why did he have to be so selfless? His sincerity was killing me.

"It's not a matter of needing time to recover," I said. "I don't want you to wait around, hanging onto the hope that I'll change my mind. You need to move on. I want you to be happy."

My voice broke. He'd whipped out his number one defence against me: his deep brown, sad-baby-seal eyes. They stared at me with watery confusion and defeat. My chest contracted.

"Tanuu, you're one of my best friends, and I love you. But I've been a terrible girlfriend."

At this, the panic on his face worsened.

"Wait, is there another guy?"

"No! Of course not. I'd never cheat on you."

But I thought of Lysi, how desperately I'd wanted to kiss her, and wondered if that were completely true.

"Well, I don't think you've been a terrible girlfriend."

"I have. I've been putting minimal effort into this relationship, and you deserve someone who'll give it everything she has. You deserve someone who loves you back in the same way."

He dropped his face into his hands. "I don't understand where I went wrong."

I sat next to him. "Tanuu, please understand me. It's not you. I have … personal things. It's hard to explain."

Tell him, said a voice in my head. *Just tell him. It'll make it less painful if he understands.*

My mouth opened and closed several times.

I couldn't keep Lysi a secret forever. I'd have to tell people eventually. Why not start with Tanuu? I trusted him, probably as much as I trusted Annith and my parents.

My heart rate quickened, like I was about to dive off a cliff.

"Hey," said a voice.

We looked up to see Blacktail beating her way through the long grass. Her smile faltered when she saw our expressions.

She seemed to guess what we'd been discussing, because she didn't give any indication that she knew something was wrong.

"Annith here yet?" she said, hooking her thumbs on the straps of her backpack.

"No," I said.

Tanuu stood without looking at either of us. He moved closer to the beach to stare at the spouts of water that rose with the tide.

"Don't get too close," said Blacktail. She made a convulsive movement with her arm, as though about to grab Tanuu and haul him away.

Tanuu raised an eyebrow. "What, are you worried about me?"

"No."

"Are, too."

She turned away. "Well, yes, but you're useless near the ocean, aren't you?"

Tanuu almost cracked a smile, but caught my eye and turned away again.

"Here comes Annith," I said, for lack of anything better to say.

We met her halfway across the field.

"Ready?" she said cheerily.

I nodded. Tanuu said nothing. Blacktail grunted.

Annith gave me a quizzical look, but I jerked my head slightly.

"Uh, I found out my family's always lived here," said Annith. "I guess that makes me a descendant of Eriana."

I stared at her. I'd momentarily forgotten Blacktail and Annith had been trying to get the same information the night before.

"That's great," I said. "I mean, if you're all right with ... a bit of your blood ..."

"Don't be dumb," said Annith. "Of course."

"I asked, too," said Blacktail. "No go. Somewhere along, my family came from Alaska."

"At least we've got Annith," I said. "I still haven't found out about mine."

Annith was staring at Tanuu, who stood apart from us, arms crossed, face uncharacteristically sullen.

"The Ravendust bushes definitely go into the woods over there," said Blacktail, motioning to the left.

She trekked onwards without waiting for a response. We followed, stepping high through the grass. Annith caught up with Blacktail, presumably to ask in undertones what was going on.

Tanuu continued brooding, misery seeping from him like a toxic gas. Trailing behind, I felt guiltier with each passing second.

Once in the woods, we stopped at each Ravendust bush and turned on the spot to locate the next. It was hard to tell whether we were following a path or jumping from plant to plant like a weird egg hunt.

The silence deepened as we zigzagged through the woods, sometimes looping in a circle, other times guessing the direction of the next plant and then happening across one a few minutes later. We passed by my house, and then the training base, and then pushed so deeply into the woods that it became hard to move without needing to clamber over huge logs and rocks. We paused here and there to snack on huckleberries, but by the afternoon we were starving and tired and out of water. We stumbled more frequently as it became exhausting to lift our feet. My coat had snagged on so many branches that I was sure I'd ripped it beyond repair.

Blacktail cursed as a low-hanging branch jabbed her in the eye.

"Maybe we should split up to cover more ground," she mumbled.

"Split up how?" said Tanuu. "There's one path. It's not like it forks."

Blacktail smacked the next branch out of the way with extra force. "I mean the next time we don't know which direction to take."

"Speaking of directions," said Annith. "Where are we?"

Nobody answered.

I hadn't spoken in so long that it took me a moment to find my voice.

"I'm sure we'll see a landmark soon," I said into the waspish silence.

I quickened my pace, putting distance between us as though to buffer their moodiness.

Eventually, we broke into a meadow. The land dropped off at the opposite end, apparently a steep bank or cliff. I hoped it would give me some indication of where we'd ended up.

A lone Ravendust bush peeked out of the centre, surrounded by grass and weeds.

I hadn't made it five steps into the meadow when a crack rang through the air and Annith let out a piercing scream.

I whirled around to see her frizzy hair disappear into the ground.

I lunged for her. "Annith!"

A splash, a moment where she stopped screaming, and then she surfaced, gasping and choking.

She'd landed in a pit, like a grave dug large enough to hold a grizzly. Around her, what must have been a cover of thatched branches had crumbled in with her. A layer of muddy, thigh-deep water roiled under Annith's flailing limbs.

For a brief, absurd moment, I wondered if she'd landed in the fissure in the earth we'd been searching for. Then sense took over as Tanuu threw himself on his stomach and reached into the pit.

"It's okay," he said. "It's an old trap. Are you all right?"

Annith was making strange gasping sounds, like she wanted to keep screaming but was too busy coughing.

"No," she said. "The sticks."

Panic rose in my chest. "The what? Sticks? What did she say?"

I dropped to my knees. Blacktail flung herself beside Tanuu and stretched out a hand, too.

"Annith, grab on," she said.

Annith reached trembling arms up to Tanuu and Blacktail. She whimpered in pain as they lifted her from the water.

I leaned down to grab her leg, and had to stifle a cry. Several of the thatched branches had sliced her open. Her jeans had torn, and one of the sticks still clung to her, penetrating through skin. Blood seeped through the wound.

Tanuu swore. He removed his jacket and wrapped it around her trembling shoulders.

We eased Annith onto the grass. She was breathing fast, panicking.

I knelt beside her.

"Annith, hold my hand. Try to slow your breathing."

She inhaled unsteadily a few times, gripping my hand like a vice.

Blacktail used her dagger to slice away the material around the protruding branch. I watched her face for a reaction, not wanting to look at the wound.

She stayed calm, thoughtful.

"I'm going to remove it," she said, and without waiting for anyone's response, she pulled the stick swiftly from Annith's leg.

Annith cried out, the sound filling the empty meadow.

"It's not deep," said Blacktail.

She unscrewed the lid of her water bottle and spilled what was left over the wound.

"See why we have hunting laws?" she said with a rare note of venom. "This trap is an illegal—"

"What's that supposed to mean?" said Tanuu.

Blacktail set her jaw, focusing on cleaning Annith's wound.

"Are you saying my father set this trap up?" said Tanuu.

"Of course not," said Blacktail. "But you were angry at my father for enforcing the law. Well, this is why."

Tanuu scoffed. "There's a difference between setting up an illegal trap that can hurt someone, and accidentally trespassing while trying to stop your family from starving."

Blacktail glowered at the wound.

"Does it need stitches?" I said.

"She's lucky," said Blacktail shortly. "The wood was old and rotting. It broke before it penetrated too far."

"She should still get it checked out," said Tanuu.

I chanced a look at it. The wound looked messy to me, the skin mangled. Blood seeped out, thick and dark. My stomach churned. I lifted my eyes to Annith's pale, damp face as Blacktail covered the wound.

"Annith, I'm sorry. This shouldn't have ..." I trailed off at the deadly expression on her face.

"No," she said. "It shouldn't have. But that's what happens when you keep wandering around places you're not supposed to with no real plan."

She wrapped Tanuu's jacket tighter to try and stop herself shivering.

"Searching these places is the best plan I have," I said, keeping my voice calm.

Annith turned her stony face away to watch Tanuu, who'd returned to the last Ravendust bush—a meagre, knee-high sapling.

No one said anything for what felt like a very long time. A thrush whistled tirelessly overhead, finding no response. I removed my backpack and handed Annith my sweater as an extra layer.

"Let's get you home. We can try again tomorrow," I said weakly.

Annith and Blacktail raised their eyebrows at me. With the Massacre departing tomorrow, time was running out.

I was considering whether I should come back and continue searching by myself that night when Tanuu gave an exasperated sigh.

"This is pointless. Are we seriously following clumps of bushes and hoping they lead us somewhere useful?"

"Do you have a better idea?" I said.

He kicked the sapling at his knee. "Ravendust bushes don't grow out of leviathan venom! They grow out of dirt and water and sunlight, like a normal - *freaking - ordinary - plant*!"

He attacked the bush, grabbing it and fighting to pull it from the ground. When it didn't budge, he kicked it a few more times.

"If you don't want to be here, no one's keeping you," I said, clenching my fists.

"We just keep running into dead ends," said Annith, with hardly more patience than Tanuu. "No one believes us, no one is helping us, nobody even wants us to succeed. The Massacre is going to happen tomorrow and we're no closer to finding this crypt. Why are we bothering?"

"Because the Massacres don't work, and we're the only ones who seem to see that!"

"Don't they work?" said Annith. "We killed more sea demons than ever on ours. Women have a lot more success out there—and that was only the first go at it. Imagine what the next batch will be able to do."

I blinked. Was she serious?

"Annith, the number of kills we made doesn't mean anything. Not when the Massacres still result in that many deaths."

"Maybe soon it won't involve so many deaths. With a new training master, there could still be hope."

I looked from her to Tanuu, to Blacktail. Even Blacktail looked mutinous.

"You're telling me you're okay with sending girls like us to battle every year?" I said.

"Why do you feel so responsible for those girls?" said Tanuu. "They're not little kids. You're only a few months older than some of the ones going out tomorrow."

"I'm one Massacre older," I said. "That's the difference. So yes, I am completely responsible for them. Just as much as you two are."

I looked between Annith and Blacktail.

"Sometimes sacrifices need to be made," said Annith. "That's the nature of war."

"This isn't about sacrifices. It's about making peace."

"What if the Massacres were a clean victory?" said Tanuu. "What if Mujihi can train those girls—"

"Human deaths aren't the only tragic ones!"

The words burst from my mouth so loudly, the wilderness around us seemed to still. The thrush stopped singing.

I regretted my words instantly. Did their expressions darken when they looked at me? Were they wondering if I'd lied about my motivations?

I hadn't lied. I simply didn't tell them the entire truth.

I turned away from their stares and stomped onwards, not sure where I was going.

Annith's low voice carried across the empty meadow. "Why do you care about that mermaid so much?"

I stopped, stiffening. I took a second to compose myself before rounding on her, chest heaving. "Don't – you – dare –"

Annith waved a hand towards Tanuu and Blacktail. "Don't act all scandalized. They were going to find out anyway."

I stepped towards her. "Wouldn't you try to save me, Annith? If I was on the enemy's side, would you shoot me because *it's the nature of war*? Would you shoot Rik?"

"Of course not. But that's … that's different."

I felt my lip curl into a snarl. When I spoke, my voice quivered. "You don't understand in the slightest."

Annith's eyes narrowed. I felt Tanuu and Blacktail's stares. Tanuu's brow was pinched—but Blacktail's mouth formed a silent, "Oh."

She had seen Lysi aboard the Bloodhound last month.

Something like panic seized my chest. My throat tightened until I felt like air couldn't pass through. Why did I have to mention Rik? Did I just blurt my feelings for Lysi to all three of them?

The thrush picked up his song again, mockingly cheerful.

I turned away so the others wouldn't see my eyes spring with tears, and continued through the grass.

"Take Annith home," I said. "Get her dry."

I crossed the field. The opposite end turned out to be a steep hill that descended into town. Closest to us was the back of the grocery store, which faced a paved lot. The other businesses there had closed indefinitely. I saw Blue Kestrel Bistro, the post office, bank, gift shop, bakery, and Windy Spit Pub. Even the gas station had closed after running dry. We had nothing left. Would the grocery store last? Could my people survive on the land alone, with no fish and so much of the wild game hunted out?

Footsteps swished in an awkward rhythm through the grass behind me. I turned to see Tanuu and Blacktail holding Annith between them.

"Take her down there and use a phone," I said, and then added stubbornly, "I'm going to keep looking."

They didn't argue. I turned away as they began a slow, laboured descent.

I trudged around the meadow, trying to find more Ravendust bushes, perhaps leading away from the town. When none crossed my path, I stopped, winding my fingers through my hair in frustration.

The bushes must have continued right through where the town now sat. I considered going around and picking up my search on the other side of the lot, but even the thought was exhausting. What if the bushes had been dug up in so many places that the path was no longer distinguishable?

A nagging voice in my head suggested there was no path to begin with, and Tanuu was right. The only remarkable thing about these plants was their ability to blacken your skin and clothes if you brushed against the leaves.

Daring to check over the hill, I confirmed that the others had gone.

I didn't need them. If they thought this wasn't important, then they were holding me back.

The thrush sang relentlessly, calling for a friend that wasn't there. I whistled back. The bird hesitated, probably wondering whether he wanted to sing to a mate who was so off-key. After a pause, he replied.

"Just you and me," I said.

Eriana came to mind, and how she'd died after a lifetime protecting the flora and fauna of this island. I wouldn't let her down.

I returned to the pit trap. Maybe I wasn't justified in thinking whoever dug the pit deserved a kick in the head. They'd been trying to get food. They wouldn't know a few unsuspecting teenagers would stumble on it—or in it.

Still, it angered me that they'd left it abandoned. What if we'd been kids playing in the woods? We were lucky we'd been able to pull Annith out right away.

I squatted next to it. The muddy water left me unable to see the bottom, but based on how Annith had landed, the pit was deep. This hunter had been after a deer, perhaps a bear. The thatched branches on top must have been disturbed enough that animals knew this patch of land was suspicious. Annith probably hadn't been watching her step when she'd fallen in.

Not for the first time, I decided animals were a lot smarter than people.

Broken branches and moss hung from the sides, half submerged. Behind them, rocks peeked through.

Frowning, I moved a few branches out of the way. The pit was lined with stones, stacked uniformly all the way around, creating a rectangular hole in the ground. This trap wasn't some random crater a desperate hunter made. Someone had put a lot of time and effort into it—and from the weathered appearance of the stones, with roots and weeds pushing through the cracks, they'd done so a long time ago.

An irregular stone caught my eye. I sat on the edge of the pit and leaned down, squinting at it. The stone had an engraving. A fanged animal head, jaws parted, with a long, narrow eye.

I yanked the bone dagger from my jeans.

There it was. The same head had been etched into the dagger we'd found beneath the Enticer. What did it mean? What was their connection?

I flipped it over to examine the other engravings. Once again, I felt that strange sense of familiarity. I rubbed my fingers over the trees on either side of the hole.

A long moment passed before I lifted my eyes, not feeling any surge of enlightenment. The world had darkened a little. The sun was setting.

For good measure, I stretched my leg into the pit and kicked at the stone with the engraving. It didn't move. Neither did the ones surrounding it. I leaned in to test all the stones I could reach. They were all wedged securely in the earth, roots and weeds sprouting between them.

"Not hiding any secrets?"

The thrush whistled.

I considered jumping down to poke around inside, but the idea was unappealing. Fat raindrops created rings in the water, now littered with decaying plant life. A cool breeze had picked up. Besides, the stone walls were built so precisely that I'd never be able to climb them to get back out. I'd need a rope.

Legs still dangling into the pit, I looked over my shoulder, grasping for ideas. Maybe we hadn't exhausted the trail of Ravendust bushes. Did the path fork somewhere? I could backtrack to the last few bushes and make a wide circle around each one. Maybe I'd find a whole new path to follow.

My feet and legs were throbbing from walking all day. I turned back to the pit, glancing between the stone and the dagger in my hand. This serpent head had to mean something.

Struck with inspiration, I stood.

Adette had mentioned a snake on Dani's wrist. What if it was the same one? Would Dani have explained the meaning of the symbol to any of the trainees?

It was a start, and a fresh one after spending all day going in circles.

We'd trekked a good deal across the island, so it took more than an hour to get back to the road—plenty of time to brood over being abandoned by my friends. I was stupid to let even a tiny part of me hope Tanuu and Blacktail would come back.

So much for Tanuu's undying support for the mission.

I reminded myself that I had just dumped him, and he'd had a crush on me since we were in kindergarten. He had every right to be miserable.

Maybe this was my fault for choosing today to dump him. But what was I supposed to do? Fake it until we were done with all of this and I didn't need his help anymore? No, I'd done the right thing. Every day I let him think we were fine, I was lying to him.

So if I'd done the right thing, why did I feel so guilty?

Relationships suck, I thought.

When I finally made it to Anyo's, I pounded on the door a little too vigorously.

Nobody answered, but a light shone through the window. I pounded again.

"Adette," I shouted. "I need to talk to you."

A long minute later, the door opened. Adette still wore her training clothes. Her eyelids looked heavy, her face clammy and pale.

"I'm sorry, I just have a question," I said.

She waited for me to continue with one hand on the door, not inviting me inside.

"Everything all right?" I said.

She lifted a shoulder, still not saying anything. The house was dead quiet.

I tried to peer around her. "Can I come in?"

Adette seemed to have a momentary, inward struggle. Then she stood aside and let me in.

The house felt like a roaring fireplace. I couldn't tell if I was just cold from being outside all day, or if they kept it abnormally warm.

"Where's your father?"

"Sleeping."

The weakness in her voice added to her air of exhaustion. I glanced around the empty kitchen. The clock showed just past 9:30. I decided to keep this short in case she wanted to go to bed.

"Adette, I need to ask you about the symbol on Dani's wrist."

Her face showed no sign of emotion. I continued.

"Do you remember what it looks like? You said it was a snake head, right?"

She nodded.

Watching her expression, I showed her the bone dagger, pointing to the animal head on the hilt.

"Does it look like this?"

Her eyes widened. At last, I seemed to have caught her interest.

"That's the one?" I said.

She met my eye, nodding once.

"How do you know it's a snake?"

"She said so."

It couldn't have been coincidence that it was a serpent. We didn't even have serpents on Eriana Kwai. This had to be related to the leviathan. But how?

"Do you know what it means?" I said, my heart beating faster.

She hesitated, seeming to contemplate something.

"One sec," she said, and left the room.

Her soft footsteps carried all the way down the hall. The clock ticked, soft and loud on alternating beats.

I pocketed the dagger and sat at the table, relieving my aching feet.

Sitting on someone's jacket, with nowhere to rest my arms on the cluttered table, I noticed how messy the house was. Dirty dishes were piled high in the sink, and I became aware of the smell coming off them. Fat, black flies buzzed around the kitchen. The floor was covered in mud. I checked the bottom of my boots, sure I'd just dragged more across the linoleum on my way to the table.

I checked the clock again. It struck me as odd that Anyo would have gone to bed already when his daughter was still awake, and the sun hadn't even set.

After a couple of minutes, Adette returned with the book Anyo had shown us.

"It's in here, too," she said. "Papa told me it's an ancient symbol once used by hunters to show their remorse for killing."

She flipped through the pages, searching for it.

"Is it to do with Eriana's punishment?" I said. "For betraying the Gaela?"

Adette glanced up at me with raised eyebrows.

"Your father told me the story of Eriana," I said. "How she used her abilities to kill all those caribou."

"Yes," said Adette. "The symbol is supposed to show the Gaela that the hunters remember what happened, and that they won't abuse the natural order of things the way Eriana did. It's a promise that they'll only take what they need—enough to keep themselves from going hungry."

She landed on a page towards the end. There was the fanged animal head.

But how much did Dani know?

"Is that it? It's just a symbol to remember the Aanil Uusha's punishment?"

Adette looked taken aback. "That ice storm was a huge tragedy. It killed all of Eriana's people."

"I know," I said quickly. "That's not what I meant."

A loud snore and a cough came from the living room behind us. Adette's face drained of colour. She whirled around, dropping the book on the table.

I started to ask what was wrong, but Adette had already dashed to the couch. Its back was to the kitchen so I couldn't see the occupant, but a wave of understanding crashed over me.

I rose from my chair. "Adette, is your father all right?"

"He's just tired," she said.

"He's not. Or you wouldn't look so worried."

She adjusted a woollen blanket over him.

"Do you need help?"

"No. He just … he had a lot to drink."

I joined her at the couch, surprised. I'd never known Anyo to be a drinker. He was lying on his back, one arm dangling to the side, as though he were simply taking a nap.

"How long has this been going on?"

Adette didn't answer. She adjusted her father's arms over the blanket.

"I had no idea," I whispered. "I'm sorry. Have you told anyone?"

She shook her head once, not meeting my eye.

"You don't have to take on this responsibility alone. My family can help."

I couldn't let her deal with this by herself—not when she already had so much to worry about.

She watched her father's chest rise and fall, keeping her face turned away from me.

"Here, let me help you clean up," I said. "This place could use …"

I scanned the floor. Despite the mess, I didn't see a single bottle of liquor or beer, or anything else that might have indicated that Adette's father had been drinking himself into a stupor.

A single teacup sat on the coffee table. It was tipped on its side, the bottom rimmed with the remnants of a dark tea.

I picked it up. The dregs were thick, almost black.

"Adette."

She saw what I'd found and jumped.

"He hasn't been drinking," I said. "This is Ravendust powder!"

"It's not—it's just a little—he needed to—" said Adette, stammering.

"You slipped it to him!"

Though I'd meant for my tone to be scolding, it came out more surprised and awed.

Her mouth opened and closed.

"I needed to help him," she said, voice high.

"Why?"

"He hasn't been sleeping. He's been having …"

Her voice broke. She began tucking the blanket around Anyo again.

"Anxiety?" I said.

She hesitated, and then nodded.

"My mother had anxiety, too," I said. "For years after my brother died. She still gets it sometimes."

Adette's watery eyes met mine.

"He panics," she said in a shaky voice. "I'm all he has."

Behind the exhaustion, her face was youthful and pure. She had so many responsibilities already.

Anyo must have felt some sense of control over his daughter's fate when he'd been training master. Now that he'd lost the title, reality must have hit him full force.

"We can get him help from a doctor," I said.

Adette took the teacup from me. When she looked down, a tear fell from her face and landed in the cup. She nodded.

"Just promise me you won't keep knocking him out," I said.

She almost smiled.

"Where did you even hear about using Ravendust powder?"

Very few knew of its power as a sedative. I'd learned about it from Annith on the Massacre, and she'd been the only one who'd known, then.

Adette lifted one shoulder. "Things get around."

I frowned. One of the girls from my Massacre must have shared the knowledge. I hoped it had been for First Aid purposes. Either way, now all the trainees knew a pinch of Ravendust could knock a person out for hours.

"I want you to take him to a doctor, all right?" I said. "I'm going to check in on you. No more knocking him out. That'll only make him sick."

She nodded.

Together, we cleaned up the piles of clothes and garbage, washed dishes, and swept the floor. By then, Adette seemed less distraught—though she looked ready to collapse. My own body felt slow and heavy.

"Do you want me to stay the night?"

She shook her head. "I'm fine. I'll go to bed and Papa will be awake in a few hours."

I hugged her, smoothing her hair away from her tired face.

"Call my house if you ever need anything. You know my mother would be happy to make you dinner, right?"

"Thanks, Meela."

It was well past midnight when I left.

As I stepped into the night, reality rippled through me with a violent shiver. The Massacre departure was mere hours away.

How many others were still awake? Were Tanuu, Annith, and Blacktail in their warm beds, sleeping soundly, resigned to the fate of those girls?

The bone dagger sat heavy in my jeans. A hunting symbol.

Even knowing this, I was no closer to finding the crypt. I was alone, one of thousands of civilians who would watch helplessly as the warriors departed tomorrow.

Time had run out. Had I really thought I could stop the Massacre—a tradition that had been ongoing since my father was a kid? It was ingrained in our society. Why had I deluded myself into thinking I could single-handedly change that?

Hunched against the cold breeze, I began the long walk home.

My time as a Massacre warrior was up. Now I was supposed to sit back and watch—and root for those girls to slay every last demon.

CHAPTER SIXTEEN
Harpoon of Death and Teeth and Stuff

"Let me get this straight," said Pontus. "We're going to lure an entire shoal of sharks into the target's path—"

"Yep."

"—surround him—"

"Yep."

"—then impale him with iron?"

"If the sharks don't kill him first."

Spio wrapped his bag with rope. He'd stuffed it full. With what, I didn't know. But it smelled like death.

We were back at the Moonless City military base. Commander Strymon and his officers had taken a day to regroup, planning to move south again that afternoon. Spio, Nobeard, Pontus, and I had ducked inside the weapons cave, masked by a calculated eruption of panic outside. Junior had yet to arrive.

"You never explained how we're getting the sharks," said Nobeard.

"Lysi and I will do it," said Spio.

Bubbles flew out of my mouth. "We will?"

"Yes."

I stared.

He turned to the group. "We have experience in this area."

I supposed it was true.

He told them about the time we managed to separate a baby orca from its pod. I drifted to the cave entrance to check for eavesdroppers and signs of Junior.

Chaos roiled as the loose great white snapped at anything made of meat. The decoy worked better than expected. The shark had not been fed breakfast yet, and Spio had gotten carried away by "accidentally" spilling dead fish everywhere after we set her free.

I smirked as Strymon shouted at the trainers to hurry up and tame it.

Meeting hadn't been possible since we got back, with Strymon and his officers tailing us like suckerfish. This meant Spio had been unable to tell us the full extent of his plan.

It would have been ideal to spend time plotting the attack, but that wasn't an option. A group from the Moonless City had come to deliver weapons at dawn, and we overheard them tell Strymon that Adaro left for his trip back to Utopia.

We had to act before he got too far ahead.

I twirled my weapon in my fists—a longblade of wood, slate, and whalebone. It was no Iron Hook of Doom, but at least it was easier to swing. Plus, it would float if I dropped it.

Spio's two remaining iron weapons, his own hook and the trident, were now in Strymon's sleeping quarters. One of Strymon's first actions as commander had been to confiscate them.

Across the military base, the shark knocked over a pile of supplies. Broken ropes dangled from her jaw. Bodies darted through the tumult, weapons and ropes flying between streams of bubbles. The dolphins cackled, spinning in their enclosure.

Satisfied everyone was still occupied, I sank back into the darkness.

"… taught it to roll over on command," said Spio. "It was awesome. But then the mom found us."

"There was also the time you lured that salmon shark to school," I said, before he could get to the part where we had to swim for our lives and ended up trapped under a reef.

Pontus and Nobeard studied us. I got the impression they were trying to decide whether to take us seriously.

"How do you plan to find a shoal of sharks?" said Pontus.

Spio lifted his bag in answer.

When Pontus still projected confusion, I said, "We'll feel for signs of a feeding frenzy. Then we'll lure them away from it with … whatever dead things Spio has in that bag."

"It could be days until we find a frenzy close enough!" said Pontus.

"With a wide enough range, we'll find one," I said. "We'll keep an eye for gulls above the surface. That'll give us a league in all directions, no matter what else we sense on the current."

Nobeard hummed thoughtfully. "Didn't consider the birds. Sharp idea, mates."

"Of course it is," I said. "Spio and I thought of it."

Spio raised a hand, which I met with an enthusiastic high-five.

"So keep your eyes and feelers awake," said Spio.

He pulled his bag over his chest and gripped his weapon, a spear of serrated stone. I glimpsed a deep gash on the inside of his arm. I hadn't noticed it before, and hoped it wasn't iron-made from the explosion.

I glanced back, wishing Junior would hurry.

The finality of the plan wrapped thickly around us. Last time, we had left on an order from the commander. This time, we were officially committing desertion.

At this point, I was ready for it. I couldn't serve under Adaro's rule any longer—especially not with Strymon as commander.

Outside was still complete bedlam. What was keeping Junior? My nerves tightened. We couldn't miss our chance. The shark would only be a diversion for so long. Plus, we couldn't let Adaro get too far north—

I slapped my forehead. "The military line!"

For a moment, the guys stared at me in confusion. Then Pontus emitted a wave of distress.

"We're going north," he said. "The border."

Spio and Nobeard caught on.

"We can fight them," said Spio.

"We can go around," said Nobeard.

"No," said Pontus. "They would slay us if we fought, and going around would add a day to the journey and make us lose the target."

"We could sneak across," said Spio. "We'll find a group of travellers—"

The cave darkened. A presence had appeared at the entrance, dimming the outside light and blocking the current.

Junior. He raised his arms in triumph. Spio's iron hook and trident were clenched in his fists.

"Ha!" I said.

"Nice job, little bro," said Pontus.

Junior glanced back. "They've got ropes over the great white."

Requiring no encouragement, we bolted for the exit. I snatched a sheet of rawhide off a work surface before ducking outside; I had a plan for the military line.

We rose, sticking to the ridge like crabs. The rocks did little to hide us.

"Pull hard!" someone shouted across the way.

We didn't stop to discuss a route. If there was a lull in the commotion, anyone would be able to feel our movement.

We scrambled from the water. The rocks grazed the surface on this side, causing violent waves. Any soldier who might have been lounging would do so on the other side, where it was calm. I hoped no one would look over and see us.

The spray crashed over me, noisy and disorienting. I held my breath against it. Each swell pushed my body in a different direction. I locked my fingers and the hilt of my blade around whatever I could find, dragging myself forwards. I recalled Spio saying something about being "a jelly in a propeller" up here. He hadn't been wrong.

My ears rang as I plunged back into the water. The guys dropped beside me in an explosion of bubbles.

We spun to face the ridge, weapons up, waiting to see if anyone had followed.

The world was silent. The current pushed at us from the northeast, steady and calm.

"Let's go," said Pontus.

We swam hard, following the plankton to the strongest current we could find.

After some time, Pontus said, "I'm concerned about our numbers. Even with Coho, there weren't many of us."

"Mate, we'll have about a million sharks on our side," said Nobeard.

"Sharks don't pick sides," said Pontus.

He did have a point. Controlling the shoal would take effort, and even if that went smoothly, we'd be five against the ten soldiers Adaro had taken.

"The Moonless City had a rebel group," I said.

"Yes," said Pontus, "but they're dead."

"There might be more."

"How do we find out?"

No one answered.

I thought back to the group at the mine. That one mermaid had swum by me and whispered something. What was it?

"*Para la reina*," I said.

The guys stared at me like I'd grown legs.

"I saw a mermaid before the explosion happened at the mine. She was one of the rebels. She said those words."

"What does it mean?" said Pontus.

"I don't know. I think it was a code. She was seeing if we were in on the plan. When I didn't respond, she disappeared."

We shared a moment of unease. Did we have time to find help? Would the risk be worth it? Even if there were other merpeople who wanted Adaro dead, most of them would see treason as a crime worthy of its punishment.

"I say we go back to the Moonless City and start yelling those words," said Spio. "See who comes forwards."

I didn't need to threaten him out of that plan. The guys knew as well as I did that we didn't have time to look for help. We had to keep going or the king would get too far ahead.

After a long silence, Nobeard said, "I want to make sure something's known. Last time, if it all went belly up—and it did—we were hidden. This time is different. Once we attack him, his whole crew will see us. We're open mutineers."

Though I knew this already, a knot twisted in my stomach. Best case, we would still have to deal with those loyal to Adaro after his death. Worst case, we'd be executed for treason.

I thought of Meela, and how much she had suffered because of this war. I thought of my brother stationed on the other side of the world. I thought of all the soldiers in the army, and all the merpeople who had been killed—both fighting for Adaro's crusade, and for opposing him.

"It's worth the risk," I said.

"Agreed," said Junior.

The other guys gave no signs of fear.

"Onwards, then," said Nobeard.

"What's the rest of the plan, Spio?" said Pontus. "What happens once you and Lysi get control of the sharks?"

"I think *control* is a loosely defined—" I began, then Spio jabbed me in the ribs.

"Allow me to explain," said Spio with an air of professionalism. "Lysi and I will chase the sharks towards the target. We'll drive them through his group like a harpoon, same as Medusa's army did to us. We won't have enough merman-power to make the sharks circle the target like they did, but that doesn't matter, because—"

"Can you drive the sharks in so you at least isolate him?" said Junior.

"If we can peel him away, we'll try," said Spio. "But I'm guessing he'll be protected in the middle. The best we can do is split the group in half."

"Also, have you ever tried to steer a shark?" I said.

Junior considered. "Fair enough."

"Anyway," said Spio. "While Lysi and I drive our shark harpoon in there, the rest of you will be in position to attack. Get your iron through the target as soon as possible. Don't worry about anyone else. We're after one body. As soon as he's dead, we turn tails to the current like a whale after mating season."

He paused, and then added, "Hope none of you is afraid of sharks."

"This sounds like a Spio plan if I ever heard one," said Nobeard.

Spio and I exchanged a grin.

I envisioned the plan—Spio and I pushing the sharks with our weapons, the other guys diving in to attack the scattering guard. I was confident in Spio's and my ability to guide the sharks, and in the sharks' ability to tear the limbs off Adaro's guards, but I couldn't help noticing how many things would need to go perfectly.

"I guess this time, we'll all go home once it's done," said Junior. "No commander to notify."

A grim moment passed between us.

"Word of this will get out soon enough," said Pontus. "We'll worry about the anarchy once it happens."

Our current veered west, so we switched to an adjacent one. I thought about Coho and Ephyra, and how they would be in Adaro's guard. As long as they stayed away from the sharks, they didn't need to get hurt.

"So who gets the iron?" said Pontus.

He eyed the trident still clutched in Junior's fist.

"You three, since Lysi and I are shark-taming," said Spio. "I'm going to suggest you fight for it."

For the hundredth time, I felt guilty for letting my iron hook get blasted away.

Spio must have read it in my aura, because he punched me in the shoulder. "Come on, buddy. There was nothing you could have done."

Junior held out the weapons to Pontus.

"You and Nobeard should take the iron. I can snap his neck with my bare hands."

"How modest," said Pontus.

Junior flexed his baby-dolphin-sized arms.

"I'll take the hook," said Nobeard. "I have a feeling it's my destiny to fight with a hook."

That left the trident to Pontus. He wrapped both fists around it with a hungry gleam in his eyes.

Though Junior probably could have snapped Adaro's neck on strength alone, he settled with taking Pontus and Nobeard's maces, one in each hand.

Then the line of guards hit our senses.

"All right, here's what we're going to do," I whispered, producing the roll of rawhide. "Surround me, weapons out. I came here a captive, so I'll leave a captive."

"Ah," said Spio. "The boys' army proved too much for you."

"I was too much for it," I said, tossing back a lock of matted hair. "Junior, hand them this and tell them you're royal guardians on a transport order."

Junior took the rawhide hesitantly.

"Why me?"

"You look the scariest."

He unrolled it. "These are assembly instructions"

"That's not important. I hope. The story is that you were instructed to bring me back to train for the Battle for Eriana Kwai."

I handed Spio my weapon, so he and Junior held two each. Nobeard and Pontus still had their iron.

They fell into place around me. I set my jaw and, thinking of Strymon's smug face, summoned all the rage I could. The guys mirrored my mood.

The floor grew shallower, locking us between surface and rocks.

As we neared the line, I began shouting.

"I tried to tell you cods I'm better off up north! I was trained to fight *humans*."

"Shut up," said Pontus, baring his teeth. "It's not our problem where you're stationed."

I snarled.

We stopped in front of a guard—a different one from last time. His thickness was comparable to Junior's. I sensed more guards on either side, hovering just within range.

Junior puffed himself up. "Royal guardians on a transport order."

The guard's eyes raked over our group. He lingered on me, and then on the iron weapons.

My heart pounded.

"This is a girl," said the guard. "Why was she here?"

"She's to return to Eriana Kwai," said Pontus.

"Why?"

"King's orders," said Junior. "We don't ask questions."

The guard was unreadable. He reached out. His hand closed around the rawhide.

Don't be difficult, I thought. *Your buddy didn't check it on the way there.*

Junior didn't open his fist. The guard had to pull the roll free.

I glanced around, pretending to look for an escape. Spio picked up on it and jabbed me with his stone spear.

"Ouch!"

Rubbing my side, I shot him a glare that wasn't entirely staged.

"Think I'm letting you escape again?" he said in his best tough-guy voice. "You already pushed your luck with that stunt back at the camp. They'll be picking iron out of the coral for the next year."

The guard eyed the iron weapons again.

"Eriana Kwai, you say?"

"Yes, sir," said Pontus. "She's to be used against the humans."

"Her specialty is irontechnics," said Spio.

I turned slightly so my scar was more visible.

The guard grunted. He hastily shoved the rawhide back at Junior and waved us through.

Spio made to prod me again as we moved forwards, but I grabbed the end of his spear, making a silent promise that I would get him back for this later.

We crossed the border and kept moving, picking up speed. Soon, we were flat out, opening as much distance as we could between the guards and us.

By the time we needed breath, we were long out of range.

We paused at the surface, panting hard.

"Nice work, Lysi," said Pontus.

Spio hesitated in giving me back my weapon. I snatched it from him with a flourish, but he submerged before I could jab him with it.

We continued northwards, travelling in silence and changing currents when we found a faster one.

The route was not without other travellers. It wasn't long until we crossed paths with a pod of transient orcas. We dove, sinking to the twilight level to make sure they wouldn't chase us.

After that, we overtook rays, marlin, and a blue whale with her calf. I checked behind us compulsively to ensure we weren't being followed.

The next time ripples hit us, we stopped. Merpeople. Their group was small, their presence too meek to be our target.

Something bulky floated in their midst—a weapons hold, maybe.

They drew closer, riding a different current than us. They must have been heading south.

We dove to avoid them.

"Weapon supplies," said Pontus once we'd risen again. "It's most likely, if they're headed for the Moonless—"

"We shouldn't have taken the main current," said Junior. "There's too much traffic. We're going to be seen, if not mauled by the next pod of whales."

"This is the only option," said Pontus. "The target is somewhere along this current."

"But if we have to keep diving, we'll never—"

"Stop," I said, holding out my hands.

They did.

I'd felt something else. I turned my head, concentrating.

"Frenzy?" said Spio.

Faint vibrations carried from somewhere far ahead. Then they disappeared.

"Moving away from us," I whispered.

I advanced until I felt them again, and then stopped. The guys followed.

"The target?" said Nobeard.

I ran a palm along my arm, as though to rub the feeling deeper into my skin.

"I think so," I whispered.

We clumped together, advancing in silence. The closeness would make our group feel like one entity, easily mistaken for a whale.

We followed, trailing as far back as we could without losing the group. The distorted murmur of conversation met my ears.

I searched for Adaro. I didn't know what to feel for. I could recognise my brother from afar, or a cousin or friend—but not a stranger.

Swimming that close together, I felt the guys' fear as my own. I tried to block it, focusing on the group ahead.

There were at least ten merpeople. Our distance made it impossible to pick out a single identity. Adaro would be in the middle, masked by the surrounding guard. The best I could do was identify gender—and they were mostly male.

Next to me, frustration seeped from Pontus. He was having as much trouble as I was.

I gave up on trying to find Adaro and scanned the vibrations as a whole, searching for anything helpful.

There. Something familiar. What was it?

I felt it out for a moment, until I was confident I hadn't imagined it.

I slowed, pulling the others back. They turned to me.

When we'd lost the feeling of the distant group, I whispered, "It's them."

"How do you know?" said Pontus.

"I recognised Coho."

A pause.

"You're sure?" said Junior.

"Yes. I don't know how. I just know. It's him."

I couldn't explain it. There was something familiar in his aura, and that was the only feature in the group I could distinguish.

"Works for me," said Spio.

"All right," said Pontus. "Now, we tail them until we find our sharks."

Tightly clustered, we followed. We stayed out of range so they wouldn't sense us, relying on the knowledge that they were heading north.

The sun crept across the sky. We ducked closer a couple of times to make sure we hadn't lost our group. I kept my feelers on Coho and the female presence beside him.

We breached often so we could keep an eye for gulls above the surface.

My stomach growled. I ignored it, irritated that my body was thinking about food at a time like this.

Finally, something notable grazed my skin. I nearly cried out in excitement.

The guys felt it, too. We stopped, senses tuned to something on the left.

The faintest of vibrations—but it was huge, chaotic, moving towards us.

"Uh, crap," said Spio.

"Yup," I said. "Dive."

Not a frenzy. Dolphins. They wouldn't be harmful, but this pod must have been three hundred in size. They breached and splashed noisily, heading straight for us from the west.

I recognised their pale bellies and dark, shaded backs as Pacific white-sided dolphins. I hadn't seen a pod of those since leaving home.

We dove to get out of their way.

"Why don't we use them?" said Junior, watching their white bellies pass overhead.

"Are you kidding?" I said. "They wouldn't fall for the bait."

"Tempting, though," said Spio, rolling onto his back.

As they passed, I thought of Axius and his dolphin ranch, and felt a pang of guilt and sadness. He might have been a giant whale turd, but he hadn't deserved to die.

The dolphins noticed us—Spio, in particular, with his bag wafting the scent of death in all directions. But they had no use for us.

Their chatter filled the water, cheerful and expressive. Distinct auras passed over my skin—a pregnant female, serene and happy; a young male, frustrated in his pursuit of a mate; an older male, annoyed by a playful tag-along; three babies enjoying a game. Most were hungry. They were after a meal.

I placed a hand over my stomach, wishing I could go with them.

We waited until the dolphins cleared our range, then rose to the northwards current again.

"Too bad this area is so foreign," whispered Spio. "Back home I always knew where the frenzies happened."

"I know," said Pontus. "This is scaring me. Notice how much colder the water's getting?"

I bit my lip. I'd been too focused on the group ahead to notice, but the water had gotten a lot more comfortable.

"You think we're almost home?" I whispered.

"We're dangerously close."

My gut twisted. I'd finally be home like I wanted.

But getting home wasn't enough anymore. It was like Spio had told me when I first arrived at the military base: *Our duty as soldiers isn't to Adaro. It's to merpeople.*

I had to get home, yes. But I was a soldier, and I had a job to finish.

"Maybe we can think this out logically," I said. "What kinds of landmarks do frenzies normally ..."

My jaw dropped. I whirled around, staring eastwards.

"What?" said Spio.

"The dolphins. They're familiar with this area. They know exactly where to find food."

Spio turned in their direction, mouth agape. Then his face broke into a grin.

"All right. Lysi and I are going to follow the pod. You guys swing wide and get ahead of the target. We'll bring the party to you."

"Aye aye," said Nobeard.

He, Pontus, and Junior took off one way while Spio and I went the other.

This had to work. Where else would a giant pod of hungry dolphins be headed in such a hurry?

We followed the trailing bubbles and caught up to the pod. The dolphins eyed us as we passed, but they remained mostly aloof. We kept going until we swam parallel with the leaders.

Then, I felt it—the faintest of ripples, but a definite change in the current.

We breached quickly. In that moment above the surface, I glimpsed white flecks in the distance. A league away, gulls were diving in.

Pulses in the current raced across my skin.

"Yup," said Spio. "That's what I call chaos."

I grinned. Predators lay ahead. With a burst of speed, we broke away from the dolphins.

Soon, a single-minded presence hit me like a wall.

I couldn't tell what type of shark—but maybe that didn't matter. The smell of hunger and blood trickled towards us.

We swam at top speed, opening as wide a gap as we could between the dolphins and ourselves. We needed time to gather the sharks and get out of there before they arrived. We had a league to do it.

At last, the frenzy came into sight.

A few striped dolphins did the brunt of the work, driving a school of herring against the surface. Birds plunged in, snatching what they could and scrambling to avoid the snapping jaws. I glimpsed a lone swordfish—and best of all, the predators we came for.

Six sharks darted in and out of the ball of fish: four threshers, two great whites.

Every instinct told me to turn and flee. All six were large and healthy, with full sets of teeth that could slice a mermaid's skin like iron. They projected such a powerful desire to kill that I swore my lungs compressed just looking at them.

The great whites drew my attention first—mouths gaping, bodies as thick as small whales. But the striped dolphins kept even further back from the threshers than the great whites. Despite their adorably large eyes, the threshers had tails as long as their bodies, which they snapped over their heads to stun the herring before devouring them. Even the smallest one was longer than me, and managed to knock out three fish at once.

I glanced back. Our dolphin pod was distant, but wouldn't be for long.

Spio turned to me. He held out a hand.

"Lysi, I feel like our entire friendship has led us to this moment."

I clasped his hand, watching the sharks gnash at the baitball and at each other.

"You ready?"

I pushed the hair out of my face. "Like you said: I spent my childhood preparing for this."

We let go. Spio opened his bag. The stench of death was powerful enough to wrinkle my nose.

A bright cloud of blood rose between us. I backed away so as not to coat myself and become living shark bait.

Then again …

I shot forwards before I could change my mind. Particles of blood clung to my skin, thick and sticky. Bits of guts floated around, too. All the better.

"What are you doing?" said Spio.

"Live bait."

"That's disgusting."

I grabbed some of the floating guts and rubbed them in my hair.

The current pulsed behind us. The pod was catching up.

"Where'd you get this much blood, anyway?" I said.

He hesitated.

I dropped the guts. "Spio."

"The chunks are just fish."

"And the blood?"

He turned his arm out, revealing the gash on the inside.

I cried out in some kind of mixture of shock and disgust.

"Where else would I have gotten so much blood?" he said. "I wasn't about to bleed out one of our dolphins. That's just mean."

I shook my head.

The pod closed in. We had moments until they would slam into the frenzy and the sharks would explode like a mine with teeth.

"I'm going to get them," I said.

Blade ready, I plunged in.

I cast my senses through the group, making sure I could track each predator. The striped dolphins projected a mild awareness of me. The sharks didn't seem to notice. Their focus was on the ball of herring.

"My, those fish are small," I said loudly. "Too bad there isn't a large, tasty mammal around here to devour."

None of them reacted. Not that I'd expected them to.

I swam closer, using my hands to waft my scent in their direction.

"Mmm."

The outermost thresher turned, distracted from its meal by the promise of something much larger, much tastier.

"That's right. Come on. I bet I taste pretty good."

I ran my fingers through my hair and flicked off a few drops of fish guts.

With competition so fierce and the prey so small, this had to work.

I glanced around the thresher, tracking the predators again. Birds continued to plunge in from above. A great white snapped its jaws around one and spat it, realising it wasn't a fish.

Dolphins, a swordfish, two great whites … three threshers. I was missing one.

The current surged at my tail. Open jaws shot at me with blinding speed. I grunted and bent backwards, curling out of range.

My heart raced.

"Okay," I said. "Okay. This is good."

A presence closed in from the side. Another thresher had abandoned the frenzy, its focus locked onto me.

They were about to surround me. Would they close in on a hunt like orcas did?

No, I told myself. *They'll fight over you and tear you limb from limb.*

Much better.

I backed away.

The dolphins arrived. They whipped past, blinding me with bubbles. Anger projected from the striped dolphins as the larger pod took over their feeding spot.

I dove, desperate not to let the sharks lose my scent.

Spio shot by, advancing with the pod and circling wide around the frenzy.

"What are you doing?" I shouted over the chattering dolphins.

"Helping!"

He plunged into the baitball. Fish scattered. Dolphins whistled their frustration at Spio for ruining their strategy. Sharks reacted with bursts of energy, catching any stragglers before they escaped.

Spio erupted from the school of fish with a war cry, swinging his spear. Anything nearby recoiled. The thresher that didn't received a whack to the face. It backed off.

Knocked away from their target, the sharks had all caught my scent. The closest thresher lunged and nearly closed its teeth around my tail.

The striped dolphins surrendered the meal and left. The sharks didn't care; they had better prey to hunt.

"Keep going," Spio shouted. "I'll make sure they follow."

He had dragged a trail of guts from the direction we had come. I led them recklessly down it. The blood was dissipating, but the scent lingered.

I rubbed my hands over my body and through my hair as I swam, scrubbing away the blood.

Feeling the distance between the sharks and me, I spared a glance over my shoulder. They swam open-mouthed, snapping up any remains they found along the way.

I was relatively clean. I pushed faster. With blood still on the current, I hoped the sharks would forget what they were chasing.

I dove abruptly.

Sure enough, the sharks kept swimming straight along the trail.

I followed them from below.

Soon, their urge to kill dissipated with the blood. Their pace slowed. They'd given up on the hunt.

I rose alongside them with my blade out. After gorging on fish, and without the scent of blood driving them mad, they seemed to decide I wasn't worth chasing.

The bigger great white led the shoal. I couldn't help noticing he was large enough to fit my entire body inside. Between the pointed snout and the pectoral fin, five gills the length of my forearm flared open and closed. In his jaws, bits of fish were caught between his many teeth. The inside of his mouth reeked of blood. I opened a little more distance between us. Sure, I had the advantage of speed, but I never underestimated a shark's reaction time.

Behind the great white, the four threshers followed. Trailing behind was the second great white. It kept trying to veer away, but something was making it fall back in line.

"Spio?"

From the other side of the trailing great white, he said, *"Never - do - that - again."*

I laughed.

We used our weapons to guide the sharks, poking them in the sides when they threatened to leave the current and swatting their tails when they moved too slowly.

Keeping them in a cluster proved hard work. I switched my focus rapidly, making sure none of them was preparing to strike. They were hard to read.

All signs of the feeding frenzy disappeared behind us. We were suspended in emptiness for a moment before the vibrations from Adaro's group brushed my skin.

"Spio, we have to make the sharks move faster."

I wasn't sure why I bothered whispering. It wouldn't matter once we bombarded him. This was the point where we became open traitors to the crown.

Two possible outcomes lay ahead: freedom or death.

I tried not to consider how many ways this plan could go belly up. What if I'd been wrong, and this wasn't Adaro's group? What if the other guys weren't able to turn the sharks around? What if the soldiers fought off the sharks too easily?

"We need to get aggressive," said Spio. "You'll have to go into demon mode."

He was right. Sharks didn't flee easily. Merpeople were a shark's biggest predator, and even that was questionable.

"Okay," I said in a small voice.

I kept pushing the sharks, steeling myself. Spio stayed at the rear, pushing the second great white from the opposite side.

"You know, Lysi, before you came here, I wished for a girl to come to the unit. Or I sent out a message to the universe. Whatever you want to call it."

I glanced back, wondering what he was getting at.

"Then you arrived," he said. "At first, I thought the universe misunderstood me. I wanted a girl I could … you know."

"Got it."

"But it was meant to be you. I don't know where I'd be right now, if you hadn't shown up. Somehow, I think something bad would've happened. We would've given up, gotten scared, been caught. I don't know."

He faltered. "What I'm trying to say is that I'm glad you're here."

The sharks created a wall between us, so I couldn't see or feel Spio, but I knew he was sincere. He wouldn't have said it otherwise.

"I'm glad you're here, too, Spio."

It was hard to imagine what life would have been like if I'd been stuck as a soldier, not a part of anything bigger. I might have tried to escape on my own and gotten caught.

Still, was I better off this way? Driving a line of sharks towards an armed guard, it was hard to tell.

Adaro and his convoy were close. I counted fourteen bodies. Based on their sudden halt, they felt us coming.

Heart racing, I tightened my grip on my weapon. "Ready?"

"Yup."

I thought of Adaro, and my eyes burst with blood. My teeth lengthened. My skin tingled as it transformed. Webs appeared between my fingers, ready to help me navigate faster.

I turned to the great white.

Some kind of hesitation passed over the sharks nearest me. They sensed my transition.

I raised my weapon and roared, sending a jolt of alertness through the sharks.

Spio bellowed from the other side.

We swiped at them, attacking near their tails. They darted away from the sting, projecting a mix of confusion and dawning aggression.

A thresher turned to me with blinding speed, jaws open, but didn't strike.

"Go!" I shouted.

As we swung our weapons, the sharks' demeanour changed. They turned from hunters to hunted.

They shot away from Spio and me.

We chased them faster. I shouted and swung my weapon, sending them off as if they were seals fleeing a whale.

The group materialised ahead. My senses found Coho at once. Ephyra swam beside him.

How determined were they to maintain their image for Adaro? I hoped they had the sense to swim away instead of trying to fight.

As expected, Adaro travelled in the centre. His soldiers spun to face us, weapons out. Katus and Ladon floated in their midst, still bearing injuries from the mine.

A moment passed where the group seemed stunned to find predators stampeding towards them. Coho reached for Ephyra's hand.

Adaro's gaze locked on me. In a blink, his expression changed from surprise to rage.

Spio and I waved our weapons beside the sharks, bringing them closer together. With the larger great white in the lead, they formed the deadly harpoon Spio had planned.

The guards roared. They rushed to meet us.

Spio and I dove at the last moment, breaking away from the sharks in unison.

But as sharks and mermen crashed together, the shoal did not have the harpoon effect we had intended. There was an explosion of bodies. The sharks scattered like they'd hit a wall, to either side and above and below—not daring to push through the line of armed soldiers.

For a moment, panic seized me as I envisioned the sharks steering around the group and continuing onwards.

But then the sharks came firing back, and I had to dive to avoid being bitten. Pontus, Junior, and Nobeard closed in, swinging their weapons and bellowing.

Though we were outnumbered, the five of us were enough to surround Adaro's group. We turned the sharks back towards them, keeping them inside.

The sharks twisted, their excitement picking up. Jaws clamped over empty water. Bodies whirled in a blinding wall of bubbles. Mermen shouted.

A thresher snapped its tail. I winced at the pulse in the current. I hadn't seen it happen, but the soldier nearest me floated limp—knocked out.

The guards tried to lead Adaro away, but couldn't without encountering jagged teeth and striking tails. So they attacked instead, swinging weapons at noses, gills, and eyes.

I hollered over the din. "Make a baitball!"

The guys sank with me. We worked together to push the group of mermen towards the surface.

The chaos developed in rings: me and the guys on the outside, a layer of sharks snapping at anything in their way, guards swinging weapons to stop teeth and tails from advancing, and then Adaro, protected in the centre and unable to move. Coho and Ephyra stayed by the king's side, weapons raised, preparing to strike at any shark that came too close.

Katus swung his good arm at the nearest thresher, driving it towards me.

I gritted my teeth and roared at the shark, raising my arms. It balked, spun around, balked again. Katus was waiting for it.

Trapped, the thresher gave a burst of speed and arched its body. The long tail whipped over its head and struck Katus in the face.

The current buffeted my chest, strong enough to shove me backwards.

Katus went limp. Blood oozed from a gash across his face.

I let him sink.

The thresher darted after him, chasing the fresh blood.

"Get in there, Pontus," shouted Spio. "We've got them."

Pontus, Junior, and Nobeard dove into the midst without hesitating.

Spio and I circled the sharks, swimming as fast as we could to keep them clustered.

Driven wild by the scent of blood, the sharks attacked everything in front of them, clamping down on limbs and tails.

Never before had I needed faster reflexes. For every swipe at one shark, the one behind it bulged away from a swinging weapon. Their movements were sporadic, fuelled by bursts of energy that I could barely keep up with.

Spio and I swam harder, faster, flitting around the sharks in a tight, evenly spaced circle.

The exertion pushed air from my lungs in gusts. The instinct to breach was becoming difficult to ignore.

Aggression flooded the scene, muddying my senses. Everything beyond the nearest shark was a flurry of bubbles. My ears filled with howls of pain and rage. Blood crept towards us, smelling and tasting like both animal and merman. Thrashing bodies and swinging weapons made it impossible to feel for anything meaningful—like the guys' whereabouts. Pontus, Junior, and Nobeard had disappeared.

I hoped desperately that the guys were getting closer to Adaro. With each heartbeat, the sharks pushed further out. Any satisfaction they felt at a fresh meal of merman had disappeared. They wanted out. Tails and jaws sent torrents at me, making it hard to control my path.

My muscles weakened. Each swing at the sharks cost me all the energy I could muster.

"Lysi!"

With a jolt, I realised I'd caught up to Spio. I checked my speed, but too late. A gap opened behind me.

On the other side of our baitball, a thresher darted away, leaving a trail of blood from a gash in its side.

"No!"

I dove below the cluster to chase it, but stopped. I'd never catch it in time.

Above, several soldiers had dropped out of the fight—either unconscious, or dead. I smelled the burn of iron. The bodies sank, blood clouding from gaping wounds. I shrank away.

My heart skipped a beat when I saw familiar faces. I didn't know their names, but I recognised them from the army. A day before, we had been allies.

Not dead, I thought. *Please, not dead.*

We had one target, and only one. Guilt squeezed my chest—even for the sharks, who pushed outwards with more force, now.

Adaro's protection was crumbling. Five soldiers remained. Two of them were Coho and Ephyra, who were both bleeding from shark bites but hadn't been hit with iron. Ladon was bleeding and burned, gritting his teeth against Junior's brute-strength attack. The other two were ordinary soldiers. It drove a hole in my gut to see Nobeard and Pontus fighting them so fiercely.

The larger great white lunged for me. A strip of flesh hung from his teeth.

I was losing wind. I raised my blade, but those jaws suddenly seemed too much for my measly weapon.

"Leave it, Lysi," shouted Spio. "He's too pissed."

I dodged the snapping teeth, expelling a spout of bubbles in the effort.

"No shi—"

"Go, Pontus!"

It was Junior. I whirled around. The great white blasted away, disappearing into the blue as fast as the thresher had.

Pontus had knocked out his opponent.

Four guards left. Junior parried Ladon while Nobeard fended off the remaining soldier. Coho grabbed Ephyra, pulling her away from the swinging iron. Whether he was giving us access to Adaro or keeping his wife safe, I didn't know. Either way, Adaro was exposed. Pontus shot towards him.

Next to Adaro's huge, imperial form, it occurred to me how young Pontus was. He was a boy, diving at the most powerful merman in the Pacific, a single weapon in hand.

Another thresher blasted through the space between Spio and me. I thought to stop it too late.

Pontus let out a war cry.

For a moment, I thought Adaro might flee through the widening gap in the sharks and soldiers. But he faced his opponent, teeth bared.

Pontus thrust the trident towards the king's stomach.

Adaro seized the iron prongs, stopping Pontus cold.

I waited for the shriek of pain. I wanted to smell flesh on iron, to hear the sizzle as he burned.

But I didn't. Had a tunnel closed around my senses, or was the scene too full of blood for me to feel anything else?

With one hand grasping the trident, Adaro drew back the other arm. That was when I noticed the weapon across his back: a stone mace, with a hook at the end. My iron hook.

I screamed. "Pontus, look out!"

Holding Pontus by the end of the trident, Adaro swung the iron hook.

Pontus saw it too late. The iron sliced across his face, blood spurting as his head snapped around.

His head lolled, the blow leaving him semi-conscious. This time, I heard the sizzle. I smelled burning flesh.

Somehow, Adaro still held onto the iron prongs of the trident. He pulled Pontus towards him.

This was wrong. Adaro should have been searing. He should have projected unbearable pain. Red beads oozed from his palms where he gripped the trident—but that was all.

He ripped the weapon from Pontus' grasp and spun it around.

"Pontus!" I yelled.

Spio and I shot forwards.

We were too slow. The iron plunged through Pontus' ribs.

I felt it. I never realised what Pontus meant to me until that moment—his last moment. After spending so much time with him, the pain he projected overwhelmed me. Fear and agony washed over my skin, bringing a cry to my lips.

Junior felt it, too, and a hundred times more powerfully. His outburst hit me like a punch in the stomach. He abandoned Ladon and shot for Adaro.

I shouted at him, but he wouldn't hear me.

Ladon made to follow. Spio and I deflected him. Ladon swung at me, giving Spio the chance to slam him with the butt of his weapon. The air left his mouth in a stream of bubbles.

The king pulled the trident from Pontus' limp body. He turned it on Junior.

The two mermen were similar in stature, but Junior had no iron. Would it matter, even if he did?

Ladon made a desperate swing at Spio, who retaliated by striking him across the chest. Another wound opened, and he backed off. He'd been bitten and slashed in several places. Blood poured from somewhere in his back. His eyelids fluttered. He would bleed out soon.

I pushed him with the hilt of my blade. He floated limp, too weak to retaliate.

All feeling seemed to have left my body. Light-headed, I glanced around.

The sharks had scattered. The last thresher tail disappeared in the distance, leaving drops of blood in its wake.

Between the floating bodies, Coho and Ephyra were hunched over, trembling, weaponless. They both bled from multiple punctures. A half-moon of teeth marks dotted Coho's forearm. Our eyes met, and regret tightened my throat.

But what had I expected? Did I think we would charge in, push aside Adaro's guards, and kill the king in one clean swoop?

Of course there would be death. Of course everyone involved—sharks included—would be slashed and beaten. The guards had sworn oaths and would do everything in their abilities to protect the king, including dying for him.

Junior slammed into Adaro with enough force to drive the king backwards.

For a moment, Adaro struggled to retaliate. Junior's two maces were blurs, striking Adaro in the face, neck, and arms.

The king straightened, trident in one hand and hook in the other, and fought back. His arms crossed as he slashed the iron weapons at Junior.

Junior ducked out of the way to avoid being seared. He came back with a heavy blow to Adaro's ribcage.

Thick and muscular, both mermen relied on brute force instead of agility to win this fight. The current pulsed with the force of two colliding great whites.

Their arms blurred, weapons pounding against each other. The dizzying speed and trailing bubbles left me blind to their movements.

Then the hook grazed Junior's arm, and the pain caused enough hesitation for Adaro to swipe again with the trident.

Junior bellowed as the iron sliced his stomach.

I cried out, dashing towards them. Spio's hand closed on my arm. He pulled me back in time to dodge a desperate swipe from Ladon.

In a fit of madness, I spun around and slashed at Ladon. Incomprehensible screams poured from my mouth. My blade sliced across his chest, his face, his throat.

His eyes rolled back. He went limp, sinking slowly.

My fingers gave out. I dropped my weapon. It drifted away in the current, and I let it.

Someone spluttered beside me.

Nobeard was slumped over, a hand pressed to his neck. Blood gushed between his fingers.

Spio darted over.

My chest constricted. He'd been fighting the merman who had given Spio and I the kelp buoys. What was his name?

He coughed up a red-tinged bubble.

"Anthias," I said.

He met my eye, projecting defeat. He brushed a hand over his lips to wipe away more blood. Mistrust and fear lingered heavily between us.

I nodded towards the open water, indicating that he should go.

He glanced to the king, locked in battle with Junior, and then to Spio, and back to me.

I raised my fists. I didn't want to fight him, but I would if he got in the way of what needed to be done.

He fled. I watched him angle downwards until he disappeared into the darkness below.

An instant later, Junior screamed. Agony stabbed every cell in my body.

I whirled to see the trident buried deep inside Junior's stomach. With a grunt, Adaro gave it one more shove before pulling it free.

I had a last, fleeting look at the kind face of Pontus' younger brother. Then the life drained from his aura, and he slumped over.

"No ..." The sound hardly escaped my lips.

"Hey, dude, you'll be all right," said Spio.

His voice seemed to come from a distance.

"Come on, I'll take you—Nobeard? Hey, open your eyes. Let's get you some air. Come on, buddy."

The hook fell from Nobeard's grip. It sank fast, vanishing from sight.

"You think iron can defeat me?" shouted Adaro. "The rightful king of the oceans is better than iron."

Spio slapped Nobeard in the face, trying to wake him up. Blood poured from his neck, more slowly now.

Spio backed off, staring at his friend. Then he dropped his eyes to where the iron hook had disappeared. Without hesitating, he dove after it.

"Spio!"

We had no time for that. We had to go, or we'd be next.

Before I could dive after him, Adaro lunged at me.

I twisted away, propelling myself around his thick body.

I wasn't fast enough. A hand closed over my fin. I cried out as his fingers dug into the soft tissue.

He dragged me backwards. I spun, swinging my fists, opening my jaws to bite him.

Adaro seized me by the hair, and then his arm was around my neck, his bicep pressing against my throat.

Rage prickled from his skin as he held me there. One massive fist gripped both trident and iron hook. He brought them up to my face, nearly touching me with the trident's prongs.

"Who else is a part of the plan?" he shouted.

"No one," I said through gritted teeth.

I tried to shrink away from the iron's sting.

"Do not lie to me! Who are you working with?"

Was that a whiff of fear in him? I cast around for Coho. He and Ephyra hovered behind us, motionless, as though hoping not to be noticed.

Adaro brought the iron closer. The middle prong of the trident hovered a finger's width from my eye.

"Tell me where the rebels are," said Adaro, "or I will give you a scar to match the one you already have."

I almost shouted that no one sent us and we were acting on our own, but I stopped myself. What would he do if he realised I had no information to give him?

At my silence, he gave a cold, deep laugh.

"Do you fear I will deal with them as I have dealt with everyone else? Pity, after all this, you find yourself alone once again. I wonder if it is your destiny to be alone, Lysithea."

I clenched my jaw, unable to move, watching the tip of the iron trident.

"Are you so arrogant that you thought you could change the entire Pacific Kingdom?" said Adaro. "Did you think you belonged to something bigger? You and your friends, destined to overthrow the rightful king of the oceans …"

"You are not the rightful king," I said, but my words came out too weak, too broken.

Had all of this been for nothing? Pontus, Junior, and Nobeard were dead. Coho had chosen his side. I'd spent a short time believing I belonged somewhere. That dream was never fated to survive.

The next beat of Adaro's pulse hammered against my flesh, and his muscles tightened, and I knew he was about to close the gap between the iron and my face.

"Wait!" I said. "Remember your deal. You can't harm me."

Adaro barked out a laugh. "All your allies are dead and still you beg to live."

I snarled. That wasn't true. I still had Spio, and my parents, and my brother, and Meela.

I clung to that.

Meela and I could spend years and leagues apart, but the Massacre had proven that no matter what, I still had her. And her determination to take down Adaro matched mine.

"She won't give you the Host if I'm dead," I said.

"Your efforts have been a waste, Lysithea. You cannot save her. Once she frees the Host, it will make no difference whether you are alive or dead."

Something in his aura sent a shudder through me. What did he mean, *you cannot save her?*

"I might have failed to mention it, but you must understand. That human of yours would never have agreed if she knew—"

"Shut up! You've got nothing—"

"Freeing the Host requires blood," he said, voice rising over mine. "A human of Eriana Kwai must sacrifice herself."

A terrible silence passed between us. My heart pounded so hard, he must have felt it.

"You're lying."

"Your human will be dead," he said deliberately. "Tell me, do you really think I am lying as I say this?"

His pulse beat against my skin, steady and even.

The blood drained from my face, leaving me dizzy.

"She won't do it," I said. "You're wrong."

Would Meela know this? Did he withhold it from her so she would follow through?

In a flash, something rose beside us.

"Well, Your Majesty, no one can say you didn't rule with an *iron fist.*"

Adaro hissed as Spio dove over our heads with the iron hook.

The impact of Spio's swing jolted us forwards, but the iron didn't draw the king's blood.

Adaro waved his weapons haphazardly at Spio. I took the opportunity to jerk away from his grasp.

I landed in Ephyra's arms. She'd grabbed a rope from one of the fallen soldiers.

Before I could push away, she pulled my wrists behind my back.

I shrieked, pummelling her with my tail.

"You two-faced—"

"Hey! Stop!" said Coho, appearing at Ephyra's side.

He tried to restrain me, but I kept thrashing, fighting him and Ephyra with everything I had.

"Cowards!" I said.

They were supposed to be on our side. If they cooperated, we might be able to finish Adaro off.

I tried to bite Ephyra. My teeth snapped where her ear had been.

Something knocked me in the jaw. I grunted, blinking away the spots in my vision.

Coho unclenched his fist, eyes wide.

"I said, stop."

Ephyra finished binding my wrists and tail, leaving hardly enough slack for me to float properly.

Still, I twisted against the ropes like a fish on the end of a line.

Spio fought hard, but Adaro's flying weapons forced him to retreat. The king slashed with both hands, pushing Spio towards the surface, where he would be cornered.

"Spio, get away from here," I shouted. "I'll be fine."

Adaro stabbed the trident. Spio barely dodged it in time. He spun around and raised the hook.

"Spio," I shouted. "Go!"

Spio hesitated. He glanced to Coho.

Adaro swung the trident. Spio darted away from the prongs.

"I'll find the others, Lysi!"

With a final glance at me, he shot backwards, leaving a trail of bubbles.

For a moment, I wondered who these 'others' were—until Adaro shouted, "Follow him!" and rounded on Coho and Ephyra.

Spio was trying to draw Adaro after him.

My chest constricted. "No!"

Coho and Ephyra hesitated, both of them weak and bleeding from shark bites. Ephyra started forwards, but Adaro stopped her with a snarl of frustration. He held out the iron hook.

"You have reached the end of your fight, Lysithea. Your human will soon be dead, and the Host mine."

I lunged at him, jerking against the ropes. I wanted to scream but fear swallowed my voice. What if he was right? I had to get to Meela. I had to stop her before she became a sacrifice.

"What should I do with her, sir?" said Ephyra, taking the hook.

"Find out where the rebels are. Use any means necessary. Then kill her."

He turned away and charged after Spio, spinning the iron trident in his fists.

CHAPTER SEVENTEEN
Eriana's Crypt

My tea had cooled long ago, but I was still clutching the mug as I watched rain slide down the window. I sat on the living room couch, listening to the downpour and the rhythm of the old clock on the wall.

A lump the size of a stone had hardened in my throat. In a mere hour, we would join the rest of the island at the docks to watch the Massacre depart.

I barely grasped the reality of it. Twenty girls from the training program were about to depart almost a year ahead of schedule. Most would die. Each would kill dozens, if not hundreds, of mermaids during her time at sea.

I blinked a few times, focusing my eyes, and dropped my gaze to the bone dagger in my lap. I turned it over, pushing my thumb against the blade. Serpent head on one side, trees on the other.

The floor creaked, and the couch sagged beside me. I looked up. My father replaced the mug in my hands with a fresh, steaming brew of pine needle tea.

"What's that you've got?"

"Found it under the Enticer," I said dispassionately.

He picked it up, examining it with raised eyebrows. "The old ship?"

I sipped my tea.

"Interesting," he said. "You don't often come across these. You know what the trees and the hole are for?"

I shook my head.

"It's like a map. See?" He held it eye level and pointed at the trees. "These should line up with landmarks."

"I thought there used to be a stone here, or a gem," I said, poking my finger through the hole.

"Nah. That hole is intentional. Looks to me like it's the real point of interest."

"It's a landmark?"

"Look at the arrow pointing into it."

I took the dagger back. A tiny groove was beneath the hole, slightly off-centre.

Was this the fissure in the earth? Did the groove mark the entrance to the leviathan's resting place?

Whether this bone dagger provided a landmark or not, I still didn't know where to find these particular trees across the expanse of Eriana Kwai.

My mother sat on my other side.

"Well, isn't that beautiful."

I let her take it from me.

My father tapped his fingers on his mug. "I do wonder whether our island has more history than any of us is aware."

I raised my eyebrows, but he didn't continue.

I didn't press. It felt too nice, sitting quietly between my parents, the three of us together.

"Mama, Papa, I'm sorry I got mad—"

My mother made a shushing noise. She wrapped an arm around my shoulders.

"But I am sorry—"

"Honey, there's no need. I was wrong to push you into something you're not ready for."

I leaned against her, breathing in the scent of mint and honey. I'd already forgiven her for that. I didn't want an apology.

"Not a day goes by where I don't miss Nilus," she said.

"I know," I said. "Me too."

She handed the dagger back. The three of us sat in silence.

My father set his mug on the coffee table and stood.

"Where are you going?" said my mother.

He held up a finger to indicate we should wait a moment, and left the room.

A minute later, he returned with his cloth-bound book.

"I never got to show you this," he said, sitting beside me. "It belonged to my mother. I don't suppose you remember your grandma."

"A little," I said, trying to lighten the truth that I didn't remember her in the slightest.

He opened the book towards the back.

"She gave me this before she died. See this? Birth certificates for you and Nilus."

My face pulled into a slight smile as I scanned the fragile papers. The pages beyond them were untouched—wanting to be marked with more family history.

"And here," said my father, flipping back a page. "You never knew my older sister. She married an American and took off for the mainland. When I was sixteen, we got word that she died in a car accident."

I blinked at the death certificate. My father never discussed his sister. I'd all but forgotten she existed.

He flipped back through more pages.

"It's mostly birth certificates, marriage records, names of siblings and cousins pencilled in where documents haven't been found. But if you go further back, you can see a few interesting stories in our family tree. Here, for instance—my great-uncle had a pet moose. See that?"

He showed me a black-and-white photo of a moose standing in a river, staring at the camera. I giggled.

"And your great-great-grand … uh … whatever he is. This man. Executed at thirty-three. Gallows."

I gasped at the same moment my mother said, "Now, honestly, Kasai!"

"He was hanged? For what?"

My father pointed to the page where a news article had been taped. "Horse thievery."

"Tough punishment for stealing," I said.

"He lived in a time and place where this wasn't tolerated," said my father.

I looked at him. "He wasn't from here?"

My father shook his head. "Saskatchewan."

There it was. Though it didn't matter anymore, a piece of me had still hoped I was a descendant of Eriana. It had become a source of pride without my knowing whether it was true. The idea was oddly magical, like I was a part of this island, right through to the blood in my veins.

Disappointment must have shown on my face, because my father said, "Now, wait a moment. Just because he's from the mainland …"

He flipped to the front page.

"Look here. The first record of the family tree on my mother's side."

I took it from him.

A picture was inked into the page in black and red. It was our national emblem, the sea lion, same as the one on the cover of Anyo's book. The next page depicted a woman, a deer on her left, a wolf on her right, an eagle overhead, and a salmon beneath her feet.

"The charmer of animals," said my father.

I tore my eyes from the page. "We are descendants. You and me. We come from Eriana."

"According to this book, yes. If you turn the page …"

I did so, revealing a few lines of text in the old language.

"Translated, it tells of our family being born from the land, always a part of it."

"A legend," said my mother.

But here was the proof. Eriana had been a real person, and I descended from her.

I sat back, watching the pine needles float around my mug.

If I had more time, could I find the Host? I could give one more shot at finding this serpent, maybe, while everyone was at the docks.

But where would I start?

I felt both my parents watching me and looked up.

"You know, Metlaa Gaela," said my father. "You've always been so stubborn. You kept telling us you'd given up, but I thought you'd keep hunting for the Host of Eriana in secret. I guess I was wrong."

I stared at him, not sure what he was getting at.

"A part of me hoped you were onto something," he said. "I'd be booted from my position on the committee if I admitted it, but I would rather end the Massacres, too."

"What?" I whispered. "You think—you believe—"

My mother clapped a hand on my knee. "Meela, I see your imagination running away again. Your father's only talking about a naive hope that there might be a better answer. Sea demons are dangerous business, and I don't want you messing around with *that man's* training program."

She huffed, face blotchy.

I glanced to my father, who stared out the window. The clouds had mercifully stopped downpouring.

"Even if this Host is real," said my father slowly, "are you convinced that freeing it is a good idea?"

"This legend is a part of us, Papa. I know I'm supposed to find it. This is the way to free our people."

He stared at me for a long time. My mother said nothing, working her jaw like she was grinding her teeth. Did they believe me? Or was that an accusation of insanity in their eyes?

"We should go," said my father. "The ceremony is in half an hour."

They stood, leaving me alone on the couch while they got dressed.

I tried to understand what my parents were thinking. Had my father supported me this whole time, or was he trying to make me feel better now that I'd failed? My mother seemed opposed out of worry, more than anything. She didn't want me getting in trouble from Mujihi.

I'd come so close. I had every piece of a puzzle except for one—and that was the big hole in the middle of the bone dagger.

We left the house in silence, stepping into air that felt much too cool for June. The dark clouds pressed down on us, threatening to open up again.

On our way down the dirt road, we were caught up by Annith, Tanuu, and Blacktail.

I studied Annith for signs of pain.

"You're all right?"

"Just fine," she said brightly, though I noticed a limp in her step.

All of them watched me. I became self-conscious of the puffiness in my face from lack of sleep.

"Can we talk?" said Annith.

I glanced to my parents, who looked away guiltily and continued on ahead of us. The four of us fell behind.

"We feel bad," said Annith. "We talked about it, and we want to keep helping."

"Out of pity?"

"No. Because you're our friend."

I shook my head. "I never wanted you to help because you felt obligated. I wanted you to believe in the plan."

"I can't speak for you guys, but I believe in the plan," said Blacktail.

"Me too," said Tanuu.

"So do I," said Annith.

I looked between their apologetic faces, somewhat exasperated.

"That's nice and all, but in case you haven't noticed where we're going, we're too late. The Massacre is departing, same as always."

"We've still got half an hour," said Tanuu. "And we know Annith's a descendant."

"Who, limpy over here?" I said. "I don't think draining more of her blood would be a wise move after yesterday."

"Whatever," she said. "I lost more blood than this on the Massacre, and I bounced back just fine."

I waved a hand. "Not that it matters, but I found out I'm a descendant."

"No way!" said Tanuu. "That's awesome."

"You guys are missing the point," I said. "We're too late. The girls are leaving and we still don't know where the Host is."

"Oh, I see what's going on," said Tanuu.

He stopped walking, forcing me to turn to him.

"What?"

"You've given up," he said.

"I have not—that's not—" I huffed.

"Meela, we're sorry," he said. "We shouldn't have left you."

"It's fine. I'm not brooding. But the whole island is ready for those girls to get out there and slaughter demons. Nothing we do is going to stop it from happening. Maybe everyone's right, and these girls will kill enough demons to ..."

My throat tightened. I kept walking. The three of them jogged to catch up.

"Remember what you told me," said Annith. "Adaro's threat if we send another battleship. He'll be pissed, right?"

"He's already pissed," I said.

"But think about what he'll do. He'll want to hurt you, Meela, in any way he can."

My heart skipped a beat. I knew it, but I couldn't think about it.

"Where do we start, Annith?" I said, voice breaking. "I'm out of ideas."

"Tanuu and I were brainstorming," said Blacktail. "We wondered if the Ravendust bushes actually lead the other way."

"What, into the ocean?"

"Yes. What if the leviathan isn't on the island at all?"

I chewed my lip. There was a real possibility that we could have been led astray.

"Think about it," said Tanuu. "Where are you gonna hide something that big?"

Not on a tiny island, I thought.

"If it's not here, how are we supposed to get to it?"

"Maybe we need to sail somewhere else to find it," said Annith. "We can take the Massacre ship and the warriors along with us, and go hunting for it."

As we neared the docks, the crowd thickened. I said nothing, surprised to find myself entertaining the idea.

But this didn't make sense. All signs pointed to the leviathan being on the island. Why would Adaro want me to find it if it wasn't on Eriana Kwai?

"Where do you think it is?" I said.

"We aren't sure …" said Blacktail.

"It's got to be somewhere no one will stumble on it," said Annith. "Like Antarctica."

"But the story mentioned an opening in the earth, like a crevasse," said Tanuu.

"Where does a person find a *crevasse*?" said Blacktail.

"Glaciers and stuff," said Tanuu.

"If it was in the ocean, Adaro would have found it by now," I said.

"Unless it's unreachable," said Blacktail.

"Okay, what about the deepest part of the ocean?" said Tanuu. "I bet a giant two-headed snake wouldn't be the creepiest thing down there."

"Ugh," said Annith. "Giant squids."

"Mariana Trench is basically just a big crevasse," said Tanuu. "It's all chasms and volcanoes because of the tectonic plates."

I stopped walking.

"You are such a nerd," said Blacktail. "Crevasse? Tectonic plates?"

"I happened to get an A in Geology," he said, throwing back his shoulders.

Annith noticed I had fallen behind and turned. The other two slowed.

"Tanuu, what did you just say?"

"Uh … geology?"

"No." I walked forwards, and something on my face made Tanuu step back. "No, not that. The deepest part of the ocean."

"The Mariana Trench?"

I pulled the bone dagger from my waistband with trembling fingers. The trees. The hole in the middle. The scene looked familiar because it was familiar. I'd spent my entire childhood there.

My mind worked furiously. The enormous puddle in the schoolyard. It never dried up. Its depth was so mysterious that kids spent recess making up stories about it.

"Eriana Trench," I whispered.

Blacktail gasped.

I looked between them, heart pounding. "You guys, it's a crevice!"

"*Crevasse*, actually," said Tanuu. "A crevice is a small crack—"

I took off at a sprint.

The crowd had thickened around us, and I had to push by a stream of people moving the other way. I veered into the woods, around the throng and into the muffled silence. I took the most direct line to the schoolyard, hopping over logs and bushes like a deer, using the dagger to slash through branches.

I stopped at the edge of the schoolyard, clutching a stitch in my side.

I lifted the dagger horizontally. The weapon showed a hole in the middle, a large tree on the right, and a cluster of smaller trees on the left.

Beyond it, the schoolyard held no cluster of trees—but there was an apple tree growing alongside the school, hugging the wall. On the far side of the giant puddle stood an enormous sequoia.

I sprinted across the field to see it from another angle, and then held the dagger up again. On the left, the school and the apple tree. On the right, the sequoia. In the middle, its shape perfectly fitting in the hole, was our beloved Eriana Trench. I ran up to the spot indicated by the notched arrow.

Tanuu, Blacktail, and Annith emerged from the woods across from me, panting hard. I stuffed the dagger back in my belt and unlaced my boots while they jogged to meet me.

"This is where I need to go in," I said, pointing at the puddle. "This side. Right here."

The three of them yelled at me at once.

"You'll freeze!"

"What are you gonna do, dive to the bottom?"

"Can we, like, talk about this for a sec?"

I pulled off my boots and socks.

"This shirt is cotton. Blacktail, you're in wool, right? Switch shirts with me."

I began pulling my arms through my sleeves.

"Meela!" said Tanuu, grabbing my wrists. "Calm down. You're freaking out."

I drew a breath, arms halfway through my twisted sleeves. "I'm not freaking out."

"You kind of are," said Annith.

"It's down there," I said, trying to keep my voice even. "We need to hurry."

"We don't know exactly what's down there," she said. "This could be dangerous."

"More dangerous than sending girls on the Massacre?"

"Maybe you should think—"

"What else is there to think about, Annith?"

"Meela's right," said Blacktail. "The ceremony's about to start. There's no time to stop and think about it."

Annith looked unconvinced. Meeting her hazel eyes, I couldn't manage more than a whisper.

"I'm afraid of what'll happen if I don't do it."

Annith crossed her arms. "That mermaid means a lot to you, doesn't she?"

I dropped my gaze.

Tanuu was removing his shoes. Blacktail scoffed, shoving him so he fell sideways.

"Don't be dumb," she said. "You're not even a descendant."

He regained his balance and straightened. "But—"

"She's right. Stay here," said Annith distractedly, still staring at me.

I felt a surge of gratitude towards them. I didn't have the energy to argue any longer.

Tanuu looked between the three of us and crossed his arms, looking bitter. "Fine. But you should take my sweater, not Blacktail's. Mine has muskox wool in it so it'll keep in the body heat better."

Annith still stared at me funny, her face slackening. Something clicked into place behind her expression.

Tanuu pulled his arms from his sleeves.

"I'd rather wear hers," I said. "Yours makes me itchy."

Annith continued to stare. Her eyes glossed over, like her body couldn't do anything while her brain was working so hard.

"Really?" said Tanuu, aghast. "But … muskox wool! What kind of person likes sheep's wool better than muskox wool?"

Annith rounded on him, making him jump back. "What do you care if Meela likes a certain kind of wool?"

Tanuu looked alarmed. "I just—"

"It's the way the wool reacts with her skin," shouted Annith, jabbing a finger into his chest. "Some people are born with sensitive skin! So what if they end up liking certain types of wool better than others? It's not a choice, now, is it? Meela has her own wool preference and you need to accept that!"

Tanuu opened and closed his mouth.

"I, for one," said Annith, looking furious at him, "love Meela the same no matter what kind of wool she prefers! Blacktail, give her your sweater."

Tanuu stuttered an apology, looking bewildered.

I looked down to hide a smile.

"It's okay," I said, patting Tanuu's arm. "We've all had a very long week."

Blacktail pulled her arms from her muskox-free sweater and we traded shirts. Her gaze darted suspiciously between Annith and me.

I glanced to Annith, who returned my hint of a smile.

"Now," she said, turning to Tanuu, "give me your sweater."

"What?" he said.

"I'll wear your sweater. I'm going with her."

"No," I said, but she cut me off.

"You can't go down there alone. One of us needs to come with you if anything goes wrong. I'm also a descendant, so I'm the best choice."

"But you're all …" I motioned to her leg.

"I've dealt with worse."

I looked between the others, trying to find an argument, but Blacktail and Tanuu seemed to approve of this plan.

"Fine," I said. "You come. You two stay. Two and two."

"Good," said Annith.

She unzipped her hoodie, which happened to be cropped, and offered it to Tanuu. He held it between his fingers delicately, like he'd been handed doll clothes.

"Am I supposed to wear this thing?"

Annith pulled on his sweater while he tried to get his arms through the hoodie. He settled with hanging it off his head by the hood. He hadn't been wearing anything underneath, so he stood shirtless with the sweater draped over his shoulders like an absurd cape.

Blacktail averted her eyes, suddenly interested in the scenery of the empty schoolyard. I supposed the last few months in the woodshop had done a lot for Tanuu's abs.

I stuck my toe in the puddle and suppressed a groan. Why wasn't it warmer out?

A fat, cold raindrop hit my head, sending a shiver down my body.

Without glancing back—I didn't want to see the expressions of pity on Tanuu and Blacktail's faces—I waded in.

Though I'd experienced icier water on the Massacre, I was unprepared for how cold the puddle actually was. The water should have been warmer at this time of year, but it was as icy as the ocean.

Annith followed without protest.

I felt along the bottom with my feet, searching for anything peculiar. The squishy ground was littered with sticks, rocks, and some unidentifiable objects that might have been garbage or toys. I made it in up to my shoulders and stopped.

"What is it?" said Annith.

I ran my toes along the length of something, wading further until I was up to my neck.

"Rope," I said through chattering teeth. "It's tight along the bottom. Think we're supposed to follow it?"

She didn't answer. I felt as far along as I could, standing on tiptoe.

The rope was strange, but would it lead to anything?

Without hesitating any longer, I sucked in a breath and plunged. The frigid water pierced me like daggers.

I kicked to the bottom, flailing awkwardly. I forced my eyes open but saw only mud.

My hands found the slimy rope. I pulled myself along it, deeper into the puddle. Annith followed, edging along behind me.

After several seconds, the muddy water began to clear and the temperature cooled even more.

The rope disappeared into the ground.

Was that it? A rope drilled into the ground at both ends?

I ran my hand through the mud, finding a thin layer of gunk over top of smooth stone. I wiped the mud away, clouding the water.

My fingers found a crack.

A fissure? I thought.

With a thrill in my chest that was something between fear and excitement, I braced myself against the ground and pulled the rope. Nothing happened.

My lungs were beginning to protest.

Annith's hand appeared, clearing away more mud.

I let go of the rope, ready to push for the surface, when my eyes fell upon a shape chiselled into the stone. Annith pointed frantically at it.

It was the same serpent head as the one on the bone dagger.

I was too desperate for air to think about it. I bent my legs and sprang upwards.

We'd travelled a considerable ways deeper and further from where we started. I cupped my hands against the water and kicked hard, the distance to the surface nearly bringing me to panic.

My head broke through and I gasped for breath, rubbing grimy water from my eyes.

Tanuu yelled something, his voice indistinct against the water draining from my ears.

"We found something," I said. "The snake symbol."

Blacktail and Tanuu came into focus. They stood knee-deep. Like me, they showed mingled terror and excitement.

Annith popped up beside me.

"The rope didn't budge," I said.

"We need to move the stone," she said, panting. "It felt loose."

"Which way do we push?"

"Down, I think."

I stared at her, wide-eyed, catching my breath. "You think it's like a trapdoor?"

"Yes."

I turned to the others.

"If we don't come up, it means we've made it inside."

Tanuu waded a step further, concern pinching his face. "If you don't come up, it could mean a lot of things!"

Blacktail placed a hand on his arm, though she looked just as uncertain.

I drew a huge breath and dove once more, kicking wildly to get to the bottom as fast as possible. I used the rope to anchor myself. Annith did the same. We kicked the stone near the engraving.

It was loose, as Annith had said.

The gunk on the bottom stirred with each push, whirling around us.

A crack appeared on either side of the rope, curving away from it. The stone was a round slab, like a manhole cover—and heavy. Each time we released our legs, it snapped closed again.

With a synchronised push, we opened a gap wide enough to squeeze through. Annith held it in place and motioned urgently for me to go in.

I couldn't afford to stop and think about it. I pushed myself through the hole, into water that felt thinner and cleaner.

The rope continued along the bottom of a wide tunnel. I grabbed it to anchor myself.

That was my mistake.

Like a slingshot, the stone behind me slammed shut, sending a current into my face and plunging me into blackness.

I dug my fingers into the crack to pull the stone away. It wouldn't budge. I slapped it with my hands, trying to wiggle it. It stayed fixed.

I couldn't see. Water sloshed in my ears, hollow and silent.

My lungs protested. I spun around. Through the clear water, dim light shone somewhere in the distance.

I couldn't be sure which option was wiser: wait for Annith to get the others and hope their combined strength would move the stone, or continue along and hope I found a place to surface.

I grabbed the rope and pulled myself towards the light. Waiting helplessly for the others to get me out in time didn't sound appealing.

Panic tightened my chest. I moved quickly, one hand in front of the other. How far could this tunnel go? What if my lungs couldn't make it all the way? Worse, what if I was pulling myself to a dead end?

I needed air desperately. I tried to meditate over the sensation like I was taught, to observe the pain in my chest and the thrill in my heart and veins with detachment. But I became all too aware that I had no breath to focus on. The grasp on my panic slipped, sending my legs into a frenzy.

I let go of the rope and frog-kicked hard.

The solid, black earth above me disappeared. In its place, the water rippled freely. The surface.

I pushed off the bottom and shot upwards. Panic closed around me like fog, blocking all my senses from functioning properly. I abandoned any controlled method of swimming, pawing the water with my hands and feet as though scrambling up a cliff face.

Finally, my head broke through. I sucked air into my lungs, gagging, thanking the goddess Eriana and the Gaela and the molecules of oxygen themselves.

Breathing hard, I treaded water while my panic dissipated. A few seconds passed before my senses returned.

I scanned my surroundings. I'd surfaced inside a cavern. The immediate area was pitch black, but flecks of light illuminated something to my right.

Latching onto my depth perception proved hard. I stared into the blackness for a moment.

It was a passageway, wide enough to fit a schoolbus. The end disappeared into nothingness. Those distant flecks of light were beams coming through holes in the earth above. Roots jutted from the ground overhead like tentacles.

I treaded towards it and bumped into solid land. A ledge separated the pool from firm, clay ground. I hoisted myself onto it.

Now that I had time to consider, I was sure I'd made the right choice in continuing to swim. By the time Annith would stop trying to move the stone, reach the surface, call the others, and wait for them to swim down …

They were probably still swimming back towards the stone door. I wondered if I should wait for Annith to get through. Would she even try, after seeing me vanish?

My teeth chattered violently. I wrung the excess water from my clothes.

I had to hurry. My friends might be panicking, thinking I'd drowned.

I set off towards the beams of light, holding the bone dagger in front of me.

The cave floor was like ice on the soles of my feet. My footsteps echoed off the smooth cavern walls. My breath came in quick, panicked bursts.

I stopped beneath the first beam of light and looked up. Roots and stones closed part of the hole, the rest of which was grey sky and the dark mass of a tree. I must have been beneath the forest, somewhere behind the school.

At my feet, a pile of dirt, leaves, and a small shoe had fallen through the hole.

A hollow sound met my ears, like a low wind pushing through the tunnel.

I continued along. The ground sloped downwards, further plunging me into darkness. The air grew colder. My breath misted in front of me, a wisp of life in the still, hollow pit. My sweater became crusty, hardening to ice. Overhead, I caught the occasional glint of light—probably a reflection off an icicle.

Even as the cave deepened, the narrow beams of light illuminated the passage just enough for me to see—and to stop me panicking from claustrophobia. I kept telling myself the outside world was not so far away.

More than ever, I was grateful for my friends. If something happened to me and I didn't turn up, they were still in that outside world. They knew where I was.

The thought seemed to warm me.

Or was the air becoming warmer?

The low, hollow sound grew louder. A warm breeze did seem to be running through the passage. It smelled faintly of the ocean.

The warmth, no matter how subtle, felt blissful.

Then the cave turned at a sharp angle, and I stopped.

What lay in front of me turned my legs to jelly.

Protruding from the darkness was something black, solid, reptilian. It was the largest head I had ever seen.

The top came level with my face, so the eye would have stared directly at me if not hidden beneath the thick, black eyelid.

Sleek scales rippled over the skull and disappeared into the darkness, giving the impression of curving upwards into a mane of horns.

The nostrils flared at the end of a square snout. I could have fit my head inside one.

Another warm gust of wind caused strands of my hair to flutter.

Only it wasn't the wind. It was the leviathan. And she was breathing, softly.

CHAPTER EIGHTEEN
Coho's Dilemma

I thrashed against the rope around my wrists and tail, trying to wiggle free. The rope strained, but refused to snap. Ephyra had wrapped it too many times.

"Let me go!"

Coho and Ephyra ignored me. Ephyra coiled the trailing rope around her hand.

"You're both traitors! You were supposed to—how could you—they're dead, Coho!"

Our allies had been killed, and Meela was about to be.

Adaro was wrong. Meela had to be alive. She would never sacrifice herself. Not when she'd fought so hard to stay alive during the battle. Not when she must know that her death would destroy everyone who loved her.

"I have to go," I muttered, working my wrists.

Coho seemed about to speak, but Ephyra held up a hand.

"I need you to give me names," she said, gentler in the absence of the king.

I gritted my teeth, tugging at my wrists and tail. Ephyra jerked the end of the rope, forcing me to look at her.

"I do not wish to torture you," she said, "but His Majesty will expect information upon his return. I can bargain for your life if you cooperate."

I snarled. "I have nothing to tell you. Coho should know that."

Coho avoided my eyes.

"It's true," he said. "Everyone who was in on the plan has been killed. Except ..."

He glanced to where Adaro had disappeared on Spio's trail.

For some reason, this infuriated me.

"He'll get away," I said.

Spio was fast. He was smaller, slimmer, and with a head start he would outstrip Adaro's bulk.

I gave another hard pull. The rope wouldn't budge. I hissed in frustration.

"Look, I'm not happy you were caught," said Coho.

"Right," I said. "I'm sure that's why you punched me."

"You tried to bite my wife in the face."

"She was tying me up!"

"I had to," said Ephyra. "His Majesty would have us killed if he thought we were allied."

"He was outnumbered! We could have ..."

I shook my head, as though to dislodge the fear clouding my thoughts. It was done. It didn't matter, now. I had to get to Meela and stop her before she became a sacrifice.

Panic overcame me.

"She can't be dead yet," I said. "No, no, no ..."

Ephyra glanced to Coho, plainly wondering if I'd lost my mind. The iron hook dangled in her fist.

"What if we tell the king we tried to stop her," said Coho, "but she stole the iron and forced us to let her go?"

Ephyra grimaced. "You know he won't believe that. Look at her."

The rope had wrapped around my neck, chest, waist, and tail, threatening to drown me. I went limp, exhausted from the struggle.

"I need air," I said weakly.

They pulled me to the surface. I was too angry to feel humiliated that they had to help me breach.

I inhaled several times, long and slow. The oxygen cleared my thoughts a little.

How had the iron failed? Was Adaro immune? I'd never heard of such a thing.

Coho and Ephyra released me. I sank again.

"None of you knew," I said. "Adaro can't be killed with iron."

"He has never mentioned it, nor have I ever seen him attacked with it," said Ephyra. "I never had reason to believe otherwise."

When neither of them said anything more, I went back to working on the rope.

"Lysi," said Ephyra. "Can I call you Lysi?"

"Whatever."

"Lysi, you must understand our position. If we let you go, we will be tried for treason. It is a risk to our entire family. To our children."

I glanced to Ephyra's stomach. It hardly protruded, but when I focused, I could feel the presence of another life inside.

In my panic, I had forgotten.

I blinked back the sudden tears threatening behind my eyes.

"But the Eriana girl will die," said Coho. "So will Lysi, as soon as the king comes back."

"And Adaro will have the Host of Eriana," I said, barely a whisper. "He'll be unstoppable."

Coho turned to his wife. I sensed his genuine fear.

"We can go into hiding. We can join a bigger rebellion—escape to the Atlantic."

Ephyra said nothing. She placed a hand on her stomach.

"We need to pick a side, now," said Coho.

Ephyra shook her head. "Your thoughts are clouded because of—"

"Eriana Kwai?" said Coho with a flare of anger. "Yeah, maybe they are. I'm sick of his attacks."

"Those will end. It is up to this one Eriana girl, now."

"They won't end!" said Coho. "Once he has that weapon he's after, his attacks will only grow more powerful, more deadly."

Ephyra said nothing.

"What does Lysi have to do with this Eriana girl, anyway?" said Coho.

"She wants Lysi alive. His Majesty is going to trade Lysi for the Host."

Coho spun to face me. I caught a quickening in his pulse.

"The girl I love," I said. "The one I told you about. She's from Eriana Kwai."

He stared at me for so long, he seemed to have frozen in place.

I flipped over, trying to untangle myself. I felt like a dolphin caught in a fishing net.

"Please," I said. "I need to stop Meela from doing this."

Coho's hands flew to his hair. He backed away, mumbling something inaudible.

I gritted my teeth, drawing blood beneath the layers of rope in my struggle.

Ephyra was staring at Coho. After a moment of his continued mumbling, I stopped struggling and stared, too.

"Coho isn't my real name," he said abruptly, voice broken. "It's a nickname the guys gave me because coho salmon was all I would eat for the first two years I was a merman."

I didn't understand why he was telling me this. I caught heartache in his aura, like a physical pain.

That familiarity grazed my skin, stronger than ever in his vibrations, expression, and mannerisms.

"I was a warrior, once," he said.

"For the Massacre," I whispered. "From Eriana Kwai."

His face crumpled, like someone had run him through with an iron spear.

"Adaro doesn't know that."

"You let your family believe you were dead," I said. "All this time, they've grieved for you."

"You don't understand. It was for love. I love Ephyra with all my heart. I could never be with her if I'd stayed human."

"So you abandoned your family? You let them mourn you all these years?"

My voice cracked. This was wrong. This was mermaid allure stealing him away from his family. Was it even true love?

"I had a little sister," he said. "She's who I miss most. Even more than my parents."

My pulse raced. I couldn't believe what he was telling me.

"You still love your family?" I said.

"Of course. I think of them every day."

"Then why haven't you tried to contact them? Why haven't you let them know you're alive?"

"They'd never accept me like this—or even recognise me."

"I think they would love you the way you are."

He shook his head. We held each other's gaze for a long time.

"What's your real name?" I demanded.

I thought I knew, but I had to hear it.

He didn't look at Ephyra or me, as though ashamed of his past as a human.

"Nilus."

CHAPTER NINETEEN
Sleeping Spirit

I stood anchored to the cold ground, unable to move, staring at the enormous head not five steps away.

I didn't know how much time passed. It might have been several minutes.

With each of those long, slow breaths, wisps of my damp hair fluttered. The gentle rhythm gave every indication that it had been moving this way, unchanged, for thousands of years.

The ocean smell was more powerful than ever—a primeval mix of animal, must, and brine.

I took a single, heavy step closer. It was several seconds before I could move my other foot.

I drew close enough to the reptilian head to see cracks between the impenetrable scales.

There was supposed to be a second head at its other end. I leaned into the darkness, trying to trace my eyes along the body. The cavern was too black beyond the leviathan's snout.

Judging by the flare at the back of the skull, its head must have been armoured with horns. How long and how many, I could not tell. I wondered what kind of armour it had along its body.

Her body. I reminded myself that this enormous beast was the embodiment of Eriana—not an *it*, but a *she*.

The thought of the spirit of Eriana, of a goddess bound with the serpent's body, made the sight less fearsome. In fact, she was strangely beautiful as she slept.

I wanted to touch her—a ridiculous urge, but I was this close now.

I extended a trembling hand, hovering beside the square snout, where I imagined a dagger-sharp fang was hiding.

No wonder you ruled the seas, I thought.

As gently as I could, I placed my hand over the scales, barely touching, as though giving myself the option to change my mind.

Nothing happened. She continued breathing.

I rested my hand on the scales properly. They were colder and smoother than iron, and somehow, more solid. This creature was as indestructible as the legend said.

Remembering why I came here, I pulled the dagger from my belt.

You're crazy, said a voice in my head. *You're about to wake this thing. How can you think that's a good idea?*

I wondered if she would be hungry when she woke. Ravenous, probably, after thousands of years.

I gripped the dagger more tightly. I had nothing to fear. I would be able to control her.

The legend had been accurate so far, and if it continued to be true in telling me I could wake the Host with my blood, then why wouldn't it be true about this?

Imagining myself with power over this monster gave me a thrill I'd never felt before.

With a leviathan—*the* leviathan—at my side, I'd be the most powerful woman in the world. I could rule the seas.

No. That's why Adaro wants her, I told myself.

I wasn't like Adaro. Once the serpent was awake, I would use her to kill Adaro, and then figure out how to destroy her. She had too much potential to be apocalyptic in the wrong hands.

But she was so beautiful.

Looking at the closed eye, a lump the size of my head, and feeling the warm air blowing from the nostril by my chest, I tried to prepare myself. I imagined how controlling her might feel.

How did it work? Did I think about what I wanted her to do? Did I tell her verbally?

As a descendant of Eriana, I supposed the instinct would come to me.

A surge of pride filled me. The goddess Eriana, who connected me to my people by blood and earth, was resting on the clay at my feet. This untameable creature she spent her life commanding was a part of me, and a part of my history— the beginning of Eriana Kwai.

I'd made it all this way to protect Eriana's children, the people of this island. How would she feel to know her descendant was here, ready to carry on her destiny?

Now the Massacre was ready to depart, taking twenty more of Eriana's children with it. I could stop it.

I, Metlaa Gaela, Daughter of Kasai, possessed the ability to waken the Host.

I turned the bone dagger in my fingers.

Do it now, I thought.

Again, a grasp on time escaped me. How long had it been? Had the warriors departed already?

My hands trembled. Was it excitement? Fear?

Cold. I was turning to ice from the outside in. The cavern had numbed my wet—now ice-encrusted—skin.

I thought of the girls aboard the ship, and their families watching them depart, and the rest of my people, including my parents and friends. I couldn't let them suffer any longer under Adaro's grasp. I thought of Lysi, and Lysi's family, who'd also suffered because of that merman's desire for power.

When I wake you, I thought, *I want you to kill Adaro.*

I knew it wouldn't work that way. I'd have to command her, somehow, once she was awake.

I placed the blade across my palm. The engraving of the serpent head stared up at me.

"For Eriana," I said.

The words filled the cavern. A chorus echoed, as though the entire island—the spirits of my ancestors, perhaps—was there with me.

I drew the dagger hard across my palm. A sting shot up my arm as the dull blade bit into my skin.

Blood seeped through the wound. I watched it pool in my palm.

I turned my hand. The blood fell. It trickled into the gap between the black, reptilian lips.

My heart hammered as I watched the blood drip down, both into the mouth and out onto the clay.

My hair stopped fluttering. The warm, rhythmic breathing ceased, plunging me into absolute, dead silence.

Slowly, the black scales overtop the eye parted. A vertical pupil narrowed into focus, a deep blue streak in the centre of a black, glassy orb.

The Host of Eriana looked straight at me.

CHAPTER TWENTY
For Eriana

Ephyra grabbed Coho's wrist, sensing his decision a beat before I did.

"Don't," she said, a dangerous tinge in the whites of her eyes.

Coho ignored her. He whirled around, scanning our surroundings.

I followed his gaze to the scene of our attack. The blood had dissipated and the bodies had sunk, leaving the water as clear as though nothing had happened.

One weapon remained, bobbing at the surface: a longblade of wood, slate, and whalebone. My weapon.

Coho pulled free from Ephyra, grabbed it, and returned. He placed the blade under the rope binding my wrists and tail.

Ephyra grabbed his wrist again, stopping him from severing the rope. "You can't—"

Coho rounded on her.

"Ephyra, I can't let my sister die. I've already abandoned her."

"What about our family?"

"We'll go into hiding. Please. Meela is our family, too."

They stared at each other, Ephyra holding tight to his wrist.

"We knew we would have to flee, eventually," whispered Coho. "Why not now?"

Ephyra's eyebrows pulled down. She softened. After a hesitation, she let go.

Without a word, Coho turned back to me. He severed the rope in a gentle way that was so Meela-ish it brought a lump to my throat.

Why hadn't I seen it before?

"She talks about you all the time," I said.

A deep crease appeared in his forehead.

Keeping his eyes down, he said, "When you told us you had to fight women in the Battle for Eriana Kwai … I wondered. I didn't let myself believe it. But it's true. She was on the Massacre, and you fought her."

The rope fell away. I nodded, rubbing my bloodied wrists.

Around us, the world was still and silent.

"They trained her to kill mermaids," said Coho.

I said nothing.

Coho dropped his gaze to the weapon in one hand, the rope in the other.

"Sorry for punching you."

"It's fine," I said truthfully.

Fear twisting my gut, I turned to where Spio had disappeared.

Sure, Spio had always escaped the tightest spots a kid could find himself in—but he'd never gotten himself hunted for treason.

I met Coho's anxious gaze. Sadness passed between us, and I knew he was also thinking of our friends.

We'd been so sure we would bring a new era to the Pacific. If the iron had worked, we would have succeeded. But Pontus, Junior, and Nobeard were at the bottom of the sea, and scavengers would be feeding on their bodies.

Meanwhile, Adaro was still alive. His Utopia lived on, and so did his plan to divide humans and merpeople.

"You should go," said Coho.

I turned northwards, wondering how far I was from Eriana Kwai.

"You, too," I said. "Take your family far away from here. I'll … I'll see you soon."

Saying goodbye felt too final.

Coho held out my weapon. When I reached for it, he shot towards me, and before I knew what was happening, he wrapped his arms around me.

I hugged him back, feeling the closeness of family in his arms. Meela's family.

I had to get to her.

Ephyra didn't hug me, but her aura was apologetic. She promised we would find each other again.

We split ways. Coho and Ephyra followed the northwest current to Utopia. I went northeast to Eriana Kwai.

Facing the open water alone didn't scare me. Not orcas, sharks, or other merpeople. The only fear swelling in my chest was for Meela, and whether I was too late to stop her.

CHAPTER TWENTY-ONE
Goddess Rising

The vertical pupil hung in space, a deep blue streak on an inky backdrop. I hardly processed that I was looking into a living, seeing eye. It was as though such an enormous creature had no place in my brain.

I was reminded of being aboard the Bloodhound. In the middle of nothingness at twilight, wispy clouds had reflected in the black water. This glossy eye now swallowed me the same way the ocean had.

A soft, breathy groan rumbled the cavern. Her nostrils flared.

I needed to make her do something, to get her under my control immediately. I decided to start with that vast ocean in front of me: the eye. I would make her blink.

I focused my thoughts on the act of blinking. I imagined the upper and lower lids meeting.

The pupil stayed fixed on me.

I blinked deliberately, concentrating on projecting the action to the serpent.

She stayed motionless.

"Blink," I said.

At the sound of my voice, the serpent raised her massive head, bringing her bottom jaw shoulder-height.

I stepped back.

She tilted her head to peer down at me.

With Eriana's blood flowing in my veins, I'd assumed it would become clear how to control her once she was awake. I'd expected to feel her presence, to instinctively know what to do. But I felt nothing—only a stinging pain in my sliced palm and that paralyzing iciness in the air.

I didn't know how to read the serpent's expression, but I thought she looked groggy, even irritated at being woken from her deep sleep.

Beyond the head, something enormous scraped over damp clay. The noise echoed. She must have been lying in a cavern as vast as a stadium.

I stumbled backwards as the second head jutted from the darkness. The square snout hovered where I'd been standing, nostrils flaring.

The heads were identical, as the legend said. Neither appeared weaker than the other.

I fleetingly wondered how much body lay coiled in the darkness. I couldn't imagine it. She was too surreal.

Two pairs of eyes watched me. I'd never felt so much like a helpless, trembling mouse.

Lower your heads, I thought.

I desperately tried to feel the words with every part of me.

The serpent drew a long, slow breath from all four nostrils. Strands of my hair pulled towards her. A shudder ran up my spine in the breeze.

"Lower your heads," I said, my voice unnaturally high.

She finally blinked of her own accord. A clear membrane crossed the eyes, front to back, and then the lids, top and bottom meeting gently in the middle. The cavern was so silent that I heard it, wet and sticky.

The lids had closed in unison, leading me to believe one mind controlled both heads. I had wondered if they would snap at each other like bickering siblings. But the serpent had full, harmonious control over her body.

The heads scanned their surroundings, mirroring each other.

I lifted an arm, extending my bleeding palm towards the second head. I concentrated on the sensation of pushing it away from me.

Nothing.

A low rumble met my ears. I checked over my shoulder before realising the noise came from the leviathan. The second head stuck out a long, red tongue, tasting the air between us. She could smell me. Was it the blood dripping from my hand?

The first head lowered to the ground. A scraping noise echoed again from the darkness. She was moving. With another flick of a forked tongue, the second head retreated into the cavern. It disappeared from my sight.

That briny, ancient scent of ocean became stronger, as though it oozed from the rippling scales.

She blinked, narrowing the vertical pupil, clearing her vision. She drew another breath that pulled wisps of hair from my shoulders.

The rumbling grew louder, coming from deep inside her.

Run, said a voice in my head.

She tasted the air, and this time the tongue nearly touched me. I backed away, clenching my bleeding fist to try and stem the flow of blood.

The jaws parted with a sound like cracking wood.

I took this as my cue. I broke eye contact and whirled around, taking off at a sprint.

For several seconds, the only sounds were my bare feet against the clay and my heaving lungs.

Then I heard her behind me—a low hiss, and the sinister rasp of her armour against clay.

I pushed harder, sprinting down the tunnel until my legs burned.

The beams of light ended. The water must have been close. Without slowing, I dove headfirst off the ledge and into the water. I frog-kicked under the threshold, putting all my strength into each stroke.

Too soon, the water pulsed, like something had been thrust violently into it. It propelled me forwards, carrying me so my back collided with the earth above.

I pushed away from the clay ceiling and kicked, blinded by the swirling black water.

I'd been out of breath before I submerged, and my lungs begged for air already.

The current drove me towards the stone door. I slammed into the tunnel walls with each pulse.

I felt like I'd been caught in an undertow. Each collision, each push to keep myself moving forwards, expelled more air from my lungs.

Ahead, a sliver of daylight peeked through the muddy water.

I hit the ceiling again. The door was in front of me. I clawed at it, frantic, until my fingers stung.

The sliver of daylight widened.

The water around me was tinged red. Blood flowed from my palm and now my fingertips.

A hand seized me by the collar. It hauled me through a narrow gap and thrust me towards the surface.

I kicked towards the light.

My head broke through. I spluttered as a wave splashed into my mouth.

The entire earth was shaking, churning the water around me like a boiling pot. The trees in the schoolyard swayed.

Tanuu popped up next to me, eyes huge. Blacktail surfaced next, and then Annith.

"Get out of the water!" I shouted, my voice so raspy and panicked that I didn't recognise it.

We swam furiously for the shore. I was so exhausted that the three of them overtook me easily. Blacktail reached the shallows first. She whirled around and extended a hand. I seized it. She dragged me out.

We waded for shore, a nightmarish struggle against the weight of waterlogged clothes.

Tanuu shouted something I couldn't hear over the rumbling earth.

Water splashed the backs of my legs and battered the mud in small tidal waves.

"I can't control her," I shouted. "I tried thinking, speaking, moving my hands. She didn't obey—"

A noise like cracking ice pierced the air.

On the other side of the puddle, where the tunnel must have spanned, the earth split. A great, jagged chunk of rock thrust skywards. A fissure opened up beside it, and the water from the trench poured inside.

I cried out, staggering backwards.

An enormous, black, scaled head erupted from the ground. A fringe of horns fanned out at the back of the skull, like a mane of bones beneath hard flesh. The serpent opened her jaws to reveal rows of curved teeth, each one the length of my forearm. Her tongue slashed the air in a streak of red.

Tanuu's profanity was drowned out by the most agonisingly loud noise I had ever heard. The serpent's roar brought my hands to my ears.

The earth stopped shaking as the sound echoed through the trees.

And I was sure, beyond doubt, that the entire island had heard—and felt—Eriana's Host awaken.

CHAPTER TWENTY-TWO
Ancient Awakening

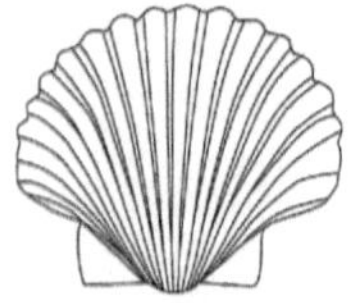

The vibrations across the water penetrated my bones, a sense like nothing I'd ever felt. Ancient, timeless, like the feel of the sea itself.

I stopped. Each breath rushed into my lungs, hot and painful.

The feeling faded.

Then a roar like thunder. What kind of animal would make a noise so terrible?

There was one explanation.

Meela had found the Host.

"No," I breathed.

Absurdly, I told myself I wasn't too late. I could still stop her. I had time to fix this.

My heart beat so fast that I trembled as I stared across the water.

Eriana Kwai was visible, a faint mark on the horizon.

Maybe Meela hadn't been the one to do it. Or maybe Adaro was wrong, and the Host didn't require a sacrifice. She could still be alive.

The current changed, dragging everything down and away from the land.

As it gathered into an enormous wave, I dove.

I angled towards Eriana Kwai, fighting the pull.

The noise, the swells, the deep reverberation might have been the result of an earthquake. But I knew it was more than that.

An uneasy feeling settled deep inside me. If I'd heard and felt it way out here, how much further would it carry?

Waves continued to rise, pushing far out to sea. Every mermaid and merman for leagues around would feel this and believe it was the result of an earthquake.

But there was one who would know the horrible truth.

I wondered where Adaro was—and how long it would be until he found out that the Host had been awakened.

CHAPTER TWENTY-THREE
Descendants

We sprinted towards the forest.

Behind us, the slab of rock jutted from the middle of the schoolyard, revealing a gaping hole into the cave below. The Host's endless body erupted from it, blacker and more solid than lava rock. Blasts emitted from her nostrils, each breath laboured. Water sprayed from her scales and flooded across the field in torrents. My ears filled with a sound like a waterfall.

Tanuu, Annith, Blacktail, and I plunged between two fat hemlocks, masking ourselves in the woods. I motioned for them to stop.

"I want - to see - what she does," I said, wheezing.

The others were breathing too hard to say anything. They leaned against the trees, clutching their ribs. Our heavy clothes dripped onto the moss floor.

The leviathan's body coiled in the trench, displacing the water and turning the field into a swamp. When the second head emerged, she raised it beside the first and paused. She surveyed the schoolyard with chilling intelligence in her eyes.

The world fell silent but for the water dripping from both heads.

She tasted the air with tongues the size of oars.

Her pupils narrowed. Her nostrils flared.

Both massive heads snapped in our direction, as though responding to a noise.

I stopped breathing. My pulse pounded in my ears.

Then the serpent lowered her head. I heard a wet grinding, like rock on mud, as she came towards us.

"Run."

We sprinted headlong through the forest, crashing through branches, ignoring the pine needles whipping our faces and brambles catching our clothes. I concentrated on my feet. Though a lifetime of going barefoot had given me tough soles, stabs of pain shot up as I landed on stones and roots.

Behind us rose a symphony of splintering trees, puffs of breath, and grinding rock. The serpent was destroying everything in her path.

Or, almost everything. In that moment, I was more grateful than ever for the vast trees on Eriana Kwai. Even a leviathan couldn't knock down a thousand-year-old sequoia. It was enough to let us stay ahead.

The serpent roared in frustration. The sound came so close that my eardrums stung, as though the sheer volume had popped them. She was much too close. Did I imagine the warm air on the back of my neck?

I didn't dare look over my shoulder in case it slowed me down.

A buck shot from the woods beside me and I stumbled in surprise. I caught blind terror in his eye before he outran us and disappeared. I veered, trusting his path through the thicket. The others stayed close behind.

With each step, my sopping pant legs chafed and clung together. My lungs screamed; a stitch burned in my ribs. Nearest me, Annith breathed so hard it sounded like whimpering. Adrenaline must have kept her pushing past her injury.

Could we dive into a cave and let the Host pass? Or would she smell us and corner us in there?

Blacktail gasped something.

"What?" I said.

"Beach. Left. Lead - to ocean."

I glanced left. If we broke the deer trail and kept running straight, we'd land at the beach. If we could get to the ocean—the leviathan's territory—maybe she would satisfy herself on a more familiar meal.

We had to try.

The thought of the end of our sprint gave me new energy. I leapt off the deer trail, back into the dense bush. The absence of a pathway forced me to slow down. I used my hands to vault over a fallen log, and again to push between the cleft of a twin spruce.

Beside us, the ground plummeted into a ravine. I knew animals sometimes ran along creeks to wash away their scent when fleeing predators. Though I doubted the trick would work here, it was worth a shot.

I ran down the steep slope, arms flailing for balance. We splashed into the creek and turned downstream. The water came to my ankles, but it was easier to run through than the uneven bush.

Something thudded behind me, and someone grunted. A splash. Footsteps stopped.

I slowed, but heard Tanuu say, "I've got you. Keep running."

Annith caught up and jabbed me between the shoulder blades. "They're up. Go!"

I did.

The sky brightened ahead. The trees thinned.

We burst from the woods. I couldn't slow down, and the drop in the earth made me trip. Reacting instinctively from years of combat training, I rolled into a ball as I fell, protecting my head. I flipped over once, twice, three times, rolling across the beach like a stone.

I hit something solid and sprawled flat, coughing. My shoulder seared where it hit, blazing through my back and arm.

I sat up, grasping for a sense of direction.

I'd landed on a rocky beach, my back to a boulder. Where the forest ended, dirt became rock, and grass became clumps of seaweed.

A dark shape loomed along the shoreline. The upturned fishing boat.

The tide was rising, splashing into the broken hull and sending a wide spray with each wave.

Lysi's beach would be just beyond that. That meant there was a hollow behind this boulder where a tide pool liked to form.

Gasping, every part of me aching, I crawled around the boulder. The tide pool rose to my neck when I sat on the bottom. My clothes were so wet and icy that the water felt warm.

I glanced around for my friends. Nearby, someone was wheezing. Hands and knees slapped the rocks. A dirt-caked arm clawed the ground beside me. I reached for it. Annith. I pulled her behind the boulder, telling her to get in.

"Annith, where's—?"

"They're coming," she said, the words a sob.

The din grew closer. The serpent was about to break through the trees.

Why weren't Tanuu and Blacktail out of the bush yet? Annith had told me to keep running. She'd said they were fine. I should have stopped to make sure.

"Annith, where—?"

"Shh!"

Trees snapped. The noise echoed.

In the tide pool, the brief feeling of warmth passed. I shivered convulsively.

"There," said Annith.

I turned. A short ways down the beach, our friends broke through the forest at full speed. They dove for the fishing boat.

The ground trembled. A roar brought my hands to my ears.

Tanuu wrapped a protective arm around Blacktail as they backed into the hull.

The serpent crashed onto the beach with a force like a mudslide. Sticks and dirt flew across the rocks.

She spotted the fishing boat and paused, nostrils flaring. The first head glanced around, taking in the beach, the treeline, the ocean. Her body and the second head still lay in the bush.

She dipped her tongue into the broken hull.

Annith tugged my arm, trying to get me to lean back. I couldn't. Tanuu and Blacktail were pressed against the rotting wood, chests heaving.

The serpent grunted, sending a blast of air over the wreckage. Fragments of wood fluttered into the waves. A long tongue traced the edges of the broken cabin.

Without warning, the serpent swung her horned head, disintegrating the top half of the boat. Tanuu and Blacktail disappeared beneath the rubble.

I clenched my jaw, trying to stop my teeth from chattering so loudly.

The serpent blinked at the rubble, as though noticing the mess she made. She tasted the air around it. Then she turned her great head towards the sea. A low hiss met my ears.

She moved towards the water.

Those intelligent eyes revealed more than hunger. Was she searching for her master? Or perhaps the Enticer?

Though she hit the water in relative silence, torrents swelled on either side of her. I held my breath as they flooded the tide pool and briefly submerged Annith and me.

The body followed, undulating across the beach. The enormous black scales clicked over the rocks.

Shivering, I curled my knees to my heaving chest. What had I done? I couldn't control her, and now this beast, large enough to destroy every ship in the sea, was free.

But the same legend that told me how to free her also told me she could be tamed. I just needed to find out how to do it. What was I missing?

"Meela," whispered Annith. "The second head is about to pass. She'll see us."

I grabbed her arm. "Go that way."

We crawled from the tide pool and around the other side of the rock, keeping as quiet as possible.

A blowing sound came from somewhere nearby. The second head was passing.

I stayed still, holding my breath. If she spotted us, it would be too easy for her to change direction and attack.

A crack split the air. Unable to stop myself, I peered around the rock. The trailing head had lunged for the fishing boat. Her teeth sunk into the weak frame and disintegrated the rest of the hull.

I hadn't heard Tanuu or Blacktail scream. Were they buried? What if a piece of steel had hit them?

I covered my mouth to stifle the panic rising within me.

Annith nudged me in the ribs. She pointed to the far side of the pile of rubble. Our friends pulled themselves from beneath it. They huddled behind the last standing fragment of wood, as insignificant as a pair of hermit crabs.

The serpent kept retreating into the water. She hadn't seen them. Rotting wood fell from her jaws, leaving a trail down the beach.

She submerged. The water puckered as she swam, her size making her easy to follow.

For a moment, waves swirled like a vortex, and then they calmed. Her wake continued onwards. She must have been feeding.

We continued to watch, frozen in place. I kept my eyes on the ocean, unsure whether the serpent would return to shore.

Annith glanced at the forest. "We need to figure out what we're miss—"

She flinched as the serpent exploded from the water, flinging something large and bloody into the air. She swallowed it and splashed back down, sending a spray as high as a ship's mast.

Every piece of me ached. My hand throbbed, blood pouring from the place where I'd cut myself with the dagger. I tried to hold the wound closed, but the blood oozed from my fist.

Annith gasped as she noticed the amount of blood on the rocks at our feet.

Too exhausted to speak, I shook my head to indicate I was fine. I hadn't cut myself deeply. I'd only used the dull bone dagger. The run must have pumped the blood through my body more vigorously.

Right now, we needed to regroup and figure out how to control the leviathan before we lost her. Or before she returned to land.

Footsteps pounded behind us. We turned.

A girl burst out of the woods.

The thin, bony figure skidded to a halt at the sight of the destroyed fishing boat. Then her gaze shifted beyond that, to the waves that thrashed more violently than the wind demanded.

Mane falling out of her high ponytail, face flushed and sweaty, Dani wore this year's Massacre uniform, clean and pressed for the ceremony.

"They did it," she said to herself.

Her wild eyes landed on Annith and me; we were hunched against a boulder, sopping wet and trembling.

"You gave your blood?"

I stared at her, panting. When she saw the blood dripping from my clenched fist, she let out a whoop.

She strode closer to the water.

"Eriana! Show yourself."

She thrust a fist in the air.

"What's she doing?" said Annith.

I had no answer. A thrill of dread overcame me.

In the distance, the ripples quieted. Then the water stirred again, closer. Scales poked out of the waves like the glistening back of a whale.

An enormous head burst from the water, sending a spray wide enough to drench us.

The leviathan's eyes bored into Dani. Her jaws opened, as though ready to strike.

She froze.

The second head emerged. All four deep blue eyes stared at Dani.

Dani dropped her arm after presenting it to the leviathan.

"The serpent head," I said breathlessly. "She has a serpent branded on her wrist."

What did Dani know about this symbol that we didn't?

Dani must have noticed the change of energy in the leviathan. She waded into the rising tide and climbed onto the highest boulder on the beach.

"*Sisiutl*," she said, in a low hiss that might have come from the serpent herself.

The waves calmed. Both massive heads lowered, as though cowering.

"You're more beautiful than I imagined," said Dani.

"Dani, what've you done?" said Annith. "What's it doing?"

Annith's voice seemed to come through a tunnel. Whether from shock or exhaustion, the world grew fuzzy. I watched in horror as Dani faced the two-headed serpent.

I was reminded of a raven perched on a treetop as she stood on the high boulder, arms outstretched.

Dani lifted her left arm. The first head twitched, following it.

"No," I said, my breathless voice carried away by the wind.

Dani lifted her right arm. The other head snapped around to look at it.

"Meela," said Annith, voice high, flooded with the panic I felt in every fibre of my body.

Dani raised both arms higher, and lower. The leviathan followed, rising up, and then down, fixed on Dani's every move with four gleaming eyes.

Dani cried out in elation. She slammed her palms forwards as though pushing the air, and both heads emitted an earth-shattering roar.

The wound in my palm seared. I hunched over, clenching my fist in vain. Blood poured from the gash. I pressed it, trying to stop the flow.

"Annith, help me fix this," I gasped.

A high wave brought the icy water to me. My blood splashed into it, clouding and disappearing.

Before Annith could take my hand, pain burst through me, coming from deep inside my hand and shooting up my arm like shattered glass. I couldn't stop the scream escaping my lips.

Someone yelled my name. I stared, unfocused, at the blood oozing from my hand. Something was wrong. I'd been cut so many times and it had never stung like this. It had never bled this much—not from a cut so small.

Sinking lower to the ground, I stared at my palm, gasping.

I shivered as another swell brought the icy water to me.

Blacktail and Tanuu were there. I didn't remember them running over. The three of them knelt beside me.

Someone yelled my name again. It wasn't any of them. It was distant. I hadn't heard that voice in a long while. For the briefest moment, warmth spread in my chest at the sound of it.

I turned towards the ocean, hearing the warning that came too late.

"Mee, stop!"

CHAPTER TWENTY-FOUR
Home

Closing that final distance to Eriana Kwai seemed to take an eternity. I swam as fast as I could, tail whipping, letting the waves control when I breached.

I let go of my weapon so it wouldn't slow me down. Whatever I was about to face, that blade wouldn't help me.

Activity stirred on the right. Idle movement and chatter told me it was merpeople going about their everyday lives.

My heart leapt. This was the town I'd grown up in. That meant I was half a league from Eriana Kwai.

The bottom grew shallower. Children playing in the coral pointed at me as I sped past.

If these families knew something was wrong on the island so close to home, they didn't show it. Their lives were too peaceful, too remote.

They had my empathy. In a few short years, those children would be drafted into the army. Like me, they would have to abandon their lives and move to Utopia to serve the king.

I kept swimming, passing over salmon, sea lions, rocks, and sand. Above, the island loomed closer. Trees became distinct against the mountains.

That rumbling carried towards me, grazing my skin and thrumming in my ears.

What was I supposed to do when I got there? How could I stop Adaro when iron was useless against him?

Our failures proved it: fighting him would not work. We needed something bigger.

Could we find another mine? Lead him into a whale's open mouth? What about the Host?

I shook my head, not sure why I was even thinking about this anymore. My allies were dead. There was no 'next time'.

Earlier today, five of us had set out with confidence. Now, three of us were dead, and Spio had been forced to swim for his life. Even if he had managed to escape, there would still be a search for his arrest. He would have to live in hiding like Coho—Nilus—and Ephyra.

I had to find them.

Nilus was a whole new reason Meela had to be alive: I couldn't let her die before telling her about her brother.

Maybe he thought it better not to tell his family, but I knew Meela. She would want to know.

I couldn't speak for her parents, but if they would rather have lost a child than accept him for what he was, I didn't care. They could deal with it.

The beach drew near. The floor rose to a few fathoms deep.

The presence of the Host closed around me like a net. Whatever this creature was, its aura was more powerful than anything I'd felt before.

She was a female form, regal and commanding. A queen?

No, a goddess—like the spirit of the ocean itself.

I hesitated, suspended. I had to get a better feel on her.

Where was she?

Her scent blended with the ocean, making her hard to detect.

Then, with a shock that drained all feeling from my limbs, I saw her.

A serpent.

Her body coiled over the floor, thick enough that she could have swallowed a humpback whale.

I traced my eyes along the body, frantically looking for her head. Stiff vibrations in the current told me her scales were harder than granite. They followed a smooth, symmetrical pattern, and I couldn't tell front from back.

A shadow fell over me and I looked up. The dark shape of the serpent's head was above surface, fixated on a large boulder. No, on a human standing on top of it.

Don't be Meela.

But I recognised the girl's thin frame from the Battle for Eriana Kwai. Dani.

A shadow materialised behind her.

For a moment, I thought the choppy water was playing a trick on me. It looked like a second head.

Suddenly, I understood why her scales were so symmetrical, her presence so disorienting.

The smell of blood met my nose. Human blood.

I snapped my head around, focusing on the source.

It disappeared as fast as it came. Someone must have been at the edge of the tide, creeping waves pulling the scent into the water.

With the next wave, their presence hit me: several humans on the beach. They were hurt.

I shot towards them, surfacing briefly.

Beyond the overpowering feel of the serpent, she was there. I would recognise her anywhere.

"Mee!"

It was her blood.

I darted past the serpent. The scent of Meela's blood grew stronger. It was noticeably stale, like an animal that had already died.

Panic swelled inside me. I couldn't think.

I surfaced again, screaming for her.

"Mee, stop!"

CHAPTER TWENTY-FIVE
The Missing Piece

Maybe too much was going on, or maybe Annith and Blacktail both recognised her, but nobody reacted when a mermaid threw herself at me and knocked me backwards.

Lysi's coppery hair sent a spray as it fell across my shoulder. She wrapped her arms around my waist in a hug as warm as it was cold.

"I'm too late," she said. "No, no, no ..."

"Lysi!"

"You didn't. Tell me you didn't."

I pulled back, too shocked by her sudden appearance to absorb what she was saying.

"You're here," I said.

I studied her face—the angle of her cheekbones, the dimple in her chin, the curve of her nose, the shape of her lips. Had her eyes always been so blue?

Even tightened by panic, her features were perfect.

"Didn't what?" I said.

Her eyes locked onto my bleeding hand. Breathing hard, she grabbed it, watching the blood seep from the wound.

"It was a sacrifice, Mee. The blood to free the Host."

I frowned at my palm. That couldn't be right. A few drops of blood had worked fine.

"The pages never said anything about a sacrifice," said Tanuu.

He reached for my injured hand, and Lysi let him take it. He pressed the cut as though he could stop the bleeding. I'd never seen him look so fearful. Did he believe it?

"It just needs stitches," said Blacktail.

"Let's wrap it," said Annith in a shaky voice. "A tourniquet."

"Good idea," I said, oddly calm.

Blacktail pulled off her shirt—my cotton shirt, as I still wore her wool one—and used her dagger to cut it into one long, spiralling strip.

"Hey!" I said. "That's the last time I let you wear my clothes."

She glanced up without amusement.

They were panicking for nothing. I would be fine, once the bleeding stopped.

I scanned their faces. They were honed in on my bloody hand as though dismantling a bomb. Why hadn't anyone reacted to Lysi? Was she even there?

I ran a hand up her arm. Smooth, cold. Yes, she was there, watching Blacktail wrap my wound.

It was as though they were all too afraid for me to care that a sea demon had appeared in their midst. I wanted to tell them to calm down, but I couldn't make a sound.

The world was discoloured, like watching everything through a haze.

It was a few drops, I thought. *The pages in the totem pole said nothing about a sacrifice.*

Dani's laugh split the air.

Lysi snapped her head around, a flash of red in her eyes. She leaned closer, as though to shield me.

Dani was facing the serpent, arms raised. It undulated below the surface a short distance away. If it weren't for the occasional head poking up for air, the glossy, black body could have passed for a breaching pod of whales.

"I feel her," shouted Dani. "I can feel Eriana! This is crazy."

High on the isolated boulder, Dani's wild expression, windblown hair, and rapid breathing gave her the appearance of someone struck by lightning.

She caught all of us staring and grinned.

"I have something for you."

From inside her Massacre uniform, she pulled out a roll of parchment and threw it at us. It landed steps away in the rising tide, where it rocked in the waves.

"No," said Annith, scooping it up. "How did …"

"Missing a page, weren't you?" said Dani.

A high wave splashed against the boulder, sending a spray over her head that hissed when it landed.

"Read it," said Annith, dropping to her knees beside Tanuu.

"I knew you'd never free Sisiutl if you understood the full details," said Dani.

Tanuu took the page from Annith. My blood smeared across it from his reddened hands. Blacktail still wrapped the cotton strip, making each turn tight and precise. My fingers swelled from the pressure.

Lysi pulled herself closer to me. Her tail pressed against my hip. I touched her, making sure she was still real. She had to stay with me. She couldn't disappear again.

Tanuu read from the page.

"… feeding Eriana's own blood to the sleeping beast, the soul hosted by the human revives the one within the leviathan. Once the beast has woken, the flesh that was slit to provide the blood will … will never …"

His voice broke.

Blacktail froze, the last strip of cotton hovering over my hand. She stared at Tanuu with wide eyes.

Tanuu swallowed hard. "… will never heal. The sacrifice of one of Eriana's descendants will ensure the reawakening of the leviathan is considered with the severity it deserves. Control of the leviathan will then be granted to a descendant branded by Eriana's Mark. The one with the Mark …"

He reached the end and lowered the page, eyes bloodshot.

"Gains control of the leviathan until death," said Blacktail, recalling the end of the sentence.

My head felt light, like everything had drained from it. I must have swayed, because Lysi placed a cold hand on my back.

"The flesh will never heal," I said. "Tanuu …"

"You'll bleed to death," he whispered.

Blacktail finished wrapping the tourniquet. I winced as she tightened the knot a bit too firmly.

"No," she said. "You won't. The cut isn't deep. Look how thick I've wrapped—"

Her eyes widened as she stared at her work. Blood seeped through the cotton. It pushed beneath and through the material, uncontrollable, like a river during a snowmelt.

"It's my fault," said Tanuu, breathing fast. "I knew a page was missing. I shoulda stopped you from—"

"We all knew," I said. "I cut my own hand. This isn't on any of you."

I couldn't look at their faces. How could I have done this to them?

Something splashed. Annith was on her feet, running towards Dani.

Dani lifted an arm lazily. The serpent coiled around the rock, an impenetrable shield.

Annith stopped, knee-deep in the tide, chest heaving. "You let Meela give her blood! You let her do it knowing she was a sacrifice!"

"Don't be selfish," said Dani. "All of this is about more than Meela. With her sacrifice, a child of Eriana Kwai now has control of the most powerful weapon in the world."

Annith tried to run forwards again, but the serpent lashed one of its huge tongues at her. I caught a whiff of ocean stench in its warm breath.

"Think about it!" said Dani. "I control the spirit of Eriana. The fate of the oceans is in my hands. I have power over who lives—and who dies."

Her pale eyes were fixed on Lysi in a way that made my stomach churn. The serpent's heads lingered on either side of the boulder, like dogs waiting for a command.

"Guys, watch the serpent," I said, barely audible.

Between the two heads and Dani, three sets of eyes focused on us. I might have been imagining it, but since Dani had claimed the Host, I thought those vertical pupils had changed, even grown paler.

"Dani," shouted Blacktail, standing in front of Lysi and me. "Meela is already dying because of you. Try anything else and you'll have four more bodies on your hands."

"So, what? In the end, when I've saved Eriana Kwai from the sea rats, a few sacrifices won't matter."

The black serpent drew taller, darkening the cloudy sky. Annith held her ground, heaving with rage.

Dani didn't strike. Somewhere beneath this reckless shell, she hesitated to kill again.

"You want to save our people," I said.

My friends stared at me like a rock had spoken. Had they heard me? My voice sounded distant. I strained to talk louder.

"You want to save our people, so start with the ones in front of you. Every child of Eriana Kwai matters. Every life matters. Making peace shouldn't mean making sacrifices."

Dani's jaw tightened, but she said nothing. The serpent stayed immobile.

A jolt of pain shot through me. I gasped. My insides felt like they were splitting into threads.

My friends knelt around me, at a loss for how to help.

Exhaustion trickled through my veins, making me dizzy, pushing me down with each desperate beat of my heart. If bleeding out meant falling asleep, Lysi holding my hand, my friends at my side, maybe this wasn't such a bad way to die.

Dani turned away. The rising tide closed around her, isolating her in the thrashing waves. She raised and lowered her arms, testing how much control she had.

Somewhere distant, Lysi said my name. I met her watery eyes, bluer than sapphires. I wanted those to be the last thing I saw.

Something was different about her.

"You're tanned," I said.

Lysi's lips parted in surprise. "That's what you're getting out of this? I got a suntan?"

I wanted to smile at her, but couldn't manage it through an overwhelming wave of sadness. I'd been prepared to die to save my people for years—but I wasn't ready anymore. This was too soon. I wasn't ready to say goodbye.

Another jolt of pain rippled through my body. I bit my lip so I wouldn't cry out. My friends spoke to me, but I could no longer hear them.

Coldness spread over the backs of my legs. The tide had caught up to us. The others noticed, too. Tanuu and Blacktail splashed around to my arms and feet as though to lift me back to shore.

I glanced down at my palm, and then regretted it. Blood oozed through the material, pouring from my hand once more. I breathed deeply, telling myself I was imagining it.

But I knew deep inside myself that this was real. I was dying.

"I'm gonna lift you," said Tanuu, squatting behind me.

"Wait," I said. "Dani needs to finish the plan."

"Finish the plan? Meela, I think we have bigger things to worry about!"

"That is the bigger thing. I won't stop until one of us—me or Adaro—is dead."

My voice rang over the hissing waves. Lysi, Tanuu, Blacktail, and Annith stared at me. I hoped they caught more determination than the fear I felt.

This was the end of it. The Aanil Uusha would claim a life today.

"It won't be you," said Lysi. "I won't let you die."

Without a glance at Tanuu or Dani or anyone, she ran her fingers through my hair. Her eyes followed her fingers across my jawline, over my shoulder, down my arm.

I squeezed her hand.

The waves calmed, sloshing gently against each other. The leviathan had stopped circling the boulder.

"Wait," said Dani. "Meela, are you—is that demon—I think I'm going to be sick!"

Hours earlier, I might have been embarrassed about Dani finding out. I might have tried to push Lysi away in the presence of anyone else, especially my friends. But I didn't care anymore. I didn't care if the whole world found out. Lysi was here, and that was all that mattered.

Annith, Tanuu, and Blacktail were also staring at Lysi—but instead of horror, I saw amazement on their faces.

I remembered the first time I'd seen Lysi. Inside and out, she'd radiated beauty. Even now, after seeing her a hundred times, that feeling of admiration never disappeared.

My lips pulled into a weak smile. Far from being embarrassed, I was proud. I wanted the world to know how much Lysi and I meant to each other.

"I thought it was bad enough you made friends with a demon," said Dani. "But you actually have feelings for one? You let her lure you like some pathetic sailor?"

Annith spun around. For lack of other options, she picked up a stone from the beach and hurled it at Dani.

The boulder was too far, and it fell miserably short of the serpent coiled around it.

Dani laughed. "Don't make me send Sisiutl after you."

The serpent answered with a rumble.

"Dani, look what you've done," said Annith. "You keep killing, and for nothing."

"Not for nothing! We're going on the Massacre with a leviathan at our heels. Don't you want to see us bring peace?"

"Yes," I said. "So don't waste this chance. Dani, we were after the Host for a reason. You need to use it to kill Adaro. Do you understand?"

"I'm going to kill more than just the king. By the time I'm done, there will be no sea rats left in the world. Starting with—"

"No! That's not what we need to do. Mermaids are not the enemy."

"Not the enemy? Who do you think is responsible for killing everyone over the last few decades?"

"You have a chance to redeem yourself," I said. "You can be remembered as the girl who brought peace. Keep going down this road, and you'll be remembered as the girl who murdered her friends and wiped out a species."

"Stop saying that!" said Dani. "I'm not a murderer!"

The serpent hissed, one head lunging towards us. The jaws snapped closed on empty air, close enough that a puff of warm wind blew my hair back. Frothy waves crashed into each other, flooding the beach and sending swells up to our necks.

The threat didn't scare me. Dani wasn't going to kill us. The fact that she hadn't attacked us yet proved it. She'd murdered, she'd made mistakes, but this wasn't her. Somewhere inside, Dani was still a child of Eriana Kwai, and a warrior who wanted to help her people. With her in control of the Host, we had to help her discover that part of herself and hope she would carry out our plan.

"How did you find out, Dani?" I said, trying to bring her temper down. "The Host wasn't easy to unearth, and you somehow got to the legend first."

The serpent's heads lowered as Dani dropped her arms. Her mouth twisted into a sneer.

"I knew you wouldn't let the issue drop after that pathetic meeting. So I kept an eye on you. I overheard what Anyo told you—the story of Eriana, the eyes in the water. The legend of Sisiutl has been in my family forever. I went to the totems to see her and figured out I needed to climb. I took the important page and left the rest for you to find."

"You can read the old language?" I said.

"No, but Hassun can. He's proven useful."

"Is that all people are to you?" said Annith. "Tools to get a job done?"

I extended a hand, signalling Annith to stop. The serpent opened its jaws and hissed as Dani's temper flared.

"So you knew you needed Eriana's Mark," I said. "How did you find the symbol?"

"The cultural centre," said Dani. "Nothing but rats and mould inside, but I did find Eriana's Mark on nearly every weapon. So I burned it into my flesh."

"Meela," said Tanuu gently. "We gotta get you out of the water."

I looked down. It had risen to my waist. I thought about standing, but even the thought made me want to close my eyes and sleep. How much blood had I lost? My fingertips were grotesquely discoloured.

"We're gonna lift you. Ready?" said Tanuu.

Annith joined Blacktail at my feet.

"While you all figure that out," said Dani, "you'll have to excuse us. I have an island to address."

"Dani, please," I said. "Don't take the serpent on the Massacre."

I had no doubt she would stay true to her word, and kill every mermaid she and the Host could find.

One of the heads drew close enough to the boulder that Dani reached for it. When she touched it, she wore an expression I never thought I'd see on her face—tender, sweet, with all the love in the world, like a mother holding her baby for the first time.

"I'd say Sisiutl's listening to me nicely, wouldn't you? Do you think she'll let me ride her to the ceremony?"

She stood on her toes to see the top of the nearest head.

Lysi's eyes flashed red, then. Her teeth lengthened. Before I understood why, something leapt from the water and crashed into us, knocking Lysi into me.

Lysi snarled like a wildcat, and then I was underwater.

A hand closed around my hair and pulled me back up. I surfaced, gasping and blind, to my friends' terrified screams.

CHAPTER TWENTY-SIX
Sworn Oath

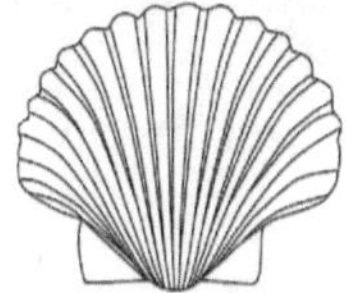

Strymon's full weight landed on me, knocking me backwards.

I braced myself in time to stop my head from slamming against Meela.

"Where is the king?" Strymon shouted over the screams of Meela's friends.

He prickled with both anger and fear. Did he think we had succeeded?

I hesitated to transform into a demon in front of Meela. Then I realised how ridiculous that was.

I snarled. "With any luck, he's dead."

Strymon reached for my throat. I tried to roll him off me but he was like a boulder pinning me down.

"You reeked of treachery since you arrived," he said, fingers closing around my neck. "Now I discover the remains of bloodshed on the way here."

He pushed me into the rocks, strangling me. I clawed at his eyes. He grunted and grabbed my wrists instead. With a force that would shatter human bone, he pried my hands away from his face.

"I warned the commander not to trust you," he said. "In the end, he was just as foul. He deserved his fate."

The tide rose, the next wave submerging me.

"You have one more chance to tell me," said Strymon. "Where is the king?"

"Gone!"

Rage flared in his aura—but I sensed the fear beneath it.

Meela was screaming. The boy, Tanuu, was pulling her away from us. My mind flipped back to her language.

"Blacktail, your dagger!"

No. I couldn't let her get involved. He'd kill her with one blow.

"Stay back, Mee! He's too—"

Strymon barked a laugh. "And you speak a human tongue! It should not surprise me. A traitor right through. I should have killed you the moment I became commander."

"Lysi, what's he saying?" said Meela.

She was fighting the boy, trying to get closer.

"Mee, stay—"

Strymon shoved my face beneath the water. While one hand held me there, the other slammed against my ribcage. The air left my lungs. He punched me again, and again, until my lungs emptied.

Through his webbed fingers, his head eclipsed the cloudy sky, agitated water blurring his face. I clawed at his arm. He pressed me harder against the rocky bottom, keeping his face out of reach.

He kept punching until I wasn't sure which was worse: the pain in my ribs or my deflated lungs. I was going to drown.

I twisted, desperately trying to roll him off me, when one of the humans launched herself at Strymon. He stopped punching to throw her off. Ripples spread out as she splashed into the tide some distance away.

At once, three more humans threw themselves at him. Pain surged from his pores. Blood dripped into the water above me. One of them must have had iron.

Strymon let go. I pushed myself up as he threw someone away from him with the ease of tossing a fish. But before I could surface, his fist came down across my face, pushing me back into the rocks.

I screamed in fury, though no one would hear it. My lungs spasmed, sending a jolt of pain up my throat.

The world overhead darkened. I thought I was losing consciousness—but then I caught a glimpse of white, shining teeth and a pink tongue. The two remaining humans scattered.

It had been a matter of time until the serpent came for us. I stopped fighting. At least this death would be a quick one.

The jaws closed over Strymon. I heard his scream from beyond the water. The serpent lifted him away from me.

I stayed still, watching through the turbulence as the head flung his body into the air and swallowed him. Droplets of blood hit the surface, smelling fresh as they spread out in front of my face.

I waited for the other head to descend on me.

It didn't come.

The darkness drew away. The sudden brightness of the grey sky made me squint.

I pushed myself up and surfaced with a shuddering gasp.

The humans were scattered in the waves. I searched for Meela, for the smell of blood draining from her body. I couldn't sense her. The scent of Strymon's death filled my nose, masking all else.

"Help!"

It was Tanuu. He staggered, fell to his knees, and then stood again, trying to lift something. A girl, face barely held out of the water. One arm was draped across Tanuu's shoulders. Her long, wet hair clung to her face.

I lunged for them, half-swimming, half-crawling through the shallow tide. I passed under the serpent's second head. It watched me but made no move.

Gasping for breath, I had no energy to fight the panic bubbling inside me.

"Mee!"

"She's conscious," said Tanuu.

Weak and groggy, she repeatedly tried to get her legs under her, only to have them give out. I let her use my shoulder as a crutch while the girls splashed over.

Annith pulled Meela's arm across her shoulder. They waded for shore, stumbling over the rocks.

Too low in the water, I could do nothing but watch. The other girl, the one they called Blacktail, gripped an iron dagger, glancing around for more attackers.

The serpent's eyes followed us. So did Dani's. Her mouth was open. With an air of surprise, she dropped her gaze to her hands—the ones that had commanded the serpent to kill Strymon.

The same hands had commanded it to spare me. Why?

Water streamed down Annith's face, which might have come from her hair or her red eyes—or both. Tanuu's eyes, too, were puffy and red. Blacktail was solemn, stony, like someone numb with shock.

Dani waved an arm. The serpent faced us, its energy rising. I braced myself, ready to break away from Meela and her friends. But the girl wavered.

One instant, she projected that blind desire for prey I only felt in animals; the next, such intense fear and dread that I might have smelled the change in her blood.

She flickered between these states as she watched us labour through the waves. I couldn't get a steady read on her. My muscles stayed tense, preparing me to flee any moment.

Then Dani turned away.

Slowly, the serpent ducked below the surface.

Above the waves, I barely heard the movement. Below the waves, soft ripples brushed my tail as she retreated.

CHAPTER TWENTY-SEVEN
One Last Chance

Tanuu and Annith dropped me just out of reach of the water. The tide would catch up to us soon, but they were panting too hard to carry me further.

Rocks groaned beneath hands and knees as they collapsed behind me.

"Are you hurt?" I said, glancing to Lysi.

"Who cares about us," mumbled Tanuu.

I closed my fingers over the blood-soaked bandage.

"Look, I lived a month longer than I was supposed to."

Lysi's eyes widened. "Don't say that!"

"We both know it was my fate to die on the Massacre."

"No, it wasn't. I would never have let that happen."

She pulled herself from the tide and sat next to me.

Every part of me seared with pain, both inside and out. My heart laboured to pump blood that wasn't there.

The world blurred. Ocean merged with cloud, the horizon broken and jagged. Somewhere closer, the dark mass of the Host swelled with the waves. Dani played with it, bringing it close and then pushing it away. I wondered if she was afraid to bring it to the ceremony. I thought I might be, if I were in her position.

The rising tide hissed in my ears, ready to coil around my chest and pull me down.

I stretched out my injured hand. Even that appeared fuzzy. Blood dripped into the waves and disappeared.

Lysi closed her hand around it.

I raked my eyes over her, grateful I got to see her one last time: her skin, smooth and golden; her greenish-brown tail, fading into her stomach like a sunset; her hair, coppery blonde, made thicker by tangles and seaweed; her perfect, arched eyebrows; her eyes, inhumanly large, white as pearls, blue as sapphires; her lips, full and rosy.

I lingered on her lips.

Might as well, I thought, *if I'm going to die anyway.*

I slid a hand around the back of her neck and tried to pull her towards me. She didn't move, resisting as easily as if I'd been pulling a tree trunk.

"I can't," she said.

"Why not?"

"You entered this world a human, and you should leave it a human. I would never forgive myself for taking that from you in your last …"

Her voice cracked. She shook her head.

"I don't care," I said. "I want to die having kissed you."

Her breath hitched. She pulled back, but I held on.

"You're not thinking clearly," she said.

"I am. I've … I've known since the Massacre."

Her eyes flicked to my lips. "You have?"

My next words came easily—even urgently. My moments were too numbered for anything else.

"I love you, Lysi."

It was as though something inside her disintegrated. Her shoulders dropped, her face softened, her eyebrows pulled down over those large, bright eyes.

"I love you, too," she whispered.

I felt her words as much as I heard them—a gust of breath on my skin, a stammer in my heart, a tingling in my lips.

"Then kiss me," I said.

Her gaze dropped to my lips again. She seemed about to speak, but then closed her mouth.

"Do it!" said Tanuu.

Lysi and I started. I'd all but forgotten we weren't alone. We turned to him just as he howled in pain, and Annith rubbed her knuckles where they'd made contact with Tanuu's jaw.

"Don't be a pig!" she shouted. "Our friend is about to die and all you can—"

"No!" he said. "I mean she's gotta be taken from her human form."

"What?" said Blacktail and Annith together.

Tanuu pulled the soggy parchment from his pocket.

"Whatever curse is acting on Meela won't harm her if she's not human."

Nobody spoke as he massaged his jawbone back in place. Lysi and I stared at each other.

"Listen," said Tanuu, flattening the parchment. "It says, *the soul hosted by the human revives the one within the leviathan.* Human! Even in the rest of it—it talked about human blood, human souls."

Annith covered her mouth.

"Oh," Blacktail breathed.

I tried to recall what the story said. I could barely focus on the present.

I glanced between my friends, really seeing them since that merman had attacked. Annith's hair dripped down her face, taking a stream of blood with it. She'd hit her head. Tanuu had a swollen cheekbone that would soon become a black eye. Blacktail cradled her left arm across her chest.

"Meela, this is how you can survive," said Tanuu.

My heart beat faster, as though renewed by the prospect of staying alive.

After a stunned silence, I turned to Lysi. "You can save my life."

"Are you sure that's true?" she said, voice high.

"No," said Tanuu. "But she has nothing to lose by trying."

Lysi's eyes darted between us, wide and fearful. "I … I haven't … Mee, I've never changed a human before."

"Good," I said.

She searched my face, seeming to gauge whether I was being serious.

Annith grabbed Tanuu and Blacktail by the hands.

"We'll be over there," she said, nodding towards the crumbled ship.

She strained to her feet and pulled the others with her, leaving Lysi and me alone.

Lysi watched them hobble away for several seconds, until I ran my fingers through her hair. She turned back to me, eyes glossy with fear.

"You're sure you want to?" she said.

I raised myself on my knees, linking my hands around her neck. "Yes."

"If this works, you're a mermaid forever."

"I want to be with you," I said.

"What if you change your mind? I don't want to be the one to steal you from your people."

"You're not stealing anything. You're giving me my life."

She opened her mouth to argue, and then closed it.

Though she could have pulled away from my hold, she didn't.

"Lysi, this is the only life I have. I don't want to lose it. I have too much to live for."

The words struck me as I said them. Despite everything my family had been through, I felt lucky to be alive. I had so much to do, and it would take a lifetime to do it all. I was not ready to have my life cut short.

Besides, this war against Adaro had yet to be won. I refused to die until I saw that happen.

Somewhere in those moments, Lysi had leaned closer. My head felt light, from some combination of dizziness and her sweet-smelling breath against my skin.

I knotted her hair in my fists.

The tide rose around us, me on my knees, Lysi sitting hip-deep. Her tail fluttered in the shallow waves.

I stopped shivering. I felt warm, despite the icy water, cutting wind, and Lysi's cold skin beneath my palms.

One way or another, my human life had come to an end.

My heart knew it, pounding wildly in my chest.

"Ready?" I said.

"Ready."

"Close your eyes."

I was reminded of a day on the beach so many years ago, sitting on these hard, damp rocks, Lysi telling me to close my eyes.

Despite everything, I smiled.

She must have remembered, too, because her lips pulled back from those perfect, white teeth.

For a moment, we stayed there, our breaths shallow. Lysi's hands were on my waist, clenching my soaking wet shirt.

Then I leaned in, and kissed her.

I held her face as our lips met, feeling her smooth skin beneath my hands. Her arms slid around my back and pulled me closer, and I pressed my body against hers.

In that moment, everything in my life came together. Everything I'd ever felt made sense, like the world had opened before me. Lysi was my childhood, my teenage years, and now my future.

I ran my fingers through her hair. My senses seemed to sharpen—a tingling in my skin, the waves purring louder in my ears, a sweetness on my tongue. Warmth spread through my body.

If this was what it felt like to bleed to death, it wasn't so bad.

CHAPTER TWENTY-EIGHT
Sea Rats

The current changed.

I pulled away.

"What is it?" said Meela.

The serpent was moving through the waves, steady and powerful. The intensity of her focus was like a shark's, but I could sense in her a deep, age-old intelligence.

I threw out an arm to sweep Meela behind me, as though I could protect her from what was coming.

"No," shouted Dani. "The Host needs her sacrifice!"

"You already have her blood!" I said.

The sky darkened as the serpent loomed out of the water.

"She hasn't died, yet," said Dani.

Tanuu ran towards us, Annith and Blacktail on his heels.

"She doesn't need to," he said. "You already have control, Dani."

She seemed to consider this, but her aura flared as Meela's friends placed themselves between us and the towering snake. Her fists clenched, hair tangling in the wind like seaweed caught in a riptide. Her pale eyes gleamed as hungrily as the serpent's.

"I gave you the chance to die with honour, Meela."

She was erratic, projecting anger and sadness and elation all at once.

"Dani, calm down," said Meela. "You don't understand."

She didn't, and she never would. Dani would never think of merpeople as equals. Her whole life had been dedicated to destroying us. She wasn't about to change that—not while her people depended on her.

Meela's friends stood ready to fight. To what end, I didn't know. Any weapons would be toys against this girl and her serpent.

"Let Meela go," said Annith. "You can walk away from this without killing anyone else—"

"Annith!" said Meela.

It had been the wrong thing to say, for Dani radiated fury.

The serpent gave a low hiss. Its jaws parted.

"Let's work together," said Meela. "You don't need to set the serpent on every mermaid. Let us tell you what we know."

I didn't like the energy coming from Dani. I needed to get to her before she acted.

Could I dart past the serpent and get to the boulder?

The double heads gave me pause. I might have outstripped a single head, but two? Could I move quickly enough? Maybe I could get beneath it somewhere.

I leaned down, scanning for a path.

Meela grabbed my arm, as if reading my thoughts.

"Look, if you wanna save our people, killing one of Eriana's descendants isn't a great way to start," said Tanuu.

"She's no child of Eriana!" said Dani with a pulse of rage.

Meela shouted back. "Open your mind! Mermaids are no different from humans. I'm still the same—"

"You've betrayed your people! You did this to yourself, knowing I have the most powerful creature in the world in my hands. Knowing I'm about to use her to destroy every last demon, starting with this one—"

Dani lurched, as though some force had knocked her from behind. Her eyes bulged. It took me a moment to feel the emotion coming from her.

Fear.

She opened her mouth as though to say more. A whimper escaped, so soft that I wasn't sure anyone else heard it.

A thick, crimson bubble formed between her parted lips. She looked down. The bubble popped. A stream of blood dripped down her chin and onto her uniform.

The smell of blood, already heavy, wafted under my nose. Warm, fresh, pure.

She fell slowly. She seemed to resist it. Her arms dropped to her sides. Her knees buckled. Her head drooped onto her chest. With the soft thud of flesh against stone, she collapsed in a heap on the boulder.

The serpent turned. Its jaws closed with a snap.

I didn't take my eyes off the rock.

A merman sat behind Dani's crumpled body.

Adaro was panting, teeth bared. Seawater poured from his black hair.

Blood trickled down his forearm—spilling out of the heart clenched in his fist.

CHAPTER TWENTY-NINE
Passed by Blood

Dani's heart pulsed in Adaro's webbed fingers. Was I imagining it? Could a heart really still keep beating when ripped from its owner's chest?

I nearly retched at the sight of it.

Blood dripped down his arm. He surveyed us on the beach, larger and more sinister than I remembered. His crimson eyes widened as they lingered on Lysi.

Dani lay on the boulder, motionless but for her dark hair, which fluttered in the wind. A dark stain pooled across her back.

Silence rang in my ears. I wanted to cry out.

I couldn't identify the feeling in my chest. Rage, shock, grief—anything but victory. Dani didn't deserve this. She was never the real enemy.

Kneeling on the rocks, my legs weakened. I fell sideways.

A low hiss came from the water. The serpent turned all four eyes onto her fallen master.

The vertical pupils darkened.

The heads turned from Dani to Adaro.

Control is passed by blood.

I drew a panicked, shaky breath.

"You need to run," said Lysi. "Go. Now. Can you support Meela?"

Tanuu leapt to his feet, not taking his eyes off Adaro.

"Come on," he said, grabbing me under the arms.

"No!" I said. "I'm not leaving—"

The serpent roared, the sound echoing across the water, bringing our hands to our ears. She drifted closer to the rock. Her pupils narrowed into slits, trained onto her new master.

"Well done, Meela," said Adaro, flashing his teeth. "Though perhaps not exactly as planned. I was not expecting to have to kill this one for it."

He waved a bloodied hand at Dani. The serpent's heads ducked, watching.

"But, all the same. You gave your blood, and the Host is mine, in the end."

He lobbed Dani's heart into the air. The serpent caught it and swallowed.

"Meela," said Annith, her voice a squeak.

"Get her out of here!" said Lysi.

She rounded on us with a red gleam in her eyes. Annith gasped. Blacktail stepped back. Tanuu's grip tightened around my arms.

"We're not going anywhere!" I said. "We can't let him get away."

Adaro swept his arm, and the serpent turned her whale-sized heads towards us. A pink tongue tasted the air.

We needed to act now. If the serpent was indestructible, it was her master we would have to kill.

Blacktail pulled out her iron dagger.

"How's your aim?" said Tanuu.

"Perfect," said Blacktail. "But he's too far away."

I tried to stand. The searing pain in my body had ebbed, but my legs were numb. I couldn't move them.

With an enormous effort, I pushed myself back up onto my knees, wobbling. I couldn't support my own weight. I'd have to drag myself across the beach with my hands.

A whimper escaped my lips. I was trapped in my own body.

The serpent advanced.

"Fine," said Lysi.

She dove, swimming straight for the serpent.

I screamed after her, but she'd already gone.

My legs wouldn't cooperate. I picked one up, as if I could move it like a puppet. I couldn't feel my fingers touching it.

What was happening to me?

Either this was it, and I had no blood left to pump through my muscles, or …

I held my injured palm close to my face. The bandage was dirty, wet, useless. I pulled the knot loose and wrenched it from my hand.

The cotton fell into the waves, where it carried back and forth like a long strand of seaweed.

The bleeding had stopped. The cut looked as it should have—small and harmless.

I lifted my gaze to the serpent. She'd stopped advancing.

Adaro watched Lysi disappear beneath the waves. His reptilian mouth curled into a snarl.

CHAPTER THIRTY
Para La Reina

I made certain Adaro would see me shoot past the boulder.

The serpent's attention locked onto me. She seemed to come from all directions.

I doubled back, travelling deeper, enticing her to follow.

At least, I assumed I would be able to outstrip the serpent. Nothing could match the speed and agility of a mermaid. Could it?

Several heartbeats passed before the current churned.

One head loomed in my vision, a black shadow. Where was the other?

I scanned the emptiness. That ancient, all-consuming presence filled the water, blinding my senses to all else.

Something gurgled in the distance. A sudden warmth washed over my skin. Then a dark shape lunged at me, jaws open.

I dove.

Teeth clamped together, grazing my tail. The current crashed into me and flipped me over. I swam blindly away.

The sky shone beside me. I spun and dove straight down. I grazed the bottom like a flatfish, leading the serpent away from the beach.

She recovered quickly and made another lunge. I veered sideways. The snout slammed against the rocks with an earth-shaking rumble.

The other head appeared beside me. A bubble blew from her nostrils, casting a veil across my path.

She was going to attack from both sides.

I used my hands to turn sharply. Both sets of jaws closed over nothing.

I pumped my tail hard. If I swam fast enough, the serpent would have to straighten out to chase me properly. Then I would have only a single head to deal with.

My muscles ached. In my whole life, I'd never swum so fast, or as far as I had in the past tidecycle. I pushed past the bone-deep exhaustion, trying to think.

If Adaro was focused on controlling the serpent, maybe the others could kill him.

With what?

As I swam headlong away from the beach, the current surged rhythmically behind me. The serpent was following.

I nearly banked south, maybe out of childhood habit. Then I remembered the families in the coral. I changed course abruptly. The serpent kept going for a moment, snapping at my wake.

I had no plan, other than to get her away from Eriana Kwai. Where could I go? How could I get rid of something so big?

A warm blast from her nostrils interfered with the rhythm of my tail. One hard puff of air and she could send me off course.

Below, the floor dropped off. I dove, following it.

The serpent's momentum carried her forwards, biting at nothing. A shadow fell over me. Then a whirlpool stirred overhead as she dove after me.

She groaned, projecting a blast of frustration.

I needed a plan. Where could I take her? Could I kill her? Trap her?

I tried to sense the bottom. The pulses behind me masked any other vibrations. I kept diving, blind.

I couldn't tell what was there until I almost slammed into the rocks.

I swerved left, saw a black shadow advancing, and flipped back the other way. The second head caught up.

They convened, but not before I twisted out of the way.

With a burst of speed helped by my hands, I followed the rocks.

A cliff materialised ahead, towering over me. Bubbles escaped my lips in surprise.

I turned before I hit it. One end of the serpent tailed me while her body curled around, drawing parallel to the cliff.

She was going to use the cliff face to corner me. I had a moment to act.

Relying on sight, I scanned the rocks. A fissure yawned beside me.

I grabbed the lip before I shot past it, yanking myself inside. The gap barely fit my body.

The black snout slammed into the cliff face. The world shook. Rocks cascaded onto my head.

I sucked back, wedging myself in place. The teeth snapped close enough to touch.

The second head caught up. She stopped snapping to eye me from two angles. The lids closed and opened with a sticky sound, adjusting to my dark hiding place.

Careful calculation projected from her. A murmur emitted from both heads.

Then a nostril pressed against the opening.

Reacting quickly, I pushed my back and tail hard against opposite walls. A bubble of air blasted at me, threatening to shake me loose.

A curved fang grazed my shoulder. She grunted in frustration. I tried to shrink further away.

Her jaws opened and closed, teeth grinding against stone.

Another rock hit my skull. I let one hand off the wall to grab it before it fell. With a grunt, I threw it hard at the serpent's mouth.

She hissed, retracting with an air of surprise. She coughed up the stone and tossed it aside, pupils narrowing.

Following the stone with my eyes, I caught a glint of light. Something moved a short distance away.

It disappeared in a blink—silent, agile, and much too big to be a fish.

The more I stared, the more I noticed other movements beside it.

At least twenty mermaids, mermen, and children had ducked behind a mound of rocks. They had long, lean frames, with tails a wide range of colours. Piercings glinted on their faces and bodies. That had been what caught my eye. The nearest one had a row of diamonds in her left collarbone. Her hair floated eerily beside her head—kelp buoys were tied to the ends of several braids.

The serpent struck the rocks. Debris swirled around us. I had no escape.

I bit my lip, thinking. She would have to breach at some point. Could I outlast her?

But as I thought it, the second head retreated for the surface.

My pulse thudded in my ears. The Host could wait outside this rock for an eternity.

Spio's voice came to mind: *If you need help, ask for it.*

I peered past the serpent. The merpeople held spears and maces.

Either these strangers helped me out of this, or this was where I died.

I stopped holding in the panic that had been building in my chest, and screamed.

"Help me!"

The serpent gave a low hiss at the noise. Her forked tongue reached for me. It tasted my skin, warm and slimy, trying to wrap behind me and pull me out.

I trembled as I held myself in place, leaning hard against the walls.

The merpeople glanced at each other, unmoving.

Did they not understand? Did they speak a different dialect? Even then, anyone could see I was desperate.

They didn't say a word.

"Please," I shouted.

The mermaid with the kelp braids nodded to the others. They turned away and, grouping together like a school of fish, began retreating.

"Wait," I shouted.

I gaped after them. They were going to leave me here to die.

But I had felt their resentment, confirming what I'd feared—that I was a part of Adaro's kingdom. I was the enemy.

Angry now, I gritted my teeth. We were allies. They couldn't abandon me.

In a last, desperate attempt, I blurted the only thing that came to mind.

"Para la reina!"

I wasn't sure why I said it. I didn't know what it meant, or if I'd even pronounced it right.

They stopped.

The lead mermaid turned, eyes wide. I stared back, trying desperately to convey everything I had done—every intention to make peace, every plot against Adaro.

The serpent picked up on my focus. She blinked, turned her head.

The mermaid's lips curled into a grin. Her skin rippled, transforming. Her teeth lengthened into an impressive row of fangs.

She raised a webbed fist and shouted, *"Para la reina!"*

The group echoed the war cry. They launched from the rocks, spears and maces raised.

The serpent opened her jaws, hissing. Bubbles erupted from the slits in her nose. The second head came to meet them.

Mermaids, mermen, and children fought with equal skill, slashing at the rock-hard scales. They darted around her vast body, under and over, swarming like flies.

I yanked myself out of the crevice and dove into the fray.

Except I had no weapon.

The serpent's heads swivelled, unsure of which target to choose.

The lead mermaid swooped in front of me before I could make it far.

"Go," she said. "We will distract it, but it is too much. We will not hold it for long."

For a moment, the words flowed by without meaning. She had that low, pronounced dialect I'd heard once before.

"Do you understand me?" she said.

"I—yes. Thank you."

She searched my face. The others continued to weave tantalisingly in front of the serpent's noses.

"Who are you?" said the mermaid.

Who was I? Not a soldier, anymore. I was a rebel. A rogue mermaid, alone and wanted for treason.

"Nobody," I said.

She inclined her head. Next to her long frame, the sharpness in her bones, and that imposing aura, I felt like a child.

"I do not think you are nobody," she said. "Will you come with us?"

A merman shouted as a set of massive jaws nearly closed around his fin.

The mermaid raised her weapon, preparing to dive in.

"I have to go back," I said, pointing towards Eriana Kwai.

She nodded, backing away. "When you are ready, come find us."

Beneath her powerful presence, I felt her sincerity. She wanted me to join them.

Was that what I wanted?

This was the resistance I'd been searching for. These were the merpeople I belonged with—more than anyone in Adaro's kingdom.

Hope bloomed in my chest. I had to find Spio. I refused to believe Adaro had caught him. My friend was out there somewhere, and together, we could join this group.

I nodded once.

"I will."

CHAPTER THIRTY-ONE
The Battle for Eriana Kwai

Arms wrapped around my waist. I screamed in protest, but Tanuu threw me over his shoulder like a bag of sand.

"Put me down!"

I punched him in the back, hearing him exhale with every blow.

"We gotta get you to safety," he said between grunts.

He made it to the shipwreck before tripping over the rubble and falling. We splashed into ankle-deep waves. I pushed myself off his shoulder, fuming.

"It's going to eat Lysi!"

I leaned towards the sea as if to swim after her.

Annith grabbed my arm. "You don't have a tail yet."

Tanuu cringed at the word.

Blacktail seemed about to place a hand on his shoulder, but stopped.

"We shouldn't take her from the water," she said. "Not if she's transitioning."

The rising tide battered the last standing piece of the shipwreck, spraying us with each wave.

"At least hide over here," said Tanuu.

I humoured him by pulling myself behind the piece of hull, out of Adaro's sight.

We needed to do something, and fast. Every second we sat here, the serpent could be closing in on Lysi.

I leaned over. Adaro was within shooting distance.

"Someone go get crossbows," I said. "The training base has enough iron—"

I ducked back as Adaro whirled around, crimson eyes flaring.

But he was looking past us, into the forest.

Then I heard it: a low, vibrating rumble. Something thundered in the distance, like a herd of galloping horses.

We turned.

My father burst from the trees, face shining with sweat. A hunting bow and arrows were clenched in his fists. My mother came behind him with a bucket of iron bolts. They stopped at the edge of the beach, panting, staring wildly around.

"Papa!"

For a brief, absurd moment, a childish feeling overcame me that everything would be all right now that my parents were here.

More arrived. Twenty, thirty, a hundred people flooded from the trees and spilled onto the beach.

They saw Annith, Tanuu, Blacktail, and me, collapsed behind the shipwreck in the ankle-deep tide. They saw Dani, lying bloody on the highest rock, Adaro behind her with his hands and arms dripping in blood. Some of them pointed to the black shape rising and falling in the distance.

Someone roared. The rest echoed. With a deafening outcry, hundreds of my people flooded onto the beach.

They carried hunting weapons, shovels, bats, anything they could find, iron or not. Even the widow from the Massacre Committee wielded a cast-iron skillet.

At the front of the crowd, Anyo stretched out his arms as though ready to conduct an orchestra.

"Fire!" he shouted.

Before Adaro could react, a shower of hunting arrows rained down on him. The wood wouldn't kill him, but they knocked him backwards.

He regained his balance and straightened. His lipless mouth parted, flashing his pointed teeth. He raised a thick arm high in the air.

"No," I shouted, panic building.

I saw her coming, a shadow beneath the surface. Ripples spread from her armoured back, growing rapidly closer.

"Mama, Papa! Run!"

They couldn't take on the serpent, no matter how many there were.

"Aim," bellowed Anyo.

Before he could tell them to fire, a monstrous head rose from the water. It reached high overhead, casting a long shadow over the beach and my people. The jaws parted, a string of saliva stretching from top fangs to bottom. She expelled a burst of air, sending hot droplets of seawater across the beach.

The roars turned to screams. Most people stopped running. Many rushed back towards the trees. A few faces remained determined—my parents among them.

"Run!" I shouted.

I pulled myself in their direction, as though I could protect them. They couldn't die because of this. Not at Adaro's hands.

Another shout rose over the din.

"Aim!"

Texas arrived on the beach, flanked by the girls who'd been ready to depart for the Massacre. They stood where the grass met the rocks, each wearing her new uniform. All twenty aimed together, holding their brand new crossbows with perfect form.

"Fire!"

A shower of iron bolts arced through the air.

All twenty hit the serpent in the face. They bounced off with *clinks* like metal on metal. She blinked, shook her head like a dog, and let out an earth-shattering roar.

Attacking the Host would get us nowhere. We needed to kill her master.

"Get the merman!"

My words were drowned by screams as the second head emerged from the water, and the serpent descended on the crowd.

With so many options for prey, she seemed not to know who to clamp her jaws around. She settled with swinging her heads through the mass of people, sending them flying. Several people screamed as they were launched into the air, scattering like leaves in the wind.

Others attacked. After the initial shock of seeing the leviathan, more people raised their weapons. The serpent was met with showers of bolts, blades, rocks, anything people could throw.

The second head closed around one man's entire body. She tossed him in the air and swallowed him, sending a shower of blood across the beach.

I searched for my parents, who had ducked into the trees to avoid what might as well have been a flying boulder. My father was firing rapidly while my mother handed him ammo.

I turned to my friends. "Tell everyone to focus on Adaro. And someone get me a weapon."

Blacktail and Annith took off into the crowd.

I glanced desperately towards the water. Where was Lysi?

The serpent raised her head, eyeing the masses below.

Behind Texas and the Massacre warriors, more girls arrived. Blondie led the pack of younger trainees.

Another cascade of bolts hit the serpent.

Tanuu cupped his hands around his mouth and bellowed at them. "Get the merman! The merman is controlling it!"

A few people heard. They passed along the message in frantic shouts.

Something tingled around my waist. My skin felt hot, like I'd sat too long facing a fire. I lifted my shirt.

The skin at my hips was broken. Or rather, covered in odd lines. Skin faded into … into what? I ran my fingers along it.

Scales.

My breath caught in my throat. For a moment, I thought I might faint.

I unzipped my pants. This was not the time for modesty.

"Tanuu, help me take these off," I said, struggling with my paralyzed legs.

He looked taken aback.

"Come on," I said. "You've been wanting to get me out of these for years."

"Really, Meela?"

He knelt to help.

He cried out when he saw the scales at my hips.

"It's okay," I said. "I was in a lot more pain a minute ago."

When the next wave retreated, revealing my legs, my stomach lurched. The scales travelled partway down my thighs. At the top of my legs, the skin had joined, flimsy, like the wings of a bat. The rest of my legs were still human.

"No offense," said Tanuu, "but that looks disgusting."

Annith and Blacktail returned with crossbows and quivers. I grabbed a weapon and slung a quiver over my chest.

"We told Texas to …" Annith trailed off when she saw my pants floating beside me. Her mouth fell open as the next wave ebbed, revealing my deformed legs.

"Aim!" shouted Texas.

We turned. All one hundred trainees raised their crossbows—this time, at Adaro.

My breath caught. Their aim was too good for all of them to miss at once. This was it. They were going to kill him.

"Fire!"

Adaro's crimson eyes flashed as he noticed the crossbows pointed at him. With a movement too fast to see, he flattened on the rock.

The serpent ducked in response to the movement. She turned to her master.

Even as Adaro flattened out, a handful of bolts hit his chest, arms, and face.

I cried out in victory, lifting my crossbow in the air.

Adaro roared—but to my horror, the bolts did not sink through him. They bounced off like hailstones, not even breaking skin. He sat up, teeth bared.

"But …" I said.

"Aim!" shouted Texas.

Fury twisted Adaro's face. He raised his arms. A torrent of seawater rained down on us. The heads loomed over the beach, one of them directly above me.

I notched a bolt and, ignoring the instinct to fire at the beast descending on us, aimed my crossbow at Adaro.

"Fire!" shouted Texas.

I pulled the trigger and dove sideways. I caught a glimpse of open jaws a mere arm's length away. Blood dripped from glistening teeth. They snapped closed around empty water where I'd been lying. The pulse in the waves sent me crashing into the shipwreck.

Crossbow in one hand, a bolt in the other, I sat up and found chunks of wood floating all over the place. Waves pummelled what was left of the broken ship, spraying me and everything around it.

Several bolts buffeted Adaro. They fell away as though made of foam.

How could he still be alive? Iron was the one sure way to slay a sea demon. This had always been the case. I gripped my weapon tighter, feeling like everything had turned inside out.

Where were Tanuu, Annith, and Blacktail?

Abruptly, Adaro scrambled forwards and plunged into the tide, where he sat submerged up to his shoulders. Shielding his head with one arm, he raised the other to the serpent.

At the blind command, the serpent lunged without an apparent plan.

Had the serpent gotten my friends? Were they trapped beneath the rubble?

I reached for a bolt. My quiver was light. I'd lost several in the waves. I cranked the lever and dropped the bolt against the shaft. In one motion, I aimed and fired. It hit Adaro in the collarbone, jolting him but not breaking his focus.

Someone spluttered behind me. I spun. Tanuu had been carried into the broken hull. He dog paddled out, wheezing.

"Meela, where are the others?"

"I don't—"

Beside us, someone rose from the water with an enormous gasp.

"Lysi!"

I reached for her, overcome with relief.

A high wave splashed against the shipwreck. I held my breath beneath its spray.

Lysi pulled me away from the debris.

"Iron doesn't kill him. We tried to explode the mine at the Moonless City, and then tried again with the Trident of Terror and the Iron Hook of Doom."

Before I could ask her to clarify that loaded statement, the serpent swiped and Lysi threw herself at Tanuu and me. We fell into the waves, briny water splashing up my nose. I made a conscious effort to keep my crossbow away from Lysi.

I surfaced, coughing. Wood splinters rained down on us.

"There!" said Tanuu.

Blacktail and Annith were on their feet, crossbows pointed at Adaro. Someone else had joined them. Fern. Of everyone on the beach, they were closest to the half-submerged merman. They fired rapidly, their bolts hitting him in the chest, throat, and face.

"You already tried iron?" I said. "When? Who's *we*?"

"Never mind," said Lysi.

Still, the impact of all the projectiles forced Adaro down. He turned as though to swim away, and stopped. Annith, Blacktail, and Fern had closed around him, trapping him between the boulder, their crossbows, and the rest of my people. From such close range, the girls' bolts drew blood, sticking into Adaro's flesh like darts.

The serpent gave a low, breathy groan, shaking her heads again like a wet dog. She turned to her master, waiting for a command.

I glanced back in search of my parents. They'd moved away from the safety of the trees.

"Be right back," said Tanuu.

He took off, splashing up the beach.

I fired at Adaro again, hitting him in the shoulder.

Lysi scanned the beach, wide-eyed. I followed her gaze.

Many people attacked the serpent, launching themselves at her indestructible body. At the treeline, the Massacre trainees fired at Adaro, along with anyone else with a crossbow or hunting bow. Not everyone had practiced aim, but enough did that a continuous stream of bolts and arrows pummelled him from every direction.

Though nobody paid us any attention amid all the chaos, I was glad Lysi's tail was masked beneath the waves.

As I thought this, the heat returned, flaring in my thighs. I looked down. The debris-filled water reached my waist. I ran a hand over my legs. My thighs had merged—smooth and scaly, one solid tail. It stopped at the knees, where that bat-like skin knit them together. Even the vague sight of the scales and their broken feel beneath my fingers made my stomach flop.

I had a tail. I would never have legs again. I would never walk or run again.

Tanuu returned with a hunting bow.

"Iron's about as effective on him as wood, right? Least this way I'll actually hit him."

"Sounds fair," said Lysi.

Tanuu let loose an arrow. It hit Adaro in the head.

The leviathan groaned as though in frustration. All four eyes were trained on her master.

Annith, Blacktail, and Fern had waded so close to the boulder that each shot had the force of a cannon fire. I was about to yell at the girls to be careful, because Adaro's next command to the serpent would be to deal with them—

Then it dawned on me.

Adaro was too overwhelmed by the attack to command the serpent. She watched him, awaiting instruction.

"Keep him busy!" I said. "Look at the heads."

As long as Adaro was occupied, we were safe from the serpent. She would not strike until her master told her to.

I fired another bolt.

"Then what?" said Lysi.

Before I could consider this, Tanuu let out a bark of laughter.

"He's gonna have to run!"

He was right. The answer seemed to be in numbers.

People had taken advantage of the serpent's immobility. They boldly splashed closer.

When the next shower of bolts, garden tools, and a baseball hit Adaro, the sheer volume submerged him completely.

Annith, Blacktail, and Fern leapt aside, aiming their weapons into the water.

"Get out of there," I shouted, but the girls didn't need telling. Already they were boosting each other onto the boulder with trained speed.

A burning sensation erupted in my palms. I gasped, dropping the crossbow. It landed on my thighs—on my tail— where the burning continued.

I swiped it away in a panic, like a poisonous spider had landed on me.

I couldn't touch it anymore. I would never be able to touch it again. Not crossbows, bolts, or any other iron.

A disturbance hit my tail. I flinched, expecting to see the Host advancing on us. But she wasn't there. I'd felt the ripples from Adaro retreating.

He had disappeared from sight, but I felt him. He was swimming away.

The serpent gave a deep groan. I caught the scent of her breath, thick and briny, more powerful than ever.

She followed. Her armour glistened in the feeble rays of sunlight. Whirlpools appeared and disappeared, each time further from the beach.

The disturbance in the water dimmed as they retreated.

"Yeah, you'd better run!" said Tanuu.

His voice rang. His pulse changed as he said the words. He was excited.

How did I know this?

The crowd roared.

I felt their elation. It bled through the air, thick and tangible, meeting my mind in the same way sweetness bursts across the tongue.

I heard their feet splashing, and just as much, felt the vibrations in the water as they chased Adaro away from Eriana Kwai.

CHAPTER THIRTY-TWO
A Journey Ended

The serpent lingered in my senses long after she had disappeared. I waited several moments, until the horizon returned to emptiness and the currents revealed nothing but fish. Finally, I peeled my gaze away from the ocean.

Though the commotion on the beach had faded, it looked as though a storm had blown through. Wooden splinters, broken trees, and weapons littered the rocks. Seawater drenched everything up to the treeline. Hundreds of humans nursed their injuries and hugged each other.

They projected pain. Bones had been broken. Lives had been lost. The air reeked of blood.

Then there was the girl on the highest boulder.

Most stared, but no one approached the blood-soaked rock. The corpse had been in the line of fire. Her uniform was shredded, her body punctured with iron and wooden arrows.

A thickset man stormed down the beach. Every thread of his focus pulled towards the girl on the rock. He waded in. His back and shoulders expanded and compressed rapidly.

A long moment passed as he stared at Dani's body.

His emotions blended, hard to read, as the girl's had been.

The crowd fell so silent that I barely sensed them beneath the wind and waves.

"Who did this?" shouted the man.

A woman splashed in behind him. Her anguish hit me before she made a sound.

"Dani! Baby!"

The woman stumbled through the tide, trying to run faster than the water would allow. Her breaths rattled with sobs.

The man didn't turn. He stayed facing his daughter.

Rage and grief drifted towards me on the wind.

Beside me, Meela lifted a hand to her cheek. She caught the tear before it fell.

Beneath the water, I grabbed her free hand and squeezed. She held on tightly.

"Who's responsible for this?" the man shouted.

His eyes found Meela.

I tensed, ready to dive if he realised what I was. But with my tail hidden beneath the surface, he didn't notice.

"Adaro," said Meela, barely audible.

"What?" said the man.

Tanuu came to her rescue. "It was Adaro. The merman. He killed her so he could have control of the serpent."

"What do you—how would killing her—why does my daughter have to do with this?" he demanded, voice breaking on the last words.

His wife clambered onto the boulder, kicking off her shoes for grip.

"Dani had control to begin with," said Annith. "She …"

Annith faltered, glancing to Meela.

"Dani finished freeing the Host of Eriana," said Meela, finding strength in her voice. "She was going to use it to save our people."

For a moment, the silence thickened. Then whispers broke out on the beach.

That was all Meela said. She didn't mention the part where Dani had used her as a sacrifice. Maybe she didn't feel the need to share Dani's final act with the island.

The man closed his eyes, rubbing a hand across them. His wife threw herself over Dani's body, shaking with sobs.

Someone splashed up behind us. I let go of Meela's hand and recoiled.

"What happened? Are you all right?"

It was Meela's father. I'd seen him once before, when I was ten. It was hard to forget the face of the man who'd nearly killed me.

"You look like you're going to be sick," he said. "Can you stand?"

A soft, pretty woman who must have been her mother waded in behind him.

"Honey, are you in shock?"

"No. I … Mama, Papa, I'm sorry. I didn't know."

"What didn't you know?" said her father.

"The blood needed to free Eriana's Host was a sacrifice," said Meela.

Her mother cried out. She dropped to her knees, flinging a hand to her daughter's forehead as though to check for a fever.

"It's okay," said Meela. "I'm not going to die. We figured out—I mean, Tanuu realised—well …"

Where Meela's toes should have been, a tail flipped out of the water. It fluttered in the breeze before sinking back into the sea.

My heart thrummed.

I'd always loved Meela the way she was, and I wouldn't have changed anything about her—but seeing her as a mermaid awoke something new inside me. We were the same, now. We could have a life together.

I wanted to kiss Meela right there in front of everyone.

"It was the only way I could survive," she said.

A stunned silence followed. Then, something shifted in the others around us.

Annith grabbed the girl with the ponytail by the elbow, pointing out a young boy on the beach who'd been injured. The two of them waded over to help.

Blacktail grabbed Tanuu's hand.

"You're bleeding," she said. "Let's go get bandages."

He let her pull him away.

Alone with Meela and her parents, I finally drew their attention. Her father's gaze travelled from my hair, to my eyes, to the iron-made scar peeking out of the water.

His aura shifted from shock, to mistrust, to fear.

He recognised me—and he clearly thought he had killed me all those years ago.

"Mama, Papa," said Meela. "I want you to meet Lysi."

Her mother squeaked. "But I thought—"

"I remember," said her father, not taking his eyes off me. "Is she the one who changed you?"

"Yes," said Meela. "She saved my life."

Her parents scanned me up and down. I resisted the urge to sink below the surface, away from their appraising stares.

Meela's heart beat wildly enough for me to feel it. I wanted to grab her hand again, but I didn't. As much as I wanted

Meela's parents to understand her feelings, I didn't know much about them or how they would react. This was Meela's territory.

"A demon," whispered her mother.

She reached for her daughter, hesitated, then touched her arm gently.

"Meela, you're freezing. Do you feel—?"

"I feel normal, Mama. I promise."

I wondered if she was lying. She must have felt stronger, quicker.

Her father cast a wary glance at me. "How can we trust you, Metlaa Gaela? Your entire biology has changed. We have no way of knowing the effects on your mind."

"It's not like that. I'm the same—"

"And what about a demon's instincts?" said her mother, recoiling as though Meela had threatened to bite her.

Meela dropped her gaze, clearly hurt.

Any elation I felt fizzled away. I had made a huge mistake.

Would I be the reason for Meela's rejection from her own family? I'd wanted to save her, but all I'd done was build a wall of ice between her and her parents.

Meela tried again. "Mama, I …"

She swallowed hard, eyes brimming with tears.

I spoke up. "This is a lot to understand, I know. But mermaid or not, Meela is the same girl you raised—"

The woman's eyes snapped to me. "She is not the same. Look at her!"

Anger flared in my chest. I closed my eyes before they could redden. This was exactly why Nilus had been afraid to tell his parents about his transformation.

My eyelids flew open. Nilus.

I opened my mouth—and hesitated. Meela's lip trembled. Her parents were slumped, shivering, as though breaking apart in the waves.

I couldn't tell them about Nilus now. Not after all this. Their family had been through too much today.

Plus, first they had to come to terms with Meela's transformation.

I drew a steadying breath. I couldn't let her parents do this to her.

"Her body has changed, but her mind and heart haven't," I said. "This is who she is. You can accept her, or you can dismiss her as a part of your family. The choice is yours. Decide what kind of parents you want to be."

Her mother's eyes widened, as though really seeing me for the first time. I sat tall in the water, challenging her to see me for who I really was: a mermaid, capable of loving, driven by emotions, empathy, and morals. I was not a demon, and neither was her daughter.

Finally, voice trembling, she said, "You don't think I love Meela no matter what?"

"Do you?" said Meela, barely audible. "Or am I just a sea rat, now?"

There was a long pause.

Then her mother burst into tears. She threw herself at Meela, hugging her tightly.

"Of course I love you," she said, sobbing. "Of course. I'm sorry."

Her father caught my eye, and there was something desperate behind those dark irises—sad, pleading.

I nodded, a silent promise. I'd brought Meela irrevocably into my world, and I would do everything in my power to keep her safe.

I backed off, letting them absorb the change that had come crashing down on their family like a tidal wave. Eventually, when her parents were ready, I would let Meela be the one to tell them about Nilus.

CHAPTER THIRTY-THREE
A Journey Begun

I sensed every cell in my mother's body as she hugged me—
the warm blood in her veins, the strong pulse of her heart, her
soft, vulnerable flesh and muscles and bones.

I flinched as my tail picked up a disturbance in the water.
Would I ever get used to this? It was my father, leaning over
so he could wrap his thick arms around the two of us. He held
on as my mother sobbed and tears flooded from my eyes.

"Honey, I never want you to feel that way," said my
mother. "We love you even as a … a mermaid."

I leaned back and pushed a lock of wet hair from her
cheek. Though I believed in unconditional love, my parents'
acceptance of me in any form—with any biology—meant
more than they would ever know.

My mother drew a steadying breath. "This is it, then.
You're going to live in the ocean with … with Lysi, here."

I nodded. That thought kept me from panicking. I could never run through the forest again, never sleep in my bed again, but I would have Lysi. The entire ocean was ours to explore. The prospect sent a thrill through my veins.

My mother dabbed at her eyes, seemed to realise she was using a shirt sleeve that was even wetter and saltier than her tears, and let her arm fall with a gentle splash.

"I expected it would be hard the day my baby left the nest, but I always thought it would be …"

"To marry a tall, dark, handsome man, and live in a house in the woods and have twelve children," I said.

My mother softened. "Maybe you can still find your dark and handsome man beneath the water. How are the mermen? Are they all like that one?"

She nodded towards the horizon.

"Uh, there's something you need to understand," I said.

I glanced to Lysi. She had backed away, not meeting my eye.

Though my heart pounded, I felt more certain about myself than I ever had. Lysi was a part of my life. The world could react however they wanted, and it wouldn't affect how I felt about her.

I reached for Lysi and grabbed her hand for them to see, pulling her back beside me.

"I love Lysi. I'm in love with her."

Lysi's pulse beat strong against my palm.

My parents looked between us, unmasked shock on their faces.

"Honey, you don't think this is just because—"

"No," I said. "It's real. I've loved her since the day we met."

My mother nodded slowly. I waited for the chill to settle between us, for the accusations to start all over again. But she smiled.

"Meela, that's wonderful."

I opened my mouth, made no sound, and closed it. After all her talk about wanting me to start a family, could she be serious?

"But what about …"

I tried to sense her, searching for disappointment.

"Honey, if spending your life with Lysi is what makes you happy, then I'm happy."

Her pulse beat steadily. She was being truthful.

"Didn't we just establish that I love you no matter what?" she said.

I threw myself at her, hugging her tightly.

"I love you, Mama."

"I love you, too. Now relax your arms a little. You're crushing me."

I let go. "Sorry."

Hesitantly, I turned to my father, who hadn't said anything in a long while.

He shrugged and said gruffly, "I think I've always known."

I stared at him, surprised. Then he smiled a little.

"You are my daughter," he said. "You always will be."

I bit my lip to stop it from trembling. I hugged him, this time carefully.

When I let go, both of them turned to Lysi.

"Take care of her," said my mother. "Make her come visit once in a while."

"I promise," said Lysi.

The three of them exchanged a smile—and that was more than I could have asked for.

My mother shivered violently. My father noticed as well, and wrapped his arms around her shoulders.

"You two should go home and dry off," I said. "I'll be here when you get back."

"You had better be, young lady," said my father.

They waded from the tide, looking weak and frigid.

I glanced back to the high boulder. Mujihi, his wife, and Dani's body had gone.

I would never forget Mujihi's contorted expression—the sorrow lined in his face.

Texas, Hassun, and a few members of the Massacre Committee had gone, too.

There would be a funeral for the victims. I would have attended, if fate had led me in a different direction.

On the beach, Blondie and Fern led the trainees in making a pile of weapons and ammo near the treeline. Others helped clean up, while many had disappeared, taking the injured with them.

Sitting among a cluster of driftwood, Anyo and Adette were hugging, father more emotional than daughter.

Seeing my parents leave, my friends splashed up. They'd clearly been waiting for the chance to swoop in.

Tanuu trailed behind, eyeing Lysi with an odd expression. I thought it might have been mistrust, but he projected something else.

Jealousy.

"I'm sorry, Tanuu," I said.

His gaze darted between Lysi and me, apparently working out the situation that had led him to this bachelor status.

Blacktail watched him. Something hopeful flickered in her aura.

Of course. Why didn't I see that before?

I bit my lip to hide a smile.

Annith slung an arm across Tanuu's shoulders. "You'll be all right. Won't he, Meela?"

"Yeah," I said. "There are plenty of fish in the sea."

I splashed my tail, sending a waterfall in their direction. Annith and Blacktail screamed and covered their heads, but Tanuu was too slow. He wiped an arm across his eyes, laughing.

"That was terrible! Your first joke as a mermaid and that's what you go with?"

I grinned.

"To be clear," he said slowly, "what you're feeling is real, right? She hasn't got some, like, mermaid lure over you?"

Lysi laughed. "That only works on men."

Tanuu squinted at her, looking as if he were preparing to run.

"I won't use it against you," she said.

Looking no less assured, he stepped behind Blacktail.

"If you do, you gotta go through her."

Blacktail laughed.

Above us, the clouds dissipated, opening up a blissfully clear sky. The ocean had quieted. The world below the surface was calm enough that I felt disturbances against my tail from a distant school of fish.

"Think Adaro will be back?" said Blacktail.

"He's got more important plans, now," said Lysi.

"Like what?"

"Once he gets back to Utopia, I imagine he'll break his promise to the Aleut people. He'll use the serpent to chase them away from his territory."

I was about to say how sorry I felt for the Aleut people when Tanuu said, "Excellent."

We turned to him in horror.

"What's the matter with you?" said Annith.

"The Aleutian Islands are a part of Alaska," he said.

"So?" I said.

Tanuu sighed. "I forgot you were all taking battle-axe throwing lessons instead of social studies."

"And what did social studies teach you?" said Blacktail.

"That pissing off the United States is never a good move."

I considered the prospect. If the Americans did get involved, would their military be the answer? Would the world start caring about the war my people had been fighting for decades?

I felt a wave of terror from Lysi. "What's wrong?"

"They'll destroy us," she said, paling. "They'll drop iron bombs on us like … snow."

"She's right," said Blacktail. "They'll target more than just Adaro. They'll want to get rid of all mermaids. Like we did."

"So we'll have to get to him before he can attack any more humans," I said.

"Destroying the indestructible," said Tanuu. "Sounds like fun."

"We'll find a way," I said.

We were interrupted by a woman's voice cutting across the beach, wondering loudly whether the Massacre would still depart today. It was the widow from the Massacre Committee. She had a gash on her forehead; I could smell the blood. She fell silent at the answering glares.

Along the beach, a few people still laboured, restoring the area back to normal.

In silent agreement, my friends and I began to help.

I relished my new senses as I pulled myself through the shallow tide, picking up scattered wood from the shipwreck. I sensed the love projecting from Annith and Rik as they shared a hug. I felt the quickening in Tanuu's pulse when he gave Blacktail a playful jab in the side. I smelled the difference between water, wood, and rock. I heard the way the wind curved around each tree along the shoreline.

And when my parents returned, I knew my loved ones were close long before they arrived.

By the time we finished cleaning up, the sun sat low on the horizon. An orange line stretched across the glassy ocean.

I said a hug-filled goodbye to my friends and parents, promising to visit often. Annith and Blacktail surprised me with their boldness and hugged Lysi, too.

"We'll leave a rock tower," said Lysi, stacking a pile of stones. "When you see it, you'll know we're close."

Annith's hazel eyes locked onto mine, brimming with emotion.

"I guess I won't be able to jump in if you need help, anymore," she said.

We shared a smile.

My friends and parents turned for home, my mother wiping tears from her cheeks.

Then everyone was gone, and it was just Lysi and me, sitting in the water, side by side. Waves gurgled over the pebbles. I felt each one coming before I saw the swell.

"You'll have to teach me how to be a proper mermaid," I said, pushing deeper into the water.

Lysi laughed. "There's nothing to it."

"You'll show me what coral looks like?"

"First thing."

"You'll show me how to hunt?"

"Until you can do it with your eyes closed."

"Good," I said, grabbing her hand.

"Hold your breath," said Lysi. "Let's go swimming."

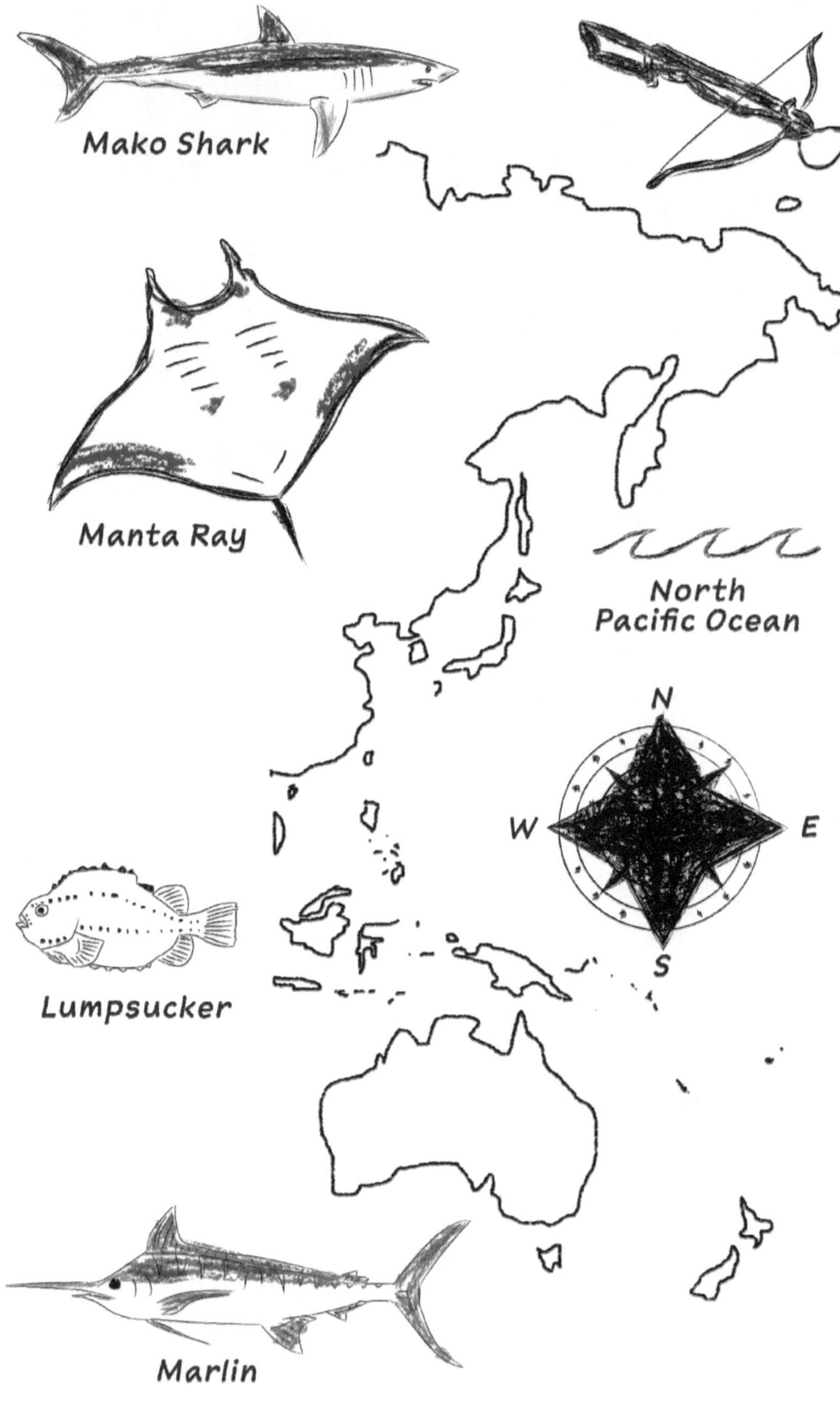

Mako Shark
Manta Ray
Lumpsucker
Marlin
North
Pacific Ocean
N
W
E
S

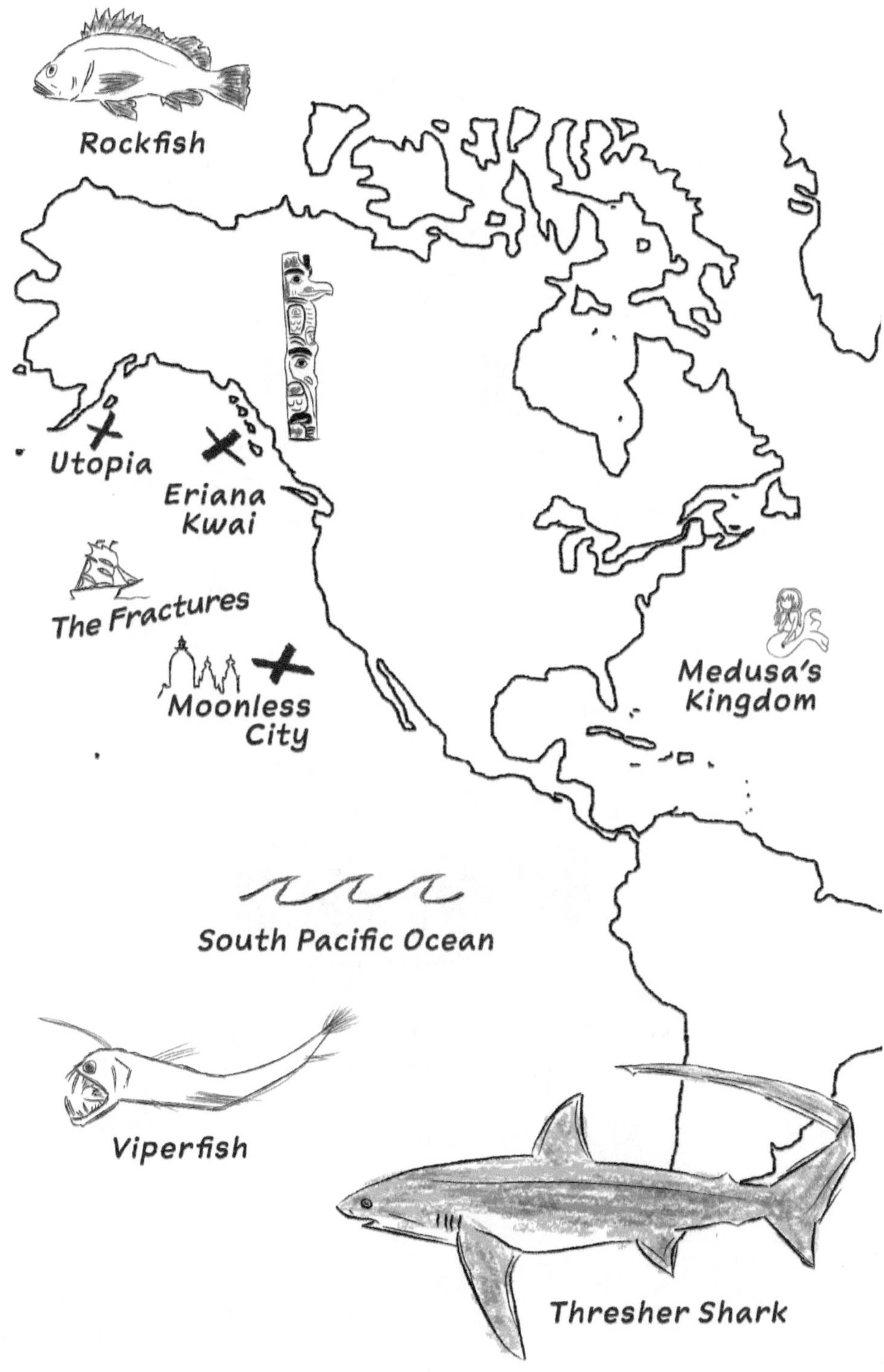

Rockfish
Utopia
Eriana
Kwai
The Fractures
Moonless
City
Medusa's
Kingdom
South Pacific Ocean
Viperfish
Thresher Shark

Also by Tiana Warner

Continue Meela and Lysi's journey in book three of
the Mermaids of Eriana Kwai trilogy.

tianawarner.com/books/ice-kingdom

Ice Massacre is now an award-winning comic!
Read it online and learn more at:

mermaidhuntress.com

Note from the author

Thank you for reading Ice Crypt and supporting an indie author. If you enjoyed Meela and Lysi's story, please consider spreading the word and reviewing it online.

To stay up to date with new releases, exciting announcements, and giveaways, please sign up for my newsletter!

tianawarner.com